GO WITH IT
SCARLETT FINN

ISBN: 9781914517181

www.scarlettfinn.com

Also by Scarlett Finn

GO NOVELS
GO WITH IT
GO IT ALONE
GO ALL OUT
GO ALL IN
GO FULL CIRCLE

EXILE
HIDE & SEEK
KISS CHASE

WRECK & RUIN
RUIN ME
RUIN HIM

THE BRANDED SERIES
BRANDED
SCARRED
MARKED

FORBIDDEN PREQUEL DUET
ALL. ONLY.
ONLY YOURS

NOTHING TO...
NOTHING TO HIDE
NOTHING TO LOSE
NOTHING IN BETWEEN: ONE
NOTHING TO DECLARE
NOTHING TO US
NOTHING IN BETWEEN: TWO
NOTHING TO SAY
NOTHING TO GAIN
NOTHING IN BETWEEN: THREE
NOTHING TO YOU
NOTHING TO THIS PREQUEL: ONE WILD NIGHT
NOTHING TO THIS
NOTHING IN BETWEEN: FOUR
NOTHING TO DO
NOTHING TO FEAR
NOTHING IN BETWEEN: FIVE
NOTHING TO DENY

THE FORBIDDEN NOVELS
FORBIDDEN DESIRE
FORBIDDEN WANT
FORBIDDEN WISH
FORBIDDEN NEED
FORBIDDEN BOND

TO DIE FOR...
TO DIE FOR TRUTH
TO DIE FOR HONOR
TO DIE FOR VIRTUE
TO DIE FOR DUTY
TO DIE FOR LOVE

LOVE AGAINST THE ODDS STANDALONE COLLECTION
SWEET SEAS
HEIR'S AFFAIR
RESCUED
MAESTRO'S MUSE
GETTING TRICKY
THIRTEEN
REMEMBER WHEN...
RELUCTANT SUSPICION
XY FACTOR

KINDRED SERIES
RAVEN
SWALLOW
CUCKOO
SWIFT
FALCON
FINCH

THE EXPLICIT SERIES
EXPLICIT INSTRUCTION
EXPLICIT DETAIL
EXPLICIT MEMORY

MISTAKE DUET
MISTAKE ME NOT
SLEIGHT MISTAKE

RISQUÉ & HARROW INTERTWINED
TAKE A RISK
FIGHTING FATE
RISK IT ALL
FIGHTING BACK
GAME OF RISK

LOST & FOUND
LOST
FOUND

ONE

HARLOW SWEETING WAS ready for bed. Her first Saturday shift as the on-call family support officer had ended a couple of hours ago. Though that hadn't meant any reprieve for her exhaustion. In her line of work, time became fluid. Leaving the family she'd been helping just because the clock had run out wasn't an option.

So being ready for bed had little to do with being able to curl up and close her eyes. Instead, she found herself trailing down a cold, dark street in the small hours of the night, making her way home one step at a time.

Her profession was more of a lifestyle than a vocation. No timecard could switch off its importance. There was no getting up and walking out just because she'd completed her allotted number of hours. People's lives were more important than clocking out.

Social service work was hard. Harlow had ventured onto the path of her current profession in high school. At a career fair, she'd discussed her interests with one of the advisor's who'd told her that social work suited the "confluence of her needs" and was a "natural evolution of her interests."

Following the advisor's suggestion, Harlow had done

some research and decided it was an occupation where she could make a difference. After college, she'd joined a suburban division and stayed there until her recent move.

No one chose social work for its simplicity. But suburbia had not been a hotbed of need.

The last thing she wanted was a job that only required her to go through the motions. More. Harlow wanted more and had been ready to leap out of her comfort zone… no matter how big the challenge.

A challenge was exactly what she'd been ready for when she made the decision to move from the easy, less demanding suburban department to the tough inner city. Much as she'd loved her colleagues and many of her clients in her previous position, there had been nothing to sink her teeth into. In short, she'd gotten bored. Transferring to a deprived urban area and taking up a post with child and family services made sense. To her anyway, her family were less understanding.

The last thing that she wanted to do was concede that they might have been right. Harlow had thought she was ready for more. Truth was, she'd had no idea how difficult it would turn out to be. Reading about desperate scenarios in books was nothing like facing them in real life. Sometimes it felt like her heart was breaking every day.

Working with vulnerable children drove her. Protecting those who couldn't protect themselves was a worthy cause. No matter how difficult she found witnessing or hearing about what they endured, she reminded herself that they were the ones enduring it. All Harlow had to do was listen and care, not live it every minute. Supporting the youngsters in their time of need, giving them a chance to realize their potential, was the least she could do.

Urban kids were savvy and street smart, even more so than her. Experience showed her how important it was to be confident, even when she was horrified. Being in the field, dealing with people hands on without fear, taught her more than she could learn from textbooks.

That didn't mean she'd given up the book learning. Harlow was a strong believer that there was always more for everyone to learn. In addition to her day job, she was doing an online criminology degree in what little spare time she could scrape together.

Harlow hadn't had the time to go back to traditional college. It hadn't helped that her parents had refused to pay for a second degree, probably because they didn't support the first one she'd chosen. And they weren't the only obstacle either. The man she'd been in a relationship with at the time saw her decision to study as a hobby rather than a way to challenge or better herself.

But it turned out that she didn't need anyone's support, just her own resolve. Her first degree allowed her to work and pay for her continued education herself. Doing it on her own meant she could be proud of the achievement no one had helped her attain.

Completing the course online took twice as long as traditional channels. Relief had come when she entered her last year. At last, she was on the final stretch. The extra work had been worth it.

Looking back, she could see that embarking on the course had probably been a prelude to her move into the city. Her need for something more challenging and dynamic hadn't come from nowhere.

Although, studying was a half-measure.

The course allowed her to read about and research dramatic, often tragic, situations full of thrills and excitement. Exactly the kind of stimulation that had been missing from her daily life.

Life had gotten harder after making the choice to move to the city. No doubt about that. Her parents hadn't supported her breaking her engagement or making so many life changes and had vowed to cut her off. Even though they hadn't paid her any sort of allowance for a long time, Harlow had lived in their house until moving in with her fiancé, and again after that relationship ended.

Leaving Rupert, and the safe suburb where she'd grown up, to strike out on her own was an achievement in itself. This was the first time in her life she was doing it all on her own. She could only rely on herself, and was proud of her financial independence, which wasn't something her sibling could boast.

Walking down the dark street in this dilapidated neighborhood, there was no one around, but Harlow couldn't say she was sorry to be by herself. Colleagues had warned her not to walk down certain streets alone, and this was one of the ones they'd named.

Still learning her way around, Harlow hadn't meant to come this way, but had been too tired to pay attention to the direction of her feet. Getting home was the only thing on her mind and her apartment was six blocks away.

Much as she wasn't paying close attention to her route, her autopilot had been smart enough to steer her away from Floyd's, a bar that was notorious for its less than savory clientele and numerous dodgy dealings. That was at least one small mercy.

Harlow smiled.

Her parents and sister wouldn't be able to comprehend what her life had become. Sometimes she couldn't comprehend it. No one in her family would be caught dead on a deserted street in the middle of a crime-ridden neighborhood well after midnight.

The odd thing was, Harlow didn't feel fear. Empowerment was what flowed through her. She was proud of herself. Shunning her upbringing hadn't been easy; few people would understand why she had done it. But on nights like this, when she was filled with a sense of purpose and pride, she remembered why the difficult path was so attractive.

Breathing in, she sighed into the calm of this beautiful night that was just perfect for a walk, even if the setting wasn't serene or romantic. Losing herself in her thoughts, Harlow took stock of where she was in life and where she might want to be next. She didn't get too far into that train of thought.

Everything that happened next, happened fast.

Crossing the mouth of an alleyway, drifting on her mental distraction, she didn't hear the rush of footsteps that must have preceded the impact of the body that hit hers hard.

Someone had burst out of the alley and crashed

straight into her. Whoever he was, he only just managed to catch her as they went into a tumble onto the sidewalk. Somehow, he had the presence of mind to twist them in the descent so she landed on top of him.

But he didn't pause. Flipping them over, he put her on her back and pounced onto his feet in a crouch.

"Get him!" someone called.

The menacing voice bounced off the walls of the narrow alley making her assailant steal a quick glance over his shoulder to check the route he'd just travelled.

Lying stunned on the pavement, Harlow couldn't breathe or compute until somehow she noticed there was blood soaking through his shirt. "Oh my God, you're hurt," she said, scrambling up.

The moment she found her feet, the stranger pulled her down again just as a series of bangs reverberated from the alley. Gunshots. That sound. It could only be gunshots.

In the cocoon of his crouch, nestled between his bent legs with his body sheltering hers, Harlow couldn't register how fast her night had become a fight to keep her life.

"Got a weapon in that purse, Trinket?"

The bass of the deep voice shook her before she could figure out that it had come from the man bracing himself around her. "I... I... a... no."

The click, click sound of an empty weapon came closer. "Good thing he's out," the voice said. "Ditch the heels and bolt."

The stranger. Her attacker and protector. Was he telling her to run? The man was alone and possibly bleeding to death while his enemies bore down on them, and he was telling her to split? That didn't gel with her instinctive urge to help those in need.

"You're hurt," she said, trying to see the blood on his shirt. The way his form was guarding hers left her in shadow and too close to see his injury. "You're bleeding."

"Bolt."

Certain as he sounded, Harlow was more certain that she wouldn't leave anyone alone in danger. "Like hell," she said, shoving away to free herself from his shielding crouch.

Thrusting to her feet, she skirted around the stooped man, putting him behind her. It was her turn to protect him. Facing the alleyway, she prepared to confront whoever might emerge from it. The stranger could have been right about the gun being empty, but the people who faded from the darkness into her view weren't unarmed.

Five guys strode from the shadows, mean and impatient. They wanted something from the bleeding man who'd sunk onto his knees on the asphalt behind her.

"Move, lady, we've got business to finish," one of the alley guys said.

The stranger had shifted onto his knees. Seeing the movement had made her twist her head, so she hadn't spotted which of the men was the speaker.

Whoever the man behind her was, he wasn't in a good way. Harlow wanted to offer comfort, to call for help. Except, that was impossible while this threat was still looming.

Putting thoughts of the stranger's possible demise to the back of her mind, she steeled herself to challenge the gang. "Not a chance," she said, raising her chin with a defiant hair flick. "You've hurt him already. You've made your point."

"Long as he's breathing, I've got a point to make." One of the alleyway gang moved closer to spearhead his group. "I've got orders to end him."

"And I've got a point of my own to make."

The alleyman sneered, probably thinking about how easy it would be to move her aside. "And what's that?"

Now she had to come up with something. "If you want to end him, you'll have to end me too." Maintaining her defiance, Harlow didn't so much as blink. Strength was crucial. "And, believe me, sir, people will notice if I go missing. You do not want to screw with the people who'll come looking for me." This was a battle of wills and she would not lose. She would not. Tilting her head to the side, Harlow showed more determination. "Do you have orders to end me too?"

Though he did his best to disguise his concern, she could tell she'd pressed one of Alleyman's buttons. Ignoring her hammering heart, Harlow kept her eyes locked on his. His tense lips moved in a show of frustrated aggravation. A breath later, she felt him stand down.

"Your girl's got your back, asshole. She won't be around to save you next time."

Whoever Alleyman was, he spat on the ground beside her and turned away, spinning a finger, indicating to his posse that they should head back the way they'd come.

Harlow kept watching until the shadows had taken them again. The moment they were gone, she whirled in a descent, ending in a crouch. Examining the man who hadn't stood since she'd left his shelter, Harlow feared his injuries could be grave.

Flopping forward, he barely managed to brace the weight of his upper body on his hands. It took him more than a few tries to lock his elbows. Scraping his palms on the asphalt, he crawled on all fours to the wall just on the inside of the alley. Wilting, he slumped against the brick and rolled on his shoulder until his back made contact with the structure.

Rushing over, Harlow scooped a hand around the back of his head. His eyes were rolling in his skull, unable to focus. Feeling the pulse in his neck increased her concern. It was there, but it wasn't strong or steady.

"Oh, God," she exhaled, letting him go to dig around in her purse that was hanging across her body, resting in her lap. "Don't worry, I'm calling 9-1-1, I'll get help—"

His hand shot up. The weight of it landed on her purse, pulling it down, and crushing her hand inside. His heavy eyes still weren't focused. "No, no calls," he grumbled, his voice weakening. "Floyd's."

Her lips parted in a quiet gasp. "I… I can't go in there, it's dangerous."

A feeble smile touched his lips at the same time his eyes closed. "You just stood up to Hagan's goons," he said and coughed, his teeth gritted in a tight grimace of pain. "You can handle Floyd's."

There were too many thoughts to comprehend; she couldn't focus, couldn't make a choice. How could she get this guy who had to be at least six three up onto his feet and to a bar that was a block and a half over? Who was Hagan? Would he or Alleyman be back?

Forgetting about the people who'd done this, she triaged the problems. No matter what, she couldn't leave this stranger here alone, not when he was seriously hurt. The most pressing matter was his life; that had to be her only focus.

He hissed, trying to pull himself into more of a seated position. "Shh," she said, stroking him from his face to his shoulder. "Don't move."

The red stain on his tee-shirt was growing into a darker hue. Swallowing hard, Harlow moistened her lips a few times, gathering the gumption to pick the fabric up so she could see the state of what was beneath.

The moment she did, she wished she hadn't.

"Fuck," he grumbled and winced in a recoil.

Just above his hip was a gash that was still spouting new blood. "Oh my God," she said, tugging off her scarf to scrunch it and push it hard against the wound.

She had no idea how he'd got hurt like this, though she had an idea about who was responsible. It frustrated her that he was refusing to go to hospital and she couldn't begin to figure out why someone would want to avoid the place that could save them.

Despite all the unknowns, one thing was clear as day. The time for speculation and indecision was over. If she left him there, he'd die either way.

"That good, huh?" Doing a double take, Harlow realized the stranger was reading the seriousness of the situation from her expression through his scarcely open eyes. "You're hot, Trinket. Does a guy get a last request?"

"Not tonight, Crash," she said, shifting closer to loop his arm up over her shoulders. "I can't believe you're on the brink of death and trying to put the moves on me."

She struggled to pull him from the wall. It took a few attempts and to get more traction, she had to press his hand onto the scarf to give him responsibility for stemming his own bleeding.

The stranger hissed again, holding the scarf against his wound. "I'm a guy with the right priorities."

He might be able to make jokes, but she didn't find

this situation funny at all. "You're going to be okay," she said, putting his mischief down to the effects of blood loss. "We're going to get you to Floyd's. But you're going to have to help me. I can't do this alone."

That made him breathe out. "Up?" he asked, bracing, despite the obvious pain behind his clenched expression.

"Up," she said, pleased that she'd managed to focus him. "On three."

Getting him onto his feet was only the first obstacle. Harlow learned fast that muscle weighed a lot more than it looked. This guy was no quarterback, but his body was solid, athletic in its ability, and definitely muscular.

His being healthy would work in his favor; he'd need all the help and luck he could muster to get out of this.

Guiding him out of the alley, they spanned the sidewalk and managed to get across the street. One step at a time, Harlow counted each as progress. This was the right block, but they still had to get to the corner and walk to the furthest end to get to Floyd's, which, if she remembered the pictures she'd seen in her research of the neighborhood, was on the opposite corner.

The stranger's shuffling steps were slowing. "What do I get?" he grumbled, maybe as a way to stay conscious.

"Get for what?" she asked, spitting her hair from her mouth, trying her best to keep her legs straight though his weight was beginning to crush her.

"Helping you out."

"Helping me out?" she said, and realized he meant getting him to his feet and moving. "You get to live."

He groaned. "Not good enough."

Keeping him talking was a good idea. The uncertainty of his slowing walk was less concerning than the slurring of his speech. His head drooped, lolling on his shoulders; he wasn't even looking where they were going. Each of his movements was blind. It seemed he trusted that she was taking him in the right direction. Though, in this state of vulnerability, he couldn't put up much of a fight against any threat.

She'd say anything if it would keep him conscious;

Harlow couldn't do this without his help. "What is it you want, Crash? Because it doesn't seem you're up to the challenge of a woman like me right now."

The faint mumble of his laugh became a grunt of pain. "Feel free to take advantage when I pass out."

"No," she said, pulling his arm further around her. "You're not going to pass out, Crash. Stay with me." All the wishing in the world didn't prevent the inevitable. Her stranger slumped further, making her stagger to the side. "Shit, you're heavy."

Sweat dampened her forehead. She could feel her hair sticking to the back of her neck where it wasn't being pulled by the leather of his jacket.

"You…" he slurred. "I…"

Determined to traverse half the block, they got around the corner but were still the length of this full block from the bar. Supporting him was getting more difficult by the second. The weight of his body shifted.

Blowing out the strain of his burden, Harlow struggled just to stop without falling over. "Crash," she said because she didn't know what else to call him. He'd crashed into her, so the moniker seemed appropriate. "I can't… are you…"

Falling against the wall of the building next to them, he didn't spend any time leaning and instead slid down onto the sidewalk.

The sight of his loose body crumpling filled her with dread. It was obvious he had little control. If he was unconscious, that was it, there would be nothing else she could do.

Desperate and terrified, Harlow dropped down beside his slumped figure. With a hand on his chest, she shuffled nearer and scooped his head up. His stubble was rough on her palm, but when she relaxed her hand, his head flopped.

His eyes were closed.

Picking up his head again, she tried to give him a shake. "Hey," she said, slapping his cheek.

Getting no response, she hit him again, a little harder.

It was useless. He was no longer conscious.

Unwilling to give up, she grabbed his shirt and pulled him forward, shaking him. Nothing happened. There was no sign of life.

Snatching her blood stained scarf from the ground next to him, she pressed it to his wound.

Panic surged through her. This man was going to die right there on the concrete if she didn't do something. "Oh, please," she whispered, crawling closer to stroke his face. "Please. Wake up, please."

The stranger didn't move, didn't respond. His pallor set fear alight within her. That spark of emotion ignited her fortitude. Harlow wouldn't let this happen. She wouldn't sit whimpering while he slipped away. Without fail, she'd always let fight win before she thought about giving in to fear. Resolve consolidated the mess of emotions warring within her. Action. She had to do something. She had to take action.

Surging to her feet, she left him there and ran down the rest of the block at full speed.

Shoving into Floyd's, she burst into the busy room, immediately drawing the attention of all those sitting around drinking. Looking left then right, she didn't even know who she was seeking, adrenaline drove her forward.

The bartender was already turning toward her. Dubious concern and suspicion gathered on his face as he scanned her. She could feel thick blood drying on her hands and was sure her clothes were covered in it, but she didn't care.

Panting, Harlow tried to catch her breath and gather the energy to speak. "Please," she said, beseeching the bartender. "Please help him."

His chin rose slowly. "Him? Him who?"

"Here," she said, taking a backward step and gesturing for him to follow. "Please, he's outside. Help him." In reverse, she retreated all the way to the door. Though there were more people out of their seats, and more looks of confused doubt, no one was following her. Frustration became anger. It erupted from her chest. "Get your fucking asses out here now!"

The desperation of her furious plea was enough to snap the bartender to attention. He disappeared around the corner of the bar, but reappeared at the same corner a moment later, this time on the customer side. Coming toward her with determination in his gait, two others materialized to flank him, matching the pace of his stride.

Harlow didn't loiter. Rushing outside, she hurried back down the sidewalk. Relief infused her when she found her patient where she'd left him. Crouching beside him, she put pressure on his wound and was stroking his face when the men from Floyd's joined her.

The first she became aware of them was a voice cutting through the night air. "It's Ryske," the voice said. Glancing over her shoulder, she saw the bartender on the phone. Of the two men who'd been with him, only one remained. The other had disappeared. "Definitely blue." He lowered the microphone from his mouth. "Is he out?" She nodded. "How long?"

"Less than five minutes," she said, feeling so protective that she twisted to prop a shoulder on the wall next to her unconscious friend. Easing Crash away from the cold concrete, she caught his deadweight and cradled his head against her chest. When she peeled her scarf from his wound, he didn't even flinch, which scared her even more. "He's lost a lot of blood. He wouldn't let me call 9-1-1. I tried. I wanted to, I…" Biting her lip, it didn't matter that she knew her sudden emotion was irrational, she couldn't control it. Harlow didn't even know this guy, yet grief was gripping her. "I should've done it, shouldn't I? I should've called 9-1-1."

The second man was about a half inch taller than the bulky bartender but was much leaner. Both were fit, leaving her to wonder if everyone in this neighborhood hit the gym.

"No," he said. "Definitely not. You did the right thing bringing him here. No 9-1-1… Let's see it."

Both men came in closer and the bartender lowered the mouthpiece of the phone again. The leaner one nodded toward her hand that was holding the scarf to the wound. Though it pained her to peel back the fabric again, Harlow wanted these men to help. Revealing the injury to the bartender and his companion, she blinked up just as they winced. The bartender turned his back to keep talking into the phone.

Harlow held the patient close, stroking his hair away from his forehead. "You're going to be okay, Crash. You're going to be okay."

The second guy hunkered down next to Crash, wearing an odd kind of smirk. "Asshole," he mumbled and socked Crash's knee with a light punch. "Even unconscious you snag 'em."

The act was peculiar. Although she couldn't figure out why anyone would want to punch or taunt an unconscious person, it made Harlow more protective. Holding Crash close, she used her body to block as much of him as she could. Whispering words of comfort, she tried to ignore the man crouched close to them.

Just as she was about to throw him the evil eye in hopes of getting him to back off, a car came skidding around the corner. Harlow tightened her embrace, praying this wasn't anyone coming to finish the job they'd started.

The bartender and the punching guy weren't concerned when the car came to a screeching halt in front of them. They opened both doors on the passenger's side, front and back, while the driver climbed out to come rushing over to her. Punching Guy stuck with the driver while the bartender stayed by the vehicle.

The bartender was off the phone and apparently the one in charge. "Get him up."

The driver and Punching Guy did as they were told, jostling her aside to pick up Crash from the sidewalk. Punching Guy hooked his forearms under Crash's arms, while the driver took his legs.

"You have to maintain pressure," she said, moving with them to press on the wound for as long as she could.

It pained her to back off. The driver put Crash's legs into the backseat and ran around to open the opposite door to pull him inside. Punching Guy kept control of Crash's upper body. Harlow couldn't tear her eyes away. She feared what would become of the stranger once they took him.

"Don't worry about that, Nightingale. You're going to be there to keep our boy going," the bartender said, putting a heavy arm around her shoulders.

"What?" she asked, but was given little choice.

The bartender urged her toward the vehicle and Punching Guy stepped aside once Crash was bundled into the backseat.

"Get in the car."

Punching Guy went around them to get in the front passenger seat while the driver leaped back in his side.

Putting a hand on her head, the bartender pushed her down, crowding her into the back. "But I…"

Almost sitting on Crash, Harlow had to grab his head up just to stop herself from landing on him.

"Keep him alive, Nightingale," the bartender said, pushing her in and slamming the door. "He's counting on you."

The second the door was closed, the bartender hit the roof twice and the car sped off, giving her no choice but to scoop up her patient's shoulders to lay his head in her lap.

Harlow was no nurse, except she was sure that if the bleeding hadn't at least slowed by now, the patient probably had no chance of making it. But for lack of anything else to do, she put pressure on the wound and looked out the window, wondering where the hell she was going and what could possibly happen next.

TWO

THEY DIDN'T DRIVE for long.

Half a dozen blocks later, they took a corner on two wheels and sped to the end of the block, coming to a skidding halt at the curb.

Adrenaline and fear kept Harlow going, but she couldn't think clearly enough to ask questions. Another man was waiting on the sidewalk to yank open the back door the moment they stopped. Autopilot made her help the trio of men pull the unconscious man from her lap.

Sidewalk Man jumped to action, helping them up the stoop. Harlow didn't remember the stairwell or entering the apartment. She was still trying to figure out what was going on or how she'd found herself there when Crash was laid on a bed in a bedroom so normal that it made the moment all the more surreal.

Sidewalk Man barked orders at the other two who were doing exactly what they were told.

Crash was stripped to the waist while Sidewalk Man, who it appeared was now in charge, went to a walk-in closet and came out with what Harlow was sure was an IV stand and a supply of blood.

"Get his pants off," Sidewalk Man said, shoving her

aside.

As though he'd just noticed her, he paused for half a beat to frown at her, like he was trying to figure out who she was. Harlow wasn't sure she'd be able to tell him if he asked because this seemed so unlike her life that she wasn't sure she was her anymore.

After that fleeting moment, he jumped back to action. The other two were pulling off Crash's boots, while Sidewalk Man bent to stick a needle into his arm. Both hands went to her mouth in an attempt to stifle her gasp. The act was so quick it seemed barbaric. Though, as shocked as she was, Harlow did feel an element of relief when she realized the patient was getting the medical attention he needed.

If there was any hope of Crash's life being saved, it was going to happen in this room.

Most of Sidewalk Man's body was blocking her view. But from his position, it appeared like he was examining Crash's wound. "Someone want to tell me what happened?" he asked.

The two men who'd just removed Crash's pants shared a look with each other. When they didn't respond, she felt obliged to say something. "I—"

"Nothing," Punching Guy said, cutting her off with a glare. "Just a mishap. You know how it is, Bale… Can you fix him?"

"Depends. How long has he been out?" Again, no one answered. The guy they'd called Bale raised his attention first to look at the two men standing at the foot of the bed. When he got nothing from them, he twisted to pin her in his sights. "The more I know, the more I can do."

"No more than twenty minutes," she said, earning herself a glare from the pair who'd closed ranks.

Bale focused on her. "Was he talking before he lost consciousness? Coherent? Oriented?"

That was difficult to answer when she didn't know what Crash was like under normal circumstances. At a bit of a loss, she opened her mouth, searching for a response. "He… he was hitting on me."

Punching Guy scoffed and the driver shook his head.

"Sounds like Ryske."

So Ryske was Crash? That was his name. "Do you know who stabbed him?" Bale asked.

Noting the professional edge to his tone, it felt like maybe this was what he did for a living. Given that he had all the necessary equipment, Harlow figured he had to be some kind of doctor.

The question was a shock. "Stabbed?" she asked, having not spent time speculating on the cause of his injury. "He… was stabbed? Oh my God."

Wobbling on her feet, she didn't realize her lightheadedness had transferred to anything physical until someone took her arm. Lifting her focus, she found Punching Guy at her side, holding her elbow.

"Just do your thing, Bale," Punching Guy said, guiding her toward the bedroom door. "Noon will help with whatever you need."

Unable to argue or fight, Harlow staggered sideways when Punching Guy opened the bedroom door and pulled her out into a darkened living room. He tugged her to the couch and left her standing between it and the coffee table while he went to check the front door was locked.

A chill went through her. Shrugging off her daze, Harlow took stock. She was alone in an apartment with four men—well, three and a half—and all of them were strangers to her. No one knew where she was and no one would know where to look for her.

Clutching her purse higher to her chest, she took a step backwards. "Who are you people?" she asked. "Why did he tell me not to call 9-1-1?"

In the moment, she'd been acting on instinct and impulse. It hadn't occurred to her to ask questions. The man was bleeding out; all she'd thought about was helping him.

With startling clarity, Punching Man's response brought things into focus. "We're criminals," he said, without compunction, coming toward her.

Trying her best to conceal the tension that began to clench her muscles, Harlow didn't let herself recoil. The man in front of her wasn't fazed despite offering such honesty.

Neither did he hesitate to offer her a hand like providing his lifestyle choice was a standard introduction.

"You're—"

"They call me Maze. Noon, he's the conscious one who drove the car. Ryske's the unconscious one who hit on you. Dover's the guy from behind the bar in Floyd's. Bale's the doc in the bedroom who's going to fix our friend right up."

Surprised that this Maze was being so open, she was nervous to shake his hand. Although, having been raised to be polite, she couldn't refuse it.

Remaining wary, she slipped her fingers into his palm. "Harlow."

"Nice to meet you, Harlow," he said, flashing her a smile that was just a little too suave for her liking. "You did our boy a solid tonight. That means we owe you…"

He didn't complete the sentence, and it seemed to be a deliberate choice. She could feel it hanging thick and unfinished in the air. "I…"

"Before we get to what you want from us, you have to tell me what you know… You tell me everything and no one else."

That statement was daunting in itself. This guy seemed to be a professional intimidator. Harlow hadn't known that was a crime, but she was beginning to rethink that assumption.

"No one else?" she asked. "I don't—"

"Ryske didn't want you calling 9-1-1 because cops ask questions. They're suspicious of guys who show up with stab wounds."

Sure, she imagined that they would be. This Maze had been kind enough to at least be honest about their profession, though she couldn't say it put her mind at ease. In fact, it raised more questions. Before she could respond, there was a knock at the door.

It was no normal knock. The sequence of different tempoed notes formed a tune. One which obviously meant something to Maze because he reversed to the door he'd just locked and opened it without even checking who he was granting entry to.

The bartender.

Dover. That was the name Maze had given for him.

Dover examined her while Maze locked the door again. "Who is she?" he asked, like she wasn't there.

"Haven't figured that out yet," Maze said, moving to his cohort's side… though "accomplice" may be a more accurate descriptor.

"Ryske gonna make it?"

"Haven't figured that out yet either," Maze said. "Noon's in there."

Dover nodded once. Both men started toward her, riveted in their focus. "You think she's one of Hagan's?"

Maze didn't get the opportunity to answer because she did. "I am not Hagan's," she asserted, offended by the notion. "His men were the ones who did this to Ryske. If I hadn't stepped in, they'd have finished what they started right there on the sidewalk."

Dover turned to look at Maze, who didn't say anything. Rethinking why the bartender had told her that he was counting on her to keep Ryske alive, Harlow began to get the impression that had been a con to keep her around until they figured her out.

"She fake named me," Maze said.

Her jaw fell. A sound of offense squeaked in the back of her throat. "I did not fake name you," she squawked. "My name is Harlow and I'll prove it."

Yanking open her purse, she rooted around and pulled out her wallet to retrieve her ID. The moment she held it up, Maze leaned forward to take it. Noticing how he took his time about scrutinizing the card, she regretted being so rash in producing it.

"IDs aren't hard to fake," Dover said, stepping forward to guard his associate who was less than discreet about pocketing her ID. "I've got a dozen of those in a drawer."

If these two thought she was going to be a pushover, they had another thing coming. "Yeah, because I'm sure your name's really Dover and Maze is the name his momma gave him," she said, thrusting one hand to her hip while the other opened to them. "May I have my ID back, please?"

"Sure," Dover said, moving to the side while Maze moved the other way, so the latter was shielded behind the former. "Just as soon as our colleague verifies your story."

"Your…" Stunned, her hand dropped. "Crash?" She shook the moniker they wouldn't recognize off her lips to replace it with the right one. "Ryske? You want to keep me here until Ryske can verify my story…" Incredulous was hardly enough to describe what she was feeling. "You're not serious… he might never wake up."

"And if he doesn't, that's bad for you," Dover said.

"I haven't told you what happened," she said, but they didn't seem interested in listening. "What do you think happened? Do you think I stabbed him? I didn't even know him before tonight! I still don't know him!"

Her plea didn't affect either of them. They went back to talking as though she were deaf. "If she's Hagan's, we shouldn't have brought her here," Maze said into Dover's ear.

Dover's chin swung toward his shoulder. "I wasn't going to leave her on the sidewalk. Ryske would be the first one to tell us to keep the variables under control."

Until that moment, Harlow had never considered that word to be an insult. "I am not a variable," she said, losing grip of her patience, which, at work, she had no trouble holding onto. Outside of work, she didn't have to worry about being professional. "I saved your friend's life! I didn't have to. I could've left him there on the sidewalk to bleed out. I could've called 9-1-1 and ignored him telling me not to! You guys might not like it, you might not trust me! Hell, I don't trust any of you! But I did a good thing tonight! All of you should be on the floor kissing my damn feet! You're the criminals! That's your choice! I am not on trial here! I do not answer to any of you! And I will not be threatened for saving your boy's ass!" Marching to them, she shoved Dover aside and opened her palm to Maze. "Give me my goddamn ID."

Maze looked past her, probably at Dover, who must have nodded because Maze retrieved the ID from his pocket and handed it over. "Ryske's always been able to pick 'em," he muttered.

Ignoring what that implied, Harlow stopped short of saying that Ryske hadn't picked her at all. The convergence of their lives meant that they'd happened to occupy the same space at the same moment in time. Neither of them had planned to crash to the sidewalk together.

Offended as she was by their treatment of her and the things they'd said as though she wasn't there, Harlow wasn't afraid of the oafs sharing this room with her.

Her lack of fear had a lot to do with her philosophy on life. Harlow believed a person was in control of their own destiny and that they had to take responsibility for their own choices. Given her training and experience, she could size people up with relative accuracy.

By their own admission, these men were criminals. Yet, no one had threatened her with violence. Other than Maze taking her out of the bedroom, no one had touched her. Whatever they were capable of, they hadn't raised her DEFCON level.

The bedroom door opened before another word was uttered. Bale came out pulling latex gloves off his hands.

Dover went toward him. "What's the word?"

"Bowel's intact far as I can see," Bale said, going into the kitchen to trash the gloves. "He was lucky."

The bedroom door was open. The guy they'd referred to as Noon was filling the frame, frustrating her view of the man who'd be in the bed behind him.

"Will he make it?" Maze asked.

Bale got a bottle of water from the fridge and took his time about opening it to drink before answering. "He lost a lot of blood. I'll run more in, give him some antibiotics and pray the wound isn't infected. I've irrigated it, but there's no way to know how dirty the blade was. I'll keep him sedated tonight, let him get some rest. I can't tell if there will be any lasting damage… unless you let me take him to the hospital."

Dover was the first to make a noise of disapproval. "You know the rules, Bale."

Harlow didn't know the rules, but she didn't care about rules. Especially ones that could end with people dying.

The same feelings of protectiveness she'd had on the sidewalk welled up in her again.

Seeing her cases through to the end was something she prided herself on. Harlow didn't abandon clients, no matter how tough things got.

"Would you like to see him, miss?" Miss. It took her a second to realize that she was the only female in the room; the only "miss" here. Her rubber-necking couldn't have gone unnoticed. Blinking at Bale, who was coming toward her, she started to nod. After registering her response, he adjusted to move toward the bedroom again. "Get your ass out the lady's way."

For a second, Bale stood facing off with Noon. Eventually, the man in the doorway sidestepped, giving Bale space to go back into the bedroom. The doctor stopped and gestured for her to follow.

While heading to the bedroom, Harlow was aware of Dover, Maze, and Noon huddling in the living room behind her. The importance of whatever they had to whisper about surpassed their concern for her and Bale being separated from them. Though given that the trio were blocking the exit, they'd know if anyone tried to sneak in or bolt.

Forgetting the distracted posse, she focused on seeing Ryske. Laid out on the bed, peaceful, with tubes in his arm and a loose dressing just resting over the wound on his hip, this was the first time she'd seen him in full light.

Compelled to get closer, Harlow moved to the edge of the bed and sank down beside him without caring about respectable distance. Stroking his hair away from his forehead, she admired his features. Dark hair, square jaw. Even while unconscious with a grave expression on his face, there was a kind of mischief that fizzed around him.

In the dim alleyway, she hadn't got a good look at him. There, in Bale's bedroom, the light from the nightstand lamp let her see that there was a bruise above his brow and another on his shoulder.

Concern made her pale fingers open on his chest. "Was he beaten up?"

Behind her, the doctor was doing something on the

dresser with supplies. "Ryske knows how to fight," Bale said. "How to handle himself. If there was a fight, you can bet he gave as good as he got… providing that was the plan."

That made her stop caressing the injury on Ryske's shoulder to turn to the doctor. "The plan?"

A slight frown tensed his preoccupied brow. "I have to finish cleaning him up," he said and nodded to the side, indicating that she should move out of his way.

In addition to what he'd been arranging on the dresser, there were various other medical supplies laid out on the nightstand. Bale put something with them and then dragged a tub chair from the corner over to the side of the bed. Sitting down, he went to work on Ryske.

For the first time all night, Harlow could breathe. "Are you a doctor?"

"I am," Bale said without taking his attention from his task.

Looking at Ryske's wound was making her queasy, so Harlow turned away and went to the window. The blinds were closed, but she used a finger to peek through them to the quiet street below.

"Are you a criminal too?"

He exhaled what could only be described as a laugh. "Every time I get a call from these guys."

The insinuation that just being around Ryske and his cohorts implicated them all made her uneasy. "I should've called 9-1-1, shouldn't I?"

"I don't know," he said. "Did Ryske tell you not to?"

"He did," she said and closed her eyes. "I don't know what I was thinking. He was there, bleeding in front of me, telling me not to call and, I don't know, it seemed like the right thing to do in that moment."

Part of her work involved building trust with individuals who were suspicious of authority. She'd often kept secrets or listened to people who wanted to get things off their chest. Respecting people and their wishes, even when they contrasted with her own beliefs, meant something to her. Judgment wasn't a part of her role, she had to be open-minded to those who did things she never would.

Thinking that maybe her acceptance was going to cause Ryske's downfall, she began to question whether she'd made the right choice.

"If Ryske told you not to, then you did the right thing," Bale said. The certainty in his voice intrigued her enough to turn. The doctor was busy with his work, so he probably didn't notice her scrutinizing him. "Ryske knows the plan."

Again with the plan. "What is the plan?"

Bale shrugged. There was a smile in his voice when he next spoke. "I don't know. I'm about as close to Ryske as anyone outside his crew can be, but he'd never think to fill me in on whatever the con is."

This night of surprises just kept on giving. "The... con?"

As if he'd sensed her astonishment, he paused to look over his shoulder. His gloved hands hovered over the wound he seemed to be dressing. "How long have you been sleeping with him?"

Ducking forward, she forgot to blink. "What? With Ryske? I... I'm not sleeping with him."

That seemed to heighten his curiosity. "Are you worth a lot of money?"

This conversation had gone in an odd direction that left her confused. "What does that have to do with anything?"

He'd loosened again. "Just wondering if you're the con," he said and went back to his work. "You weren't the one who stabbed him, were you?"

She bit her lip instead of rolling her eyes. "No." Though maybe if she'd gotten to know him better, she might have been tempted. The man was unconscious and managing to cause her aggravation. "What do you mean I'm the con?"

"I was exaggerating... sort of," he said. "Ryske will do almost anything for a job, but I'm sure this is a step too far, even for him. Though it's not the first time he's been stabbed, so if this was for a con, he knew what he was in for... Course it wouldn't be the first time he's taken things too far either."

Going to the end of the bed, she was astounded by

the man lying on it, and wondered what had brought him to her. His athletic body had been pressed into her while she'd tried to coax him to Floyd's. That's when she'd learned Ryske was in shape. Seeing him now, wearing nothing but a pair of dark boxer-briefs, his ripped physique was more conditioned than she could have imagined.

A black tribal tattoo arched around his uninjured hip in sharp curved claws that stretched across his defined abs. Covering half his abdomen, it stopped just beneath his ribs. Adorning the shoulder opposite his abdominal tattoo was another tribal design. This one cut across his collar bone and continued down to his elbow and forearm. Beneath the claws that extended beyond his elbow was a wide black wristband tattoo of zigzags and what looked like arrowheads.

Her curiosity about what the ink meant peaked when Bale picked up Ryske's wrist closest to the center of the bed, presumably to check his pulse. On the back of that forearm, extending from elbow to almost his wrist were four thick black stars. They had to stand for something. Harlow was sure of it.

The doctor put Ryske's arm back down and went back to his work. Not finished with her inspection, Harlow noted that just under his watch was the only piece of jewelry he seemed to be wearing. A narrow, rounded braid of black leather circled his wrist. At the front was a dark metal cylinder that seemed to be engraved.

Tipping her head, she squinted to try reading what the bracelet said. "On his wrist, what does the—"

"Carpe noctem," he said and then translated the words. "Seize the night." Harlow had known what carpe noctem meant, but didn't interrupt. "That's Ryske, and maybe explains why he's got scars all over."

It seemed that the doctor had picked up on how curious she was about the patient. Though given that he was still working, she didn't know how he could. Finishing with what he was doing, Bale reached over to curve a hand around Ryske's leg. Rolling the patient just a little, the doctor showed her the outer side of his patient's thigh where there was a healed scar.

"How did—"

"That one's a stab wound."

Either this was Bale proving his previous point, or him trying to warn her about the man she'd saved. "A stab wound?"

Nodding, he pushed Ryske's starred arm up to show a thin slice of a scar front to back on his ribs beneath his arm. "That was a bullet, just grazed him, but still bled bad." Putting his arm back down, Bale began to clean up the supplies. "I've patched 'em all up at one time or another."

After putting the used and dirty things aside, he took a blood pressure cuff from his bag that was on the nightstand.

"You're their doctor," she said, trying to figure this whole warped scenario out. "But if they're criminals, why would you—"

"It's a long story, and not one I want to tell," he said.

She wasn't quickly dissuaded. "You implied you weren't part of his crew."

"I'm not," he said, then breathed out. "I guess I'm peripheral. I don't doubt that they have a lot of people who help them out. But Ryske, Dover, Noon, and Maze, they trust each other and only each other."

"That's the crew? The four of them?" she asked. Bale nodded, going through his checks. "And they con people? Rich people? That's what they do?"

He stopped to look at her. "If you want to know more, you should ask Ryske."

Quizzing the doctor was putting him in an awkward position. There was no sense of fear coming from him and he'd stood up to the crew in the living room. But Harlow had no idea how these men got the doctor to look after them. The last thing she wanted to do was endanger him in any way.

"Thanks," she said, hoping Ryske would make it through to tell his tales, even if she wouldn't be around to hear them. "But now that I know he's safe, I think I should probably just go… if his buddies will let me leave."

Wearing a smile, he returned his focus to his patient. "Don't worry about them. No one's being falsely imprisoned in my apartment. If they try to restrain you, I'll call the cops myself."

Bale seemed normal, rational, sane. In short, not like the men in the living room. It was nice to have an ally.

With the reassurance she'd be allowed to leave, Harlow took what could be one last look at the patient. "Is he going to be okay, Doctor?"

"There's no rush for you to cut ties. No one here will hurt you and Ryske will want to thank you. Why don't you go home, get some rest, and come back tomorrow to check on him yourself?" The doctor was more than sane, he was warm and kind. "Some sleep wouldn't hurt and I think you could probably do with cleaning up."

Scanning her, his smirk grew before his attention returned to his patient. Harlow had forgotten about the blood on her clothes and on her hands. Bale was right, she should clean up, and she did need rest.

"Okay," she said, without lying to herself that she wouldn't be curious about Ryske. Follow up was part of her job too. Checking on a person she'd helped was engrained in her. Harlow wanted to keep on helping Ryske, despite his less than savory choices. "You're sure that would be okay? He'll be here?"

"The Floyd's crew trust my medical choices," he said. "Best case scenario, there's no organ or brain damage from the blood loss, but Ryske will still have to heal, and finish the course of antibiotics. I'll be keeping him here for at least two weeks."

"Two weeks? You think you can keep him here that long?"

"I think if he goes against medical advice they'll lose their doctor pretty fast," he said. "I take a huge risk treating them like this. If something goes wrong, I lose my license, possibly go to jail, and have to live with the guilt for the rest of my life. They know I'll keep doing everything I can to help them, providing they respect my professional opinion. That includes convalescence instructions. I've fought with them about this too many times. They know I win or I won't be here the next time." He flashed her a fast smile. "This is not our first rodeo, Miss…"

"Sweeting," she said, hearing the question in his voice. "Harlow Sweeting."

"Do you have a boyfriend waiting for you at home, Harlow Sweeting?" She shook her head. "Kids?" Again, she shook her head. "Good. Do you live alone?"

"Why does that…"

"I'm checking how wide the circle is," he said. "I just told you that what I'm doing could get me into trouble."

As a doctor, it was his responsibility to treat the person in front of him. Just as she'd felt it was her responsibility to support the person in front of her when Ryske had bowled her over in the street.

Decisions made on impulse weren't always the most reasoned, or easy to explain later when someone was trying to rationalize them… like in an interrogation room.

"Your secret is safe," she said, wondering if she could get into trouble for what she'd done too. Technically, nothing she'd done was illegal, but unethical could cause her problems in her professional role. "If mine is safe with you."

His smile became more genuine. "Creeping around with criminals not your usual bag?"

Relaxing, she returned his ease. "Not exactly."

He stood up, removing his gloves. "Then I guess you're part of their toolkit now too, just like me," he said and came over, raising his open arm to her shoulders. "Welcome to the club. Come on, I'll get Noon to drive you home."

"Noon? I don't need a ride."

Pausing with a hand on the bedroom door handle, he smirked. "Noon does the driving… always."

THREE

HARLOW HADN'T EXPECTED Noon to show up the following morning in spite of him saying that he would come to pick her up. But when she came around the corner from the deli that Sunday, he was there, waiting on the sidewalk.

The previous night he'd driven her home and actually thanked her for bringing Ryske to them. She wouldn't exactly call him warm and fuzzy, but she'd felt comfortable enough to tell him that she wanted to come and see Ryske again. That was when he'd offered to pick her up and take her back to Bale's.

Getting into a car with him again was a much calmer experience that day and conversation on the ride over to Bale's was civilized if inconsequential. When they arrived at the doctor's apartment, Harlow wasn't surprised to find Dover, Maze, and Bale in various states of tired and grumpy strewn around the living room. They'd obviously been up all night.

Harlow won friends when she put down the tray of coffees and box of fresh pastries that she'd collected from the deli before finding Noon outside her building.

Like a pack of desperate hyenas, the men attacked the feast. "Did Ryske wake up? How's he doing?"

"He's still on the IV," Bale said, slurping coffee. "But

I withdrew the sedative, so he should be waking up soon."

Unlooping her scarf, she laid it on the back of the couch and then took off her jacket. "Can I go in?"

Bale nodded. The other three were too busy fighting over pastries to object.

Keeping her purse and a sports bag hanging across her body, Harlow went into the bedroom. Ryske was exactly where she'd left him. His general color was better, but the bruises were more developed. On the floor by the nightstand was an open trash bag filled with various used medical supplies and dirty dressings.

Taking the straps of the two bags she was wearing off over her head as she went closer, she put both on the floor and sat down in the leather tub chair that had been angled toward Ryske just in front of his IV stand. This wasn't like any hospital she'd been in. The set up made it feel like visiting a patient, which she guessed it should because that was what she was doing.

Sliding her hand under his felt a little odd. They weren't friends, didn't really know each other at all. Yet, she felt a connection to him; one that told her she'd be devastated if he didn't pull through.

Sitting beside him felt natural, even though taking physical liberties should feel awkward. In contradiction to that rational, reasonable thought about containing herself, her fingertip stretched out to graze the curve of his tattoo just above his elbow. The black ink mesmerized her, drawing her in. Turning her nail against the edge, she traced the shape of it further up his arm, over the bulk of his bicep.

She didn't know how long she'd been sitting there, outlining the pattern on his arm with her fingernail because the hypnotic act pulled her into a trance. Ryske was clearly strong and capable. If he was smart enough to be on this side of prison walls, he had to be intelligent enough to know what he was doing.

That left her to speculate: what caused someone to choose crime as a way of life?

Harlow was a trusting person. Many colleagues and clients had accused her of being naïve. She'd be the first to admit that her upbringing was more sheltered than most. But she was savvier than her sister and had seen more than she was given credit for. Not rushing to judgment was a point of pride for her.

On the job, she'd learned plenty about people and appearances and how they could be deceiving. Just because she accepted people didn't mean that she believed everyone was redeemable or wanted to be saved. But choosing a life of crime had to be a sign of a deeper pathology. Was Ryske punishing himself? Did he enjoy the thrill?

No one was flat evil; that was one truth she was certain of. Blaming inherent wickedness like it was unavoidable was a cop out as far as she was concerned. People had to take ownership of their actions. She couldn't deny that there were people who took pleasure in cruelty. Too often in her job, she met selfish people who would choose their own wants over another's needs.

But was anyone truly selfless? It was a truth she hadn't yet figured out, but that didn't stop her from trying every once in a while.

"Was I good?"

The croaking masculine voice pulled her out of her philosophical pondering. Ryske's eyes were open to slits and were definitely fixated on her.

Harlow's hand fell from its exploration. "Good?"

"When I was out and you took advantage," he said, his voice rough.

Moving made his expression distort in discomfort. Realizing that he was trying to sit up, Harlow panicked and leaped to her feet. "No," she said, pressing his shoulders to prevent him from rising. "Lie down, Ryske."

Giving up the fight, he relaxed onto his back, taking the time to check out where they were. "Guess we made it to Bale's."

"Would you like me to get him?" she asked, shuffling backwards a half step.

His hand shot up to grab her wrist before she could get too far. "Floyd's," he murmured, intent on her. "Did anyone hurt you?"

That he even thought to ask stunned her enough that she sank back down into the chair she'd left just a moment ago. "No one hurt me," she said. He loosened like that was a relief and closed his eyes. "I had to curse at them to get them to move. You should've introduced yourself before you passed out, that might have helped."

Pain and exhaustion joined the scratch in his throat. "Crash was just fine, Trinket."

His grip on her wrist slackened, which gave her the chance to slide her hand beneath his. Holding his palm over hers and wrapping her fingers around his thumb didn't make her self-conscious. It should because they were strangers, yet, it felt familiar.

Taking it as a good sign that he remembered their meeting, she guessed that was an indication there was little chance of brain damage.

He cracked an eye for a second. "It's daylight. Have you been here all night?"

"Noon took me home," she said. "I had to get cleaned up. I came back with food a while ago. Your crew are eating in the living room... They'll want to know you're awake."

"Just give it a minute, Trink," he said with a groan that betrayed he wanted a minute to orient himself before everyone descended with questions. "Just talk. Keep talking."

Unsure what to say, she licked her lips and ran her gaze down over his tattoos again. "You gave everyone a scare," she said. "We didn't know if you were going to make it. I don't think your friends wanted to answer Bale's questions. For a minute, I think they suspected that I'd hurt you. I don't know, maybe they still do... Bale's nice. He was nice to me anyway. He likes you, said you were close... At least as close as you could be to anyone outside your crew. Maze told me that you're criminals." Shifting closer, she clung to his hand, but a fingernail from her other hand began to move around the lines of his arm tattoo again. "He didn't go into detail, but Bale implied there was a plan and you like to con people out of things... Guess that's why your friends were suspicious of me. If you go around duping people, you have to accept that one day someone's going to dupe you right back."

The sight of his chest expanding was startling. The loud, sharp whistle that echoed from his lips a moment later gave her a jolt. His eyes weren't open, but he tightened his grip on her hand when she tried to withdraw it.

A moment later, the bedroom door opened and everyone from the living room poured into the room with them.

Off-kilter and braced to see what would happen next, Harlow was on the edge of her seat. Her attention flicked from the expectant men at the end of the bed to the one lying down who'd opened his eyes again, but this time their intensity was trained on his crew.

"You fuckers talk too much," was the first thing Ryske said.

Bale came around the bed, forcing Ryske to let go of her when she pushed the tub chair back out of the doctor's way.

Grabbing a penlight, the doctor used it to test Ryske's pupils. "What day is it?" Bale asked.

"Fuckday," Ryske said and had enough strength to push the doctor so hard that he stumbled. One more step and he would've ended up in her lap. "Get out my face. What you doing running your mouth?"

Glancing over his shoulder, Bale looked from her back to Ryske. "She said you weren't sleeping together."

"Not yet," Ryske said. Cradling his injury, he pushed up into a seated position. Though he was fighting through obvious pain, no one stepped up to stop him. "We get any whisper?"

"No," Dover said.

Maze and Noon flanked the bartender at the end of the bed. With slow, tentative movements, Bale went about taking Ryske's blood pressure. The patient glared at the doctor but didn't put up a fight.

"You deliver the package?" Maze asked.

"I did that," Ryske said. "As per the plan, I lost ten grand to the bastard... then his slave stabbed me."

"Ophelia?" Maze asked, ignoring the shocking thing he'd just been told.

If Harlow had heard it, the others had to have heard it too. Instead of caring about their friend and his near death experience, the crew were focused on this "plan" talk.

"Present and correct," Ryske said. "For a minute, I thought I'd have to go deeper, but they took the bait." He hissed when Bale peeled back the dressing on his wound. "Maybe a little too well."

"You played dirty?" Maze said.

"Like he expects me to."

"The guy is desperate for any excuse to spill your blood. Violence is his first impulse whenever you give him an opening," Dover said. "It's amazing that you made it twelve blocks."

"Made it more than that. I had to try losing them. Took them in circles a while. Thought it was no big deal, the knife went in smooth," Ryske said. "Brash doesn't know how to fight clean. Animal took pleasure in pleasing Hagan. Prick."

Whatever Bale was doing, it made Ryske wince and push at the doctor who was trying to help him. Despite the patient's obvious discomfort, Harlow didn't leap to his aid. She was too busy trying to put together the pieces of what they were saying.

"I have to check it, Ryske," Bale said, but that didn't quell the mood of the man on the bed. "If infection eats its way down to your dick, you won't have anything to fuck the pretty social worker with."

That statement stopped Ryske's objections. While he sagged back, letting his head fall and his eyes close, she perked up. "Social worker?" she asked, gaining the attention of the men at the end of the bed. "You're talking about me?" Rising slowly, she wasn't sure whether to be livid or offended. "You checked up on me?"

"Turns out you didn't fake name me," Maze said.

It was galling that these people thought it was acceptable to investigate her without cause. When she'd come in to find them awake, she'd been touched that they cared for their friend so much. Now she learned they'd spent time trawling her past.

"I can't believe you assholes," she said, leaping from her chair. She shoved Bale aside and grabbed the two bags she'd dumped onto the floor. After tossing the strap of her purse over her head, she threw the sports bag at Ryske, without caring that when it landed on him, he cursed and braced against it. "Save yourself next time, Crash."

Ready to spin and leave them all to their insanity, she was once again stalled by Ryske grabbing her wrist. "Clear out," he said.

Dover, Maze, and Noon immediately turned to filter out, but Bale held back. "I still have to—"

"In a minute, doc," Ryske said, softer this time, with less impatience and aggravation.

Bale went out after the others. Dover ducked back in to close the door. Harlow was still fizzing and couldn't imagine what Ryske thought he could say that would appease her.

"Coincidence doesn't happen in our world," he said. "We doubt anyone who occupies the same time and space as us. Serendipity is suspicious. They were looking out for me. That's all, Trinket. They thought their friend was dying and needed to do something…. They had to do something."

Damn. But she understood his point. Relaxing her resistance, she exhaled and turned slowly to see that although he was trying to hide it, he was still in pain. The sports bag lay beside him on the bed. She shouldn't have thrown it at him. It could've really hurt him. Rage wasn't usually part of her repertoire, but she'd been hurt by the intrusion on her privacy.

"Your friends could learn to strike up a conversation," she said, sitting on the bed by his hip to reach across him to unzip the sports bag.

"That's usually my job," he said, and surprised her by scooping his fingers through her hair at her temple to draw her attention up. "Didn't you promise me something if I made it?"

"No," she said, noticing the deep green of his eyes for the first time. If she hadn't just seen him wake up, she'd wonder if he was wearing colored contacts. "You got to live, that should be enough."

"Not enough," he said, trailing the pad of his thumb down her cheekbone to the front of her chin.

It was incredible to see such heat and desire in his magnetic gaze. The man had been unconscious only a matter of minutes ago. Yet, somehow, he was making her feel like they'd just come to the end of an intense date and there was only one thing he'd be capable of, and it wasn't related to any injury.

"Just back from the brink of death and you're still making moves," she said, taking his hand away from her face and shifting back to lay his hand just above his wound. "Your friends might have confidence in your abilities, but there's only one thing you should be thinking about and that's getting better."

Leaning forward, his hands seemed to be en route to her waist. "Don't worry about that, we'll work around it."

All she could do was laugh and avoid his attempts to get hold of her. Pushing his hands away, she reached into the bag to pull out the sweats she'd bought that morning. "Work around a knife wound," she said, almost shaking her head. Leaving the bed, she went toward the end to feed his feet into the pants. "Yeah, that's hot, Ryske. Really hot."

It seemed like a smart idea to avoid looking into those eyes while she struggled to get him into the clothes. "What happened to my sponge bath?"

This guy just didn't let up, and it wasn't easy to keep concealing her smile. "I want approval from the doctor before you even think about moving," she said, deciding that being firm was the only way to handle him. "You should drink something and probably eat. You'll need to keep your strength up."

Ryske was intent on his flirtation. "You like it energetic, Trink?"

Any opening would only encourage him. As much as she was tempted to laugh, Harlow knew his behavior was probably a result of him being high on whatever Bale was feeding into him.

"Yeah, that's it," she said. "You're useless to me in

this state."

"Tell me how you like it, baby," he said, letting her pull the pants over his ass and take water from the sports bag.

Opening it, she put a straw inside and sat on the bed next to him to hold the bottle and direct the straw so he could take a drink. "Have more," she said, hoping the liquid would help him.

"I'll have more if you give me something."

He was worse than a taunting teenager. "I'll slap you if you keep playing."

"Playing is what I do best," he said, sliding a hand up her leg.

Catching his digits, she pushed them down to her knee. "You're lucky you're an invalid on drugs," she said. "If you were a client, I'd be lodging a complaint."

The deep purr of his voice was seductive in itself, but she had to ignore the tingle vibrating through her. "Let go of my hand and I promise you'll have nothing to complain about, babydoll."

The last thing Harlow would do was let his hands wander. Even though he was just teasing, there was something endearing about his drowsy eyes. He wanted to be himself to seduce her like he was on top form and able. But the poor guy was so tired he couldn't even lift his head from the headboard at the back of the bed.

It wasn't typical for her to wander into ethical gray areas; it wasn't typical for her to be spending time with a man like Ryske either.

Changing the subject seemed to be the best way to give both of them a break. "What happened last night?" she asked. "Will you tell me that?"

The patient wasn't distracted. "Will you tell me what turns you on?"

"Maybe," she said. "Answer my question and maybe I'll answer yours."

"I got stabbed," he said, managing to thread his fingers through hers.

At least while they were linked, his hand wasn't seeking anything more intimate. "I got that. Why did you get stabbed? Hagan's men were the ones who hurt you. Who is he? Why did you want to lose ten thousand to him? Who's Ophelia?"

His eyes closed again. "Not your competition."

Edging further up the bed, she kept his hand, but used her other to touch the bruise on his brow. "How did you get this? Seems the guy taking ten thousand dollars from you should be enough. Why did he want a pound of flesh too?"

"Didn't have the cash," he said. "Lost in a card game, didn't have the money to cash out."

"But…" Harlow didn't understand. "Why play if you didn't have it to lose? Didn't you show him the cash up front? Wasn't it a friendly game?"

He smirked. "Friendly? Hardly. Stakes were more than cash."

Frustrated again, Harlow couldn't figure it out. She wanted to ask more, but felt guilty pushing so soon after his injury and while he was vulnerable.

"I can't figure you out, Crash," she murmured, combing her fingers through his hair.

His hand loosened from hers; he was slipping back into sleep. "Don't give up trying, Trink," he said, his whispered words slow and heavy. "My guardian angel."

"Shh," she said, letting her fingers drift down to touch his lips. "I'll be here when you wake up. Get some sleep."

FOUR

HARLOW SAT WITH Ryske for another few minutes until she was sure he was asleep. She didn't like that he was still in a seated position because that put pressure on his wound. But she wasn't going to try to move him herself. Doing that would cause more harm.

Inside the sports bag, she'd packed a few essentials and added the things she'd bought before going to the deli. Most of what was inside fell into the toiletries or clothing categories. But she'd also brought a blanket. Pulling it out, she spread the soft material across his chest. Tucking it in and running her hand into his hair one last time, she was actually reluctant to leave. Forcing herself to go, she left the bed and headed out to the living room.

The guys were on the couches and chairs, arranged around the coffee table that was still strewn with the remnants of the breakfast she'd brought.

Wearing a frown, she marched across the room to stand in front of the fireplace, and raised her hands to her hips, giving them all a dose of her disapproval. "I know you were afraid of losing him," she said, scanning the men. "I understand that and I know you had no idea who I was or if I was a threat to him. But you had no right to go checking up on me, not without at least asking me for honesty first."

"It's Maze's default to dig," Dover said, slouching deeper into his armchair to her right. "And we had to know if you were connected to Hagan."

"If I had been, I wouldn't have gotten into the car outside Floyd's," she said.

"Sure you would," Noon said from the couch next to Maze opposite where she was standing. "If you were doing recon for Hagan, finding Bale would be a coup."

"It's a competition," Dover said. "It's complicated, Nightingale. You don't understand what's going on. We're in deep."

"We have to protect ourselves," Noon said. "And while Ryske is down, it's our job to protect him."

Harlow understood that too. She couldn't understand why they didn't see that she had been protecting him as well. Maybe her reasons were different from theirs, but she hadn't done Ryske any harm, she'd only helped.

Before she could say any of that, Maze snapped, "I don't see why we're groveling," he said, suddenly sitting up straight. "She's no threat, we know that. She is a potential target, but that's not our problem. If she's pissed off, she knows where the door is."

"Ryske seems to like her," Bale said.

Maze just smiled. It was an ironic twist to his lips, not rooted in happiness. "And if he wants her, he'll go get her, we all know that. I'm not going to grovel, Harlow. I am grateful that you helped our boy, and if you need a favor to even the score, you'll find one of us in Floyd's any time. But you don't have to be here. If you hate us, leave. If you're pissed, leave."

Telling them that she didn't like what they'd done wasn't about hate or anger. She'd told Ryske that she would be here when he woke up and she planned to be. Maze was tense about something, and she had a feeling it wasn't her.

Ignoring Maze's temper, she switched her focus to Bale. "Ryske's asleep. I gave him some water, is that okay? He only had a sip."

"That's fine," Bale said.

Sometimes the doctor seemed to be the only sane

mind present. "He's still sitting up. I don't want him to get hurt. Could you help me lay him down?"

"Maze will help the doc," Dover said, nodding at his friend who hadn't expected to be volunteered. "Go help."

His jaw moved, but he got up and went into the bedroom with Bale not far behind him. After the door closed, Dover breathed out and raised his hands to the top of his head.

Noon was the one to move to the front of his seat. "Ignore Maze, he's being an asshole," he said to her. "We do have to protect the crew, but it's not you he's pissed at."

"Though he's right," Dover said. "You should probably go. This isn't your life."

Getting rid of her wasn't going to be easy. "What isn't my life?" she asked, walking to the chair that Bale had vacated at the opposite end of the coffee table from Dover. "I chose my career because I wanted to help people. I'm here to help."

The way Dover and Noon looked at each other was intriguing, though she couldn't quite figure out what it meant. Were they still suspicious of her or worried about drawing her in deeper?

"How long have you all been friends?" she asked, trying to break the ice.

It took a moment before anyone answered, but eventually Dover drew his eyes from Noon to her. "A long time," he said. "A very long time."

These men were protective of their friendships. The default seemed to be more about habit than suspicion. It had become clear that they took their cues from Ryske. As long as he was out of service, they were going to feel at a disadvantage, which would probably make them defensive.

They'd witnessed their friend hurt, they were shook up, and for some reason, she was too. Ryske's crew had a reason to worry, Harlow didn't. She hadn't known him before last night. Yet, for some reason, she felt like she too would be more grounded if Ryske would come around. It was a crazy thought; she'd never known him as himself at his full strength.

But she was intrigued. Maybe too intrigued. Whether or not it was healthy, Harlow didn't plan on going anywhere until her curiosity was satisfied.

***

RYSKE'S CREW KEPT to themselves. Most of the time when she walked into a room they were huddled together and either shut up so she wouldn't catch a word or lowered their volume, making it clear that they didn't want her to be part of their discussions.

Bale was a pleasant host though. He let her help with the checks on sleeping Ryske and after popping out to the store, he gave her free rein to cook in his kitchen. It was a distraction; one she needed to clear her head. Going through the motions in the kitchen was easier than trying to figure out why it was so important to her to keep her promise to Ryske that she'd be around when he woke up.

Harlow didn't like to make promises. In fact, it was one of the first things she'd learned at work. Promises were easy to break and sometimes it wasn't anyone's fault; some things just weren't possible. So while it was a nice idea to tell a family they'd get to stay together or to promise kids that they wouldn't be separated from their parents, it wasn't possible to make that happen when courts said otherwise or parents went to jail or died.

Maybe that was why she was so determined to keep the promises that she did make. Staying for Ryske wasn't a hardship; she had nothing but homework to do that Sunday. If time got on and she really had to, she could do some of her research on her phone.

The soup she'd made was cooling on the stove when Dover poked his head out of the bedroom to whistle at Noon and Maze, who got up to go scurrying into the bedroom. The door was closed and she was left alone in the kitchen to guess that Ryske had woken up.

Harlow was still frowning at the bedroom door a minute later when the timer went off, indicating that her cookies were ready. Taking them from the oven, she placed them on a cooling rack and then ladled some soup into a bowl.

It wasn't just Ryske who intrigued her. She had an

odd compulsion to get to the bottom of what had happened. If these men were acting in a way designed to hurt them, it was her professional duty to help them avoid destructive behavior.

Retrieving a spoon from the drawer, she carried the bowl of soup to the bedroom. She didn't even care that the men bristled when she opened the door and entered to join them.

Harlow ignored the trio and went to sit by Ryske, stirring the soup as she walked. Focusing on the food meant she didn't have to look anyone in the eye, and it let her keep up the appearance of being relaxed and unaffected by the crew's annoyance at her presence.

Bale wasn't in the room. The shower was on in the adjoining bathroom, so she guessed that's where he was.

"You want to give us a minute, Harlow?" Dover asked.

Scooping some soup into the spoon, she circled her lips and blew on it gently, leaning closer to Ryske. "He has to eat," she said, offering the spoon to the patient's lips. "Bale said it was okay."

"I'm sure he can work a spoon," Maze said without disguising his impatience.

Matching the half-smile that hinted on Ryske's lips before he opened them to accept the soup, she inched a little higher. "It's okay, she can stay," Ryske said, licking the soup from his lips. "That's good, Trink."

"Made it myself," she said, scooping up some more and testing the temperature on her lip before offering it to his.

Crooking a brow, he showed he was impressed and accepted the food.

"She really is a regular Florence Nightingale," Dover muttered.

Harlow chose to ignore him and kept feeding Ryske. "I baked cookies for you too, if you're strong enough." The intimate mood that had been building between them was shattered when Ryske lurched forward, choking in a cough and putting a hand under his chin to catch the soup that tried to escape. Panic made her shove the soup onto the nightstand.

Standing in a stoop, stroking his back, Harlow cupped a hand around his cheek. "Was it too hot? God, I'm sorry, Crash. I'm sorry."

A blink later, he'd recovered. His chin rose. The feral look he pinned on her brought her up short. She wasn't quite sure why he was suddenly so aware of her.

"Clear out, guys."

That tone was a more serious variation on the purr he'd used before falling asleep.

"Oh, geez," she heard Maze mutter.

Glancing back, the trio were slipping out of the bedroom. Harlow was still confused about what had happened when Ryske's fingers curled around her wrist. He drew her back down to sit on the bed. Pulling her hand across his lap, he held it down on the mattress by his uninjured hip, forcing her to lean across him.

"Are you okay?" she asked.

With his eyelids low, his gaze managed to be intent on something, but it wasn't her face. With a loose hand, he swept her hair from her shoulder and leaned forward. A brief moment of discomfort made him pause to grit his teeth, but it passed and he kept moving until his breath warmed the crook of her neck.

"Cookies, huh?" he murmured a moment before pressing the heat of his mouth to her skin.

Shock and arousal jolted her. "Ryske," she said, planting a hand on his shoulder, but he still had her other wrist in his grip and she couldn't get it free. "Oh my God, no. No!"

"Don't fight, Trink," he said, kissing her neck again. Just like before, his fingers began to slide up the inside of her knee toward the hem of her skirt. "I'm gonna make you feel so good."

The spell of sleep had given his brazenness a boost. "No," she said, grabbing for his hand to force it away from her leg. Leaning away as much as she could, Harlow got her neck out of the reach of his entitled mouth. "Ryske, I want to take care of you."

His alight eyes were trailing across her body. "It's my turn to take real good care of you, babydoll."

"No," she said, flattening his hand onto his chest. After what was meant to be an anchoring press, she skimmed her fingers down to his dressed wound. "You're injured."

That wasn't the only reason that she was saying no to his advances but figured it should be the most relevant factor in *Ryske's* decision making. "Everything works, baby. I promise. No problems."

There was no way she believed that he actually knew that every part of himself worked after experiencing such trauma and blood loss. Not that it mattered, there was no way that she wanted to find out.

"No," she said, being more forceful about putting his hand to his chest when he tried to reach for her again. "God, Ryske, if this is what you're like at half-strength, I dread to think about how vigorous you'd be if you were yourself."

A renewed sparkle shone from him. "Is that what you need, baby? Vigorous?"

He might be talking in that purr he reserved for seduction, but her interest in being alluring wasn't as high as his. In her attempt to dissuade him, she took on an almost schoolmarm persona and sat straighter to chastise him.

"I need for you to eat your soup. If you finish it, I might…" She held up a straight finger. "*Might* let you have a cookie. But you are going to keep your hands to yourself and your mouth too, definitely your mouth. You should keep that to…" she cleared her throat. "To yourself."

Sinking back against the pillows propped on the headboard, he smirked again. "You're in charge, Trinket," he said. Thinking that her resistance had exhausted him might have been premature. "But when I'm myself again, I'm gonna have you… and you're not even going to fight it."

He didn't fight to keep her wrist when she took it from his grip against the mattress. After adjusting her position, Harlow picked up the soup again and began to feed him. "You're lucky that you're on drugs or I'd be offended by that presumption."

Harlow had been given an excellent education, her parents had insisted on it. But she didn't usually speak quite so properly. Maybe Ryske's lack of compunction increased hers. She'd shake it off. She would. Once she got used to being around Ryske… if she ever got used to it.

"You've got some big words there, baby," he said. "But, I gotta tell you, other than whatever you put in that broth, I'm not on any drugs."

It wasn't a broth, but that wasn't really the point. Lowering the bowl an inch, she noticed that the IV was no longer in his arm. The stand was there, but the needle was gone.

"You're… what about the antibiotics?"

Either he was confused or didn't care, maybe he'd been talking about illegal drugs. Reassuring as it was to know he wasn't an addict, Harlow hadn't thought for a second that he was. In addition to the antibiotics, she'd guess Bale had Ryske on some kind of painkillers. Though it might not be so easy to get his hands on the narcotics without a patient to declare.

Shrugging off her question, Ryske sighed. "Bale's the doctor," he said, walking his fingertips onto her knee again. "You worry about playing nursemaid."

"That hand goes any higher, and you'll need the doctor all over again."

"Good," he said, accepting another spoonful. "We're defining our boundaries. Keep telling me what works for you. How's this?"

Sliding his hand higher, he flattened it out, until his fingertips touched the hem of her skirt. "Keep it out of my clothes and I'll let it stay there."

The soup was cool enough now that she didn't have to blow. Even though Maze had probably been right that Ryske could work a spoon, Harlow kept feeding him.

After another few spoonful's, he spoke, "Why did you choose social work?"

"I wanted to help people. Why did you choose crime?"

"Same reason," he said.

His fingers bent and straightened on her leg in an almost constant caress, but he didn't let them ascend beneath her skirt, just as she'd asked.

With the spoon in the soup, she narrowed her eyes on him. "You chose crime to help people?"

"Yeah," he said and smiled. "Me."

Dragging the back of the spoon against the rim of the bowl, she scraped off the drips. "It can't be that satisfying," she said. "Don't you feel guilty about hurting people for your own gain?"

"I don't hurt people," he said, curling his fingers around hers on the spoon to guide it to his mouth. After slurping from it, he licked the spoon. "Not the kind of people you help anyway."

When he released his grip, she put the spoon back in the bowl, and lowered it to her lap, cradling the ceramic in her hand. "Dover said you were in competition with Hagan. What does that mean?"

Before he answered, he considered her. Rather than playing him by projecting innocence, she tried to appear as neutral as she could.

Opening his mouth, he inhaled a deep breath, and took his time about blowing it out. "Floyd's belonged to Dover's father, a man we all knew, a good man… At least, good by our yardstick, maybe not by yours."

Putting the bowl on the nightstand, she curled a leg up onto the bed to twist further toward him. Though that gave his hand access to a little more flesh, he still followed her instruction and kept it out of her skirt.

"I have no yardstick," she said, resting her hand over his on her leg, mostly as a way to get his fingers to stay still given that they were beginning to awaken her skin. "It's my job to be impartial. You can talk to me."

One side of his mouth stretched. Either he thought she was cute and innocent, or wading into something she'd never be able to handle. "He died a few years ago, and when he did, Dover took over running the bar." She nodded. "For as long as I can remember…" He paused, maybe lingering over the decision of how much to tell her. "There's been an underground casino in the basement."

She didn't expect him to say that. The dark, dirty conditions of the bar she'd gone into didn't scream glamorous casino, not even close. "Cards?"

"Yeah," he said. "Among other things. Floyd's has held the monopoly in the neighborhood for decades. Any upstarts who think they can take our business don't last long."

"Hagan wants to take it?" she said, trying to figure things out. "I don't understand though. You said you lost money to him. You must have played at his place. Why would he let you do that if you're on Dover's crew? He must know you're loyal to Floyd's."

Slipping his hand out from beneath hers, he curled his fingers against her jaw. "A sweet middle-class girl like you shouldn't be in bed with a man like me." Glancing around at the bed they were seated on, she wondered what her upbringing had to do with their association. His laugh made her attention snap back to him. "Man, those big innocent eyes are killer. Clueless or scamming, I don't even care. I bet you've never met a man who wouldn't fall to his knees for you… You ever done any grifting?"

Though he probably thought the suggestion was a compliment, it made her laugh. "Are you trying to recruit me?" She tilted her head. "Bale said you don't let anyone new on your crew. Are you thinking of using me once and then ousting me? If you're asking me to do what I think you're asking me to, I think they call that pimping, and much as I appreciate the offer, I have a job, Mr. Ryske."

"One that doesn't allow you to reach your potential," he said, caressing her jawline with his knuckles. "And I'd never pimp you, baby."

Crooking a brow, she didn't take his reassurance at face value. No one could accuse her of being naïve today. "Not until you've had the pleasure yourself, right?" she asked. The act of leaning closer let his hand slide a fraction higher on her leg. "It's never going to happen, Crash."

The curve of his index finger glided down her jaw. "No?" he asked, raising his chin to align their mouths. "I think you'd be surprised by what we're capable of, Trinket."

"We?" she asked. "You think your crew will help you to seduce me?"

He didn't blink, but his eyelids were getting heavier

by the moment. "Fuck them, Trink. I'm talking about us. You and me, baby… We are gonna own the world… I'll show you… Lemme help you…"

"Last time I asked you to help me, it was to get you onto your feet, and you wanted something in return."

Satisfaction twisted his lips. "This time, I'll give you something," he said, using his loose, curled fingers to try tempting her mouth closer.

The act of licking her lips fired a glint of triumph in his eyes. Except Harlow wasn't preparing to kiss him, she was preparing to call him out.

"You just can't help yourself," she murmured. "I don't know what's worse, that you think I'd believe this was real or that you believe I could be desperate enough to fall for it. Do you ever switch it off?"

Though the light of victory was gone from his gaze, he didn't come across as disappointed. Remaining where they were, in close proximity with their mouths only an inch or two apart, they both took the chance to reassess their assumptions about the other.

"Oh, shit, Ryske," Bale's voice came from behind them. "In my bed? Really?" Sitting back, Harlow twisted to look over her shoulder. The doctor stood just outside the bathroom, a towel wrapped around his hips, his hair wet. "I agreed to take out the IV so you could use the bathroom, not for… this."

Unapologetic, Ryske was more amused than smug. "You gift-wrapped and hand-delivered a beautiful woman to me, doc. A man's got to keep his skills polished."

Yeah, and that's what Harlow had meant when she asked if Ryske thought she'd believe the seduction was real. Being a female, in proximity to a male who obviously enjoyed them, was enough for him. Not for her. The last thing she'd ever be for any man was a practice mannequin.

"Polish them with your fist in the shower as soon as the doctor clears you for solo bathing," she said, rising from the bed and flattening her skirt. Going to the end of the bed, she smiled at Bale. "If the others haven't finished them, there are cookies in the kitchen. I'm going home to finish my research."

Bale nodded, moving closer. "You'll let Noon drive you?"

"I will. Saves me cab fare."

"Are you coming back tomorrow?"

"After work," she said. "I'll come straight from the office."

"I'm on second shift at the hospital tomorrow, but one of the guys will be here to let you in." Bale glanced toward the bed, but she was pleased not to have to look at the patient. "I want him off his feet for at least the next couple of days. Can you stay until about ten thirty? I should be back by then, I don't trust the others."

"I understand," she said and took his hand. "Of course I'll stay."

"Whoa, hey, wait," Ryske said, making them turn. The patient wasn't so at ease anymore, he was struggling to straighten his position. "You don't trust my guys to what? And why the fuck is she holding your hand?"

Drawing her attention away from Ryske, Harlow showed that she wasn't afraid to ignore him. "I'll leave my number by the phone," she said. "Call me if you need anything. And make sure he has his IV in before you leave."

"I will," Bale said, switching a glare to Ryske. "If it's gone by the time you get here, we'll know he went against medical advice."

She let Ryske see her smile. "Which I know you're not allowed to do or you lose your doctor."

Defeated, and maybe a little petulant, Ryske slumped against his pillows. "Aren't you people supposed to help others not conspire against them?"

"For you, we make an exception," Bale said.

Stepping forward, Harlow took Bale's hand to guide him down so she could kiss his cheek, shocking both men.

Bale's smile began to slope upwards.

"Yeah, you smile, doc," Ryske said. "Just don't forget how much time that mouth is gonna spend wrapped around my cock in a few weeks."

Forgetting to be offended, Harlow let herself be

amused by Ryske's audacity, maybe because it horrified Bale so much. Turning to Ryske, she kept her tongue pointed against her upper lip while she absorbed the arrogance in his gaze.

"Never gonna happen," she whispered just loud enough for him to hear and backed toward the door to slip out.

Ryske was her friend; the crew he ran with would come around to being her friends too. They weren't her usual fare of people. Although she hadn't been in the city for long, but already she was broadening her horizons and learning it was a hell of a lot of fun.

FIVE

BY FRIDAY NIGHT, it had become routine for Harlow to head over to Bale's after work. Usually, she went straight there. But, that night, she had taken a detour to her apartment to change her clothes before swinging by to check on the patient.

"Hey," she said, walking into Bale's apartment to find him alone at the dining table with files spread out around him. "Are you okay?"

Harlow took off her jacket and hung it up by the door. Bale ran a hand through his hair. Concern drew her closer; she'd never seen him look so disheveled. Taking care of Ryske while maintaining his regular schedule had to be taking its toll.

Moving into his peripheral vision made him raise his attention from whatever he was working on. When he noticed her, and what she was wearing, he perked up.

"Wow," he said, his amazed eyes moving over her body. "That's some dress."

"Do you like it?" she asked, turning on the spot to show off the pale blush pink Bardot bodycon dress that crisscrossed over her chest.

"Are you sure you want to go in there wearing that?" Bale asked, fixating on her legs.

She'd stopped asking to go into the bedroom at the start of the week. Ryske had zero modesty anyway and was used to various people wandering in and out around him. Dover's comment about the crew knowing each other a long time was accurate if their familiarity was anything to go by. They all seemed incredibly used to having each other around in close quarters.

Heading for the bedroom, Harlow had no hesitation. With her hand on the door handle, she twisted to face the doctor again, propping her arm on the door. "Why wouldn't I be sure? It's Ryske."

A man she was far from scared of. "It's Ryske. That's exactly what I'm getting at," Bale muttered, hunching over his work again.

Shaking her head, she left him to his task and swept into the bedroom.

Like he'd been expecting her, Ryske started talking before he'd even looked at her. "Trink, I've been—whoa, fuck!"

It wasn't difficult to pick out the moment he'd spotted her dress.

Slouched, facing the TV that was on the wall by the door, Ryske was quick to turn off the screen and sit up straighter.

"Do you like it?" she asked, turning in a slow spin like she'd done for Bale.

Like a kid at Christmas, his glee was almost palpable. "Hell, yeah," he said, rubbing his hands together in anticipation. "You didn't have to dress up for me, Trink. I've been ready for you all week." Slapping his uninjured hip, he held his other hand toward her. "Come to papa, baby."

Laughing at his enthusiasm, Harlow bent over to lift her feet and pull off her heels in turn. Once they clattered onto the floor, she crawled onto the empty side of the bed next to him.

"I can't stay long," she said, propping her head on her hand when she stretched out on her side. "I have somewhere to be."

Rolling onto his side to face her, Ryske was higher in

the bed, and sort of loomed above her. Being near to him made her feel protected. That was probably why she didn't object when he ran his fingers through the length of her hair from her temple to the ends. Letting it slip from between his digits, he draped it down her upper arm. From there, it cascaded across her back and chest.

She couldn't take her focus from him as he watched her hair fall. "Date?" he murmured, capturing a loose section of her locks. She shook her head. "Good, 'cause I'd hate to have to come out of hiding just to kill a guy for wanting you… You are too beautiful." Bowing closer, he breathed in the scent of her hair. "You always smell so expensive."

"I'm more than you can afford."

"As you like to remind me," he said.

Putting a hand to his shoulder, she eased him onto his back. Teasing was fine. Flirting was the norm. But she had to be in charge of boundaries because Ryske didn't have any.

Checking on him was supposed to be the purpose of the visit. "How have you been today?"

He groaned. "I'm so sick of being in this bed. Bale won't even let me go on the fucking treadmill."

Being glued to one place was driving him nuts. Every day, she witnessed his frustration level ratchet up a notch. Like a tiger pacing in a cage, he was ready to take a swipe at anyone who looked at him the wrong way. Anyone except her. There was no way he'd ever take a swipe at her.

Reassuring him, letting him vent his irritation, was her role. "He was letting you do weights," she said, swaying across him to tug his waistband from his hip to check his dressing. "Do you want me to change your dressing?"

Bale had showed her how to do it. Ryske seemed to prefer her doing it for some reason, probably for the variety. The doctor spent a lot of time poking around at his patient; Ryske had less patience with him.

"Not in that pretty dress," he said, stroking her hair again. "But if you want to take it off…"

Flipping her hair so she could look up the length of his torso at him, her chin was just above the line of his sweatpants. She wasn't surprised when he winked at her. The mischief of his eyes complemented his smirk.

"I can change your dressing without getting my dress dirty."

His mind didn't seem to be on the practical. A moment passed. Each second grew more charged than the last.

Eventually, he exhaled a long breath. "Goddamn, I've never met a woman so good at teasing me," he said through his gritted teeth.

"I don't tease you," she said. That wasn't the first time he'd accused her of doing it though. Passing the blame onto her seemed to be his way of justifying what happened when there was an awakening in his pants. Planting a hand on the bed by his wound, she pushed up to reach for the pillow he wasn't using from the head of the bed and slapped it onto his lap. "And we've talked about that."

Sitting up, she curled her legs at her side and supported her upper body on one straight arm.

"You encourage my blood flow better than anyone else," Ryske said, sliding down on the bed and slipping a hand to the back of his head. "One day you'll let me show you."

His ease and assurance were, in a lot of ways, admirable. "I have never known a man as confident as you," she said, almost in awe of him. "I've known arrogant guys, met plenty of them through work or my family. You're so… easy about it."

His fingertips drifted up her locked arm. "Trinket, for you, I'll always be easy," he said, picking her loose hand from the bed to put it onto his abs. "Do that thing you do with my tats and your nails."

Skootching closer, she lay down on her side again, curling her elbow beneath her head for support. With her other hand, she traced the outline of his tattoo over his hip to his abs and his ribs, taking her time, moving her nail slowly. He groaned again. Although a smile warmed her lips, she didn't look up; she was too comfortable to move.

"You don't know how good that feels," he said. "Can't wait 'til it's your mouth."

"You will never feel my mouth on your body, Crash,"

she said, but kept drawing around the tattoo with her nail.

For whatever reason, it soothed him to feel her fingernails move on his skin.

"You said never about lying in bed with me and you fell asleep there last night."

She had.

Earlier in the week, when she'd asserted she would never lie in bed beside him, Harlow hadn't realized they'd be watching movies and hanging out as much as they had. Each day this week had been dedicated to Ryske and his crew and been spent in this apartment.

Harlow had done her homework on the floor on Monday night, while the crew shouted at some sports thing on the TV. Tuesday, she'd spent some time talking with Ryske, telling him about her work and education, including the course she was close to completing. Whether he was or not, it felt like he'd been listening; she got the impression he was interested. Although, he was a sort of a conman, so that was an important tool of his trade.

On Wednesday, she'd been happy to chill and watch movies with him. To do that, it had just been easier to lie on the bed with him. Although she was overt in her efforts to leave obvious space between them, at some point during that movie night any illusion of distance or decorum had been erased. Harlow couldn't remember how.

After putting on an action movie the previous night, she'd fallen asleep. It had been a long week and the toil had caught up with her. Didn't help that the movie wasn't all that good either.

Her blossoming trust in Ryske had proved to be founded. Although she'd woken up with a start next to him, her clothes were still in place and undisturbed; he'd kept his hands to himself.

With her nails dancing across his skin, Harlow wasn't returning the favor. "What does the one on your wrist mean?" she asked.

Trailing her fingernail up, down, and around on his abdomen, she paused at the waistband of his sweatpants to reverse course.

"If you want to see how far the one you're playing with goes," he murmured. "Take my pants off."

The claws of the tattoo did extend to his thigh. "I've seen you without your pants," she said. Keeping her hand on the outside of his sweats, she slipped a hand beneath the pillow that was still over his lap to trace the area of the scar on his thigh that Bale had shown her. "How did you get the scar?"

"Messed with the wrong girl."

"A woman did it to you?"

"Her protector," he said, letting his fingers tangle in her hair while her nail returned to tracing his abdominal tattoo. "You sounded surprised. Do you think women can't wield a weapon? Soon as I'm out this prison, I'm buying you a piece. You shouldn't be walking around in neighborhoods like mine without a weapon."

A smile curved her lips, though she tried to keep it to herself. "Maze promised if I needed help, I could track him down in Floyd's. Besides, I wasn't the one who wound up with a knife in my gut. That was you… I did pretty well in your neighborhood. I go to work in your neighborhood every day."

"After that day is over, it becomes a playground for men like me."

"I'm not afraid of you," she said on a half-laugh. "You're not dangerous."

In a snap, his hand shot out to grab her wrist. Yanking her upward with his bruising grip, he forced her body onto his. The sudden move had taken Harlow so by surprise that adrenaline streamed into her system, firing up her heart. There was no time to react; her gaze landed on his and her mind blanked.

Strewn across him, her chest on his ribs, it once again felt as though their mouths were seeking each other out. They were being drawn together by an invisible magnet she struggled to resist.

Easing her higher, his strength made short work of narrowing the space between their mouths. "I am dangerous, Trinket," he murmured. "More dangerous than you know. And I'm in your arsenal now. Me and my crew."

If it had been his intention to scare her, he'd failed. That didn't mean her baser instincts weren't firing. Choosing to resist, she acted like she wasn't aware of the thud of his heart rocking her ribcage.

Just the taste of his breath was enough to intoxicate her. "Where are the guys tonight?" she asked.

Smirking, he tightened his hold on her wrist, making her lips open further. Harlow had never been with a man who'd physically hurt her. Ryske was doing it now, though not in anger; he was a man overwhelmed by the moment. That pain he was causing, that niggling sensation in her wrist, she was surprised to find... she liked it.

He didn't answer her question. "Conversation's a diversion," he said, watching her lips as he licked his own. "You're still fighting it. Stop fighting, Trink."

One solid tug on her wrist would bring their mouths together. He tried to do it, to pull her higher, but she resisted. Feeling the pull of his strength working in opposition to hers did something to her gut. More than that it warmed her, tormenting her hormones and sending a buzz of need down through to her core. It wasn't right that he turned her on, or that she liked his insistent strength and that twist of pain. But there was no denying it. At some point in the week, she had admitted to herself that her intrigue had become attraction, irrational though it was.

"You're injured."

"My mouth's just fine."

If Harlow let him kiss her, if she kissed him, she wouldn't be able to control what came next. Before being forced to make a choice between surrendering or resisting, there was a knock at the apartment's front door in the room beyond, which she supposed Bale would answer.

"Guess that's your crew."

Harlow didn't knock when she arrived at Bale's apartment anymore. As far as she'd seen, Ryske's crew didn't either. In all the time she'd spent there, she'd never seen the doctor have another visitor. If the crew were knocking, she supposed Bale must have locked the door, or maybe she'd done it by mistake, which would be why one of the guys would have to knock to get in.

Ryske must have thought the same thing. "They won't interrupt us," he said, keeping her wrist locked in his fist while sliding his other hand down her spine to cup her ass.

Trying not to notice how his large, entitled, capable hand squeezed her closer with an almost territorial grip, Harlow kept talking. "Noon promised to bring me Kung Pao chicken. I didn't want to drink on an empty stomach."

"Hitting the town to have yourself some fun?" he asked, squeezing her harder with both hands. "I won't let another man have you."

To win this battle, she had to be strong… stronger than him. Ryske was more practiced, but Harlow knew how to be stubborn. "I told you, it's not a date. It's drinks with colleagues," she said, thinking about how long she'd been lying on him, putting so much of her weight on his body. Sure, she was draped against his uninjured side, but being under her couldn't be comfortable for him. "Let me go, Crash. I don't want to hurt you."

His brows rose in amused surprise. "Is that a threat, Trink?"

Taking control, he flipped her onto her back. The sudden move made her gasp, but when the weight of his body settled on hers, it stunned her into silence. The pillow on his lap was still between them, which she guessed frustrated him. A kiss would've been one thing. It wasn't like there was a chance of them doing anything else, not with…

Recalling what had brought Ryske to this bed in the first place, Harlow yelped. "Ryske, your wound! It's healing so well…"

The noise of a scuffle came from beyond the bedroom. Though his eyes didn't leave hers, she knew that Ryske had heard it too. Maybe staying put was his way of trying not to scare her.

The bang that followed erased any hope of staying calm.

Harlow thought she'd seen Ryske move fast; that was nothing to what happened next. Shoved aside and flipped over so she was face down on the bed, Harlow didn't have time to do more than turn her head before Ryske pounced across his side of the bed to drop onto the floor in a crouch.

A nightstand drawer opened. A moment later, Ryske spun toward the door, still hunkered down, checking the clip of a gun she'd never seen before.

"Ryske," she hissed.

"Get in the bathroom. Lock the door. Stay in there until I come for you."

"No," she said, bouncing onto her knees on the bed.

Making himself a bigger target, he surged to his feet, the gun firm in both hands. "Harlow—"

The bedroom door opened. In a single leap, Ryske put his body between her and the door, while extending the gun to aim at whoever was entering.

When they registered Bale was the person coming in, Ryske lowered the gun, though he kept it in his grip.

"What's going on?" Ryske demanded of their host.

There was a frantic air about the doctor who was wide-eyed. "I guess they know you're here," Bale said. "Two guys came to the door. They asked for you. I told them I had no idea what they were talking about. One pulled a gun, it went off in the struggle—"

"Is anyone hurt?" Harlow asked.

Ryske didn't flinch while Bale's wild eyes went from Ryske to her and over his shoulder toward the living room. Clearly, he wasn't a fan of this kind of excitement.

"No," he said. "They ran off. But if the neighbors heard, the cops will be on their way."

"If they know where I am, they're onto you, doc," Ryske said, stooping to grab the sports bag she'd brought him on Sunday from under the bed. "You can't stay here."

It had taken Ryske no time at all to make a plan and jump to action. Harlow was still reeling; Bale too.

"I would say I can stay with a friend from the hospital," Bale said. "But I don't know how I'll explain my patient."

"Watch your own ass, I'll worry about mine," Ryske said, sticking the gun in the bag. Other things from the nightstand followed.

Giving him a medical problem focused the doctor's mind. "I told you two weeks under medical supervision," Bale said, moving deeper into the room. "It's been less than one."

"Adapt, doc," Ryske said. "You've gotta be willing to bend the rules when lives are at stake. Know who said that?"

Bale wasn't buying it and just narrowed his unimpressed focus. "Probably you, asshole. Don't feed me your crap like I'm one of your marks. Stop believing your own bullshit. It's bad for your health."

Sidelining their sniping, Harlow scrambled over the bed. Stopping high on her knees, she leaned over the bag and scooped her hands under Ryske's jaw, forcing him to look at her. The depth of concentration and concern in his focus startled her. It shouldn't have given how serious this situation was. But, for a second, he didn't look like the Ryske she'd come to know.

That said, Harlow didn't feel like herself either. But she was so used to Ryske being happy, laidback, mischievous… Ryske. With him, she felt safe. With this stern Ryske, she got a new respect for the gravity of the situation.

"Crash," she whispered, pulling his head up when he tried to look to the bag again. "I don't want you to get hurt."

"Trink, we don't got time for—"

"Yes, we do," Bale said, rushing across to the closet to begin pulling out medical supplies. "You have to change the dressing at least once a day, Nightingale. Twice would be better. Keep an eye on the wound, watch for redness, swelling, pain, fever."

The doctor was on a mission, and it was one that daunted her. "Wait. Me?" Harlow asked. "You want me to care for him?"

Bale turned to dump a bag on the bed to zip it up. "Yes, you," he said. "You're the only one I trust to look after his medical needs. Do you remember what I said?"

If anything happened to Ryske, Bale's ass was on the line. Hers too. "I remember."

Taking that as acceptance of his request, Bale nodded once. "I've put antibiotics in there, instructions are on the label." He picked up the bag of medical supplies to thrust it toward her. When she didn't take it, he shook it. "You're running out of time, Har. You have to go."

The cops would be here any minute. Ryske pulled on a tee-shirt and then tossed the strap of the sports bag over his head to arrange it across his body.

The sight of that strap cutting across his torso and the possible weight in it prompted her to take action. "No," she said, snatching the medical bag from Bale then spinning around to yank the sports bag off over Ryske's head, using the height of the bed to give her reach.

Clambering off the furniture to stand at Ryske's side, she arranged both bags across her body, adjusting the straps as she did. "Trink, what are you—"

"I'm carrying these," she asserted.

The decision was non-negotiable.

While they stared each other out, the doctor came around the bed, pausing only to grab up her shoes. "You guys have got to move," Bale said, thrusting her shoes at Ryske then herding the couple toward the door.

Difficult as it might be to explain the gunshot to the cops, it would be harder to explain the busted criminal in his bed. Harlow didn't want to explain her presence either, especially when she was just beginning to build up relationships with the law enforcement officers she came across through her work.

Harlow was in front as they crossed the living room. Ryske seized her hand just as she grabbed her jacket from the hook by the door to tuck it over the sports bag. Taking her shoes from Ryske, she put them on in a flash.

"Call me if you need anything, Nightingale," Bale said and kissed her cheek just before Ryske pulled her out into the hallway and to the stairwell.

They got to the street. Harlow tried to step out to hail a cab, but Ryske didn't let her stop and instead kept on dragging her down the block.

"Crash," she objected, trying without success to tug her hand out of his. "You'll tear your wound. We need a cab!"

"Not outside Bale's," he said, intent to keep striding on. "We don't leave an evidence trail."

If the cops asked questions, if Bale said something to make them suspicious, catching a cab right outside his apartment could implicate them or at least betray their presence.

A block later, Ryske stepped into the street and raised a hand to hail a cab. One stopped almost immediately and he pushed her into the back. Harlow took off the bags, dumping them on the furthest seat, so she could settle in the middle. Ryske got in after her. The moment he closed the door, she started to peel back the waistband of his pants to check that he hadn't damaged his wound.

Ryske slid down in the seat to give her better access and spouted her address for the driver. Giving him a passing glance, Harlow let him know she'd registered that he knew something about her she'd never told him. But, in fairness, she was sort of used to that by now.

"Do you think he'll be okay?" she asked, struggling to see beyond his dressing in the dim illumination offered in the back of the cab. She didn't want to take off the dressing all the way until they got inside.

"The doc will be fine. You got a phone?"

Her phone was in her jacket pocket. It had been dumped with the bags. After rooting around for a few seconds, she pulled out the device and handed it over to him. "Here."

As he began to dial, she retrieved a hooded sweatshirt from the sports bag and fed his arms into it. Gallivanting around the city in nothing but a tee-shirt and sweats wouldn't be good for him. He was wearing sneakers too, though she had no idea where they'd come from. Under the bed? By the door? She had been too swept up in getting herself together to notice him slipping his bare feet into them.

"Flip," Ryske said into the phone. "Yep... It's black... Yep... I've got her." She paused in zipping him up, wondering if he was talking about her. He winked. "Tomorrow. I've got a debt to pay tonight."

He hung up and slid the phone into his pocket before putting an arm around her. Instead of settling against him like he tried to get her to do, she picked up his arm and guided it away from her shoulders.

Although their positions were inverted, having his arm over her shoulders in that way reminded her too much of the night they'd met. That wasn't a memory that she liked to relive.

Clasping his hand in both of hers, she held it in her lap.

He kissed the top of her head and didn't force the issue. He linked his fingers through hers and held her hand while they rode the rest of the way in silence.

SIX

AFTER GETTING OUT of the cab, Ryske put his arm around her again. Instead of shrugging it off, Harlow took his forearm in both hands and pulled it further around her body, nestling it between her breasts. It wasn't like he'd be explicit about asking for support; all she could do was assume that he needed it.

Guiding him up the stairs and into her apartment, she worried about why he was being quiet, fearing he could be in pain. Turned out, she was worrying for nothing because he was full of confidence from the moment they stepped over her threshold.

Ryske boosted her forward out of his way so he could close the front door and plucked the keys right out of her hand. Forging ahead, flicking on lights as he went like he'd made himself at home there a dozen times, he checked the kitchen and closet. Having no idea what he was looking for, Harlow stayed by the door, just watching him, waiting for his curiosity to be satisfied.

Once he was done with his inspection, Ryske came over and linked their fingers. The man had purpose, she couldn't deny that. His grip was sure and strong as he pulled her past the breakfast bar and into the living room. Much to her relief, he ignored her messy corner desk, and kept on going to stop by the open arch that led to her bedroom.

Well, what had been her bedroom. She'd have to give it up to the patient who'd been thrust upon her. Caring for Ryske for the remainder of his recuperation was a huge responsibility that she hadn't expected to shoulder.

Ryske scanned the living room, but she didn't let him loiter. He'd been on his feet for too long already. Squeezing his hand tighter, she swiped aside the beaded curtain of transparent crystal beads that covered the arch to lead him to the bed. Pushing him down, she wanted him to rest.

Ryske didn't interpret her actions that way. "Love a woman who knows what she wants."

Her sense of humor was dormant. Adrenaline was still too potent in her bloodstream for her to relax enough to joke. This might be run of the mill for him, but Harlow needed some time to calm down and get herself together.

"Good, then you won't mind stripping for me," she said, sitting on the end of the bed to check what supplies Bale had packed into the med bag.

"I've been waiting all week for you to ask, Trink," he said, kicking off his sneakers and wasting no time stripping to the waist.

All week, he'd proved time and again that he had no modesty. The moment his tee-shirt hit the floor, he raised his hips to drive his thumbs into the waistband of his pants.

As soon as she saw his thumbs disappearing into the elastic, Harlow stopped rifling to hold up both hands. "Ah, that's enough. I can see your wound from here."

With a sly smile, he tilted his head. "But, Trink, I've got so much more to show you."

Already she was beginning to feel more at ease. "So much more, I don't have to see," she said, leaving her seat to turn on the lamp by the bed. "Lie down."

He leaped onto the bed and locked his fingers behind his head. Kneeling on the floor next to the bed, she carefully edged the waistbands of his pants and underwear down just enough to give her space to work. Being as gentle as she could, Harlow began to pick off his dressing.

"I think this is the first time we've been all alone," he said. "We've got the whole place to ourselves, Trinket."

Keeping her concentration on inspecting his wound, she couldn't be as chilled. It was on her to keep this man alive; Bale was trusting her. "Just because I haven't called the cops on you yet, doesn't mean I won't," she said, peering closer. The wound was one problem, but his constant flirting and cajoling would have to be monitored and handled too. "Bale put a couple of syringes in that bag. Don't know what's in them, but I'm sure one of them will subdue you."

In Bale's apartment, with the gun, Ryske had been a serious, almost menacing guy. The man in her bed was the relaxed, teasing Ryske she'd hung out with all week.

"Wow, baby, you surprise me," he said, breathing out and closing his eyes as a smile curved his lips. "Was that an offer to get high with me? I had no idea you were the type. Let's do it."

"I do not want to get high with you," she said, not satisfied that the dressing she'd started to take off was clean enough to put back on. Ripping it off fast, she got a shot of pleasure when he tensed in a recoil that proved he hadn't been expecting the action. "What drugs do you do, Ryske?"

He didn't answer her and seemed to have moved onto something else in his mind. "You know what I love?" he asked, settling against her pillows again, satisfaction written all over his face. "I love it when you use that sexy stern tone on me. Tell me off, Trink. Damn, it gets me hard."

So not really something else. Sex. That was where Ryske's mind seemed most comfortable.

Just the threat of him getting aroused was enough to make her rise and bow over him. She meant to show him that she wasn't to be messed with, but he took the opportunity to stroke her ass. Telling him off was exactly what he'd told her to do. Instead, she reached past him to retrieve a pillow from the opposite side of the bed and thrust it onto his lap.

"I really don't want to be acquainted with that part of you," she warned.

Walking to the end of the bed, she dug around the med bag for more gauze and tape. The wound was red, but was still sealed, so she hoped that was a good sign.

"Why are you so afraid of it?"

She kept sorting the supplies, putting things in places where she knew she'd be able to find them in a hurry. "Of what?"

"Sex."

She stopped sorting to look at him. For once, it didn't sound like he was teasing, but that only made her more suspicious. "I'm not afraid of sex."

"Sure you are," he said.

Seeing him slip his hand beneath the pillow on his lap made her swallow hard. Whether it was inside or outside his pants, he was definitely making contact with… himself.

"Can you not do that while I'm in the room, please?"

Intrigue eclipsed his usual smirk. "Maybe it's my dick you're afraid of."

"I am not afraid of it," she said.

Raising his brows like he didn't believe her, he flipped the pillow off his lap and showed that not only was his hand inside his pants, but he was holding the imposing member tenting his sweats. "No?"

Rolling her eyes toward the ceiling, she tipped up her chin. "Oh, God."

"Definitely afraid."

Glaring at him, she might be getting used to his triumphant leer, but that didn't mean she couldn't resent it. "Your penis doesn't have special powers."

"You don't know that."

"What do you think I'm afraid of exactly?" she asked, going back over to kneel by the bed, taking her wares with her, and ignoring whatever was going on beyond her work area. "I've had sex before. I've seen dicks. Plenty of them."

"Yeah? How many?"

Pausing with the tape extended, she blinked at him. "What?"

Whether it was genuine or not, his expression didn't seem to be mocking. "You brought it up, so tell me… How many have you seen, Trink?" She couldn't even make her lips part. "Guess with porn that's a tough one to answer. Better to tell me how many you've gotten to grips with."

It took effort on her part to blank her expression, and she wasn't sure she succeeded. "You want to know how many penises I've touched?" He nodded. After a second of silence, the corner of his mouth twitched. He quickly flattened it again, but the brief crack in his mask was enough to snap her from her discombobulation. "You're mocking me." Picking up her scissors, she clutched them tight. "You think that's a smart thing to do to the woman in charge of your care."

"You saved me from a stab wound last week, no reason you wouldn't this week."

Except if she was the one who inflicted it. "Last week, I didn't know you. This week, I do," she said, but turned her scissors to cut the tape. "I don't doubt that I have less sexual experience than you. I also don't doubt there are rabbits with less experience than you, given how sex seems to be on your mind twenty-four seven."

"Not twenty-four seven," he said, locking his fingers behind his head again. "I don't think about it when I'm with my crew."

"Lucky for them," she said, affixing his clean dressing. "Maybe you should initiate me, so I can be saved the trouble."

He laughed. "It's trouble for you to hear that a guy's attracted to you?"

"It's trouble for me to hear *you're* attracted to me," she said, tipping her head to admire her work, hoping it was good enough. "Especially since I don't believe it."

"I'm not going to lie and say I can't lie. But why would I—"

"It's some weird Florence Nightingale thing," she said, gathering up her supplies and trashing the used dressing. "Just like Dover says. You think you're attracted to me because I was there at the right moment and because I'm the only woman you've seen all week. You don't really want to be with me."

"Let me be the judge of what I want."

Breathing out a laugh, she tossed what she hadn't used back into the med bag and sat on the bed by his feet.

"What I should really have said is that you and I have different definitions of what being with someone means. You believe in casual sex."

"It's not my religion," he said, pushing his fists into the mattress to sit up straighter. "But, yeah, I think it exists."

She shrugged and zipped up the bag. "I'm not a casual sex kind of woman… I'm not afraid of your penis, and I am attracted to you. But I'm smart enough to know what kind of man you are and I know we want different things."

"Want? If you're attracted to me, you and me want exactly the same damn thing. But if you're talking about a future…" he said, a snicker in his voice. "Baby, you should be happy I have no plans for you beyond this bed and your body. The only thing I plan beyond the moment is the con. If I haven't made plans for you that means you're not on my professional agenda."

Trying to subdue what would probably be a condescending smile, she licked her lips. "And that is exactly how I know we're incompatible. I want to be on the agenda of the man I'm sleeping with. I don't want him to trip and fall into bed with me just because I'm around and then forget me the minute I'm out of his sight."

"You want a relationship? Baby, we've known each other a week, and I'm not the type of guy to—"

"You're not my type of guy," she said, making eye contact. "Isn't that the point we agree on? You want an easy, fun girl to be casual with. I sleep with men I see a future with. I'm not frivolous and fun, Crash. I'm a serious professional."

For the first time, she saw a glimmer of offense on his face. It made him appear petulant; it was almost cute. If a man with the physique and demeanor of a tough guy could ever be considered cute.

"I'm a professional," he grumbled.

A professional law-breaker, yes. "But what are you serious about?" she asked. "Other than whatever scheme you have going on."

"Okay, so I'm not your white picket fence guy, but I can be the ride of your life."

His wink made her laugh. "That's some claim when

you've no idea who I've ridden before."

"I know you've never ridden me."

She leaned toward him, lowering her volume. "And I never will, Crash."

Ryske wasn't dissuaded. If anything, whenever she asserted her opposition, he only grew more assured. "Baby, you are gonna taste so sweet."

"Do you think I'm some sort of prize or is it just the challenge you crave? You've been laid up all week when what you want is to be out on the street, running your con. I'm here, that's why you want me. As soon as Bale's clock runs out, you'll forget that I exist."

For a breath, it seemed like he was going to say something. But when his eyes moved toward her covered window, she knew that she was on the money. It was ridiculous to be stung by the silent confirmation that she was right, especially when she simultaneously appreciated him not bullshitting her with pick-up lines or platitudes.

Ryske was a dynamic guy, always ready to move, whether it was for a con or onto the next mark. His lifestyle intrigued the immature part of her which was excited by danger. In spite of that, Harlow was smart enough to recognize that letting herself be seduced by the novelty of him would lead to heartache and humiliation in the long run.

He hadn't said anything else, so she decided to give him some space. "I have to call and let my colleagues know I won't be joining them. Get some rest."

Harlow stowed the med bag in her closet, then headed for the dark living room again. "You gonna join me, Trink?"

The guy never switched it off. Keeping her smirk to herself, she didn't slow. "You're an invalid, Crash. I need a man who can go all night and not break a sweat." Sweeping the crystal ball curtain aside, she tossed a sultry look over her shoulder. "If I said yes to you, you'd be too busy drooling and bleeding all over the place to satisfy me."

She kept on going out of the room, but he called after her. "Come back in here and say that to my face, babydoll!"

Harlow hadn't intended for Ryske to ever be in her

apartment. Now, somehow, he was semi-naked in her bed probably still sporting a semi.

While exerting little effort, the man had a way of diverting the course of her life. Astounding as it was, Harlow wasn't really complaining.

Whenever Crash was around, life wasn't boring, anything could happen. Thinking fast, accepting a challenge, was exhilarating. Thrilled by the twists and turns, this wasn't life like Harlow knew it, but it was every day for Ryske.

As soon as the patient had completed Bale's ordered recuperation time, he'd go back to his vibrant life and she'd return to the stresses and strains of social work. Normal, boring life, helping people who often didn't want to help themselves. That was her life; the only one she knew.

SEVEN

HAVING RYSKE AS a permanent feature in her apartment meant taking on more than just entertaining and feeding a single patient. It didn't mean having one roommate, it meant suddenly having four of them.

Every day when Harlow came home from work, Ryske's crew were dotted around her place. Usually, in her bedroom or living room, making plans or messing around. They filled her fridge with half-eaten takeout, left wet towels in her bathroom, and never cleaned up after themselves.

Odd thing was, it didn't make her angry. She actually liked the energy of the abode when it was filled with the Floyd's crew.

Growing up in her starched parents' house, there was never as much joy and camaraderie as she felt when the crew were lounging around in her apartment. Not even during joyous or festive times when there was more activity.

Having four men around full-time was a steep learning curve. Ryske was Ryske. And she was learning more about each of the others. Maze was the most discerning, and from what she could figure, the one with the most in terms of a formal education. Dover was a jack-of-all-trades, skilled in a variety of practicalities. Responsible and smart, he was aware, yet discreet.

Noon was like the little brother of the group. The one the others liked to pick on, but in a light-hearted way. He often spoke before thinking, which gave the guys plenty of opportunities to josh him.

Entering her apartment after work that Friday, a week after Ryske had arrived, Harlow heard the TV and the murmur of masculine friendship and laughter. The quartet loved to clown around. As serious as they could be, especially if they had an audience, they could be such big kids in private.

Hanging up her things by the door, she slipped her laptop from her bag and crossed to the living room, pausing by the first armchair. "Maze, my computer crashed again," she said.

Harlow didn't expect the multi-tasking pro to look at her and he didn't disappoint. Maze just lifted a hand to take the machine from her without ever moving his attention from the TV. When her hands were free, Noon took one to guide her over his straight legs that were resting on her coffee table. Kissing Dover's cheek signaled her final greeting.

After that, Harlow dropped to her knees in front of Ryske who was seated at the end of the couch. The other three guys in the room all whooped. Ryske didn't react to them. With his eyes on the TV, he did as she'd trained him to do every time she got home and slid his hips to the front of the seat to let her lift his shirt and peel back the waistband of his pants.

Checking the dressing was her priority. By now, it was just there to stop the wound being aggravated by his clothes. Bale had told her it was okay to take it off. She might have neglected to tell Ryske that yet.

"You've got her trained," Maze said, though he was half-lost in her computer, while still catching glimpses at the TV. "She goes out to work all day, earning the bacon, and comes straight home to blow you."

"If that's what she was doing down there, you guys wouldn't be here when she came home from work," Ryske said, stroking her hair. "She does look damn good down there though, right?" Drawing her eyes from the dressing, she let him register her displeasure before going back to her task. "Did you have a good day, dear?"

Tearing off his dressing in one swift move, she enjoyed startling him. "Let's keep this off tonight."

"Guess that's an answer," Ryske said.

Twisting around, she didn't bother to get up, just slumped on the floor between Ryske's feet to stare at the TV. Noon pushed a box of Chinese food down the coffee table and she grabbed it, using the chopsticks that were in it to eat the delicious chicken inside.

Ryske's fingers tangled in her hair, stroking through it. Her body was tired, but not as exhausted as her mind. With the food box in her hand, she chewed the chicken and let her head fall against the inside of Ryske's knee.

In her exhausted hand, the food box sank to the floor by her hip. "Still not the best I've ever had," she murmured.

"I'll keep trying, Nightingale," Noon said, making her smile.

Noon had promised her the best Chinese food she'd ever tasted. So far, he hadn't managed it. But he was tenacious, she had to acknowledge that he wasn't giving up easy.

Harlow sighed. Ryske's hand stopped in her hair. "You need me and the guys to go kick someone's ass, baby?" he asked. "You're not yourself tonight. If someone upset you—"

"I'm tired," she said and stifled a yawn with the back of her hand.

"Take a nap."

"There are four men in my apartment and there's no lock on my bedroom door."

"Babe, there's no door," Dover said and the men snickered.

Harlow's eyes closed. "Exactly," she said, thinking this was a nice cozy nook that she could get comfortable in.

"Your virtue's safe," Maze muttered.

Noon laughed. "Yeah, we've all jerked off today."

She wasn't sure how he knew that, but figured it had been part of some odd conversation they must have had while she'd been at work. "Do you think I'm worried about you thugs violating me? Hardly. I won't sleep for the commotion of you people making a mess, teasing each other over nothing, and apparently conversing about your masturbation habits."

Ryske's fingers sank deeper into her hair to curl around the side of her neck. That meant he was leaning forward, but she couldn't bring herself to open her eyes to chastise him. "The guys are clearing out in a minute. Go lay down. I'll wake you up in a while for that college assignment you were talking about."

Another sigh. "I'm supposed to be looking after you."

"There's less than forty-eight hours left on the clock, Trink," he said. "You've done your duty by me."

"Not a minute before Bale says I have," she said. "I had lunch with him today. He was explicit. You don't get out of here until at least Sunday… He's coming over to check on you in the afternoon."

"If you're going to be spending another two nights with me, you better keep your energy levels up," Ryske said, strengthening his grip until his tangled fingers were digging into her neck.

The security of his firm grasp stimulated the simmering heat that had become a familiar sensation in her gut whenever he was around. "Tighter," she groaned before she realized the word had slipped out.

It wasn't until he complied that Harlow figured out what she'd done. Tightening his grip sent a searing pulse of awareness shimmering from his fingers through her torso to her clit… and he'd done it at her request.

Her eyes snapped open. Though she tried to level out her breathing, Harlow was achingly conscious of the faux pas she'd just made. All week, even in the rare moments they were alone, she'd fought hard against her growing need for him. It wasn't easy, especially given how obvious he made his want for her, but she'd been strong.

Except what she'd just done revealed too much of herself. It would let Ryske peek beneath the surface and get a glimpse of what he kept telling her, but she kept trying to ignore: they were electric together.

Harlow didn't know what Ryske had told his crew about their relationship. While she knew they didn't sleep together and that they hadn't even kissed, she guessed Ryske had implied there was something going on because his crew always talked as if it was a done deal.

Hoping to maintain her dignity, she straightened up. "I will go and lie down," she said, pulling his hand away and tossing the Chinese food box to the table while getting to her feet. "Excuse me."

She'd have preferred to hear the guys jeering Ryske about her instead of the hushed whispers that proceeded the crystals falling back into place after she entered her bedroom. When the crew huddled and whispered, something serious was being discussed.

Harlow did not want to be something serious. If they mocked her or her association with Ryske, it was one big joke. She could handle the humiliation of that. What she couldn't take was the embarrassment of the truth; her feelings for Ryske were more than sexual.

She cared about him, and his friends.

In a few days, this extraordinary chapter of her life would be closed forever. Coming to terms with that had been playing on her mind, but there was nothing she could do about it. It would be over for her.

***

WHEN SLIPPING BENEATH her covers, Harlow had expected to find her scent intermingled with Ryske's. She'd become accustomed to it. Though it made no sense, it was a comfort. Sharing the bed while not sharing the bed was how their routine had settled.

Each night, she'd go to bed early, but set her alarm for around midnight or one AM. After the alarm went off, she'd wake, kick out whoever of the crew were loitering, and put Ryske to bed before finishing her night's sleep on the couch.

On that night, she hadn't set an alarm because Ryske had told her that he'd wake her. The point hadn't been to sleep for long, but somehow, when she next became aware of reality, Harlow's internal clock betrayed that she'd been sleeping for a while.

Something moved her head, so her eyes opened a fraction. Being still half in the fog of slumber, all she registered was darkness. There hadn't been an alarm… what had woken her?

If Ryske was trying to wake her, he wasn't being direct about it. Rolling her head to the side to blink up into the shadows of the room, it took a few seconds to identify Ryske's outline next to the bed. His arm was outstretched, taking the pillow she wasn't using from the other side of the mattress.

The pillow he'd touched was overlapping the one under her head, which must have been the movement she'd felt. He hadn't intended to wake her.

"Crash," she murmured on a slow blink.

The back of his fingers drifted down her temple. "Go to sleep, baby," he whispered.

Catching his hand as it was about to ebb, she unfurled his fingers to press his palm to her cheek. Her eyes closed. "Crash."

"Mm," he said like he was figuring something out. "I like tired Trinket."

In a warm and snuggly mood, she let him go. "Lie down."

Her eyes didn't open; the proximity of cozy slumber was too pleasant to resist. The mattress moved and the heat of his body neared hers. Instinct helped her to lift his arm to hook it around her shoulders. Skootching closer to nestle against him, Harlow rested her head on the front of his shoulder.

Under the covers while he was on top of them, she didn't let the full length of her body make contact with his. But a thrum of satisfaction at the contact they did have helped her to relax.

"I definitely like tired Trinket."

His wound was on this side of his body and she didn't want to aggravate it. "Am I hurting you?" she asked, wriggling just a little closer.

"Yep," he said. "I think you should kiss it better."

Her lips curled, but it was about ten seconds before she brought herself to speak. "Don't push your luck." They lay together for a minute or two. "Are the guys gone?"

"Couple of hours ago," he said, his fingers trailing up and down her arm. "I didn't want to disturb you. If I'd known this was waiting for me, I'd have come through sooner."

Despite promising to wake her, he'd let her sleep. Harlow was too tired to scold him; she could do her college work tomorrow. It would just mean canceling her mani-pedi.

Another minute passed and her thoughts coasted. "In two days you're going to be gone from my life," she murmured. "Do you think I'll ever see you again?"

"If you want to," he said. "You know how to find me anytime you need me."

"Need?"

"Or want," he said with a thread of confusion in his voice. "Trink, baby, do you want something now?"

His hand started to edge aside the covers, apparently intending to slip beneath them.

What she wanted, she couldn't let herself have. "Tell me about your family."

His hand stopped. "What?"

Opening her hand on his torso, she felt his heartbeat. "I want to know something about where you come from. I want more than the player, more than the grifter. I want to know something about the man who's been in my bed all week." This truth made her eyes open. But she didn't dare move her head, not when tension was moving through him. This was a make or break moment. "Trust me, Ryske… I don't even know if that's your real name."

A charged minute of silence passed. She held her breath, waiting to see how he'd react to her probing. "It's my real name."

"And your parents, what are they like? Do you still see them?"

"No," he said. "My dad was a drunk, violent fucker. My mom was a whore, not a hooker, a serial cheater. One day she fucked off with some rich cunt, left me with the prick.

Only saw her once since then. I didn't even recognize her."

Others might be shocked to hear of a mother abandoning her child. For Harlow, who saw it happen almost every day at work, it was no surprise. Didn't make the idea of a young Ryske handling his aggressive father any more appetizing.

"She didn't take you with her?"

He scoffed. "No chance. There was some satisfaction in finding out the cunt was playing her. He wasn't rich, not even close. Least she was smart enough not to come back with her tail between her legs."

"And your dad?"

"Soon as I was old enough to hit back, he kicked me out… Stayed with Floyd after that."

Twisting to tip her head back, Harlow risked making eye contact. "Dover's dad?"

He nodded. "I didn't mind slinging cards or drinks, not when his roof was safer to be under than anything I'd ever had at home. Turned out I was the best kid in the state with a deck… Even though I'd win every time I played, I could always convince bastards to play and give up their cash. That's when I learned about the con… that I was good at it. Dover and I had guys from the high school in Floyd's basement first during school lunchbreaks, then kids started cutting to come over and the place was full dawn to dusk. We sold beer and took the rich kids cash teaching them blackjack. We had a full op running and were making more in daylight than Floyd was making in the dark."

Propping her fist between his shoulder and her chin, she found herself fascinated. "And Noon? Maze?"

"Noon taught me everything I know about stealing and chopping cars. We built a career in swiping keys and picking pockets. We met when he tried dipping my jacket." A glance of nostalgia crossed his face. "Not knowing I was as crooked as him, he tried to talk me out of calling the cops when I caught him. I made him a deal, we'd cut the deck, high card got the wallet… there was more than a thousand bucks in there."

In the pause that followed, her anticipation rose.

"What happened? Who won?"

"Both of us. As we were about to cut, the prep school let out. I knew I could take those kids. So I told Noon to watch, he took my lead and we cleaned up in three-card Monte. Ended up doubling my money and splitting the pot with him. Never looked back. On the street, we were a double act. He'd do his thing taking car after car, I'd keep owners distracted, divert the cops, whatever was needed."

She had no trouble imagining Ryske using his charisma to distract and facilitate Noon's work. The man could talk his way out of anything. Awe-inspired and humbled, she was incredulous and impressed.

Whether or not someone agreed with Ryske's tactics, no one could doubt his skill. "You could charm the panties from a queen, couldn't you?"

"Doesn't seem to be working with you," he said, offering a wink. A second went by and his teasing became something more solemn. "Don't know what it is about you, Trinket. I know what you want to hear, but I... I can't play my game with you. I always know what people want to hear; that's the key to grifting. You tell people what they want to hear."

"What do I want to hear?"

He watched her tongue slide across her lips, curling his fingers around her arm again to pull her closer. "You want promises... Indiscriminate compliments make you feel good, they flatter you, but they don't seduce you. Reliability seduces you. You want a guy who'll be there for you every minute. A guy who won't do stupid things and take crazy risks... I can make you promises and convince you I'm exactly who you want me to be. I could do that. I could talk you into it, make those promises and convince you to give me exactly what I want."

Digging her elbow into the pillow by his head to pull herself higher, she looked deeper. "Then why don't you?"

"I wouldn't mean it," he said, caressing her cheek. "I wouldn't be able to keep my promises."

"And that bothers you?"

His lips curved in a resigned, not joyful, smile. "Not

with anyone but you."

Unsure if Ryske was doing exactly what he was claiming not to be doing, Harlow did feel drawn to him.

Honesty seduced her. If she could be sure this was genuine, that he was telling the truth, and showing her this vulnerability, she might let it work and surrender.

But Ryske had admitted how good he was at what he did, and he had promised to have her. If she gave in, and let him take her all the way, she could be walking into a savvy grifter's carefully constructed plot, and it wasn't like she could claim he hadn't warned her what he was capable of.

EIGHT

JUST BEING IN her bed with Ryske went against what Harlow had been asserting since the night they'd met. But he had wormed his way into her affections. As much as she wanted to believe him, Harlow wouldn't be naïve.

Ryske was no romantic hero. It would be her own fault if she was dumb enough to cross this street without looking both ways.

Touching his brow with a fingertip, she wondered if anyone truly got inside this man's head. "How many women have you made fall in love with you, Crash?"

"Love?" he asked and shrugged, finger-combing her hair to the back of her shoulder, though it fluttered down onto his bare chest again the moment it left his digits. "I don't know. But I've hurt more than I'd be proud to admit."

Stroking her fingernail through his eyebrow, Harlow concentrated how the hairs moved rather than his gaze beneath. "My father owns an investment firm," she said. "Sweeting Securities."

"I know," he said, curling his fingers around the side of her neck.

"He's not a one percenter, but he has access to a lot of money."

A twitch in his eyelid made her gaze drop to his. "What are you trying to tell me, baby? You want me to run a con on your dad? You got beef there?"

"I'm saying you could," she said, slithering down his body to use her fingernail on the lines of his shoulder tattoo that stretched across his pec. Whenever she traced his tattoos, his voice got heavier, and his focus wavered. "I could get you in."

But if she thought she was manipulating him or going to get him to admit to something he meant to keep secret, she'd underestimated just how shrewd he was.

Catching her off guard again, he threw his arms around her and flipped her onto her back. The covers tangled between them, but there was no pillow for protection this time.

"Trink, I know what you're thinking… what you think this is. But if you saw the con coming, I wouldn't be doing it right."

So he recognized what her attempt to tempt him was. Yes, it was a test. Harlow didn't want him to steal from her father and she sure didn't want to be party to it. Finding out if Ryske was for real, if his choice to be here was personal or professional, was her goal. But he was wise to it.

Hearing his assurances did make her feel better. There was no point trying to trick him if he was just going to see through it. "How do you do it?" she asked. "How do you decide where to… you know?"

"You've heard of means, motive, and opportunity, right?" She nodded. "I know you have because I've read it in your textbooks."

While she was at work, he had access to everything in her apartment. She hadn't thought that meant reading her college work, but it didn't upset her that he had. It was just lying there on her desk after all, it wasn't confidential.

The warm weight of his body was calming… and intimate. "You always have the means. You're skilled and capable. That can't define what you choose."

"No, but the other two do. Sometimes a situation presents itself and we have to deal with it, like this Hagan bullshit. Other times, we get a tip and find our way in. We're always listening for opportunity. Sometimes we have to create it."

For him, it was simple. For her, it was riveting. "And how do you do that? Why do you do that?"

"Well, that's motive, sweetheart. If I need the money, I have the motive, and that's when I go looking for opportunity."

"That's when you go looking for a mark," she said, captivated and intrigued. "How do you pick a mark?"

If he sensed the depth of her interest, he didn't mock it. "I have my own triangle for that," he said and pressed a fingertip into her as he counted off the three points. "Means, weakness, and karma. Means: does the potential mark have the ability to sacrifice something I need while absorbing the hit? I won't leave anyone destitute." That surprised her. Harlow's expression must have changed to betray her emotion because he added clarification. "Doesn't mean what I do doesn't cause the mark problems. Usually does. Sometimes they lose a lot. Destitute to me isn't the same thing as it is to them."

Coming from the streets and living his life surrounded by poverty, Ryske understood what real need was. By going after the rich, who'd probably care more about embarrassment than losing money, their marks would be able to absorb the financial hit of whatever was stolen from them.

The Floyd's crew didn't wipe people out, which was what she took from what Ryske was saying. It was smart; maybe not so selfless. Hitting any one person too hard would bring unwanted attention to them, both from potential future marks and law enforcement.

"I suppose the weakness is how you get what you want," she said. "Is there a weakness you can exploit to get in or extract what you need?" Wearing a smile, he nodded once. "But karma." Harlow narrowed her eyes and gave a quick, shallow head shake to show her confusion. "I don't—"

"Do they have it coming," he said. "Every couple of years or so we do one big job; something that takes serious planning and a long con. There's nothing more satisfying than giving some sick, rich bastard a taste of his own medicine."

"Like a regular Robin Hood."

"Nah, I don't give it away," he said. "Though, I guess you could think of me and my crew as poor and needy…"

"If you're poor it's because you spend so much on takeout and beer," she said, opening her hands around the curve of his shoulders. "I have never known a group of men in better shape, yet you all eat so terribly."

"I eat well when you cook for me," he said.

"Something I won't be doing anymore in a couple of days," she said, feeling a pang of sorrow. "You will take care of yourself, won't you, Crash?"

"Always have."

Maybe because he'd never had parents or family to look out for him; his crew were his surrogate family. "I'm worried about this Hagan mess. His men are looking for you. Bale can't go back to his apartment. He said today that he thinks Hagan's men are following him, probably looking for you…"

"Probably," Ryske said. It dumbfounded her that he was so casual about the potential danger waiting on the streets preparing for the next time he showed his face. "Hagan's had a guy in Floyd's for the last couple of weeks."

Though her body tensed, her jaw loosened. "You know that? Why wouldn't Dover kick him out?"

"Because while he's keeping an eye on us, we're keeping an eye on him." His smile didn't make her feel better. "Don't worry, Trink. Soon as I run out Bale's clock, I'll deal with it."

"That's what worries me, Ryske. Hagan's men favor weapons. Did you forget getting stabbed and shot at a couple of weeks ago? They brought a gun to Bale's too. They're serious men; don't screw around with them. You'll get hurt again."

Swagger warmed his expression. "You worried about me, baby?" he asked, but she wasn't messing around. "I won't get hurt. I have my crew behind me. This is war, baby. You've got to be willing to take a few licks."

Being stabbed was not a lick to her. Fearing for his

safety, she wanted them to stop being stubborn and just make things better. No competition was worth losing their lives.

"Maybe if you just pay Hagan back the money," she said. "I know it's a lot. I can help. I could ask—"

"I could come up with ten grand if I had to… if I wanted to. Losing the money was the plan."

Bale had told her Ryske would do anything for the job. Hearing that in action scared her. "Was getting stabbed part of the plan?"

"Just a slight detour."

He was so glib that she was offended. "If it means so little to you, why did I bother to save your life?"

"It never hurts to let your enemy stew," he said, trying to trail his fingertips into her hair, but she swatted his hand away. Seizing her wrist, he pinned it to the bed and bowed lower. "Tighter?"

The reminder of her slip up earlier became less embarrassing when his fingers strengthened. Need took humiliation's place as it began to pulse through her. A squeak left her lips. His feral look of knowing was pure smug satisfaction.

"Ryske," she gasped when the pain of his grip grew, enhancing her arousal.

"What is it that fascinates you about criminals, scholar?" The question surprised her. "That's right, Trink, I read your essay. Their motivation. The excitement. The thrill… You don't get it. Least you didn't. Not until you met my crew. You want to know if I'm conning you? Well, I want to know if I'm just an academic exercise."

It hadn't even occurred to her that getting close to him and his friends was anything other than altruism. Not at first anyway. "No! Ryske, I wouldn't—"

"Why didn't you call the cops?" he asked, not soft and safe anymore.

For the first time, she realized he had questions of his own. About her. Questions about who she was. Not simple facts like names and dates, but on the inside, in those deep recesses of her that she'd never revealed.

The growl in his voice and glare in his eye made her

more aware of her vulnerable position beneath him, trapped by his strength. Yet, in spite of the adrenaline coursing through her, she didn't feel fear. She felt just about every other emotion there was. But not fear.

"You told me not to," was as much of a response as she could muster while entranced by him.

"You didn't give a fuck about me. I was bleeding out. I could've died on that street, but you risked your freedom by following my instructions… Was that it? The risk? Does taking risks excite you, baby? More than a good little girl like you wants to admit, right?"

This was too much. Too close. Too intimate. In bed with him. In the dead of night.

Grabbing her last thread of resistance, Harlow swallowed and tried to push him away, but he was too strong. "Stop it, Ryske," she protested. "Why are you doing this?"

"You like it tight?" Another squeak came from her throat when he squeezed her wrist so tight that she was sure he was close to crushing bones. "I like it tight too, baby… and I bet you can deliver."

Suddenly, he pounced to his knees. Harlow froze. Ryske yanked the blankets from between their bodies and thrust them out of the way.

"Ryske," she said, panting. "Ryske, what are you doing?"

Her nightgown was next to be pushed aside. He parted her legs with one rough hand while the other kept its conquering hold on her wrist. "For two weeks you've been hiding behind the excuse of my injury… tonight I show you that excuse is bullshit. I'm capable, baby. So damn capable you'll forget how to breathe."

She wasn't sure that she could remember now. This was happening so fast. From sleep, to conversation, to… he dropped down over her. Against her inner thigh, she could feel his hand slip into his sweats, either to take them off or free himself.

Harlow was still trying to catch her breath and couldn't figure out what to do. "Crash," she said, and he paused for long enough to look her in the eye. Trying to distinguish his need from his determination, she slid a hand to his cheek to stroke him. "Make me a promise. Say it and mean it."

Could he do it? Harlow knew he could say it. He was a conman capable of saying anything. If he said it, would she be able to tell if he meant it? She could pretend to believe it whether she did or not and let herself give in to him.

But she wouldn't.

Harlow had been strong for the last two weeks. Desirable as he was, this man wouldn't be able to give her what she wanted. Sure, a short-term fling would light up her world and, he was right, it would be the thrill of her life. But she wouldn't give him her heart, not for nothing.

Though he seemed to be searching her, she couldn't tell what he was looking for. She needed something from him, but he needed something back. Until she knew what it was, there was no chance that she could give it to him.

A light on the nightstand beyond her shoulder drew his eye. A moment later, the sound of her phone ringing pierced the air.

Ryske surged up to snag the phone from the nightstand and answered it. Using the camera rather than the mouthpiece showed it was a FaceTime call. "What?" he snapped.

"Need you, man."

Harlow recognized Noon's voice and took the phone to turn it to her. Ryske came down to lie beside her so they could both see the screen.

"You're not getting him," she said, guessing that Noon was in a dark corner of Floyd's from the noise and what was going on around him.

She couldn't see many details, and didn't know the bar that well since she'd only been there once. But their underground dealings were at their busiest on a Friday night. She'd overheard the crew talking about it earlier in the week and figured that was probably why the guys had snuck away from her apartment without her coaxing them out.

Something like pride and relief crossed Noon's face; he didn't look as relaxed as he usually did. "I know interrupting Ryske when he's getting laid is like a cardinal sin, but this is no joke."

Trying her best not to be outraged, Harlow was about to tell Noon she was referring to Bale's medical advice, not the bed that he'd be able to see they were sharing. Noon flipped the camera before she could speak. It took her a minute to figure out what she was supposed to be seeing through the shadows of the smoky place, but when she picked out the features of Alleyman, she gasped.

Ryske must have figured it out in the same second that she did. "On my way," he said and disconnected the call.

Leaping from the bed, it took him just a few seconds to snatch up the clothes he'd discarded on the floor. Dressing as he strode from the bedroom, Ryske wasn't thinking about anything except being where his crew needed him to be.

Snapping out of her shock, Harlow followed in his footsteps, scrambling from the bed and dashing out of the room. "Ryske!"

He was at the end of the breakfast bar, using it as support to step into his boots. "Save it, Trink."

Glad that he had to bend and tie his boots, she used the delay to hurry across the room and put herself in front of him. "I don't… I don't want you to get hurt."

"The wound is sealed. You said it yourself," he said, straightening up. "The dressing is off. I'll square things with Bale."

He tried to go past her, but she got in his way, splaying both hands on his chest. "Crash, I…" Panic and fear were making her tremble. Harlow didn't know what to say or how to get what she wanted, that was Ryske's forte, not hers. "I don't want you to get hurt."

Touching her chin with a gentle caress, he didn't lose any of his determination. "Only one thing stops me walking out that door."

"One thing?" she asked, but her flash of hope was dashed when he curled a digit under the strap of her nightgown to draw it down her arm.

He'd stay if she offered her body to him.

Tilting his head, he began to descend. Before his

mouth could make contact with hers, she turned her face away.

He didn't argue or mock, just accepted that he had his answer and let his hand fall. "Take it easy, Trinket."

This time when he skirted around her, she didn't block his path. His friends needed him; that was all he cared about. Even if she'd offered him her body, he hadn't promised to stay away from danger. The sad truth was, there would always be danger.

Providing his friends weren't injured by Alleyman, they'd forgive Ryske for not showing up if he could declare he'd been busy screwing her. Or maybe he'd known she'd refuse, so the ultimatum was moot. There would be nothing stopping him from having sex with her and splitting the second they were done anyway.

Even if he didn't, there would be more danger, maybe new danger, tomorrow, and the next day, and the next. Every risk lined up just waiting to bring peril to Ryske.

Hearing him leave broke her heart.

After two weeks recuperating from being stabbed, Ryske wasn't at peak fitness. He'd been taking it easy, not working out or training. But her concern was about more than the level of ability.

If Alleyman was at Floyd's for Ryske, or even if he wasn't, and he just saw him walking in, he could do what he'd promised to in that alley and finish what he started. Ryske could be stabbed again, or shot, and though he'd be surrounded by his crew, that wouldn't guarantee he'd be okay.

What boiled the acid eating her guts was that she'd never know. Harlow might never know what became of any of them.

Slumping back against the end of the breakfast bar, she struggled to hold herself up. As the adrenaline began to subside, she wrapped her arms around herself, guarding against the chill it left in its wake. Life without Ryske had happened as suddenly as he'd crashed into her life.

He was gone.

He wouldn't be back. There would be no point in him coming back to her apartment after showing his face in

Floyd's again. Knowing he was practiced in what he did was all she could hang her hopes on. He'd be okay. She was probably panicking for nothing. His crew would see him safe.

Alone and feeling sorry for herself, being in the city had never felt so isolating. Harlow was free to go back to her life as it had been before. Life in the fast lane was over.

NINE

THE FIRST WEEK that followed Ryske's departure was odd.

Harlow had been living alone in her apartment for a couple of months before meeting Ryske, so it shouldn't be weird to be there by herself. But, for some reason, without him and his crew around taking up space, the place seemed to echo.

During the second and third week, she tried to adjust, telling herself on a regular basis that she had to move on. A month after he'd told her to take it easy and slipped out into the night, she was beginning to feel like herself again.

Though Harlow still found herself thinking of Ryske when she shouldn't. Every time her mind wandered it ended up landing on him. On his inability to pick up after himself or make a bed. On his love of Szechuan and greasy blue burgers. On his smirk. His scent. His long showers, broad fingers… his strong grip.

Cajoling her mind away from her former houseguest and back to the moment, Harlow glanced around at the family services bullpen she'd been working in for two and a half months.

Seated outside her supervisor's office, she was waiting

for her boss, Gina, to get back, so they could do an urgent review of one of her current cases. The file on her lap contained the details she'd need for the meeting. In the meantime, all she could do was sit there and scan the busy space that was bustling with the colleagues she'd been trying to bond with since she got there.

Harlow sought a friend, but came up short. In ten weeks, she hadn't met a single person who wanted more than a professional relationship. Considering herself friendly, she didn't understand why it was so hard to connect with people.

Sometimes she got distracted and blinkered in work. Maybe that made a bad impression on her peers. That focus should make a better impression on Gina. Though it didn't seem to. Despite being productive and efficient and thorough, Harlow doubted that her boss could pick her out of a line-up.

Gina came around the corner and stormed down the perimeter of the room with a look on her face like she was ready to take on the world. That certainty and determination was enviable. Gina was a hard woman, tough, maybe a little cynical, but she got the job done. Harlow admired how, despite coming from a difficult background, Gina stayed in the trenches to help the kind of people she'd grown up with even though the job was thankless and never ending.

Leaping to her feet when Gina passed, Harlow stayed close and followed the woman into the office, holding her file in one hand.

"Felipe Soto," Gina said, dropping into her seat and pulling herself in at the desk. "I just got off the phone with the detective in charge. They've still got nothing. Our relationship with the police department is currency."

Putting pressure on the already stretched police department wouldn't win her team any friends. "I know," Harlow said, feeling a little like a kid in front of the principal.

"You saw the kid the day he disappeared. His dad goes to jail and then the kid vanishes. The cops thought it was payback. Pablo Soto has enemies; he's not an easy guy to warm up to." Felipe's father was a nasty piece of work. Harlow had never met him, reading the file was enough to bring her to that conclusion. "You said you got a sense of something else."

Though there was a chair right beside her, she hadn't been invited to sit, so Harlow just stood there, clutching her file. "I did. I… I told the police. Felipe spoke about his responsibility to his mom. How he wanted to look after her."

"You know Clyde was working with him for a while, that he helped keep him away from the gangs in that neighborhood." Gina laid her forearms on the desk and gave Harlow something of a condescending look. "I know you're not from the city and some of the things you've seen have probably shocked your little suburban eyes."

"I—"

"You're still in your probationary period and losing a high-risk kid puts you on the watch list, you know?" That didn't sound like a threat, but Harlow did get the sense that her boss wasn't confident in her newest employee's abilities. "We've worked with you a lot, everyone in this department has."

Was that a complaint? Was Gina telling Harlow she was a burden or about to fire her ass?

"I appreciate everything you've done, I—"

"It's Friday night; everyone gets together for a drink on a Friday." Harlow had never quite made it to one of the weekly gatherings and got a sense she'd been judged for that too. "I want you to spend some time with Clyde. Talk to him. While our relationships with official agencies, like the cops, are important, it's just as important that we cultivate relationships on the ground, in the neighborhood. Means when things like this happen, we can reach out to our own network. You know how it is, or you should… sometimes folks will say things to people who aren't cops, people like us."

"I know."

As soon as she'd gotten the message that Felipe had been reported missing, Harlow had gone to see his mom, Martina. The cops were already there and after finishing with Martina, they'd taken a statement from Harlow too. Given that she had been working with the boy, she'd been on their list of people to talk to. Doing it at the Soto's apartment just saved them from tracking her down at the social work office.

Harlow had suggested hitting the street to look for him herself. Both the detective in charge and Gina had told her not to.

Seemed that advice was about to change. "Tomorrow, if there's been no news, we're going to go by the neighborhood, see if we can get anyone to talk. You won't be able to do much, but Clyde and I will introduce you around. It will help you to see how things work on the street. A day or two of following leads will be good for you. Part of our job involves playing detective sometimes. This is not your cushy little suburban office."

So that was why Gina didn't like her? Harlow came from an affluent home and a safe neighborhood. She'd expected it would take time to gain respect, but was at a greater disadvantage if no one would give her the chance to do that.

Gina was biased, it didn't take a genius to see that. In their few encounters, Clyde had always been nice to her. Maybe some of his ease would rub off on the boss if they spent the next couple of days working together. If not, this was going to be the weekend from hell.

***

HARLOW WASN'T DISAPPOINTED, but only because she'd been right.

The weekend wasn't off to a great start. Standing on a cold street corner, she tried shuffling her feet and rubbing her arms to heat herself up. The last thing she wanted was to be accused of complaining, so she tried to be subtle about combatting her discomfort.

Clyde was an interesting man. She'd spoken to him before but had never spent much time in his company. Last night, during their drinks with colleagues, Harlow had little choice except to bond with him. All through the Friday night, Gina had kept steering Harlow back to him, reminding her of Clyde's experience on the streets.

There hadn't been any word on Felipe overnight. Given that, Harlow had agreed to meet with Clyde and Gina that Saturday evening, on their own time, to canvass the neighborhood, asking questions about the youngster.

They'd learned that most everyone knew a neighborhood kid had been reported missing to the cops, but that only seemed to make the community more wary about answering questions.

Harlow hadn't done a lot of talking; she'd done a lot of listening. It turned out that Felipe's mother, Martina, had called the cops to report him missing, but had then tried to retract the report for some reason. People in the Soto apartment building had nice things to say about Felipe, and fewer nice things to say about some of the other kids who they seemed to think it was necessary to talk about.

As for pinpointing Felipe's whereabouts, they'd had no luck.

After trying every apartment in the Soto's building, and managing to speak with someone in maybe two thirds of the residences, they'd moved on to other buildings on the block. Without any leads there, the next thing was to try some of Felipe's hang outs.

Someone Gina knew had walked past them on the opposite side of the street. Thinking she was more likely to get somewhere on her own, Gina had told Harlow and Clyde to wait while she went across to see if the woman knew anything useful.

Gina had been over there for at least three minutes. Whatever the woman was talking about, she was animated. Maybe rather than having something vital to say, the woman just over-exaggerated her movement to keep warm. Harlow figured she couldn't be the only one who was cold.

"Would you like my jacket?"

Clyde's question took her attention away from Gina who was still chatting on the other side of the street. "Your… no, thank you… Then you'll be cold."

"I'm trying to be a gentleman over here," he said and when he smiled, she did too. He nodded toward Gina. "Do you think she's getting anywhere?

"I hope so," she said, though wasn't optimistic given how they'd struck out consistently over the last four hours.

Pushing back the cuff of her jacket, Harlow checked her watch. It was closer to five hours since she'd met Clyde and Gina out here. Five hours of wandering without hope, feigning enthusiasm, asking questions and facing nothing but resistance.

As Harlow was righting her cuff, Gina bid her contact farewell and checked for traffic as she crossed the street. There were no cars in sight. For some reason, Noon popped into her mind. She wondered if people around here kept their cars parked somewhere else just in case he chose to swipe them.

"Anything?" Clyde asked when Gina reached them.

Gina shook her head and started down the street in a stroll. Harlow and Clyde fell into step on either side of her. Harlow had never seen Gina walk so slowly, usually she was in a rush to get from A to B. If her boss was sauntering, Harlow guessed either she was thinking about their next move or coming up short.

"It's after midnight," Gina said. "We can't knock on anymore doors."

"Probably not a good idea to keep walking the streets either," Clyde said. "It's dangerous around here after dark. We've been pushing our luck."

It didn't seem so scary when they were in lit buildings, talking to people. It didn't feel so late either. Not until she thought about the young teen who could be out there somewhere scared and alone.

Still, Harlow agreed with Gina's assessment that it was too late to go knocking on people's doors. "So is that it?" she asked. "Time to go home?"

"Time to give up," Gina said with a thread of judgment.

Despite her efforts, Harlow hadn't won over her boss.

"There's one place we haven't tried," Clyde said, slowing when they reached the corner.

He didn't elaborate with words, but nodded across the intersection to the diagonal corner of the crossroads.

Gina laughed. Harlow turned to see where he was

talking about. Floyd's. Her reaction was immediate, but somehow, she managed to internalize it. They'd come at it from the opposite side, so she hadn't recognized where they were.

This was the neighborhood where her department did most of their work. She'd known Floyd's was close by but had been so preoccupied with her concern for Felipe that she hadn't grasped they were about to come upon it.

Her heart began to race. Standing there, on that open corner, she was exposed. Any member of Ryske's crew could come out at any second and see her loitering.

Since Ryske had left her apartment, she hadn't heard a peep from him or his friends. Still, all of them invaded her thoughts at different, sometimes inconvenient, times. Concern for their welfare made Harlow go so far as to check obits and scan the internet for stories about tragedy in this neighborhood. Each time she didn't find the name of anyone she knew, she'd been relieved. Though, that didn't really mean anything. There were no guarantees.

No amount of reading could give her assurances about their safety. Without talking to them, Harlow couldn't be sure that Ryske, or his crew, was even alive. Anything could have happened on Ryske's return to Floyd's. A confrontation with Alleyman could have ensued and maybe one of them had ended up with more than a scar.

In the nights, lying in her bed, where Ryske had slept so many times, she wished she knew more about the man… and where he called home. Without knowing anything about his regular life, his life that didn't include her, Harlow couldn't picture him anywhere but in her bed or Bale's—both places she'd slept with him.

As far as she was aware, he was alive. That was what she told herself anyway. Letting her mind run wild with other possibilities would drive her insane. Coming to terms with the fact that she'd never see him again had been harder than convincing herself that Ryske was still breathing, still out in the world… somewhere.

Having gone out of her way to avoid walking by Floyd's over the last month, Harlow didn't expect to be looking at it again that night. Before Ryske, she'd been afraid of the place that her colleagues told her was dangerous. Since meeting the crew who called the bar home, her motivation for avoiding it wasn't about fear… not for her safety anyway.

"That place is full of adults," Gina said. "Criminals. The dregs of the neighborhood. Why would they know where a kid was hiding? Why would they care?"

"You know why," Clyde said. "A lot of gang members graduate up into more organized crime, which means those criminals have links to the kids that run errands for them. Felipe talked about wanting to look out for his mom, to provide for her. Martina Soto said if Felipe's father ever went to prison again, she'd never take him back. So now Felipe thinks of himself as the man of the house."

That had pretty much been what Harlow had told the police. The notion of a kid feeling responsible for a family saddened her. Clyde seemed more accepting, but that just left her incredulous.

Resigned and pained in equal measure, Harlow didn't like Felipe's vision of the future. "He's thirteen," she said.

Both Clyde and Gina gave her looks containing varying degrees of sympathy and pity. They thought of her as naïve. Maybe she was. Their reactions drove Harlow to raise her chin in defiance. Her opinion was that no thirteen year-old should have to shoulder adult responsibilities, not those equivalent to supporting a whole household. Wavering or shrinking wouldn't win her respect. She had something to prove in this city, not only to her clients, but her colleagues as well.

"Doesn't matter how old he is," Gina said. "He's not been showing up to school, and if he wants to earn money, there are plenty of ways he can do that around here."

"Illegal ways," Clyde said. "And if someone wants to earn a quick buck or work a long con, there's only one place around here for that."

He and Gina turned their sights to Floyd's. Harlow couldn't work out if Clyde was waiting for Gina's go ahead, or if Gina was even considering going inside. But Harlow was about done standing out here in the cold. Dithering wasn't making progress. She didn't want to go home without knowing she'd done everything she could to find Felipe. The kid could be in serious trouble.

All night she'd been sidelined as an observer and hadn't been allowed to lead conversations or even ask questions. Taking a secondary position, deferring to others, was part of what she'd wanted to get away from both in her personal and professional lives in the suburbs.

In the city, she had promised herself to be proactive. To take control. To pursue her own path.

"I'll go," Harlow said and took a step toward the curb.

Gina caught her arm. "Whoa, no. No way. You don't know what you're walking into in there."

Oh, but she did. Much as she'd vowed never to force herself into Ryske's life, Maze had said he owed her one and this was about a kid's life. Someone in Floyd's could have an answer that would help Felipe.

Gina had told her to cultivate relationships in the neighborhood. Harlow would never gain anyone's respect if she kept being afraid of offending others.

Ryske's crew might not be like any friends she'd had in the past, but during the two weeks of Ryske's recuperation, they'd become the closest thing she'd had for a long time.

"Typically only men hang out in Floyd's," Clyde said. "Any women are fair game or connected to a man. So, yeah, uh… either you're a girlfriend or a hooker."

"I'll be fine," Harlow said, peeling Gina's fingers from her arm. "Beats standing out here in the cold."

"They'll tear you apart," Gina said.

Clyde at least had the decency to look worried as opposed to Gina who just appeared skeptical. "Anything could happen to you in a place like that. It's not safe."

Harlow smiled. "It was your idea, Clyde," she said. Her colleagues weren't moved. She sighed. "Look, I'll go in and if I'm not back in a half hour, come and find me."

Asking the Floyd's guys about Felipe was meant to help the youngster. Harlow wasn't prepared to advertise her connection to them for fear her boss would assume she could just go in and ask for favors all the time.

Having connections was one thing, exploiting them was another.

For the sake of the kids who she might need to support in the future, Harlow had to be careful about asking for help and ensure she didn't do it too often.

Clyde bowed forward in shocked opposition. "A half hour? How about we wait ten minutes?"

"It will take me that long to find the bar," she said, omitting the fact that she actually knew something about the layout of Floyd's. "And another ten to fend off whichever drunk hits on me before I get any chance to talk to someone who might be able to help."

"Twenty minutes," Gina said, taking a step back. "I think this is a bad idea."

That didn't take a rocket scientist. Gina may have been hoping Harlow would chicken out or fall on her face. Didn't matter, Harlow wasn't going to lose her determination.

TEN

TURNING AWAY FROM her colleagues, Harlow checked four ways for traffic and headed to the bar, trying not to think about the adjoining street where Ryske had slithered down the wall and passed out. The last time, her first time, in Floyd's was something of a blur, even though it hadn't been that long ago.

Wiping her mind, prioritizing focus, this wasn't the time to be reliving the traumatic memory of that night. She had to get her poker face on.

Harlow had never played poker, but when she walked through the corner doors of Floyd's and paused to let her eyes adjust, she thought she did an okay job of keeping her expression blank. It wasn't easy. Dozens of eyes scrutinized her. The place was packed. Music played on the jukebox, loud, but not as loud as the conversation filling the room.

The wooden furniture was painted black, just like the floor. There was wood paneling up half the walls that matched the color of the bar, which, although it was chipped and scratched, was still glossed enough to have a dull shine. Opening a hand on it when she got there, Harlow made a mental note to compliment Dover for taking care of it.

None of the stools matched, but neither did any of

the tables and chairs. If what she'd heard about Floyd's was accurate, there were fights in there almost every night. Replacing individual items probably made more sense than refitting the whole establishment every time a table was cracked or a chair smashed.

The first man she noticed behind the bar wasn't one she recognized. Vigilance prickled the back of her neck. Coming in under the assumption that Ryske's crew would be around might have been a mistake. If they weren't, she was a chicken who'd just wandered into a packed foxhole and from the looks of it, these foxes were hungry.

Lingering for a moment before taking a seat, Harlow was reconsidering whether or not this was a good idea. Just then, a familiar face walked around the curve of the bar. Dover. He didn't immediately notice her, he was too busy frowning at his patrons, probably wondering what had them so fascinated.

Relieved that her bold move hadn't been a bust, Harlow took the opportunity to slide onto a stool, acting like she hadn't doubted her decision to come for a moment.

A second familiar face came around the corner; this one on her side of the bar rather than behind it. Noon. Harlow didn't focus on him. Instead, she looked past the unfamiliar bartender who was heading toward her, and fixated on Dover whose attention was drifting her way.

Dover was almost upon her by the time he noticed she was there. Seeing him smile was encouraging. The unknown bartender asked if she wanted a drink, but she ignored him. Dover did too.

"It's about time you came home, babe," Dover said, nodding his worker-bee out of the way. The guy did a double take, but did as told and scurried off. "I should dock your allowance, Nightingale."

Not only a smile, but a tease too. That was big praise and such a relief. "Does that make you my daddy?" she asked, broadening the curve of her lips.

The man sliding onto the stool by hers paused halfway on and off. "Uh, I don't think I was supposed to hear that," Noon said.

Slipping a familiar hand onto his thigh, a friendly pat completed their reunion.

"Why?" Dover asked. "You afraid to admit that makes you her stunted little brother?"

There was no more than a couple of years between the men, but Noon was a lot less mature and more impulsive than business owner Dover.

Heading them off before they could descend further into playing, Harlow was aware of her clock and put both forearms on the bar to bring herself closer to it. "Am I allowed to be in here?"

Dover put both hands on the bar. "Any guy who doesn't remember your performance the last time you were here, is probably just impressed that you had the balls to walk in at all. You won't get into any trouble, babe."

"Yeah," Noon said, swigging from the beer bottle he must have brought with him. "Chick like you classes up the joint."

"Which is probably exactly what your clientele doesn't want," she said and raised a shoulder in apology. "No offense."

Dover laughed. "You think I confuse this place for a fancy Manhattan wine bar? Forget about it, Nightingale. We got what we like and we like what we got." She loved that philosophy. "What do you wanna drink?"

She shook her head. "I shouldn't. I just came in for—"

"He's not here," Noon said, turning to Dover. "We could buzz Maze, but—"

"I'm not looking for Ryske," she said. Whatever their assumptions about the why, Harlow didn't insult the men's intelligence by pretending she didn't know who they'd assumed she was looking for. Seeing their expectation made her cringe. "Maze is the one I want to talk to actually."

"Your computer broken?" Noon asked, puffing up a little. "I'm okay with electronics."

Dover scoffed. "Yeah, if that were true, what would we need Maze for? Oh wait, I forgot, you're an asshole. Always handy to have one of those around."

The way they beat up on Noon was always in good fun. In secret, the crew adored him. But her maternal side was always stirred when the others poked at him, even in spite of Noon being older than her.

"I don't think you're an asshole," she said, picking up Noon's arm to put it around her. "I think you're adorable."

"Yeah, see, I'm adorable," Noon said, pulling her closer while making a face at Dover. She didn't see it, but Dover repaid Noon in kind.

"Puppies are adorable," Dover said. "She thinks you're a pathetic slobbering mutt who's not smart enough to know where to piss… Hmm, guess she does know you."

Ignoring Dover, Harlow put her head on Noon's shoulder. "I was thinking about you earlier," she said.

"No kidding?" Noon said. "You want to come upstairs with me, Nightingale?"

Dover blanked his face. "No women allowed upstairs. And you do know Ryske would kill you dead if you tried it, right?" he asked Noon. "With his bare hands, you'd just be dead."

Ryske had told her what was under Floyd's floor, not what was above. "What's upstairs?" she asked, curious about why women weren't allowed and why Ryske would have a problem with Noon taking her there.

"Among other things: beds."

Harlow could only laugh. She didn't believe for a second that Noon would ever make a move on her.

"I wasn't thinking that," Noon said. "Thought I could order the lady some Chinese food. Wait with her for Maze."

Dover wasn't buying it. "Yeah, and liquor her up."

"I really can't stay to get drunk," she said and checked her watch. "Or at all really… will Maze be around tomorrow?"

"He'll be around tonight," Dover said. "Just doing a recce. He should be back any minute."

A recce? Reconnaissance? Harlow wasn't going to ask. At least wherever they were, Ryske and Maze were together. Should help if anyone thought to stab one of them.

"Is this a computer specific problem?" Noon asked.

"No," she said. "He just always said to me that he'd feel better when his debt was paid." Appealing to them both, she ensured to make eye contact. "I never considered what happened with Ryske a debt, you know that. But I need help and—"

"If one of us has a debt to you, we're all on the hook for it," Dover said, bending down to rest both forearms on the bar. Noon got closer too. Harlow realized she was enveloped in the covert huddle of Ryske's crew. Well, half of them anyway. She was in the coveted and privileged huddle. *In* it. "Why don't you fill us in?"

She didn't have a lot of time, her colleagues could walk in any second. If she went out there to say she got nothing and set nothing in motion, Harlow would lose respect not gain it. Though surviving in Floyd's should score her some points… in theory.

She took a deep breath. "I—"

"Wait," Dover said and turned around to duck down.

When he got back up, he was pouring chilled white wine into a glass.

Smiling, Harlow accepted the drink and took a sip. "How much wine do you serve in here?" she said, licking her lips and nodding in approval. "It's good."

"Got it just for you. We knew you'd be back…" Wow, she was stunned. Not only that he'd ordered something for the bar for her, but that they'd had faith. In the time since she'd last seen Ryske, Harlow had assumed the crew had forgotten about her. Apparently they hadn't. "Tell us your story, Nightingale," Dover said, leaning close again.

Getting over her surprise, Harlow was quick about filling them in. Knowing that there wasn't much time, she gave them the cliff notes version.

"So basically…" she said, having brought them up to speed. "I need to know if this kid is in trouble. No, let me rephrase. I know he's in trouble, I just need to know how deep."

Neither man spoke, but she recognized the solemn expression they exchanged. "You came to the right place," Dover said.

Hope made her sit up straighter. "You know where he is?"

Noon shook his head. "No, but we will within twenty-four hours."

Dover was confident too. "We'll come to yours with what we find. It's safer."

Alarm struck her. "I thought you said I was safe here."

"Here you're golden," Dover said. "Especially with us around."

Noon leaned in to bump his shoulder on hers. "And at least one of us is always around Floyd's."

"But getting here isn't as safe," Dover explained. "You know what this neighborhood is like more than most outsiders."

After what she'd gone through with Ryske. The acknowledgment that she had some experience was the most respectful thing anyone had said to her that month. Funny that the criminals should be kinder than the non-criminals.

Now that she was in Floyd's, Harlow was enjoying herself. Just spending a few minutes with Dover and Noon had been more fun than a whole night with her work colleagues. It made her realize that she didn't want this to be the last time she was ever there.

"I don't mind visiting," Harlow said.

"You haven't visited until now," Noon said. "What took you so long, Nightingale?"

Dover cleared his throat and she caught him shaking his head. "You sure you don't want us to come to you?" he asked when he noticed her peering at him.

Still curious, she just shook her head. "I want to visit... Unless you think someone will have a problem with me being here?"

The look he tried to disguise was telling, but didn't reveal enough for her to figure it out. "No. No one will have a problem," Dover said. "I guess the way you keep looking at that watch, you have somewhere you need to be. You want Noon to give you a ride?"

"I have colleagues waiting outside."

Noon hit his chest. "Oh, I'm wounded."

But he was smiling, so she smiled along and drained her glass before slipping off her stool. "What do I owe you for the wine?"

Leaning over the bar, Dover touched his cheek. "Lay one on me and we're square."

Noon steadied her as she boosted up to kiss Dover's cheek. Despite having done it plenty before, it made her blush to kiss him in front of this many witnesses. Since Noon had been as kind, she was compelled to offer him a cheek-kiss too.

"Thank you both. This means so much to me. You have no idea."

"Our debt will never be repaid with favors like this. You saved Ryske's life. Show your face any time."

Backing away from the bar, Harlow was pleased to have accomplished something and done it without coming across as a crazy stalker. It was a relief that Ryske hadn't been around; she hadn't needed to embarrass herself by looking like she'd used an excuse to see him again.

Except, Harlow would be back tomorrow and had no idea what that would bring.

ELEVEN

WALKING INTO FLOYD'S the previous night had been nerve-wracking. But it had been impulse, there had been no time to overthink it. Since leaving, she'd had time to obsess about what might happen when she returned.

Last night, Harlow had slipped out of Floyd's and gotten back to Gina and Clyde without having to face Ryske. But she wouldn't be so lucky on night two. Ryske would have spoken to his crew and learned that she'd been around. Dover would have filled him in and told him that she was coming back.

Although she'd received a warm welcome from Dover and Noon on her impromptu visit, Harlow feared the hospitality she received on the second night might not be so warm.

If Ryske was there, it was because he wanted to see her, and she wouldn't be able to avoid him. If he wasn't there… It was difficult to decide which would be worse, being forced to face him or learning he had no interest in seeing her ever again.

Gina and Clyde had been surprised to learn that not only had she come out alive and unharmed, but that she was going back to receive an update on Felipe. Her confidence in her contacts was unwavering; they'd come up with the goods.

It had been fun to see Gina incredulous, though Harlow tried to be magnanimous. Clyde was more dubious about her trusting whoever she'd spoken to. That made sense given he didn't know she had a previous relationship with the crew.

Gathering her wits, Harlow ran down her stoop, thinking about getting to Floyd's and what might happen if she did make it there alive.

The blast of a car horn startled her to a halt.

There by the curb was Noon hanging out the window of what looked like a Pontiac. "Looking for a date, Sugar?"

Broadening her smile, her stress level dropped. She went over to skirt the car to get in on the passenger side. "You didn't have to come pick me up."

He blended into traffic. "I was cruising anyway," he said, though she didn't know whether or not to believe him.

Pulling on her seatbelt, Harlow checked out the dash. "This is a nice car."

"Yeah, that's what I thought too," he said. "When I walked by and saw the rims, I had to have it."

She'd been going to ask about the dealership he'd got it from and the cost, but her mouth closed before the words came out. Ryske had been clear about Noon's hobby. Bale had told her Noon did all the driving and always had.

It was possible that this car didn't belong to the man driving it. If she asked, did that make her party to the crime even though she hadn't been there when he committed it?

"Maze was sorry he missed you last night," Noon said, before she could decide whether or not to ask about the ownership of the vehicle.

Her train of thought changed suddenly; he'd omitted a name she might have expected to hear. "Maze was?"

There wasn't quite a smirk on his face, but there was definitely something on his mind. "Your family are rich, right?"

"Middle-class," she said. "We're not the Rockefellers."

He coughed out a laugh. "Maybe if you were Ryske

would get his thumb out his ass."

Speculation about her and Ryske's relationship might have been expected while she was in their lives, but it had been a month since she had been. Obviously, it was still on Noon's mind.

Given that she hadn't seen Ryske for so long, she was out of the loop. Noon would've seen his friend, probably that day, so his opinion on her worthiness was likely to be more accurate than anything she thought.

Her mood soured. "You're saying I'm not rich enough for him?"

Glancing to her in a sudden panic, he checked the road, then looked at her again. "What? No! I... I didn't mean that. Shit, that would be something, wouldn't it?" His smile was awkward. "There were times growing up he and me couldn't afford to eat for a week. He's no prince."

Her curiosity was almost suspicion. "I thought he stayed with Floyd and Dover... didn't you stay with them?"

That she knew anything about Ryske's past seemed to surprise the driver, enough that he tossed her another look, this one more astonished than panicked. "Ryske told you that?"

"He told me a lot," she said, allowing a knowing smirk to warm her lips. "Like how a little game of three-card-Monte brought the two of you together."

Laughing, he relaxed and stretched a loose hand to the back of her headrest while tossing her another look. "Maybe it's not as lost as we thought," he said. "Sure, yeah, we stayed with Floyd a lot. Sometimes we got restless, you know? We were kids, no responsibilities, and sometimes flush. So we'd take off on what we called 'Wild Adventures.' At some point, we'd run out of money, and out of luck. We'd be stranded in a random shithole in some crappy corner of the planet. Didn't matter how desperate I thought our situation was, Ryske always had a plan, always had a way out."

Thinking about what Ryske had said to her the night he left her apartment, Harlow straightened the line of her skirt on her thigh. "Let me guess," she said. "It involved a con."

A few seconds went by. "Is that the problem?" he

asked, his hand sliding away from her seat to return to the wheel. "You snap about not being rich enough for him; maybe he's not righteous enough for you… I get it, he's not good enough. You think he's not good enough for you… You don't want a guy who's damaged goods."

Although there was anger in his voice, she didn't feel the need to backtrack. In fact, in an attempt not to exacerbate the situation, she tried to conceal her kneejerk smile by turning towards her side window to hide it. Apparently, she wasn't quick enough because Noon made a sound of disgust.

His quick judgment made her angry and erased her smile. "That's it, Noon, yeah, he's not good enough for me. That's why I took him in and looked after him for a whole week," she said. "I think he's evil and demented and completely beneath me." Bouncing around to face him, a surge of infuriation enflamed her. "The bastard walked out of my apartment without so much as a thanks for the memories. You called and then he was gone. Just gone. All of you were. Do you think that if I thought you were damaged or inferior that I would have let you take up residence in my home? I didn't cut ties with you. All of you abandoned me!"

"Night—"

"Spending time with Ryske, getting to know him, it was the most… enlivening time of my life. He never made me feel judged, something my family specialize in, and he never asked for anything I wasn't capable of giving."

Capable, though not always willing. Harlow could have slept with him; it was within her ability to yield. She'd just chosen not to.

"Was sex all you wanted?"

"Sex was all he wanted," she said, losing some of her gusto and angling her body toward the hood while taking her attention back to the side window.

It seemed ridiculous to confess that they'd never had sex. They hadn't, but maybe Ryske hadn't told his crew that. With how Noon was talking, she guessed Ryske hadn't said much to his crew about them. It sounded like there had been some speculation on their part though. Confirming or denying anything wasn't her place. They were Ryske's people. What they knew was his call.

Saying less felt more normal than revealing anything that might contradict Ryske. Maybe she was covering for him, but could admit to herself that there was a corner of her psyche that liked the idea of being a grifter's girl. That was another reason she didn't correct Noon.

"Is that what he said?" Noon asked. "That he just wanted to be casual?"

"He didn't have to say it," she said, ready to cut off this line of questioning. "I want to be your friend. Yours, Maze's, Dover's and yes, even Ryske's too. Bale said I was part of your toolbox, and I'm fine with that. I understand the trust and dedication you have to each other. I admire it. But… I'm never going to be special to him."

Just saying it out loud was difficult. It was insane that Ryske could hurt her when he wasn't even present. He'd been nothing but honest. It wasn't his fault that she'd got more invested than him. Yet, there she was, trying not to squirm in her chair or reveal just how deep that truth cut her.

His lack of response revealed that she hadn't been completely successful. There was no double take or glib retort, Noon kept his eyes fixed on the road ahead.

"I'm sorry, Nightingale," he said. "I had no idea… Maybe he is damaged."

"Damaged goods is what my ex called me when I told him I wouldn't give up work to play the dutiful wife. My mom went insane when she found out I'd told him before the wedding. Really nuts. She'd advised me not to. She wanted me to trap him into being with me, I guess. It wasn't malicious, she was never as explicit as that. Rupert was a good man. Maybe she thought I'd change my mind about working, I don't know."

"I… I don't know what to say."

She inhaled through her nose, becoming reflective. "Maybe I am too independent for my own good… I did value Ryske's honesty, I did. I'm just not casual about relationships," she said. "Not because I have some righteous sense of virtue or because I want every man I care about to fall in love with me. The truth is, I still haven't figured out what I want from the rest of my life. Ryske isn't damaged, at least, if he is, it doesn't change what he means to me. But that's not why we're not… I don't know what he told you guys about us, but…" Expanding was just going to take her further down the rabbit hole. She had to stop rambling. "All he wanted was something casual, and I'm sorry, but that's not who I am."

They drove past a gang on a corner and closed in on Floyd's. Noon pulled in around the back and she twisted to reach for the door handle.

Noon caught her hand to hold her back. "Dover told me to tell you something."

"Okay," she said, dubious of what it might be. "About Felipe?"

"No."

The drive had been nice, but now that she thought about it, she should've just asked Noon for the update and then she wouldn't have had to come near the bar at all. "Noon, what did he say?"

"Go with it."

That might have been supposed to mean something to her, except she didn't follow. "I don't understand. What do you mean? Go with what?"

"In Floyd's, tonight, any time you're back, any time you're here…" Giving him some time to figure himself out, she stayed quiet. Eventually, he sighed. "Just always be careful what you say outside the crew, you know? Even if something doesn't make sense to you, never question or contradict, just go with it."

Putting a hand over his, she smiled. "Don't worry about that, Noon. If you think I'm going to blow one of your schemes, I'm not. I'd be surprised if I ever have reason to be in Floyd's again after tonight… unless another one of my kids goes missing."

His face set in a scowl. "I thought you said you wanted to be our friend."

She touched his cheek. "I do," she said. "And if you want to show up with Chinese food, my door is open any time. But I can't force myself onto Ryske. I don't want it to get weird, and it will if he thinks I'm stalking him."

Telling a guy that she didn't do casual and then showing up everywhere he hung out might give him the wrong idea. Ryske intrigued her and it would've been fun to explore what had been between them if she was a few years younger, or pre-Rupert. But her ego couldn't take another bruising.

"He's been in a bad mood for the last month," Noon said, fidgeting like maybe he wasn't sure he should be saying anything.

"He was stabbed," she said. "Has Bale been keeping an eye on him?"

"Bale's out of town."

The way he said that and then let her go made Harlow think there was more to the story, but she didn't ask. Noon got out of the car and came around to open her door. It wasn't an act of chivalry, she got the sense he just didn't want to be alone with her anymore. Maybe he feared getting into trouble for telling her something that was possibly a secret.

But if she covered for Ryske, she'd cover for Noon too.

Linking their hands, he led her toward the alley that would take them to the street and the corner entrance. "I'd think you guys would have a secret back door for your underground gamers."

Pausing, he turned to examine her. "Shit, Ryske doesn't usually talk so much, even when he's high. What were you pumping into him?" He laughed. "No, wait, I don't want to know."

TWELVE

ROUNDING THE BUILDING, they were seconds away from disappearing through the corner doors to go into Floyd's when she noticed a lone figure loitering by the curb about ten feet away. Probably registering movement, the man turned to them.

Harlow's eyes met the loiterer's. Recognizing him, she stopped. "Clyde?"

At her side, Noon grew taller and more rigid while tightening his grip on her hand. "You know this schmuck?"

"He's not a schmuck, he's my colleague," she said and stepped around Noon. Instead of letting her go, he tugged her to him. Disguising her bounce back, Harlow put a hand to Noon's chest. "Clyde, what are you doing here?"

"This is how you got your information?" Clyde asked, frowning at Noon. "Your boyfriend comes here?"

"Yeah, he does," Noon said, too confrontational for her liking. "You better fucking remember that, asshole."

Noon yanked her behind him. Terrified that he was going to hurt the astonished Clyde, she grabbed for his arm with both hands. "Noon, stop it," she said, stepping in so close that she was almost talking against his arm. Clyde's scrutiny of the familiar act made her lean back to address her colleague. "Are you here for a reason?"

"I didn't want you going in there alone," Clyde said, his words stunted with wonder. "I wanted to be here in case you needed backup."

"She doesn't need backup. We're her backup. Floyd's is her home."

"Stop getting defensive," she said, tugging on Noon's arm. Clyde's scrutiny intensified when Noon slid an arm around her shoulders. "Why don't you come inside and have a drink, Clyde? You're here anyway."

If Dover said she was welcome, then her friends should be as well. Sure, she and Clyde were hardly bosom buddies… she didn't even know his last name… or, come to think of it, his first, maybe Clyde was his last name.

"He's not drinking with us," Noon grumbled.

"Stop your BS," she said, lacing her fingers through his. Gesturing at Clyde, she encouraged him to join them, but kept talking to Noon. "He's my friend, don't be rude."

As they went inside, she noted that Floyd's wasn't quite as busy as it had been the previous night, though most of the tables were occupied. The lights and the volume of the music were lower, giving the place a more intimate feel.

It was odd that she should think of a place she'd once feared as cozy. The probing eyes, tattoos and muscles of patrons didn't intimidate her anymore. Neither did the scent of beer and body odor surprise her.

Given the right mood, she could imagine a time when she'd feel comfortable there. If she wasn't waiting for Ryske's reaction to her invading his life that was.

All that considered, Harlow kept her head, and played it smart. Fixing her eyes on the bar, she thought of how children were instructed not to look aggressive dogs square in the eye in case they thought they were being challenged. Harlow didn't fear for her own safety; Noon was at her side. But she wasn't stupid enough to give off any hostile vibes. It was impossible to know who was watching and who might hold a grudge.

After Harlow took a stool at the bar, Clyde slid onto one beside her. "I can't believe you know these people," her colleague hissed.

Noon ran a hand down the back of her hair and kept going. He disappeared around the corner but reappeared on the other side of the bar a minute later. Without asking anything, he produced a glass of wine for her like Dover had last night. The growl on his face betrayed how he begrudged tossing a beer in Clyde's direction.

"I'm going to look for the guys," Noon said. "Wait here. Don't move."

Scanning the bottles lined up on shelves at the back of the bar, Harlow wished she'd insisted on a tour last night. If she had asked to be shown around, maybe she'd have some idea of where to run if things went south.

Seconds ago, when they'd come inside, she'd been thinking of how safe she was there. But watching Noon disappear around the curve of the bar chilled her. Suddenly, she was without protection.

In her peripheral vision, she saw Clyde's head was bobbing in a nod. "These are the people you came to for help last night," he said, fixated on completely the wrong thing.

They were alone in what could be an unfriendly place. Clyde should be focused on the potential danger, not his shock of her connection to the notorious establishment. Figuring maybe it was different for guys, and that Clyde was confident he could handle himself in a fight, Harlow told herself not to worry about him. She hadn't promised him protection and he hadn't asked for it.

"Yes, they are."

"And you couldn't have just told us that?" he asked. "You couldn't have been honest and said, 'Hey, you know what? My boyfriend hangs out in Floyd's, I'll be perfectly safe.' Why not just tell us about Mr. Friendly? I can really tell what you see in him."

Blowing out a breath, she hated judgment, but passive aggressive was even less attractive. "The man you just met is not my boyfriend. But he does know people who may be able to help us track down Felipe, which is the point, right? We're doing this to find a teenager who could be lost or up to God knows what."

"I could've helped you," he said and laid a hand over hers on the bar. "You didn't have to get yourself mixed up with the people in here to do your job. When did you meet him? Was it after Felipe went missing? Let me guess, you tried to go looking on your own without telling anyone, before you came out last night with me and Gina, didn't you?"

Thinking she was some sort of crusader was giving her more credit than she was due. "Clyde," Harlow said, shaking her head.

He continued before she had a chance to finish. "What did they ask you to do?"

Picking up her hand, he took it to his lap. Just the act of putting her hand in such a personal place seemed intimate, so much so that it startled her into looking down, though the shadow of the bar made it too dark to see anything.

"I don't think—"

"I've seen you around the office, read some of your notes. I know you. I'm not sure you're ready for a neighborhood like this. These guys will eat you up and spit you out if you're not careful." The cool caress of his damp fingers moved from his beer bottle onto her cheek. "You can't let them take advantage of you."

Blinking up into his soft eyes, that were almost pitying, she knew he thought her to be naïve, probably verging into stupid. In his narrative, she would deserve anything she got for wandering into a dangerous place like this and demanding answers.

"Clyde, I—"

Harlow wasn't sure what she'd been about to say, and she never got the chance to find out. Her words were cut off when her colleague was suddenly yanked from his stool. Before she could even think to leap from hers, the harsh thwack of a fist smacking into flesh echoed through the air.

Clyde flew back into her view. Spinning around, he flopped over the bar, smacking his head against it, then slithered to the floor.

Fear and confusion pumped through her, fueled by a surge of adrenaline. Whipping around so fast that her neck cracked, Harlow expected to find an out of control drunk or maybe a strung out sociopath.

Instead, she saw a tall, broad, and terrifying Ryske.

With his fists balled and his arms tensed, she could see his shoulders rising and falling as he inhaled and exhaled, deep, furious breaths. All his focus was on Clyde; she wasn't sure he was even aware of her.

"Get up," Ryske hissed, beginning to advance again.

Anyone within spitting distance scrambled away, pushing aside tables and knocking over chairs in their haste to get out of Ryske's periphery.

Rushing to intercept him, Harlow threw all of her body weight against him. "No," she said, slapping her hands to his chest. "No! Crash, stop!"

Clyde was still cowering on the floor. If he was smart, he'd stay there.

"Out of the way, Trink," Ryske growled.

With one arm, he managed to sweep her aside like she weighed nothing, clearing his path to Clyde.

Harlow was still finding her footing when she spotted Dover coming in with Maze just behind him. "Dover!"

Her exclamation made him and Maze jump to attention. Knowing his own place, Dover had noticed there was something going on, but hadn't zoned in on it until she called out.

With moist palms pressed to her upper chest, all Harlow could do was watch with wide eyes. Dover and Maze rushed over and fought with Ryske to pull him away from Clyde who had his arms up protecting his face, fearful of Ryske's next punch.

"What the hell's the matter with you?" Dover screamed, shoving Ryske back.

Maze pinned his confused anger on her. "What the fuck were you doing? Blowing the guy?"

Ignoring Maze, she went to crouch at Clyde's side. "I'm sorry," she said, trying to coax his arms down from blocking his head. "I'm so sorry."

"Don't fucking touch him, Trink," Ryske spat with visceral fury.

Crash didn't have the monopoly on rage. Tossing her

hair over her shoulder to look back at him, she saw Dover and Maze still fighting to hold their friend back. Surging to her feet, Harlow marched over, glad that Dover was still holding onto the manic Ryske, not because she was afraid of him, but because Clyde didn't deserve another hit. He hadn't deserved the first one.

"How dare you treat my friend this way!"

Dover struggled against Ryske's strength but managed a glance at her. "What happened? What the fuck did—"

"Your buddy came from nowhere and smacked my friend in the face for no reason!"

Surprise made Dover relax enough that Ryske almost got past him. The bartender managed to strengthen his grip again just in time to catch his friend. Maze rushed in to back him up. Harlow didn't think that Ryske was really fuming enough to force his way past his friends. It seemed like he was trying to reinforce his point by blustering and making it difficult for them to keep him still.

Maze hadn't lost his confusion, if anything, it grew. "I have never seen you throw the first punch," he said and glanced to Dover who gave Ryske a shake.

"Who is he, man?" Dover asked. "What happened?"

"I told you what happened," she said and shoved Maze aside to sock Ryske's shoulder. "How do you like it, asshole?"

Ryske's agitation narrowed into laser precise focus that zoned in on her. His hand shot up to grab her by the throat. His grip was sure. Not tight enough to restrict her breathing or hurt her. Enough to possess her. To claim and own her.

Fixated on each other, their shallow breathing sank into sync. She stilled, like an animal playing dead.

"Whoa, hey," Maze said.

Dover tried to grab Ryske's hand away from her, but the first move Harlow made was to brush him aside.

Still transfixed on the other, Harlow was sure she and Ryske made quite the spectacle, or she would think that if she could focus on anything other than the intensity of his gaze.

Ryske walked her backward, anyone in their path scrambled. He didn't stop until her back hit the bar.

"When I told you I won't let any other man have you, I meant it. So either you brought him here to get my attention, which you have, or you want me to take him out, which I will… Which is it?"

"Neither," she said, not taking her eyes from his while seeking his loose hand. Threading their fingers together, she had hopes of calming him. "I didn't bring him, Noon brought me. Clyde was waiting for me outside, he's my colleague."

His attention dropped to the floor at their side where Clyde was still cowering. "A stalker? Is that right?" he asked. "You lured him to the right place."

With a finger on his jaw, she brought his attention to her. "Not a stalker, Crash, a friend," she said. "Will you please be reasonable?"

Ryske didn't answer. If he wanted to beat on Clyde, he could. That he wasn't taking that chance showed they'd made progress. She hoped. They would stay in this face-off all night unless someone broke it. So Harlow pushed Ryske back, demanding enough space that she could bend over to pull Clyde to his feet.

Clyde cleared his throat a few times, wary of those around him, and what he'd just endured. "Your, uh… boyfriend, I guess?"

There was no time to respond.

"What the fuck happened in here?" Noon's voice exploded behind her. "I was gone five fucking minutes."

"You thought it was smart to let guys hit on her at the bar?" Maze asked, stepping up behind Clyde to pick up a stool and sit down. "Least we know who can't keep her safe now. You need a fucking sitter of your own, Noon. Use your damn head."

THIRTEEN

THE MUSIC STARTED again. People began to pick up furniture and shuffle back to their previous positions. Harlow tried to take a step toward Clyde, but Ryske's arm snaked around her waist to jolt her back against his chest with such power he forced the air out of her lungs.

"Maybe you should go," she said to Clyde, pushing at Ryske's locked arm that held her fast. "As you can see, I'm completely safe here."

"I'm not sure about that," Clyde muttered.

Something like a growl sounded above her head. Twisting to peek up, she wasn't surprised to see Ryske's distaste pinned on Clyde. Too short to make a dent in his view, the top of her head only just reached his chin.

Though she knew she should be more concerned about controlling him, enchantment was never far away when Ryske was close by.

"I'm so used to seeing you lying down that I forgot how tall you are," she murmured.

His arm tightened around her waist. Her initial resentment for his uninvited embrace was turning into something more primal. "So used to seeing him lying down," Clyde said, reminding her that she wasn't actually alone with

Ryske. "That tells me all I need to know about your relationship with him. You're lovers."

Ryske used the way his arm was coiled around her middle to slide her body behind his back. With a deft move, he'd pulled her one way, side-stepped, and then just slotted her in at his back. Before she'd even realized he'd inverted their positions, Ryske was standing up to Clyde again. "And what the fuck does her pussy mean to you?"

"Crash," she said, wrapping her arms around his torso, fearing he could fly for Clyde again at any moment. She wouldn't be able to hold him back on her own, so again, she looked to Dover for support. "Did you get any word on Felipe? If you tell me what you know, Clyde and I can get out of here."

"You're going nowhere with this jerkoff," Ryske said, glowering at Clyde.

"Let's everybody calm the fuck down," Dover said and came closer to lay a hand on her shoulder.

Leaping around to swipe it away, Ryske sent a shockwave through their group. Getting defensive with his crew was unheard of. He'd seen his guys kiss her and touch her; he'd never been possessive of her with them.

For some reason, he was so on edge that instinct had made him strike one of his own.

"Okay, someone needs a timeout," Maze said, leaving his stool to go around everyone. "'Scuse me, Nightingale."

He eased her aside and grabbed Ryske's shoulders from behind. Instead of just going with his friend, Ryske yanked himself free of Maze's grasp. "I'm not leaving Trink out here unprotected."

"Your trinket will be fine out here," Maze said, putting an arm around Ryske to grip his opposite shoulder tight. "Anyone touches her and we'll introduce his insides to the outside."

The thread of warning in Maze's voice was ominous. As it was supposed to be. Maze was showing solidarity with Ryske. Letting Clyde know he wasn't off the hook. If Ryske went over the edge and threw all in to take down Clyde, Harlow would bet that the Floyd's crew would leap in too.

Even if they didn't agree with him, they had a 'one in, all in' kind of strategy.

Getting Ryske out of the bar would diffuse some of the tension, which she needed if she wanted any answers. But if he didn't *choose* to walk out with his friend, she had no idea how far he'd go in resisting his crew.

Dover came to her side. "We'll keep her safe, man."

Moving around the bartender, she got close to Ryske. "Crash," she murmured, picking up his hand and pressing it to her upper chest. "Go with Maze… please, baby."

She'd never called him that before or referred to him as her boyfriend like Clyde had. Their discussions to date had only included her assertions that she wouldn't ever be intimate with him.

Yet, something about her words or her proximity did the job. "You don't leave these premises without my word."

Nodding, she wanted to find out what had happened to Felipe, and would worry about that before trying to settle the tormented grifter. Sliding his hand higher, he curled his fingers around her throat to squeeze her tighter than he had before.

Of their own volition, her lips parted in a pout. Being in his hold felt so damn good. "Tighter, Crash," she whispered.

Strengthening his grip, he pulled her to him. Holding her body to his, their mouths hung just an inch apart. "Tease me, Trink."

Teetering on her tiptoes, she was at his mercy. Yet, somehow, she had all the power. "Later," she said, slipping her fingers beneath the hem of his tee-shirt to graze her nails over the area of his abdominal tattoo. "Later."

Maze pulled Ryske from her. Harlow didn't dare break eye contact. Staring into Crash seemed to distract him from Clyde's presence. Back in his right mind, at least for that minute, Ryske let Maze draw him away. In the shadow at the end of the bar, the men disappeared.

At her back, Dover was the one to inhale and blow out a breath that ruffled her hair. "Shit, babe, you make him lose his fucking mind."

"Does he have one to lose?" Clyde piped up. "I've never seen a more unreasonable man."

Whipping around almost in unison, Harlow was alarmed by the glare Dover set on Clyde. "That's what happens when you move in on another guy's girl."

Harlow hadn't seen Ryske for a month. They'd never had sex. Never kissed. But his crew believed they were together in some way. And no wonder when Ryske had adopted the role of jealous lover.

As far as she was concerned, after he'd walked out of her apartment, he'd never thought about her again. Showing up at Floyd's had not been her plan. For the sake of Felipe, Harlow had been willing to take the risk even if it meant Ryske assuming she was using the kid as an excuse to see him.

In a flash, Ryske had changed her mind about him having ideas of unwelcome advances. After what had just happened, Harlow was thinking they'd need to have a conversation about who he was to her and who he wasn't allowed to punch on her behalf.

In the car in the way over, she'd just been telling Noon that she wouldn't be coming back because if she did, Ryske might believe she was stalking him. Then, as soon as Crash had seen her, he'd had a crazy irrational reaction like he might be a little unhinged himself.

"Night," Noon said and it took her a second to realize he was talking to her, shortening her nickname from Nightingale. "Come and finish your drink."

Holding up her topped off wine, Noon gave her an opening that she welcomed to get things back to a state of normality. She slid onto her stool and took the glass he offered.

"You better be driving me home tonight," she said, sipping the wine.

Harlow didn't even have a car and hadn't driven here, so it was silly to imply that she'd be stranded without Noon's help. Her apartment wasn't that far either. If she had to walk it, she could. If that wasn't an option, she could use a cab... if one would come here to pick her up.

"Are you going home tonight?" Noon asked.

The implication wasn't ambiguous. If she didn't go home… The alternative was Ryske's bed. With the way he'd reacted to Clyde, he'd made it obvious that offer was still on the table.

Taking another drink, she didn't realize her mind was drifting, but became swept up in what it was to be near to Ryske again… how his grip had felt on her neck… his skin under her nails.

Harlow shivered.

"Yo!"

The exclamation startled her into turning around. Dover, Clyde, and Noon were all looking at her. With her fingertips stroking her throat and the likelihood of a blush in her cheeks, she doubted it took them long to figure out who she'd been thinking about.

"How long have you been with him?" Clyde asked.

The obvious judgment in his voice was a surprise to her. His profession was the same as hers; they were trained to be neutral or at least to exhibit objectivity. Taking her eyes from Dover to Noon, the pair didn't seem prepared to bail her out of the conversation.

Projecting her request for them to divert the discussion, she blinked her eyes back to Dover. That was when Noon spoke. "You seem very interested in our girl," he said. "Why do you care who she's fucking?"

Apparently, she hadn't conveyed the message. Noon was taking on Ryske's mantle while all she wanted was some peace. "No one cares who I'm fucking," she said and focused on Dover, taking control of the conversation herself. "What did you find out about Felipe?"

"We came through."

Relief. "Good. I knew you would," she said, and leaned closer, expecting him to elaborate.

Rather than give her more words, Dover took her hand and led her from her stool.

Snatching for her wine glass, she tried to take a gulp before he took her too far from it. "Bring the wine, babe."

Not one to refuse, given that she was enjoying the buzz of the alcohol now that the adrenaline was wearing off,

Harlow held the glass to her chest and let Dover take her past the other patrons. Winding through the tables, ignoring the faces monitoring their progress, she smiled when the song changed to a tune she loved.

Pulling herself closer to Dover, Harlow was safe in his shadow mouthing the words to the song when they got to the end of the bar. Dover took a right to head down a passageway.

To the immediate right was the open entry to behind the bar, another door on the solid wall further down wasn't marked. To the left was the men's room with the powder room next along. It was the door at the head of the passageway, perpendicular to the ladies' room that they seemed to be heading for.

Dover opened the door and led her through. Harlow held her breath, wondering what would be inside.

In the opposite corner was a curtain covering a gap in the wall. Thick and red, it was nothing like her crystal beads. The light was low. It originated from the TV on a unit against the back wall. Couches were arranged around a coffee table in front of it. This seemed to be some kind of den.

There was another door to the right, but when her eyes caught on the sight of a figure sitting up straighter on the couch, she was intrigued enough to move closer. Letting her eyes adjust, Harlow registered a mop of dark, possibly black hair atop the head of someone watching the TV. This was none of Ryske's crew; it wasn't even a man.

"Felipe?" she asked, hurrying around the couch to see more of the kid's profile.

He turned and grinned when he saw her. "Miss Sweeting," he said and held up the remote control. "Man, you have some cool friends."

"I have some…" Shock made her look from the exuberant teen to Dover who was still by the door. "What the… how did you?"

"Yeah, we found the kid," he said, heading for the couch and giving the kid a shove so he had space to sit down. "Turn that off."

Felipe did as told and turned off the TV. "Yes, sir."

Dover turned on a lamp. Harlow was relieved and surprised and taken aback. "Felipe, your mom—"

"We took him to his mom tonight," Dover said. "She was damn relieved to see him."

"Embarrassed me," Felipe mumbled, slouching against the back of the couch. "She was crying and everything."

"That's because you scared her," Harlow said, propping herself on the arm of the couch, facing him. "You scared us all. What were you thinking running off like you did?"

"I wanted to take care of my mom," Felipe said. "I'm the man of the house. Last time my dad went to jail, Mr. Clyde said I had to be strong, to man up and stay with my mom until my dad got back. But, this time, my mom said she's not taking him back, no way. So we can't afford to wait. I needed to earn some money."

It might be useful to have Clyde there for support. But Dover hadn't invited her colleague to join them. This was a private space, not part of the public bar. Noon hadn't come with them either. Under other circumstances, she might assume he was working the bar, but she speculated to herself that he might have been tasked with keeping Clyde under watch.

Clyde was a grown man and shouldn't be in physical danger with Noon. Felipe was the problem right in front of her. She decided to deal with him and then worry about Clyde. As long as Maze kept Ryske away from her colleague, he should be fine.

"But, Felipe, where were you? I don't understand what—"

"Let's not get into that," Dover said, with a quick shake of his head. "We talked to his momma, and she's gonna call off the dogs tomorrow."

Nice as it was that the crew had calmed Felipe's mom, it wasn't enough just to flash the kid around for a night, and then let him vanish again.

This kid needed a long-term care plan and ongoing support. "Felipe, you have to go to school. I know you think that it's your responsibility to earn money for your mom, but—"

"He's going to go to school," Dover said. "It's one of the rules."

At a loss, Harlow didn't want to stutter again, but found herself confused. "The… rules?"

"He goes to school, does his homework, and respects his mom. If he does all that, we'll let him come over here and make a few bucks. Weekends, he'll do errands, chores, fix up the furniture, whatever we say."

Felipe was eager. More than eager. "Yes, sir, Mr. Dover, sir," he said and nodded. "Whatever you say."

"Good, kid. Now scram. Go ask Noon to take you home to your momma. Tell him to take the chump with him."

Felipe surged to his feet, but faltered. "The… the who?"

"He'll know," Dover said and lifted his hips to take out his wallet. Thumbing out a few bills, he stuffed them into the kid's hand. "Be back tomorrow on time. On time or the gravy train will be gone, you get it?"

Felipe nodded. "I should speak to Mr. Ryske before I—"

"Mr. Ryske is busy," Dover said. "I'll tell him you left. Now get out."

Felipe offered her another smile before dashing out of the room to head for the bar.

For a few seconds, Harlow just sat stunned by what had happened. "I can't believe you—"

"I didn't. Ryske did," Dover said, standing up. "Soon as him and Maze heard you'd been in and what was wrong, he hit the streets. He found the kid, brought him back, cleaned him up…"

"Where was he?"

"Exactly where you didn't want him to be," Dover said.

Harlow had feared Felipe had been taken in by a gang who'd exploit him or sell him on to one of the organized crime syndicates who specialized in much more depraved dealings. That Dover didn't go into details was either to spare her or

Felipe. Whichever it was, she was glad Dover hadn't discussed it in front of the youngster.

"You rescued him."

Dover closed one eye in a sort of subdued wince. "Ryske won't like that description, but… yeah, I guess… The kid is right, he'll need to earn money. His aunt's pregnant and just moved in with them. The three of them have no one else."

This was a different world. The kids in her old suburban division wouldn't be thinking about supporting two women and a baby, but Harlow had left that world behind.

Gratitude and wonder filled her. "So you gave him a job here," she said, sliding off the arm of the couch to sit on the seat. "Shit, Dover, I don't know what to say."

"It's no picnic here. We won't let him serve or work out on the floor when we're open. There's plenty of other stuff to keep him busy… But, babe, if the gangs want him it'll be hard to keep them away. They'll offer more money and more excitement… something he'll want more of as he gets older and sees his friends allying themselves with that shit."

Smiling, she raised a fist to her temple for support, propping her elbow on the backrest. "You don't think your little posse is a gang?"

Dover wasn't moved. "We don't go around shooting people because they wear colors different to ours."

Recalling how she'd gotten involved with this bunch erased her smile. "No, they just stab you and leave you for dead."

"That's not exactly an everyday thing," he said with a loose half-shrug.

Opening the hand that had been in a fist on her temple, she rested her palm on the top of the couch and let it slide down. The lives of Ryske and his crew were dangerous, she'd always respected that, understood it. At least as much as someone on the outside looking in could appreciate it.

They'd helped her, maybe saved a kid. A lot had been on her mind over the last month. Something in this moment made her want to share.

"I've been worried about him for a month," she said. "I had no idea if he was dead or alive."

They'd been discussing Felipe. But when she made eye contact with Dover, she could see that he understood she'd moved on to talk about someone else.

"You could've come over."

Shaking her head, she let out a sigh. "If he wants her, he'll go get her… that's what Maze said the night we met."

Clarity crossed Dover's features. "You've been waiting for him to come to you."

Had she? Harlow didn't know. Putting words to all the thoughts she'd had over the last month was near impossible because they'd been so conflicting and had pulled her every which way.

Squinting at the back of the couch, she stroked it again, and shook her head. "No, no, I… I know it would never work between us. I wouldn't have anything to offer him… He didn't really want me anyway. I was just… there." Confusion and exasperation were making her words run away from her. "That's what I said at the time, and I was right… I shouldn't even be thinking about him like this."

Behind her, from the edge of the room, a deep masculine voice interrupted. "Like what?"

Twisting fast, she saw Ryske standing alone in front of the red curtain.

Dover stood up, straightening his jeans. "I've got a bar to run, clean up after yourselves."

FOURTEEN

RIGHTING HER POSITION on the couch to put her feet flat on the floor, Harlow listened to Dover depart the room and close the door. Now they were alone. Alone. Being by herself with Ryske had not been part of the plan. Nothing ever went to plan where he was concerned.

Go with it. That's what Noon had said. Though this may not have been exactly what he meant, she went with it, even in spite of her nerves sparking and fizzing with a vengeance.

Ryske began to cross toward her. Spreading her hands on her thighs, Harlow flattened her skirt and kept her eyes on the low coffee table a couple of feet from her knees.

She expected him to go past her, to take a seat on the couch where Dover had been. Instead, he stopped in front of the arm she'd been perched on a few minutes ago and offered a flat hand.

"Come upstairs with me."

Noon had invited her upstairs; Dover had told

her what was up there: beds.

Tipping her head back, Harlow tried to decipher if the beds were what he was suggesting. In bed with Ryske again, she'd never thought… It would never stop at watching movies or fingernails on tattoos.

It may have been a month since she'd seen him, but she straight away recognized the purr of seduction in his voice and the heavy drowsiness in his eyes was unmistakable.

He was thinking about sex. He was always thinking about sex.

"Nothing has changed," she said, stemming his seduction before it reached full steam.

Resisting his persistence might not be so easy with him at full health. Harlow had to hold on to the reasons she'd refused before. No matter how much she wanted to begin a torrid affair, or how much he claimed to want her, nothing had changed since they'd decided not to be together a month ago.

Like it was enough, he contradicted her. "You're here, Trink."

Just sharing the same air wasn't enough, Harlow had told him that already. "Yeah, I am," she said and stood up. "I came here to help a kid and you…"

"Gave him a chance," he said. "The kid is good, we won't corrupt him."

"I appreciate that."

A smug kind of teasing grin rose on his loose lips. "I'm using him to impress you. Grateful enough to lose your panties?"

"Crash," she exhaled, shaking her head. He didn't let her retreat or scold; he moved closer, so close that she could feel the beat of his heart. Being strong was easier when there was some illusion of space between them. Any thread of strength left her voice. "Don't, Crash."

"I'm teasing, Trink," he murmured. "I'm teasing you." Which only lessened her resolve. Vulnerability made her chin dip, but he caught it on a single-digit caress. "I have nothing for you."

Her heart screamed, caught between desperation and melancholy. Somehow, her hands found their way onto his chest. "I don't know what that means."

His arms began to settle around her. "Promises. The future. Plans. All those things that mean something to you… I have nothing to give."

"I know," she said, filled with the urge to reassure him. Smiling made it easier to relax. Harlow just couldn't be near this man without being happy. "You are exactly what you're supposed to be, exactly who you are. I don't want that man to change… It would break my heart if you changed."

Her ease wasn't contagious. Tension thrummed through him. She read it in the mixture of pain and hunger on his face. "If I don't, I'll never taste you."

Oh, he knew how to provoke her heart and her hormones. A coil of need swirled in her belly like a whirlpool growing in an ever-lengthening string, circling down and down until it anchored itself between her legs.

"I want to be your plaything," she confessed. "But you'll only break my heart."

"I know."

Another shot of honesty. If it wasn't enough that just being near to him, feeling him, smelling him, touching him, got her hot and made her lose her senses. He also insisted on giving the most arousing thing a man could give: the truth.

"I don't want to break you, any part of you, but… I can't get you out of me. You're in my blood," he said and peered deeper into her eyes as his arms fell from around her. "How did you do this to me, Trink?"

His arms bulged, telling her that he was balling

frustrated fists at his sides. While she couldn't take her gaze away from his, she could offer comfort by dropping her hands from his chest to curl them over his fists, urging them to relax so he could lace their fingers together.

"Shh, Crash," she soothed. "We have this… this way we make each other feel. It's not going anywhere."

"That's the goddamn problem," he snapped, yanking his hands free of hers. Turning his back on her, he stalked toward the curtain, stopping a couple of feet from it. "Shit, Trink, I knew I wanted you… but when I saw you out there tonight, and that guy, with his hands on you…" His hands fisted again, but that was nothing to the way he grinded his teeth in a show of hatred and rage. "If I'd had a gun, I'd have put a bullet in him."

"Don't say things like that!" Marching over, she went around him, making him look at her. "You are not going to commit any crimes for me." His scowl deepened. "Not for me, Crash." She shook her head. "No."

Snatching her arms, he forced her body against his. "You want to know what I learned tonight?"

Licking her lips, she tried to control her anxiety. Controlling her need was harder. The two warred within her. Only the former stopped her from giving into the latter. "What?"

Bowing lower while pulling her higher, he hissed the truth in her face. "There's no damn thing you couldn't drive me to."

Rushing her backwards, he slammed her to the wall and lunged down, aiming for her mouth.

Grabbing for his shoulders, Harlow fought to hold him back. "I'm scared."

His brow strengthened. "Of me?"

"This won't end with a kiss," she panted, frantic and desperate.

"No," he said, catching her wrists to squeeze them in his possessive grip, urging them to the wall on either side of her head. "But it's gonna start with one."

He was a fool if he didn't know this had started six weeks ago. Even while he'd been bleeding to death, she'd felt the spark between them. Controlling this was on her. Only her. He'd live in abandon if she let him. But she couldn't let him.

Shaking her head, Harlow turned her face down so he couldn't reach her mouth. "I can't, Crash. I just… I can't…"

In frustration, he let her go and punched the wall above her head, making her jump. The power of his infuriation pulsated through him, heating the air around them.

Shoving away from her, he strode to the couch then spun, opening his arms. "What the fuck do you want, Trink? What the fuck can a guy like me give you? You want a promise? Why the fuck would you want to tie yourself to a guy like me? You should be begging for a promise that I *won't* fall for you, a promise that I *won't* force you to be with me. You should want the promise of here and now. The promise that we have no future."

"Why?" she demanded, pushing off the wall.

"Because I'm a crook!"

"That's one thing about you, Crash, and it was never the thing that meant the most to me."

"What was it then, huh?" he asked without disguising his skepticism.

"You opened your eyes, you looked at me…" Slowing her breathing, she calmed herself as she tiptoed toward him, finding her control. "You wanted to know if I'd been hurt… You didn't ask about yourself, didn't ask if you were going to be okay or what damage had been done to you or even for the doctor… You asked about me."

No one had ever cared about her like that. Ryske had given her honesty and it had revealed so much of him to her.

"Didn't I ask if the sex was good first?"

Pressing her lips together, she nudged him. "Crash," she chastised in a whisper.

Since he'd walked out on her a month ago, she hadn't been able to make sense of her feelings or her thoughts about him. But staring into him now, Harlow felt grounded, anchored, and suddenly, it all made sense.

Putting aside the teasing, he became more serious. "You think I care," he muttered.

"I know you care," she said, looping her arms around his neck. Being near to him, touching him, was a pleasure she wanted to take advantage of, even if she couldn't go as far as she wanted to. "And, yes, you're a crook. You're a conman and a liar." She smiled. "But you don't lie to me."

Though he rested both hands on her waist, he raised his chin to look down his nose at her. "I should. Maybe if I did, I'd have had you naked by now."

"Maybe," she said. "If naked was all you wanted from me, you would've lied. Just like you said before. You'd have told me what I wanted to hear, and you know what, Crash? I'd have lapped it up because it would've given me the excuse I needed to let this happen. But you didn't, because you don't only want me naked, you want my respect. You want my heart."

A quirk of amusement followed. "Sure of yourself, aren't you, Little Trinket?"

Harlow had to laugh. He didn't deny it. He couldn't. He'd told her that he couldn't lie to her. Maybe he hadn't realized the reason that he felt that way, but he had figured out that she was different. He'd confessed that he couldn't make her promises because it bothered him he wouldn't be able to keep them.

"Do you think that this would be done if we'd had sex already?" she asked. "Would you be over me if I'd just given in?"

"Maybe," he said. "Want to try it and see?"

Warmed by confidence, she slid her hand from the back of his neck to rest it on his chest. "Be careful," she purred, pouting up at him. "Don't forget, I like having your attention. If getting naked with you will take that away, I'll never do it."

But Ryske didn't scare easy. Wearing a smirk, he cupped her breast and squeezed, his gaze measuring hers, judging how she felt about having his hands on her. Harlow didn't shrink. He felt good. Amazing. But she couldn't let him know that. Any hint that she wanted more would encourage him to strain her already stretched resolve.

"You want my attention," he murmured, seduction seeping from his every pore. "You want promises. You are a demanding woman, Trink."

"Only of you," she said, leaning in. "I'll demand and demand and demand… Still want to screw me?"

"Screw you, yes. Make you promises, no."

Pushing her breast into his caressing hand, his growl of appreciation valued her being bold. It hadn't taken her long to lose her anxiety.

A month apart might have made her wary at first, but losing herself with him when they were alone had always been simple. Their days away from each other faded to nothing.

"Then I guess we're at an impasse," she said and tried to turn away.

Ryske snatched her arm and hauled her back. "You're not gonna walk away so easy, Trink."

Pulling her arm from his grip, she was happy to counter his vehemence. "Like you walked away from me? A month, Crash. You left me swinging in the wind for a month… Were you ever coming back?"

"No," he said. Given his line of work, being so honest probably wasn't normal procedure for him, especially with women. With her, for some reason, it was automatic. "I thought of you." He drove his fingers through his hair. "Shit, Trink, you can tease me even from way across town."

She hadn't done anything to tease him, and she'd never asked him to leave her forever. Walking away from her had been his choice. If he wanted to blame her, he could. But she wasn't going to apologize for his insanity… even if she was the cause of it.

"Did you dream of me, Sailor?" she teased, walking her fingers up his chest.

"I dreamed of quieting that smart mouth," he said, leaning down. "Of tying you to my bed and keeping *you* locked up for two weeks."

Harlow hadn't locked him up, and she hadn't tied him to anything. Bale's rules had made him feel like a prisoner, he'd told her as much in the past. "Maybe you should stab me."

One side of his mouth rose higher than the other; the light in his eye became sinister. "If that's an invitation, I'm gonna take it." Seeing her confusion made him grab his groin to explain. "I've got something real special I wanna drive deep into you."

"Oh, Crash," she muttered. "That's just crude."

Again, she tried to turn away. This time when he grabbed her upper arm to haul her back, he cupped the back of her head too. Before she could catch her breath, he wrenched her to the tips of her toes and sealed his mouth over hers.

Harlow had told herself not to kiss him, not to give him any encouragement until he could give her something more than sex in return.

That ideal evaporated when he plunged his

tongue into her mouth and bonded them in the way she'd been resisting for weeks. The warmth of his mouth was luxury like she'd never known it. Security circled her, pulling her to him, attaching her essence to his like her sanity depended on him too.

If she'd been able to hold onto a thought beyond the incredible texture of his lips owning hers, she may have regretted being glib about how she tormented him. After this, she'd never be sure of her lucidity without him at her side to keep her grounded.

She'd never given credence to the helplessness of addiction. Harlow was strong-willed and had spent her life arguing with her mother because she wouldn't conform for the sake of it. If she had an opinion that differed from someone else's, she had no problem voicing it.

That fortitude served her; it combined with her overwhelming desire to drive her on and encourage her in everything she did… which at that moment seemed to be this man.

Grasping for the hem of his tee-shirt, Harlow wasted no time in pulling it off over his head. While Ryske was still freeing his arm from the fabric, she thrust him back, knocking him off his feet. Ryske landed on the couch. Before he could think about catching his breath, she climbed onto his lap to straddle him and ran her fingertips down the center of his bare torso.

Avoiding his mouth was supposed to prevent this. His breaking of that seal shattered her resolve. They'd crossed the line and he didn't seem sorry. Driving his hands into her hair, he pulled her mouth back to his and consumed her with his desire.

Habit made her fear for his wound but reminding herself that it had been healing for six weeks, it shouldn't be painful anymore. His kiss didn't slow or drift, so she made herself forget about any vulnerability and let herself trust the strength and capability of the man owning her.

"I figured it might be time to—"

The sound of a male voice made her break the kiss. Planting her hands on Ryske's chest, Harlow pushed away, blinking the daze of desire from her eyes. Looking over the back of the couch, she found that Noon was just inside the room.

"Fuck off, Noon," Ryske said, without sparing his friend a glance because he was too busy trying to coil his arms around her.

The sight of another person made her remember herself. Looking at Ryske, the reality of what they'd just been doing became all too clear.

There was no solace in being right. Harlow had known that if she let herself kiss him, or be kissed by him, that her body would take over and instinct would make it impossible to resist going all the way.

FIFTEEN

"SHIT," NOON murmured. "I, uh… didn't mean to…"

Taking the interruption as an opportunity to regain her senses, Harlow clambered off Ryske's lap, running one hand through her hair and the other over her hip.

"Oh, come on!" Ryske groaned, trying to catch her legs, but she pushed his hands away. "Come back, baby."

"No, I… I have to get going."

Noon pointed over his shoulder. "I can fuck off. I didn't know you guys were screwing around in here. I—"

"No," she said, pulling her top down over her stomach. Ryske had explored more than she'd realized; the fabric had been bunched under her bra. "Can you give me a ride home?"

"I'll give you a ride," Ryske said, touching the inside of her knee.

Swatting at his hand, she didn't make contact. "No, thank you," she said, crossing one leg over the other to side step away from him. "Noon does all the driving."

Heading for Noon who was still by the door carrying an awkward air, Harlow tried not to show just how grateful she was to him for interrupting what would only have ended one way.

Grabbing Noon's hand, she took him out of the room and through the bar, the same way Dover had brought her. Harlow didn't slow down when she got to the other side of the bar, even when she noticed Dover frowning at the view of her dragging Noon along behind her.

The bartender probably expected if she was going to be stealing any man out of Floyd's, it wouldn't be this one. But she wasn't going to hang around to explain herself. That would give Ryske time to put on his shirt and chase after them… and she wasn't all that sure she had an explanation anyway… not a believable one.

Bursting out onto the street, Harlow was determined to get home as quickly as she could. "What's going on?" Noon asked, lolloping along with his hand linked in hers.

It occurred to her that there was one man she'd forgotten to worry about. Stopping, she whirled around to point back the way they'd come. "Clyde?"

"Stayed with the Soto's," Noon said.

Whether or not Clyde had volunteered to go with Felipe or to stay with him, he'd be able to call a cab from the Soto's meaning he was safe, which was a step up from what he'd been at Floyd's. She'd have a lot of explaining to do when she got to work the following day, not only to Clyde for Ryske's behavior, but to Gina about Felipe. But that was a problem she'd worry about in the morning.

Returning to her previous determination, Harlow clung to Noon's hand, using it to pull him into the alley at the rear of Floyd's where they'd parked the car.

There seemed to be no urgency to Noon's movements; his dawdling was driving her nuts. "Can we get going?" she asked, glancing at the building beside them.

The closest window was making her nervous. The ones further along that were fogged and emanating some light would be the restrooms, but the one closest to the street was darker. That was the window next to the TV unit in the den… where she and Ryske had…

Trying her best to swing Noon toward the car as she let him go, she followed the move with a push then hurried around to the passenger side. "I don't have my keys," he said, touching the hip pockets of his jeans.

After a moment of panic made her mouth open in a silent gasp, her skepticism flared, and she folded her arms against the car. "You're a car thief."

His brows rose. "You want me to jack my own car?"

Shaking her head, she grinned. "Your car? Really? Is that the line?" It only took a moment of staring for his smile to crack. Pushing off the car, she opened her hands to it. "Come on, impress me, Cowboy."

"That's her line, Noon," Ryske's voice came from nowhere, erasing the smile from her face. "Don't fall for it."

Movement from the direction opposite to the one she and Noon had come caught her eye. Ryske was emerging from the narrow space between the far end of Floyd's and the next building. That had to be a dead end alley; there was no space between the two structures on the street side.

So she guessed she'd found Floyd's secret entrance.

"What are you doing here?" she asked.

The question was moot. The car was the only thing on his current path. When he got to the trunk, Ryske tossed something to Noon. It had to be the car keys because a second later, Noon was climbing into the driver's seat.

Ryske had come around and startled her attention away from where Noon had been by opening the back passenger door and gesturing for her to get inside.

Though he seemed to think he was being chivalrous, she tilted her head. "Oh, because you're the guy, you get to ride up front?" she asked.

Rather than make it a big deal, Harlow settled for scowling at him and started to round the door. But just as she was about to lower into the backseat, he sprang forward, using himself and the door to pin her in place.

"You asking me to get in the back with you? I can do that, baby... What you wanna do back there, Trink?"

Bending his elbows, he leaned in, giving her even less space. The smirk on his face was enough to make her think about kneeing him in a sensitive area, but she restrained herself and sneered instead.

"You'd really do it, wouldn't you?" she asked. "You'd

have sex right there behind your friend."

He shrugged. "Noon's seen me do worse."

Grabbing his arm, she dug her nails in deep while pushing it out of her way. "Oh, I don't doubt that for a second."

Climbing into the car, Harlow was quick to turn and reach for the door, holding up a hand to prevent him from getting in with her. "Ah!"

Twisting her wrist, she pointed to the front of the car. Without hiding his amusement, Ryske stepped back and closed her door before getting in next to Noon who had already started the car.

They drove a couple of blocks before the silence got too much for Noon. "So what's the story with you two?" he asked. "You back on or…"

"She was on me," Ryske said, messing with the AC. "And I'm happy for her to be on me any time, any day."

"In your dreams, Crash."

"Every night."

"We've never had a woman on the crew before," Noon said, like he was pondering the future and how it would play out. "You tell her about Ophelia?"

The next silence was far more loaded. Ryske's anger fizzled, heating the air, which made Noon tense up as he figured out that he'd just put his foot in his mouth. Difficult as it was to hear that Ryske had another woman in his life, she chose to laugh instead of cry.

"Go with it," she said, sliding down in the center of the backseat. "That's what you said to me earlier, Noon, honey." If this was what he was talking about then he should have been more explicit. "Is that what Dover meant? Ryske and his women? I'm supposed to go with that? You don't have to worry, Noon, he can keep his women and keep making you all rich. It means nothing to me."

Twisting to look over the shoulder of his chair, Ryske pinned her in his sights. "Nothing? You had enough?"

"Oh, I have had enough, Ryske. More than enough."

Folding her hands in her lap, she turned her attention to the street. Noon might be annoyed at himself for opening his mouth about this Ophelia. Ryske might be pissed at his friend for telling her that there was another woman. But if Harlow had stepped back from her attraction to look at his life, she'd have realized that there was a reason Ryske kept saying he couldn't make her promises.

Considering his life and the things he had to do to fulfil his role with his crew, Harlow saw that his refusal to promise her anything was about more than just his own selfish need to be promiscuous. Dover, Noon, and Maze, all had roles. She didn't understand what they were exactly, but Ryske was the man they sent inside to infiltrate or to charm.

That being the case, she imagined there were plenty of times his role involved seducing a woman. Harlow had once asked him how many women he'd made fall in love with him. While he'd refused to be specific, he'd been man enough to admit that he'd hurt women. Whether he felt bad about that or not, he was aware of his power. Though maybe not aware enough, because she'd put good money on most of the women he charmed and seduced falling in love with him.

It wouldn't be a hard thing to do. If Ryske had told her what she'd wanted to hear, she'd be in his bed, enjoying their affair and she didn't doubt she'd have handed him her heart by now. Sure, he'd have handed it back at some point and she'd have ended up hating him. But he'd still have made her fall in love with him in the first place.

They pulled up outside her apartment. Harlow didn't wait to hear what Ryske said to Noon after she kissed the driver's cheek. She was out of the vehicle and on the sidewalk heading for the stoop when she heard the other car door close behind her.

"Trink."

It was her intention to ignore him. There was nothing he could say that would change things between them. Finding out that this Ophelia was a part of the equation too, Harlow knew that even if she'd been tempted to say to hell with it and give herself to Ryske before, there was zero chance of it now.

She was on the third step when he grabbed her and pulled her back down to the first one. That was when she noticed Noon was no longer there, the car was gone from the curb.

"Do you think I'll feel sorry for you and invite you up?" she asked. "You told Noon to leave, that's your bad. Get a cab."

"I'm not sleeping with her."

Frustrated and tired, she was aware of the hour and that she'd have to get up for work in the morning. Harlow didn't have time to deal with drama like this.

"I don't care, Crash," she said on a sigh. "Sleep with whomever you like. One of us should be getting some."

Something like swagger touched his expression. "If you want some, I'm right here to give it to you."

"Go find Ophelia," she said, but was pulled back again when she tried to retreat. "Damnit, Crash, stop doing that. I'm going upstairs now. Alone. I don't want you to join me. I don't want you to follow me."

For a moment, he examined her. His look of concern became one of admiration. "Wow, I actually believed that. You're a natural."

"This again?" she asked, trying not to groan. "I do not want to be on your crew, Ryske. I want you to leave me alone."

Turned out he did start to believe her. His concern returned and was followed by anger. "So that's it? A month goes by with nothing, you need something, we drop everything to help and then you're just gone again?"

Doubting his outburst was really any demand for payment, she set a hand on her hip. "What would you like? Because I'll tell you what you're not getting. You're not getting a date. A blowjob. A hand job. Sex of any variety. Or any kind of kiss. If you want any of that, go call Ophelia."

Frustration flavored his words. "I'm not sleeping with her," he said, and still hadn't let go of her arm. Pulling her down the last step onto the sidewalk, he lowered his volume. "She's our inside man. We're in because of her."

"Good. Great," she said, without an ounce of enthusiasm. "Why do I care?"

Angling his head, he peered into her. "I don't know, Trink. Do you care?"

She didn't hesitate to shake her head. "No, I don't care, because in the car just now I realized you're right. You can't make me promises and I don't want them. We can't be together, but it's not because you won't promise me forever, it's because I'll never be able to trust you to be faithful."

That made him let her go and step away. "If you're done wanting promises, invite me up. Let's fuck. Let's get it over with."

The demand was too angry for her to believe that he wanted the invitation. "You should be pleased this has happened," she said. "You didn't want me to want a future and now I'm saying I don't… That doesn't mean I want to drop my panties for you either."

Unimpressed and still angry, he bobbed his head. "You want your reliable guy."

She smiled and took her keys from her pocket. "I would never have considered you to be a reliable guy. I could've got over that. I might even have gotten over the flirtations you'd have to engage in for your work, maybe even some of the physical stuff…"

His eyes narrowed. "But?"

All along he'd been honest with her, so she gave him the same. "I always thought I'd go crazy with worry. We met after you were stabbed for goodness sake. It makes sense that I'd be terrified that could happen again. I told you that when you left my place. But I think I could handle that better… I could handle worrying about you being hurt easier than I could handle the idea of you falling for another woman."

Searching her eyes, he didn't respond for a score of seconds. "You think we'd get together and then I'd fall for another woman and abandon you?" Though she didn't say it out right, she lifted one shoulder and closed her eyes in a slow blink of acceptance. "Like my mom you mean?"

That changed her confidence and clarified his anger for her. Making assumptions about the kind of man he was hurt him. Especially when those assumptions clashed with the thing he hated most about one of his parents.

"I didn't mean—"

"You don't think that maybe that's why I don't make

those promises?" he asked. "You were special. You were something real to me, something tangible. In a world full of bullshit. You were real. My Trinket… I told you I couldn't make you promises… but fuck, I was close, baby… Shit, I was rethinking my whole damn life for you."

Numbness hollowed her out. "All of that was past tense."

He was shaking his head in a shallow arc, looking into her like he didn't recognize her. "If you think I'm capable of that… If you think I'm the type of guy who would make you a promise, a for real promise, and then break it for the next piece of ass I touched… Shit, baby, you don't have a damn clue who I am."

His words stopped. Like he couldn't look at her anymore, he turned and walked away, never once looking back.

She'd offended him. No, she'd hurt him. Confessing the truth of his parentage to her probably hadn't been easy for him. Harlow had heard the words as he'd said them, but had failed to absorb what they meant to his psyche and how they'd shaped who he was.

Ryske was a professional. He understood the difference between pretend for professional sake and real in his personal life. That was why he was so adamant about what he would and wouldn't say to her. Harlow wasn't professional to him. If she was, he'd say anything to her to get what he wanted, even if it was just sex.

She'd been personal.

Ryske, her Crash, would only be with a woman in his real personal life if she understood he was hers completely, even in spite of the professional bullshit.

He hadn't made her a promise. If he had, it wouldn't have mattered how many females he touched for the job, how many he seduced, he'd always come home to her, always love her.

Harlow watched him go until she couldn't see him anymore and didn't even notice the cold air biting into her skin. He'd accused her of abandoning the crew as soon as she'd gotten what she wanted. But after how things had just ended, there was no way she could never see them again. She had to fix this. She just didn't know how.

SIXTEEN

THE IDEA THAT she had to fix things with Ryske stayed with Harlow until the next day at work.

Calling wasn't an option; she didn't have a direct number for him. Floyd's was probably in the book. Even though the bar wouldn't be open yet, she took a guess that Dover or Maze or someone would be around to pick up.

Except a phone call wouldn't be enough.

Dumb as it was given the barriers she kept putting up between them, all Harlow could think about was how much she wanted to be lying next to Ryske, tracing the outlines on his inked skin with her fingernails. If he'd let her get that close, she'd be able to beg his forgiveness.

But if she did get that close, he'd want more, and her actions had given him the perfect excuse to demand it of her. Demand and submit. Command and yield. They weren't accurate descriptors for what she had with Ryske. What she had with him was different from anything that she'd had with any man before.

Harlow had discovered that she liked it when there was hurt involved… of the physical variety anyway. There was something alluring about feeling in control when Ryske had his hand around her throat. It wasn't like he tortured her or took pleasure in her agony. She didn't understand it, not all the way, but couldn't stop thinking about how her Crash made her feel.

After ending her relationship with Rupert, Harlow had taken the time to consider what she wanted from life. Some decisions were harder to make than others. Moving into the city had been a practical decision. Still, it wasn't an easy process. Breaking the news to her parents, finding a new job and an apartment, each came with its own challenges. As difficult as the transition had been, she didn't regret making it.

Harlow was learning about herself and figuring out that maybe she wasn't only the sum total of what her mom, dad, sister, and ex-fiancé thought. In spite of their reservations, her practical decision was working out… for the most part. Emotional conclusions weren't as easy to reach. She still didn't know what she wanted from love and romance and men in the future.

Rupert had wanted her to be a stay at home mom. He earned enough money to support them and saw her work as more of a hobby than a necessity. His marriage proposal had been expected. More than that, it was overdue. In truth, Harlow had been finding ways to head him off for years before the unavoidable happened.

After five years, she'd run out of ways to bob and weave from the path of his inevitable blow. He'd landed it good, speaking to her mother first and arranging the whole thing with her family so they knew about it in advance. Her mom, Jean, had been eager for them to tie the knot. Her whole family had. Saying no hadn't been an option.

Not that she'd been bulldozed into it. Marriage had been the next logical step for them and they were happy together… well, they weren't unhappy. It wasn't until after she'd said yes that everything had snowballed into an out of control avalanche.

In private, the only place she could get a word in edgeways, Harlow had been clear with Rupert that the engagement was a trial. That she didn't want to rush into anything.

But there wasn't anything he could do to pull it back

once the ring was on her finger; there wasn't anything either of them could do. As soon as her parents and his mom got involved, they'd started making plans. Her mom made excuses to take her shopping where they'd invariably end up in bridal stores trying on dresses. Rupert's mom took on the task of calling venues and caterers. Her father hadn't been exempt from the meddling, he'd begun advising Rupert on real estate in the best school districts.

The train had left the station and Harlow had been the only one trying to pull the brakes.

The morning it came off the tracks, Rupert had taken her pack of contraceptive pills from her hand. He'd asserted that she didn't need them anymore. The statement had broken the dam and they'd never mended it again.

Neither she nor Rupert had made it to work that day.

The conversation had fast become an argument. Harlow had really thought that it was over between them almost straight away. Rupert had asked her to stay and they'd spent a whole day trying to negotiate what their future would be.

But he wouldn't budge. Rupert wanted her pregnant; wanted her to stay at home and do the school run. To him, her future was as a soccer mom who'd rely on their mothers for advice and lunch with her socialite friends after a morning at the beauty salon.

She couldn't do it.

Harlow had been patient in explaining that she wasn't sure she wanted to have kids at all. Horrified as he'd been by the idea that they might not have a traditional family, Rupert listened. She talked about travel and experience, about taking risks and trying new things.

Needless to say, their day of discussion and negotiation might as well have ended after the morning's argument. By sunset, they'd figured out that, actually, they weren't the people they each thought they were. They wanted completely different things from life.

Harlow had known the decision to end the relationship was right by how quickly she got over it. She found losing the habit of being coupled up more difficult to deal with than breaking the emotional connection.

Rupert had been a fun guy to hang out with when they met. Sure, he could be dry at some of the corporate functions they attended, but her dad had always been like that too, so it seemed normal to her.

Friendship was how their association had begun. Reverting back to that hadn't been difficult for her and these days, friendship was as far as their bond went.

She'd gotten with Rupert in the first place because he was a good listener and sympathized with her over her parents' attempts to control her. His situation with his mom was much the same. Bonding over their familial frustrations, they'd built a friendship. After he made a move, a relationship seemed like a natural progression.

Harlow didn't know where along the way Rupert's views had become so traditional. Maybe they'd always been that way and she just hadn't noticed. The more perplexing question had been: where along the way had they lost their friendship?

On reflection after the end had come, she could see that the excitement had long since gone from their relationship. There had been no thrill, no overwhelming desire. The sex was fine. Sometimes a hit, more often a miss. Harlow just figured that's what happened after being with the same person for so many years.

Talking had been a big part of their relationship at the beginning. By the end, they'd been going through the motions for quite a while.

All this time spent contemplating her relationship with Rupert had to be motivated by her newer association with Ryske. Dating hadn't been on her agenda while she'd been busy with her college assignments and moving both home and job. Switching from suburban to city living wasn't simple, especially without support around and everyone telling her it was an impossible and ridiculous thing to do.

Harlow was proud of herself for not wavering and battling through their objections. Hard work didn't scare her. While getting herself setup, there hadn't been time for men, or any kind of social life, which was probably another reason why she'd neglected to form any friendships.

During the time of her breakup and her subsequent decision to move, she'd learned that any females who she might have considered friends weren't particularly loyal. Most of her suburban "friends" were appalled that she'd let a prize like Rupert go. In a lot of ways, given their aspirations, Harlow could understand why they felt that way.

Maybe her choices were insane. That was always a possibility. But her choices were hers. Whether she flew or crashed and burned, at least Harlow could be confident that she was the only one to blame for the path her life was on.

Sitting in the deli a few blocks from her work, Harlow was pondering these things, her past decisions and what the future may hold, while enjoying her lunch.

After taking a sip of iced coffee, she reached for her sandwich and found the wax paper empty. She was finished and had barely noticed eating.

Bundling up her trash, she slipped off her stool and took her phone from her pocket to check the time… and with hopes that maybe Ryske had found a way to get in touch with her.

He hadn't.

What Harlow did find on her phone was a message from her boss, Gina. It contained an address and instructed her not to come back to the office but to go straight to a meeting. The "urgent" heading further confused Harlow.

Gina often rescheduled appointments or passed her work off. The nature of what they did meant frequent emergencies cropped up that someone would have to cover.

Taking this development as a sign of trust and progress on her journey to getting her boss's respect, Harlow trashed her empty sandwich paper, gulped down the rest of her coffee, and set off to the urgent appointment, determined not to let her boss down.

*****

GIVEN THAT SHE wasn't from the city, Harlow wasn't familiar with the different streets and districts. If she was in the office and a new address popped onto her docket, she'd do some internet research or ask her colleagues about it.

Gina's abrupt and unexpected message hadn't afforded Harlow the chance to do that. After getting out of the cab at her destination, she wished she'd made the time.

The building she found herself standing outside was not the caliber of place she'd been visiting since starting work in the city.

Examining the sidewalk canopy and the doorman who wore a swish uniform, Harlow was intrigued. Pedestrians were walking by, probably wondering why she was on the curb gawking. But she couldn't figure out what to think about why Gina would send her there.

Another car pulled up behind her, forcing Harlow to put one foot in front of the other and get over her surprise. Though it wasn't the last one she'd have.

She expected the doorman to ask her name, he didn't. Stepping aside without a word, he opened the glass door for her and she walked into a marble lobby. Taking her phone from her pocket, she checked Gina's message for the apartment number and glanced to the security desk by the elevator bank.

"I—"

"Go straight up, Miss Sweeting," the guard on the desk said, wearing a broad, welcoming smile.

That was nice, and she returned his friendly greeting, feeling a little out of her element. Staggering toward the elevator, the glossy gold door opened the moment she pressed the call button like the carriage had been expecting her too. She got in to select the floor.

Leaning against the back wall of the elevator, she tried to figure out why she'd been given this assignment. Harlow wasn't naive enough to believe that only poverty-stricken kids were abused or that they were the only ones who could lose a parent to death or jail. But if this was a high profile client, or sensitive situation, she'd have expected Gina to deal with it herself.

Considering that it could be an adoption case, Harlow didn't like being unprepared. But she was here on the orders of her superior, and had no choice except to keep moving forward when the lift doors opened.

In the large square hallway, there was a single front door. Having only one apartment on this whole floor was unexpected and gave her no excuse for dawdling or delay.

An odd surge of anxiety welled up inside her. Something about this whole situation felt wrong. More wrong than a typical case. There was nothing around to suggest anything sinister was going on, something just niggled at her gut.

Telling herself that a little paranoia could be healthy when walking into a new setup, Harlow tried to shrug off her uncertainty, and crept toward the door, preparing herself to knock.

Mayhem could be ready to greet her on the other side. It was almost funny that she was more nervous here than she'd been walking in to Floyd's. Though walking in with Noon the last time had given her a confidence that could be dulling her memory of how it had felt to walk in on Saturday night when she was tentative about the reception she'd receive.

Floyd's and Noon. Thinking of them brought her back to Ryske. Damn, she'd feel better if she'd made up with him before having to face the hurdle of a new and unexpected client. Just having him on her side, even if he wasn't near to her, made her feel stronger and more confident. But Harlow had screwed it up. He wasn't on her side anymore.

Before she got a chance to knock, the door in front of her opened, startling her out of her thoughts. "Miss Sweeting," the man facing her said, raising an arm. "Please, come in."

His tailored suit screamed wealth. But as he ushered her across a wide entryway and took her up two curved marble stairs toward glorious light, Harlow realized he wasn't the man she was there to see.

In the vast space at the top of the stairs, there was a bar to one side and a grand piano to the other. Throw rugs separated couches from the desk that was angled in the glazed corner of the room. This room didn't seem to know what it wanted to be. A living room? A study? An entertaining space? She had no idea.

"Thank you for coming at such short notice," the man who had invited her in said. "Please, take a seat." He gestured toward one of the couches on the far wall, while he himself headed toward the bar. "Would you like a drink, Miss Sweeting?"

Relaxed as he was, she was wary. "I'm sorry, can I ask… do you know why I'm here?" she asked, taking her phone from her pocket again to open her notes app.

The downside of coming straight from lunch was that she had no notepad or paperwork. In her last job, they'd had company tablets with access to their systems and all the forms they could need for any scenario. This district didn't have as much money or access to the same resources, which made sense given that the budget was stretched much thinner in the city.

"Oh, yes, I know why you're here," he said, doing something behind the bar that she couldn't make out.

Harlow expected him to continue, to elaborate and fill in the blanks for her. Instead, he finished what he was doing, and surprised her by coming around the bar carrying a glass of white wine. Hoping that the drink was for him rather than her, she didn't quite know what to say when he came over and sat beside her while offering her the alcohol.

"Thank you, but I… it's the middle of the day. I'm working." Trying a laugh to lighten the mood, nothing about this was putting her at ease. "I'd be fired if my boss knew I was drinking on the job."

"You're off duty, Harlow," he said, leaning over to put the glass on the coffee table in front of her. "Gina isn't expecting you back at the office. You can drink as much as you like."

Nodding at the glass, he seemed to have some expectation that what he'd said would reassure her. It didn't. The alarming statement didn't reassure her at all.

It didn't occur to her until that moment that this stranger had used her name. That wouldn't be unusual for a client if they'd been told who was coming to assist them. Gina might have told this man her name, but he had no reason to know that she drank white wine. As far as Harlow knew, Gina didn't know her alcohol preferences. Even if she did, she shouldn't be giving out personal information.

Something didn't add up. Beyond what the stranger knew about her likes and dislikes, there was definitely no reason he should be arranging for her to have the afternoon off.

Harlow cursed herself for not paying attention to her instincts. "I have to make a quick call," she said, lifting her phone, wondering if she should try calling Bale, who Noon had said was out of town, or if she'd have time to search for Floyd's number.

This guy should think she was calling the office—

"You won't need that," he said, plucking the phone from her hand and turning it off.

Stuttering and blinking, Harlow couldn't believe he'd been so brazen. "Excuse me, but that's my phone."

When she tried to reach for it, he stood up and took it with him to the bar. Going around behind it, he crouched; she heard some noises that she couldn't quite decipher. The next time he stood up, the phone was gone.

"Maybe I should introduce myself."

Anger overtook her unease. "Yes, I think you should," she said.

Stealing her phone took some nerve. Whoever his boss was, he obviously had money, which meant he was probably used to having people's undivided attention when they visited him. Harlow wasn't intimidated by money, or influenced by it, and she'd be telling him that if he ever showed his face.

She planned to have a word with Gina too about rearranging her schedule at the whim of an obnoxious client. Picking up the slack by taking a random meeting was just fine with Harlow. What she did mind was any one client demanding more of her time than anyone else got.

Harlow had paperwork to complete and other clients to call. She'd planned to go see Felipe and his mom at the end of the day too, just to check all was well and that he'd gone to school.

"My name is Adonis Brash."

Handsome and strong, he was. Adonis, he was not. Wait. Harlow moved past the first name and tried to figure out why the last name was familiar. He was coming toward her wearing an expression of knowing and patience like he was waiting for her to figure something out.

Brash.

She'd heard it before. Brash… Brash… Oh, shit. Ryske had said it. In context of the man who'd attacked him on the night he'd been stabbed. While she couldn't remember if Ryske had specified which man had held the blade, he'd referred to both Brash and Animal.

Sinking onto the couch beside her, closer than he had before, his vibe grew cocky. "Figure it out yet?"

Swallowing, she thought of what Noon had told her, *go with it*. Perched on the edge of the couch, she crossed her ankles and picked up the wine. Not out of any desire to drink, but to project ease.

"I'm sorry, no… I don't believe we've met, Mr. Brash. Will your boss be joining us soon?" she asked, doing whatever she could to unnerve him, knowing it had been his goal to unsettle her. "He will return my phone before I leave, won't he? Taking it is more than a little rude. Is he used to getting his own way?"

Witnessing his growing confusion was satisfying. It didn't matter that he wasn't overt. The way he peered at her betrayed how he couldn't decide what to make of her confident response.

"Mr. Hagan is a busy man, and he doesn't like others to be distracted in his presence," Brash said, his voice distant, proving he couldn't make a decision about her ignorance.

"Mr. Hagan," she said. "What is it that Mr. Hagan does to make his money?" Brash wasn't instantly forthcoming. She crooked a brow, almost daring him to lie. "Mr. Brash?"

SEVENTEEN

BRASH WAS SAVED from answering by the sound of another door opening. It took Harlow a minute to locate where the noise had come from. At the end of the bar, tucked down at the bottom of a couple of stairs that probably matched the sweep of those she and Brash had ascended from the entryway, she noticed the top corner of a door moving.

Brash stood up and started heading that way. Harlow took the opportunity to put the wine glass down without drinking. She'd love a drink to bolster her courage but wouldn't trust anything handed to her in this place.

The man ascending the stairs was blocked from her view by Brash who stood at the midway point between her and the bar. Holding her breath, Harlow waited to see the man responsible for Ryske's injuries, but wasn't sure she could trust herself to keep playing it cool after she did.

Brash might have held the knife, or maybe he was responsible for some of Ryske's bruises, either way, he was no friend of hers. For Hagan, she held a different level of contempt. Anger and disgust ate at her guts, she wanted to scream, to grab the wine glass and smash it in his face. The moment she had the thought, Harlow heard Ryske's voice in her head, telling her that wasn't a good idea without an exit strategy.

"Is she here?" a masculine voice asked. "Did she make it?"

Rising from the couch, Harlow knew he was talking about her. While it wasn't easy to keep her chin up, her only chance was to stay calm and in control. If one of these men wanted to tell the truth about what they'd done, she'd listen. If she was here because they wanted forgiveness, they'd be disappointed. No way was Harlow going to make this situation easy for them. They'd already made her life difficult in so many ways; it seemed only right that she return the favor.

Projecting nothing except ease, Harlow wanted to keep these men as far off their game as she could. "I assume that you are talking about me, Mr. Hagan," she said, speaking before Brash could answer his boss.

Brash turned toward her, a scowl on his face. If he was beginning to figure her out, he wasn't happy with what he was learning.

Without disguising her satisfaction, she drew a feigned smile away from the man she'd displeased to look at the other. At least ten years older than her, Hagan wasn't what she'd expected him to be. Given what he'd done to Ryske, or ordered done, she wouldn't have been surprised if he'd had horns and a tail.

As it turned out, he had neither.

With a little gray at his temples and distinguished eyes that sparkled, Hagan appeared intelligent, dashing even, and that wasn't a word she could remember ever thinking about another man.

"Miss Sweeting," he said, his voice a deep, purring lilt. "I apologize for our heavy-handed tactics."

Coming to her, he passed Brash without giving him a second glance and held both hands toward her. Harlow tried her best not to let him get an advantage, but couldn't think of anything to do except offer her hand in return.

Cradling it in both of his, Hagan raised it to his mouth and pressed his lips against her knuckles, prolonging the contact like he appreciated the moment more than he should in an initial meeting with a stranger.

"I wouldn't say your tactics are heavy-handed," she said, doing her best not to pull away although the longer he lingered there, the more tense she became. "I would say they are rude."

"Rude?" he asked, straightening his spine, keeping her hand sandwiched between both of his. He tossed a quick glare over his shoulder to Brash, but was smiling again when he turned back to her. "I apologize for my underling."

"It's not him who you have to apologize for," she said. "Unless it was him who decided to rearrange my schedule with my boss and steal my phone."

Nodding slowly, Hagan seemed to be catching up. "Yes, I appreciate that may have unsettled you."

His arrogance seemed limitless. "Unsettled? No," she said, unwilling to be dismissed or to have the truth downplayed. "Like I said, it's rude."

Still, there was no apology. "Everything will be explained and you'll see why I acted the way I did," he said.

Using only one hand, he gestured at the couch like he was inviting her to sit. Before she could decide whether or not to accept the invite, he sat down and forced her to join him with the grip he had on her hand.

Harlow didn't like sitting so close to him. It only got harder to be there when he twisted and his knee touched hers. Acid churned in her stomach. This Hagan guy was good. Practiced, professional, and ignorant. He played it smooth, showing no indication that he knew he was irritating her.

His harmless act was fooling no one. The seal of truth hadn't been breached yet, but it was only a matter of who broke first. They all understood more than they were letting on. No doubt they each knew pieces of the puzzle. Though there was one obvious piece: this polite, passive thing was bogus.

Harlow supposed there was a chance that Hagan didn't know she was aware that he was the person responsible for Ryske's injuries. But there was no way she'd buy this meeting as a coincidence. Especially not after the way Brash had acted with her.

"Would you like a drink?" Hagan asked, stroking the

back of her hand with his soft fingertips.

"Your boyfriend already tried to liquor me up."

He stopped stroking to show her his shock. "Brash and I are not… we're not…" He turned his chin to his shoulder, addressing his colleague without looking straight at him. "Get out of here. Get on with your duties."

She didn't mind Brash's annoyance or the venomous glare he tossed her way. In fact, the act of revealing his irritation only encouraged her to keep on pushing buttons. A moment later, he'd disappeared down the stairs Hagan had used to enter and a door closed.

"So you're in need of social services," she said. Playing it straight had been the best policy so far. "I admit to being a little behind the ball on this. Perhaps you could explain your predicament, so I can get to work solving your issues."

Hagan observed her affable demeanor. Clearly, he hadn't expected her to project the image of a capable professional. But if he was expecting a simpering victim, he'd cornered the wrong woman.

"Social services," he muttered.

"Yes," she said, finally managing to extricate her hand from his. Slipping further down the couch, Harlow settled in the corner like it was simply more comfortable there, which, of course, it was. Anywhere away from this Hagan was more comfortable than being up close. "It is what I do."

His head moved a few degrees to the left. "But is it all you do?"

Harlow didn't understand the question. "I'm sorry, I don't…"

"You must have a social life, activities that you enjoy, hobbies, that sort of thing."

Giving him credit where it was due, she watched him reorient himself at the opposite end of the couch as though he was settling in to spend time getting to know a new friend.

"I don't like to discuss my personal life with clients," she said. He arched his brows. "It detracts from your need. I'd be grateful if you could explain why you are in need of my department's help. Obviously, you understand, we help many people in need. It's important that our time is maximized. I can't sit here gossiping all day. I would like to know why you called for help today."

"I called," he said. "Not for help. I called because I had to see you."

Now they were getting closer to the truth. Still, she feigned innocence. "Me? We've never met."

The side of his mouth curved. "Not exactly, but I believe we have a mutual acquaintance."

"If we do, maybe I'm not the best person to help you in a professional capacity," she said, holding her skirt to her knees as she rose. "I shouldn't discuss personal matters during business hours. And, forgive me for saying, but it's inappropriate and unprofessional to assume that I would."

"I bet he likes the prim thing, doesn't he?" Hagan asked, sinking deeper into the couch. "I wouldn't have guessed it about him, but looking at you here like this." He nodded his head in appreciation. "I see it."

"Mr. Hagan—"

"Jarvis is fine," he said. "I think it's okay to be informal with the person who ordered your boyfriend's murder, don't you?"

Murder? That was harder to stomach. Try as she might to maintain the impenetrable façade, the sense of loss and horror that idea conjured narrowed Harlow's throat.

Her lips parted. "What do you want?"

"Nothing terrible," he said and inhaled. "Answer my questions to the best of your knowledge and I'll let you walk away as soon as we're done."

"If I don't?"

"Then your boyfriend won't be the only one to suffer," he said. "And don't worry, I know what you told my colleague about people coming to find you. But once we're done with you, you'll be in too many pieces for them to put you back together. No one will come after me for taking you off the board."

Clearing her throat, Harlow scratched her temple with a single nail. "I don't want to undermine your threatening… because you are very good at it," she said, delivering the compliment like it was genuine. "But… I don't have a boyfriend."

EIGHTEEN

HAGAN WASN'T FAZED and actually laughed. Not a full body, over the top laugh, just a poised snicker. "After his reaction in Floyd's last night, I don't care what label you put on it," he said. "I know you're the woman I need."

Acting like his statement was an advance, she cringed. "I'm not looking for a boyfriend either."

"I'm a man of means," he said, raising his hands from the couch to let them flop down at the wrists, presenting the room to her. "I have business interests all over the city. I could be helpful to you in your endeavors."

"And what endeavors are those?" she asked. "Did you call me here to interrogate me or to seduce me?"

"Why can't I do both?"

That was an easy one to answer. "You can try to do either. Neither will be successful."

Drawing in a breath, he considered her for a few seconds before speaking with a new kind of light in his eyes that made her wary. "I do see it. Oh, Ryske does enjoy presenting me with a challenge."

"Then you should attempt to corral him into coming here and presenting himself. I won't answer your questions or give in to any advances. Trying to change my mind will be a waste of your time, which I'm sure is valuable."

"It is," he said, sitting up to reach for her wine to take a sip. "But time spent with a beautiful woman is never wasted." He offered her the glass. "I assume you feared drugs or poison, I wouldn't have drunk either. Now you know it's safe… In any event, I like an opponent to have their wits. I am far more direct if I choose to eliminate them… as your boyfriend can attest."

Harlow took the wine and sat back again. The glass was the closest thing she had to a weapon. If this turned ugly, she'd be prepared. If not, she might take courage from the alcohol. Though she'd wait to see if Hagan's demeanor was changed by the liquid first.

Watching him like a hawk, she tried to spot any signs he could be under the influence of drugs. Except it seemed he was as keen-eyed as ever.

"Why don't we call him up and ask him?" she said after a moment.

He tilted his head. "Thought you didn't have a boyfriend."

Ryske didn't have that title in her life and probably wouldn't want it given how things had ended between them the previous night. But if Hagan would let her near a phone to get anyone on the line, Ryske would be the man she'd choose to call. Regardless of how mad he was about what she'd said last night, or how she'd offended him, Harlow didn't doubt for a second that he'd do whatever it took to make her safe.

That realization took her out of this tense moment and gave her clarity. Finding herself there, in the clutches of the crew's enemy, Harlow's perspective began to shift. Ryske wouldn't make her promises. He wasn't convinced they could have a future. This setup helped her to understand his point of view. She got it. Hagan conning and cornering her epitomized why Ryske was reluctant to put words to what was between them.

Carrying the weight of his upbringing, Ryske didn't want to be his father or his mother. He'd made it seem like he didn't want to commit to her because he wanted to be free. And it wasn't like either of them could deny that he was independent and a bit of a player. But his aversion wasn't about any overwhelming desire to play the field. He wouldn't lie and promise her things that he couldn't deliver on.

Ryske didn't want to promise fidelity and build a life with her and then renege… like his mother had done to his father. He didn't want to tell her he'd be faithful, because once that promise was made, nothing would make him go back on it. Promising himself to her limited his ability to do his job and to support his crew.

Except, somehow, even without the words, Harlow was convinced of his depth of feeling for her. Maybe she couldn't put language to it, maybe Ryske couldn't either, but they had an affinity. She meant something to him.

"Is something wrong, Miss Sweeting?"

There wasn't concern in Hagan's tone. Instead, it was curious. The question snapped her out of her reflection. "No," she said, more aware of her man's psyche than she had been before. With the new clarity, her viewpoint was clearer. "Why don't we speed this up? Ask me your questions, so I can refuse to answer them and get out of here."

"If you don't answer them, you don't leave."

A threat. Overdue, but not unexpected. "What if I don't know the answer?"

"Whether you know the answer or not is irrelevant. Whether I believe you know the answer will decide your fate," he said, and left the couch to go toward the bar. "Your boyfriend believes him and his little gang own the monopoly in underground activities in this city…" He rounded the bar and paused to make eye contact. "They don't."

Hagan had already referenced the bar, so he knew where the crew called home. "I would hardly call Floyd's a monopoly."

With his hand halfway toward a bottle, he stalled, and just kept his attention on her. Surprise made the way for scrutiny. "If you're lying, you're good at it," he said. "Your boyfriend, he has connections… Useful connections… widespread connections in areas that are less than… sophisticated. Connections beyond their flea hole of a base."

Floyd's was not a classy joint. It was shadowy and

sinister, exactly like its clientele, but she wouldn't call it a flea hole. It was Ryske's home. His friends had become her friends and she cared about them. Harlow didn't appreciate this elitist insulting them.

It was difficult to admit how far up her ass her head had been. No man had excited her hormones like Ryske could. Crash was a powerful man; strong, dedicated, and infatuated with her. Why hadn't she let herself be infatuated with him?

Because she'd feared someone expecting to take over her life and make her decisions. That was why. She should have been honest with Ryske. He was a dominant guy, but she doubted he'd want a mute, obedient housewife who he could impregnate before going off to a typical nine to five.

Ryske was everything Rupert hadn't been. He was dynamic and cool; a risk taker with an adventurous personality.

Yes, he was a criminal, and that hardly screamed stability. But how he made his living wasn't the definition of him. Just like she'd said to him on the street last night, his occupation had never been a problem for her. By her nature, Harlow wasn't a judgmental person. On top of that, she'd been trained not to leap to conclusions or be prejudicial.

People chose their path based on their own personality and desire. It had taken Harlow a long time to come to terms with the truth that she didn't want the same life her parents had lived.

Children? Maybe she'd want them one day, maybe not. Sure, she was no college kid with nothing but time to while away, but she was sure of what she didn't want: a normal, traditional life. It followed that if she didn't want one of those she couldn't be with a normal, traditional man.

"You keep drifting off," Hagan said, surprising her with his proximity. She hadn't even seen him approach, but he was seating himself on the couch with her again, carrying a glass containing what looked like bourbon. "I hope that means I'm getting through to you."

A light began to grow in her. Priorities shifted, aims realigned. Meeting Ryske had changed her. Until now, Harlow hadn't faced that. Figuring out the truth of where she was supposed to be, and who she was meant to be with, heated her resolve.

Much as she didn't usually believe in coincidence, she was coming to the conclusion that Ryske hadn't run into her by accident. Fate had been watching out for her and forced them into the same space in time.

Pinning her focus to him, Harlow showed no fear, and sipped her wine. "Are you married, Mr. Hagan?"

"Married? No. If you think there will be an interruption to save you, you'll be disappointed. The only people here work for me and they're professionals who won't be swayed by manipulation. They know what they're doing."

"Apparently not," she said. His expression betrayed his confusion. "You've admitted that *you* are not the best; that means your team is not the best."

His sneer wasn't one of a threatened man. "Do you think I'm threatened by Ryske and his team?" he asked. "After hearing what happened last night, I believed you had to be integral to his life… I'm reconsidering that theory."

Crossing her legs, she raised the wineglass to her lips. "Oh, what a shame for me," she said, without masking her sarcasm.

"I assume your relationship is sexual. When my associate reported Ryske's vicious reaction to seeing you with another man…"

Clyde in Floyd's last night. Damnit. Ryske knew that Hagan had men watching him, men positioned in Floyd's to monitor him. At least that's what he'd told her while he was still under Bale's orders. Maybe Hagan had rotated his men and Ryske didn't recognize whoever had been switched onto the recent Floyd's duty.

If he thought Hagan wasn't watching him anymore, he wouldn't be as careful as he should be.

Still, Harlow couldn't let Hagan see behind her poised façade. "Ryske's reaction shouldn't matter to anyone except me."

He laughed, swirling his liquor in the base of his glass. "And the man he floored."

Conceding that with a nod, it just made sense. "At the

time, yes. But I wouldn't worry about him. He's capable of worrying about himself."

Harlow had gone into work determined to speak to Clyde about what had happened in Floyd's. As she'd reached his desk, another of their colleagues had called out to say he'd come in early and left again to see a client prior to a court appearance. Court could take all day, she knew that from experience.

Gina had been out of the office that morning too, everyone had visits to make, and the two hadn't crossed paths. Because she didn't have his phone number, Harlow had intended to speak to Gina, to find out if the boss would share Clyde's contact details. Beyond the personal, it would've helped her to speak to her colleague before going to visit the Sotos. Though, given her predicament, it seemed none of that was going to happen.

"That's a callous attitude," Hagan said, bending to put his glass down. He stayed in that position to rest an elbow on his knee. "Do you like the attention of men, Miss Sweeting? Do you like to string many along?"

So this wasn't only an opportunity for him to probe her for information on Ryske, he was trying to decipher her too. "You'll have to be more subtle if seduction is your goal."

"Perhaps you'd prefer a direct question."

"If it will speed the process…"

"Are you in love with him?"

With Ryske? That was a question she was only just beginning to answer for herself. But no matter the state of their relationship, or the stage it was at, she had no reason to share her feelings with Jarvis Hagan.

"Whatever is going on between you and him, it's nothing to do with me," she said. "I don't see why I should be compelled to share my personal feelings with you. Is that why you're holding my phone hostage?"

Leaving the couch, she put her wine on the table.

"What are you doing?" he asked, looking up at her.

"I'm leaving," she said. "I'd appreciate it if you'd return my phone, but if you choose not to, I'll make a police report."

Harlow noticed the flare of horror on his face, though she didn't sense that his reaction was rooted in fear. Offense drove his affront. There probably weren't many people who would say such a thing to him.

It wasn't a threat, it was a statement of fact. Harlow couldn't overpower him and wouldn't make a fool of herself trying. But something had been stolen from her and she could identify the perpetrator, so why shouldn't she report the crime?

As she tried to go past him, he leaped up and grabbed her upper arm to halt her. "I can't let you leave, Miss Sweeting. I won't."

"You can't stop me," she said. "Unless you plan to keep me prisoner."

She'd meant for the statement to be so ludicrous that he'd have no choice but to let her walk out. Except, he didn't flinch. His grip stayed clamped on her arm; his gazed bored into her.

Hagan leaned down. "That's exactly what I plan to do."

Spinning around, he strode across the room with purpose, dragging Harlow along in his wake. She tried to pull her arm away, yelping in objection, but he didn't slow. Passing the bar, he went down the stairs and through the tucked away door.

The space they entered was a curved hallway full of light, floored with the same marble that was in the rest of the apartment.

"Let me go," she said, fighting to free her arm.

The success of liberation was a short-lived victory. She turned, intending to return to the other room, but came up against a bulky man who had to be some kind of security. He must have been lurking by the door; she hadn't even seen him, and that was a wonder given his size.

Backing off, Harlow looked left to right, seeking another way out. There were other doors leading from the hallway, but she didn't know what was behind them. Redemption or rescue seemed unlikely. Looking up, the light that flooded the cavern was coming from a skylight twenty feet above.

She had no way out.

"This way, Miss Sweeting," Hagan said.

Whirling in the direction of his voice, she fizzed with resentment at the sight of his ease. Holding a door open for her, Hagan gestured for her to go inside a new room.

"Does being polite ease your guilt?" she asked, struggling to contain her rage. "You won't get away with this."

His lips curled. "I will… I already have. You're here. Your boss isn't looking for you and if your boyfriend comes looking…"

Sweeping his arm toward the room, he tried again to encourage her inside.

Seeing little option, Harlow took a couple of small steps in his direction, giving her mind time to work. "Do you want him to know I'm here? Do you expect him to come and get me?"

If the answer was yes, she might be able to negotiate. Harlow didn't want Crash anywhere near this man who'd already hurt him once. Taking him out of the running, she considered who else might be able to help. The cops were the obvious choice. Rupert was another, he could come over and maybe embarrass Hagan into releasing her.

His answer gave her little hope. "No," he said. "I plan to keep you… When I'm ready, I'll return you to him. What happens here will send a message to him. You will send him a message."

"What message is that?"

Closing the space between them, he brushed her hair from her cheek. Swiping his hand away, she leaped back, but the guard was there to hold her in place.

"He's not the only one who can screw with people he shouldn't," Hagan murmured.

Yanking herself free of the guard, she didn't like being sandwiched between these males. "What does that mean?"

His eyelid twitched. "You think he walks on water, but I know different. He fucks women, wrecks their lives, and tosses them to the curb. He destroys them. Decimates them and anyone who cares about them… You are just the latest on the list. Ryske never gave a damn about a woman he stuck his dick in, not in his life. This time I'll be the one to show him what it's like to hurt."

Grabbing her, Hagan thrust her into the room while the security guy rushed up to block any escape.

The door slammed shut.

Rushing the door, Harlow gave it a tug, but it was locked.

Damn. Damn. Damnit.

Scanning the space Hagan had trapped her in, Harlow was surprised that it wasn't a medieval cell. Rather it appeared to be a den, and quite a comfortable one.

Searching was useless, drawers were locked or empty and although there was a bathroom, there was nothing in it that could be used as a weapon and no route of escape. There was no phone or even wiring.

Seating herself on the couch after finding nothing of use, she tucked her hands under her legs and set her focus on the tall windows. This apartment was several floors up and given that she couldn't hear any street sound, it made sense that the street wouldn't be able to hear her.

Hagan had a plan, something to do with using her against Ryske. Harlow didn't like it. In fact, that was a massive understatement. She'd never been madder in her life. Being used as a pawn was insulting. It didn't help to know that she was being manipulated to hurt the man she'd just realized she wanted a chance to be with.

At least her anger wasn't fear. Hagan was an asshole, but he hadn't hurt her in any serious way. He talked a good game, but had revealed his hand in his last outburst. From what he'd said, it didn't take a genius to deduce that Hagan wanted to hurt Ryske because Ryske had hurt a woman in his life.

So much of this didn't make sense, but knowing she'd see Ryske again was a comfort. Hagan had told her she would. When she did, Harlow was going to ask questions and find out the truth of what was going on. Apologizing would be first on her list, and if Ryske could accept that and trust her, they'd get this figured out.

Whether Ryske wanted her to be or not, Harlow was on his side. With his behavior, Jarvis Hagan had seen to that. Harlow was for Ryske, but she had no idea if he was on her team or done with her for good.

NINETEEN

HARLOW DIDN'T EXPECT to be locked up in Hagan's den for long.

Turned out that assumption was wrong.

Day faded to night and the security guard brought her food without offering her a word. Eating wasn't an attractive idea, so she ignored the meal and just waited.

There was no clock and Harlow wasn't wearing a watch. All she could do was think. Being alone with her mind didn't help keep her calm.

To break up the time, she went into the bathroom to splash water on her face. By the time she returned, the food tray was gone from the unit by the door. On the off chance the guard might have been neglectful, she went over to try the door again, but it was still locked.

Turning her back on the door, she was about to slump against it when she noticed that the couch had been pulled out into a bed.

Alarm shook her.

Ryske.

All she wanted was to see Ryske and be free of this room. Realizing that Hagan's promise to imprison her was going to stretch beyond a few hours was a blow that she couldn't comprehend. A bed. That meant Hagan wanted her to stay the night.

Harlow shouldn't have made assumptions. This was serious. More serious than she could've imagined. It didn't matter that the room wasn't so different from a hotel room, she wasn't in it by choice. That made it a prison cell.

This was so far removed from any life she knew. In suburbia, being locked up and held against her will wasn't a realistic possibility. Now it was her reality.

Without knowing Hagan's plan, Harlow couldn't anticipate his next move or design an escape. That meant she wouldn't be able to warn Ryske either, and she cursed herself for not keeping in closer contact with him and his crew.

Since he'd left her place, they had only seen each other when she went to Floyd's. With the way things had ended on the street, Ryske probably assumed they were finished for good. That's what she'd implied while rebuking his advances. Ryske wouldn't be looking for her, none of them would.

Clyde wouldn't care if she disappeared, not after the way he'd been treated by her friends. Gina would notice if she didn't show up for work, but Hagan seemed to have some kind of influence there that didn't fill Harlow with confidence. If he called Gina and asked to have her as his own personal social worker, pertaining to whatever story he'd spouted, would she fall for it?

Harlow's nightmare only got worse. Hagan wasn't satisfied with holding her for a single day. One day became two, became three, and she began to lose hope that she'd ever leave the den. No one was coming to her rescue, hope for that dwindled with each day that passed.

Security guards brought her food and clothes, and the bathroom was available for her to use as needed and for water. Brash came in a few times to taunt her and just be annoying, which seemed to be his specialty. She hadn't seen Hagan, and had lost her sense of humor... not that she'd really had one about being locked up.

According to the number of nights that had passed outside the windows, Harlow figured out that they'd reached

Saturday. Her theories about Gina had grown more sinister by the day. Before this Hagan mess, Harlow had wanted her superior's respect, now she had little regard for the woman in return.

If she was irresponsible or a recluse, it might be understandable that her work could accept her disappearing after, or rather during, a client meeting. But Harlow had never missed a minute of work either in suburbia or since starting her new job in the city.

When she got away from Hagan's and back to the office, she was going to talk to Gina about security measures. In her head, she'd already drafted a memo recommending that it would be a good idea to have some sort of alarm system instituted whereby everyone had to check in, in person, with their supervisor or colleagues every hour or two. They certainly shouldn't be able to vanish for a week, no matter the excuse they were given by clients.

There was a chance she was jumping to conclusions and was willing to be proved wrong. The cops could have been to Hagan's to ask questions. Maybe Gina had reported her missing.

The obstacle to her freedom was Hagan's wealth and potential influence. If he said she wasn't at his apartment, law enforcement may just accept his word. Especially if he gave them Ryske's details as a new lead and hinted that there was a romantic connection.

But she doubted Hagan would be that dumb. If the cops showed up in Floyd's asking questions about her, Hagan's hand would be tipped. The Floyd's crew would learn from the interrogation that she was missing and that could prompt them to start looking.

Could. But it wasn't guaranteed.

Maybe Ryske had heard she was missing and thought to hell with her. But no…

The den door opened, interrupting her contemplation. Lifting her head from a pillow, she didn't expect to see Hagan entering.

It wasn't enough that he was present, he'd come to visit wearing a tux and carrying something that looked suspiciously like a dress.

He tossed the fabric onto the arm of the couch. "Put it on."

Picking it up, she untwisted the red silk, and found it was a maxi dress with a plunging neckline and a leg slit that ran far higher than any she'd ever choose for herself.

"Why would I do that?" she asked without doing him the courtesy of even standing up.

"Because you want to see him," he said. "Put on the dress or spend another week in here while I decide what to do with you."

Though it was a threat, it wasn't one that involved shedding blood… necessarily. After a week of being trapped in this room, she was eager to get out. Getting out was progress. Defying Hagan just for the hell of it would mean staying locked up and helpless. Changing her clothes and going with him would at least be a change in circumstances.

Even if Harlow got out there and learned that Ryske wanted nothing to do with her, she still wanted to warn him about Hagan's venom.

"Fine," she said and got up to head for the bathroom.

"Where are you going?"

Holding up the dress in her fist, she didn't even care that she'd be crushing the silk. "If you want me to put on the dress, I'll change in private. Otherwise, I'm just as happy to go wherever you want me to go in what I'm wearing now." Which was gray sweatpants and a black vest. After checking out her apparel, Hagan stepped aside. "Yeah, that's what I thought."

"And make some sort of effort," Hagan said.

Harlow had to think fast after facing him. He tossed something at her, which she only just caught.

Flipping it over, she took a few seconds to recognize it as a compact makeup kit. "What's this?"

"Think classy," he said and looked at his watch. "And hurry up."

Earlier in the day, she'd been given hair products and a narrow window of time to wash her hair. With this visit and the dress, the reasoning behind the products became clear.

Hagan had dictated his regime to her and she hadn't even realized it.

Tonight was more than progress, it was part of his agenda. Harlow just had to figure out a way to make sure it suited hers too.

***

CLINGING TO THE SILK of her dress, holding the two sides of the leg slit together, Harlow didn't want anyone ogling her.

If she'd been alone in the back of the sleek limo with Hagan, she may have made an attempt to leap from the vehicle and run at the first set of lights. But, as it was, she was flanked by two broad security guards who didn't leave much room for her to maneuver. Hagan had also made a show of locking the doors while glaring at her as soon as they got in.

After almost a week locked inside Hagan's apartment, it had been nice to feel the air on her skin in the short walk between Hagan's building and the car. The relief had been too brief and the pendulum had swung back the other way. With so many people in the back of the vehicle, stifling her, Harlow was uncomfortable in the humidity created by body heat and breath. Not that she'd have expected to be comfortable in the presence of Hagan and his minions.

Harlow tried to forget about the lack of space and began to speculate about what might happen when they got to wherever they were going. Throughout the ride, she held onto the hope that Ryske might be the prize at the end of this journey. Though that would only be a positive if she was allowed to speak to him... preferably before he threw a punch.

If Ryske reacted to Hagan the same way he'd reacted to Clyde, it could cause problems for all of them. But given that their last encounter had ended with him walking away from her without looking back, there was a chance that his fondness for her had dwindled.

Time to reach conclusions was short. They only drove a few blocks before the car pulled to a stop. She tried to lean forward to see where they were, but couldn't pick out many specifics. There was a red carpet on the sidewalk, and a posse of people in groups of various sizes.

The door was opened for them. After Hagan got out, a security guard followed and then the one left inside forced her out and straight into Hagan who crowded close while security penned her in against him.

"If you think about doing anything stupid," Hagan said. "I'll see to it that your lover gets more than a scratch. Smile and play nice."

Snatching her wrist, he forced her hand into his elbow and smiled, waiting for her to reciprocate. Once she did, exaggerated as her false grin was, Hagan was satisfied enough to take them inside what appeared to be a hotel lobby.

Everyone was moving in the same direction, towards the open double doors of a grand ballroom. They went into the bustling space. Over the susurration of conversation, classical music was being played on stringed instruments, and it seemed everyone held a flute of champagne. Harlow didn't care about that. Nothing about this meant anything to her.

Although her only choice was to stay next to Hagan because he still had her in his clutches, her eyes were wild. Her frantic gaze searched left and right, looking for any sign that someone she knew might be around. Someone like Ryske or Maze or any of the Floyd's crew.

Despite his heritage and the place he called home, Harlow had no trouble believing that Ryske could fit in here. With a suit and a smile, he'd fit in anywhere. It was harder to imagine him coming here looking for a good time.

But Hagan had implied that he'd be here, hadn't he? Ryske had to be up to something, general networking or maybe a specific meeting… could be he was just plain working. Maybe someone in the ballroom was a mark. Was she going to find him in the midst of a seduction? How did she feel about that?

Harlow didn't know how she'd feel. Well, yes, she did. It would sicken her to see him with another woman. She'd feel jealous and angry and uncomfortable, but wasn't that exactly why Ryske didn't want to make her promises?

Hagan took her to the bar and ordered drinks. Once the bartender turned to fill the order, Hagan retrieved a glass of complimentary champagne from further along the bar. "Drink this," he said, putting the glass in her hand.

"Why?"

The liquid wasn't likely to be tainted, he'd pulled it from an anonymous pack of other glasses that were being picked up by others at random. It would've been extremely difficult for Hagan to ensure the one he'd arranged to be tainted for her wasn't picked up by someone else. With the ever changing grid of glasses, it would also be difficult for him to know which the tainted glass was.

She took a sip, it was good, but Harlow still didn't understand why he wanted her to drink it. "The drunker you are, the better."

Under other circumstances, she'd say there was something admirable about honesty. This time, it just turned her stomach.

Putting the glass aside, Harlow propped herself on a stool. "Is that your idea of a seduction?" she asked. "I could believe it's the only way you can find a willing woman."

He laughed. The sound was warmer and seemed more intimate than his previous attempts. "Not at all," he said. "Though if the evening goes that way, I wouldn't object."

Almost snorting, she wasn't hesitant to deliver a truth of her own. "It won't."

"Then I'll have to settle for loosening your tongue in a different way."

"That's a risky strategy," she said, smiling at the bartender who brought their drinks, though she had no intention of drinking from the new glass he'd provided either. "You might hope to get information from me that serves you. But I'm as likely to start mouthing off about what you've done to me."

"What have I done?" he asked. "You've spent a few days living at my hospitality, that is all. No one has hurt you."

"Imprisonment is imprisonment. Torture comes in different forms."

The warmth of his gaze cooled. Receiving a glare

from him was satisfying. Harlow wanted to push his buttons and didn't want anyone in this room to think they were friends much less intimate. The more time he spent glaring the better, and she'd return the sentiment without hesitation.

In an abrupt change, his scowl flipped to a glorious smile and he took a half step to the side. "Oh, you are beautiful," he said, opening his arms. "A vision."

The words weren't for her, and neither was the smile. His attention had switched to something, or rather someone, behind her. Suffering proverbial whiplash from his sudden change in demeanor, Harlow twisted in her stool to see what had taken his attention. A gorgeous blonde was coming toward them, returning Hagan's smile. The woman went into his arms, and they kissed each other's cheeks.

"You are as handsome as ever," the blonde said, her voice a sultry purr.

Her smile became a begging pout, making Harlow wonder about this woman's connection to the man who'd held her prisoner all week. If the two were lovers, the blonde wouldn't be pleased to see Hagan at this function with another woman. Harlow knew the woman had no need to be jealous. There wouldn't be a cat fight tonight. If the blonde wanted Hagan, she could have him.

"I know that face. What do you want?" Hagan asked the blonde.

Whoever she was, Hagan knew her well enough to read her expressions and address her with a fed up groan that was familiar and almost teasing.

"Do you have a minute for Christian Hyslop?"

Oh, a new person could mean an opening for her. Harlow perked up. Neither Hagan nor the blonde looked at her, but she was already scanning the room trying to pinpoint the nearest exit. Except, his security guards were no doubt still watching her. Would she get away with sneaking out?

Hagan exhaled. "I suppose you…" The blonde stepped aside to sweep an arm toward a man standing about fifteen feet away. "Okay, but no more. I don't want a night of this. And just one minute."

Nodding, the blonde kissed his cheek again, and spun

around to watch Hagan head for the man she'd referred to as Hyslop.

TWENTY

AFTER WATCHING HAGAN and Hyslop for a second, the blonde turned to order a drink at the bar. Harlow didn't pay much attention, she was more interested in Hagan who'd positioned himself to face in her direction so he could keep watching her.

Could she make a break for it? Maybe the scene would be worth it. Hagan could run after her and tackle her to the floor in a mist of flailing limbs and desperate screams, but did he want to make a fool of himself like that in this room of his peers who probably admired him? She doubted it. But he may have a plan B, and—

"You're sleeping with him, aren't you?"

It took Harlow a second to realize that the question had come from the blonde and that the woman was talking to her. It hadn't been immediately obvious because the blonde was leaning on the bar, staring straight ahead. The beauty was nowhere near as friendly or simpering as she had been a moment before.

"No," Harlow said, which she would've said regardless of the blonde's affect because, A) it was the truth, and B) she hadn't been instructed to say otherwise. She couldn't imagine any motivation for Hagan wanting anyone to think she and he were intimate, other than to hurt Ryske, and Harlow wouldn't be party to that if she could avoid it. "No, I promise you we've never—"

"He's been different recently. Distant. And all this week, he's been edgy and angry, like something's on his mind," the blonde said, her cold eyes drifting in Harlow's direction. "It's you. You're what's different. Are you in love with him?"

Shock made Harlow blink. It was hard not to gasp in horror. "No! No, I could never—"

"He's in love with you, I can tell," the blonde said, switching her focus to her drink and breathing out an ironic laugh. "I didn't think he was capable."

Glancing past the blonde to Hagan, Harlow found she was still under his scrutiny. "I'd probably agree with that assessment. Well, except himself. He's in love with himself."

"He never shied from flirting with me, and his hands would wander, you know, like they do when a man's interested and wants to push for more."

Harlow would take the blonde's word for that. She was pleased to have never had the pleasure of Hagan's hands on her. Him just holding her hand was enough to put her off.

"I can promise you—"

"He's just been so angry for the last month. He disappeared after the stabbing and I… it didn't matter how many times Maze told me he was safe, I couldn't believe it until I saw it with my own eyes."

Maze… Slowly, her head turned to fixate on the blonde's profile, though Harlow only watched for a moment before she turned to make eye contact. This woman wasn't talking about Hagan at all. She knew Maze. Who would know Maze and about the stabbing? Someone who'd been there. Present and correct. Ophelia. This was Ophelia, it had to be.

"What's your name?"

The blonde smiled. "He didn't tell you about me?" she asked, flashing furtive eyes Harlow's way. "I shouldn't be surprised. I've heard how he likes to keep his women separate. Guess that's why I never had a chance. After Anwen he was never the same. I suppose I remind him of her… maybe that's why he trusts me… I always thought she was why he'd let us only go so far, but never all the way."

Questions flooded Harlow's mind about this Anwen and how Ophelia was connected to both her and to Hagan, and to Ryske.

"You're in love with him," Harlow murmured, though she hadn't really meant to say anything.

The blonde didn't answer her question, but there was a forlorn kind of pain in her gaze that broke Harlow's heart. The woman did have feelings for Ryske, and he didn't return those feelings. Or, if he did, he wouldn't let himself act on them because of this Anwen.

"Ophelia."

Neither of them expected to hear Hagan's voice. Both were startled and turned in the direction of the sound to find him striding over. Once he was there, he put himself between them. The move, she supposed, was meant to look casual. Harlow saw it as a ploy and wondered if Ophelia saw through it too.

"How did it go?" Ophelia asked, impressing Harlow with how quickly she became the social butterfly again.

"The man is an oaf as always," Hagan said, pushing his empty glass onto the bar and gesturing the bartender over. "But he's a rich one with good ideas."

"You'll hear him out?"

"I'll let him pitch."

"Pitch what?" Harlow asked, seeing an opportunity.

Hagan couldn't know that Ophelia was in cahoots with Ryske. There would be no reason for Hagan to be so friendly with a woman who was providing access and information to a person he despised. And given that Harlow was supposed to be his date for the evening, there would be no reason for him not to answer her question and share the story. Making the enquiry was normal small talk for a date.

"Hyslop is an amazing man," Ophelia said, like she was simply filling her in. "He has a brilliant mind, but he's just not personable. He can talk to people he likes one on one, but try to get him into an investors meeting…" She waved an airy hand. "Oh, it's a disaster. I swear, he could pitch a spacecraft intended to get astronauts to Mars and back in a day, for the price of a popsicle, and he'd still find a way to mess it up."

"So he's an inventor," Harlow asked and focused on Hagan. "Do you have something against him? If he's going to make you money…"

"My brother doesn't like dealing with erratic people."

Clarity changed Harlow's expression. "Your… brother?"

Ophelia laughed and put an arm around Hagan. "Yes! You didn't think there was something salacious between us, did you? Goodness, that's disgusting."

Picking Ophelia's arm from around him, Hagan eased her back a step. "You need to be careful what you're saying," he said to his sister. "This woman is connected to someone we both know."

"We know plenty of people," Ophelia said, gulping her drink and leaning past her brother to stage whisper to Harlow. "He doesn't like his dates to know how ruthless he can be. I wouldn't put it past him to take Hyslop's idea and sell it as his own." Ophelia laughed like she was joking… or was she? "Oh, I'm kidding, brother, wipe that displeasure from your face."

"You've had too much to drink," he said, plucking the glass from her hand. "Ophelia, you shouldn't—"

"I think I'm allowed to get a little bit drunk."

"Because he stood you up again?" he said.

Ophelia wasn't as drunk as she was pretending to be, but Harlow could respect what she was doing. Lowering her brother's expectations meant she could act in a less than responsible way and get away with it because he believed she was under the influence.

"Who stood her up?" Harlow asked, fearing what the answer might be.

Hagan's glare snapped around to her. "Stop asking questions."

"You brought me here," she said, picking up the champagne she'd put aside earlier, figuring a couple of sips wouldn't hurt. "Why shouldn't I amuse myself?"

"You're being rude."

Taking the flute from her mouth, she caught a drip of champagne on her lip with her fingertip. "I'm being rude? You're the one who…"

Just as she felt like she was getting into the spirit of the night and finding her groove in how to aggravate Hagan, a random partygoer in her peripheral vision stepped aside. The movement may not have registered if it hadn't revealed someone she knew.

Ryske.

There was no frown on his face, his expression was blank. Although he appeared to be alone, she wondered how close the rest of the crew were. On the night he'd been stabbed, he'd been by himself. Harlow hoped that they'd learned from that error. Around others, on other ops, it might be safe for him to fly solo. Hagan had proved he was willing to be lethal, making him an unsafe mark for Ryske. Yet, there he was.

Ryske wasn't just there, he was approaching them. It didn't seem that Hagan had noticed him yet because he was whispering something to his sister, and wasn't facing Ryske's way.

Harlow felt a surge of panic. She didn't know what to do. Her instinct was to go to him, to talk to him, to explain, and hopefully escape with him. It was impossible for her to know what he thought about the sight he was witnessing. Now he was within just a few feet. Her mouth opened, but she didn't know what to say.

Ophelia gasped and leaped from her stool, hurrying past her brother to throw herself against Ryske. "Oh, you naughty boy, you kept me waiting," Ophelia said, stroking his face. "Why must you always be late?"

"Like to keep you on your toes, Fi," he said and dipped to kiss her.

Vomit almost touched the back of Harlow's throat. While it wasn't a full kiss, it was more than a friendly peck on the cheek.

Harlow didn't mean to gawp or blanch, but she was still focused on the lip-locked pair when a voice filled her ear. "Did I forget to tell you about my sister's ridiculous crush?"

Being discreet about shaking herself from her daze wasn't easy. Though the speed of her recovery impressed even her. "Who says I didn't know?" she asked Hagan, turning her back on the couple now whispering to each other.

The kiss was sickening to watch, but it was easier to witness that physical act than it was to observe the way Ryske smiled at the simpering Ophelia who wouldn't stop touching him.

"Everyone's waiting," Ryske's voice rose.

Harlow knew he wasn't talking to her and did her best not to react to the deep sound that had been such a tormenting comfort to her so often since they'd met.

"Then what are we doing here?" Hagan said and put a hand to the small of her back. "Come with me."

Still facing the bar, Harlow kept her lips on her champagne flute while she hissed at him through gritted teeth. "Why don't you go to hell?"

Leaning in, he brushed her hair from her shoulder and kissed her ear provoking her instinct to pull away. Her recoil prompted him to slide his hand across her back and onto her opposite hip to tug her to him.

"I would rethink your attitude," he grumbled. "The target you care about is within my sights. Do you think I would hesitate to hurt him?"

Turning her head was her only option. The rest of her body was locked in the clamp of Hagan's half-embrace. With her shoulders tensed and her elbows on the bar, there was no room for maneuver, but she was grateful Hagan only had access to her hip.

"What would that get you?" she asked and took her time about drinking some more champagne before discarding the flute. "What's to stop me from walking over there and sticking my tongue down his throat?" Pushing Hagan back, she twisted her body to face him, ignoring how his hand found its way into the slit of her dress. Letting Hagan provoke a reaction from her would provoke one from Ryske, she'd bet that was what Hagan was banking on. So Harlow focused her glare on him and blanked out the feel of his fingertips on her inner thigh. "Better yet, what's to stop me walking over there, dropping to my knees and—"

"I'm not the only one watching," Hagan said. "You or him. Do you want to take the risk of blowing his cover? You know how precious he is about that."

Pressing her lips together, Harlow wasn't sure if there was steam coming out of her nose; it felt like it. She hated this. Hated being out of control. Hated being under Hagan's control. Hated what Ryske must think of her.

Though he hadn't reacted to seeing her, he must have been hurt, or at least pissed, to see her with the man who'd ordered the stabbing. Hagan wasn't only a mark, there was history between the men that she hadn't understood. Now, given that Hagan wasn't forthcoming, and Ryske probably hated her, she may never learn what had gone on between them.

"I will scream rape if you touch me again," she said, sliding off her stool and resenting how close Hagan stayed to her.

Harlow held her breath when he inched closer still. When he touched her cheek and smiled at her like he was a boyfriend complimenting his girl, she had to clench her jaw.

"I'm not a man who takes to being taunted," he murmured like they were words of love when they were anything but. "The more you say it, the more you make me want to show you just how helpless you are. I get what I want, your feelings are irrelevant to me."

"What's the delay?" Ophelia asked, approaching with Ryske at her side, her arm around his waist.

"No delay," Hagan said and took Harlow's hand to put it inside the crook of his elbow again.

"Good," Ophelia said, opening a hand to the man at her side. "Harlow, I'd like you to meet Ryske."

Turned out they all had roles to play in this crazy game. Fine, she was a newbie, but she'd figure it out. Harlow hadn't introduced herself to Ophelia, though there was no reason for Hagan to know that, so Ophelia's introduction should go under the radar.

Disgusted as she was, Harlow wasn't going to endanger herself or Ryske. That didn't mean she planned to make any of this easy for her jailor.

Widening her smile, she pinned it on Ryske. "Your boyfriend is extremely attractive, Ophelia," Harlow said, offering her hand to Ryske.

A pro at appearing neutral, this was his job. It was no surprise that he could do passive. Ryske took her hand and bowed to kiss it.

Ophelia laughed. "Oh, he's not exactly my boyfriend."

"Not exactly?" Harlow asked, keeping Ryske's hand even after he tried to release hers. Building a façade like she was just a flirt who didn't want to let him go gave her the opportunity to be close to him for another few seconds. "Then I may have to fight you for him." She licked her lips. "Ophelia, how do you restrain yourself?"

"Okay, ladies, form a line," Ryske said and winked at her, making her giggle in a way she never had before.

Hagan yanked her hard against his side, shaking the smile from her face. "Behave yourself."

"Not something I'm known for," Harlow said out of the corner of her mouth.

"Trouble in paradise?" Ryske asked.

Hagan snatched Harlow's hand away from the man in front of her. "No," Hagan said. "Everything is as it should be."

Ryske looked to her, more intrigue and concern on his face than there had been before. There was no outward sign that he was asking her, as himself, if she needed him to intervene. Yet, that felt like the opening he was giving her.

Pasting a smile on her face, she didn't want to risk anyone getting hurt. "Just peachy," she said.

"Then we should join our friends," Ryske said, turning to put an arm around Ophelia's shoulder to lead her through the crowd.

TWENTY-ONE

HARLOW AND HAGAN followed close behind Ryske and Ophelia as they moved through the partygoers. Wherever they were going could be full of friends or foes, she had no idea if their destination would be hostile or jovial. Though Harlow wouldn't put money on it being the latter.

On an op, Ryske liked to have a plan. Being an unexpected variable didn't make her feel good. Neither did knowing that Ryske probably resented her for getting involved. Not that any of this was her choice. Hagan wanted to use her to hurt Ryske; a man she cared for and respected.

Her infuriation didn't matter, neither did Hagan's motivations. Harlow resolved herself to being an asset for her friend. Whatever it took, she'd keep Ryske safe, even if that meant playing along with Hagan or going home with him.

Unless it meant certain death for Crash, Harlow wouldn't sleep with Hagan. But she was pretty sure it wouldn't come to that. She couldn't think of any situation in which sex would be necessary to keep Ryske safe. But, no matter what, that was her priority. Safe. She wanted him safe.

Having Ryske close, yet, out of reach, was torture. Like she'd said to Hagan, it came in many forms. She wanted to touch him and explain how she'd ended up crashing the op.

But with Hagan watching their every move, that wasn't possible.

Doing her best to keep her mind switched on, Harlow memorized their route out of the ballroom and into a corridor. The thick carpet beneath her feet threatened to envelop her heels and make her wobble, which didn't make it easy to walk with grace.

Ryske swung a right, stopping at a door with a security lock. It didn't slow him down; he keyed a code into a panel and opened the door that led to a very different kind of corridor.

The new hallway didn't scream swish, expensive hotel corridor like the last one had. It was a cold, industrial space; long with a gray vinyl floor and off-white walls. Even the doors were non-descript in their plainness.

Nothing was signposted. There were no carts standing around or monogramed panels. If she had to guess, Harlow would say this was an employee-only space. Yet, there they were and, as far as she knew, none of them were employees.

Noon came to her mind. Go with it. That's what he'd said. That's what she had to do.

Acting as though this was normal, or she knew exactly what to expect, Harlow didn't even blink when Ryske stopped at a second door to key in another code. Watching his fingers, as she had on the first panel, she memorized the number he put in, noting that it was only one digit different from the previous code, which would make it easier to remember.

Memorizing the numbers was probably stupid. Certainly, if she never came back to this place again, it would be too soon. It wasn't like she had plans to use either number. Still, they'd be good to know in case a quick exit was needed.

Opening the door, Ryske stepped aside to let Hagan enter first. That meant letting her enter in front of him too; her hand was still locked inside Hagan's elbow. Harlow's trust didn't waver, but she didn't like being sent into a viper's nest before Ryske checked it out for danger, especially since she didn't necessarily know what danger might look like.

The sight presented to her inside, sinister as it was,

didn't appear immediately dangerous. There were no weapons trained on her, no thugs hiding in corners. No thugs, but they weren't alone. Three other people were already there, two men and one woman.

Two couches with end tables and a coffee table between them dominated the space in front of her. The three people sat facing them on the furthest couch, which had a large table behind it.

To the left, the room opened up to accommodate a bar and there was another door up there too. Another door could mean another exit. But her gaze snagged on the desk in the corner. On that desk was a phone. A phone. Harlow almost laughed. All week she'd wanted access to a line so she could reach out to Ryske and the first time she came across one, he was in the damn room with her. Yet, he was no more accessible.

There were no windows, which was maybe the most striking thing. Though the corridor that had brought them to this room was internal and meant to be functional not impressive, the room itself was the opposite and clearly meant to be impressive, as it was decorated like an upscale drawing room.

Everything about this op and the things she learned were a juxtaposition of contradictions.

"It's about time," one of the men on the couch said and turned to whisper something to the woman seated between him and the other man.

The woman got up without uttering a word and crossed the room to sit alone at the bar.

"I think the women should be excused," the second man said.

Harlow wasn't sure what to think of that. Being excused would give her an opportunity to flee—providing she wasn't intercepted by one of Hagan's agents or detained by Ophelia. Much as it seemed Hagan's sister was working with Ryske to some extent, Harlow would guess her compliance only went so far. Ophelia could still have some loyalty to her brother. Her aid may be conditional and dependent on some kind of intimate agreement.

"Suits me," Ryske said, leaving the group by the door to go over and take a seat on the empty couch.

"You know damn well I won't be cut out of this, Anthony," Ophelia said, holding her head up as she followed Ryske.

Sitting at his side, thigh to thigh, Ophelia didn't let a slither of light break between their bodies.

Intimate, whether it was their agreement or not, was certainly what Ophelia wanted from the man she pinned herself to.

The first man spoke up again. "You're a tenacious woman, Ophelia, but—"

"Keep your insincere compliments, Gilbert Parratt," Ophelia spat. "You're a misogynist hell-bent on controlling every woman in your life. You can't control me, and I don't give a damn what you think."

Wow, that woman had spunk and balls too. The man, Parratt, appeared to be in his early forties, too young to be considered an old fool who might try to get away with holding onto nineteen-fifties views.

"We don't know this new woman you've brought," Anthony said. "Strangers make me nervous."

"Everything makes you nervous, Yarker," Hagan said, resting a hand on her lower back to urge her forward. "She's here on the clock. You don't have to worry about her interest in this." He gave her a shove. "Go sit at the bar."

Had he just implied that she was… What the hell? Glaring over her shoulder at Hagan had no effect. He didn't respond to her venom and just kept looking at her as she stumbled her way towards the bar. Ryske hadn't even glanced her way, so he apparently had no problem with everyone believing she was a hooker.

Instead of being like the lady already perched on a bar stool with her legs neatly folded, Harlow went around the bar and began to poke at the bottles. All those years spent studying and building her career, and it had taken just a few seconds to reduce her to a working girl. Her father would be mortified by the implication.

Although it was frustrating to be belittled, it wasn't

worth the fight. Harlow couldn't care less what these men thought about her.

"So…" Parratt said.

Hagan had taken a seat at the end of the table behind the couch Parratt and Yarker were on. Doubting his choice of location was meant to intimidate the other men in the room, she resented that he'd positioned himself to keep an eye on her. Part of her was tempted to go and try the door in the corner next to the bar. Just to see if she could provoke him into leaping up and running the length of the room.

"Yes," Yarker followed up. "So… are we all in? On course?"

"Yes," Ryske said. "And yes. You?"

"I once again wish to raise my objections to this man being present," Hagan said. "He can't be trusted."

"This again?" Parratt groaned and sighed. "I think we all know the source of your objections."

Fixing herself a drink, Harlow tried to be subtle about stealing glances over the bar to observe what was going on between the members of the meeting. Ryske was drumming his fingertips on Ophelia's knee and letting them slide a little higher, distracting her from the meeting, but she appeared happy to be distracted.

"He's sleeping with your sister," Yarker said.

"And slept with my fiancée, but that's beside the point," Hagan said.

The ice Harlow had been holding in the metal tongs fell in a clatter, skidding across the bar and smashing on the floor. Without lifting her head to see if she was the focus of the room, she allowed her legs to buckle, and dropped onto the floor, giving the illusion that she intended to clean up the mess.

Harlow didn't really care about cleaning up. For appearance sake, she grabbed the larger pieces of ice and tossed them over her head into the sink, which succeeded in causing another loud rattle. Damn. Drawing attention to herself hadn't been the goal, but it seemed to be all she was capable of.

Staying in a crouch, she squeezed her eyes closed and

covered her face with both hands.

The meeting continued, offering her some relief.

"Hagan—"

"There isn't a woman in the room he hasn't slept with," Hagan said. "Is this the kind of man you want to trust with our investment?"

"He's... had your hooker?" Yarker stuttered. "When? Just... tonight?"

"What do you think caused the delay?" Ryske asked, but his voice was flat and unimpressed. "My sex life is irrelevant to our business deal... I don't seem to recall you having a problem with me screwing your wife, Yarker... How much did you get in that divorce settlement? Evidence of infidelity was what you wanted and it was what you got."

"I... don't think we should discuss—"

"Why not?" Ryske asked. "Hagan brought it up."

"Yes, and he was the only one," Parratt said. "I don't give a damn what you do with your dick. All I care about is that you pony up. Do you have the cash?"

"Yes," Ryske said. "Do you?"

Hagan interjected with a loud bluster. "No, now, wait a minute... This is what I take exception to," he said. "I know he doesn't have the money. I know it for a fact."

Letting her hands slide from her face, Harlow folded her arms on her bent knees and laid her temple against them.

"Okay," Parratt said with measured patience. "Show us the proof."

Some of the gusto was taken from Hagan's tone. "I... I can't show you proof of a negative."

"Then I guess you're up the creek," Ryske said, the satisfaction of his smile obvious in his intonation. His amusement grew into teasing. "Come to think of it, Jarvis, I'm damn sure you don't have the cash-on-hand either."

Parratt's patience was stretched. "Thirty days, a million apiece," he said probably tired of the men baiting each other.

Wondering at the finality of his tone, Harlow rose to her feet to check out what was going on. Looking beyond the peering woman seated on the other side of the bar, Harlow didn't expect for Parratt to be on his feet.

"Since when did you become defacto leader?" Ryske asked. "You're as liable for this as us… We're not done here. I want to discuss Hagan's creeping."

Parratt sat down again. "What do you mean?"

"His third-rate operation."

Hagan sat up straight like someone had prodded his spine. "My… my operation is—"

"Rigged? Illegitimate?" Ryske wasn't shy about being blunt.

"Do you have evidence?" Yarker asked.

"That there's cheating?" Ryske asked. "Yes."

Parratt opened a hand to him, giving him the floor, while settling back and crossing his legs. "Then show us."

"I lost," Ryske said. "That's all the proof I need."

Lost on purpose, that's how she'd taken what had been said at Bale's. Except Ryske was using his loss as evidence that Hagan's operation was shoddy.

Managing an illegal casino had to be risky enough. To be accused of fraud, cheating, running a sham establishment, could lead to all sorts of problems for Hagan. Customers may not want to visit at all if they didn't think games were fair or winnable. Those that did, wouldn't have to worry about Hagan running to the law if they got violent after an unjust game or decision.

Hagan scoffed. "Because you can't play the game and win, doesn't mean there's cheating."

Both Parratt and Yarker were looking at each other like they weren't so sure about that. "When was this?"

"Seven weeks ago," Ryske said.

That made Parratt incredulous. She wondered if any of these people trusted each other. Though, given how many deceptions she was aware of between them, Harlow thought a little suspicion was healthy.

"And you're just coming to us with it now?" Parratt asked. "Why the delay?"

"The fucker had his man put a knife in my gut," Ryske said. "I wasn't feeling chatty."

The truth hit Parratt and Yarker who took a few

moments to absorb it, though they couldn't hide how disturbed they were.

"You… you were stabbed?" Parratt asked, then switched to Hagan. "You injured your own colleague?"

Colleagues was an odd title given how much animosity existed between the men.

"He has no evidence of that," Hagan said, an edge of desperation flavoring his words.

Ryske wasn't done. He wasn't going to just let it go, and he shouldn't either, someone had to answer for what he'd been through. "Want to see the scar?"

"I do," Ophelia said in sync with the woman at the bar, who said the same thing.

Harlow hadn't realized the unknown woman was paying such close attention to the proceedings. She hadn't said a word. Apparently, Ryske's scar was the catalyst she needed to break her silence.

Ryske ran a hand down the length of Ophelia's hair and twisted to wink at the woman seated at the bar. "Form a line, ladies."

That was the line he'd used in the hotel ballroom, she'd guess it was a practiced one. But given what she'd heard tonight, Harlow began to think maybe it wasn't only a line, maybe he really would service them if they did just wait their turns.

TWENTY-TWO

"A SCAR PROVES nothing," Hagan asserted. "You know what kind of man he is. God knows how many wives he's seduced away from their husbands and how many lowlifes he pisses off every day."

"I've pissed off a bunch of lowlifes and husbands," Ryske said. "'Cept it doesn't matter if the scar holds up. You've done me a solid and brought me a goddamn witness."

In all the time they'd been in this room, Ryske hadn't looked at her let alone spoken to her. Being a rookie, Harlow wasn't sure when she was supposed to speak up, or if she should wait to be questioned. Ryske's statement showed his faith that she would back up his story. Showed his faith in her. Which was amazing. Humbling. The last time they'd been alone they'd argued and effectively ended things.

His faith had endured even though she'd shown up with Hagan.

Sure, Harlow knew that her jailor hadn't won her loyalty, but Ryske had no way to know how she'd ended up at Hagan's side. Yet, his confidence in her hadn't wavered.

Hagan's confidence was misplaced. "Harlow will not—"

"Harlow will," Ryske said. His position seated in the

corner of the couch, angled against the arm, facing away from her meant they couldn't look at each other. That didn't matter. Just the sound of his voice was enough to make her shiver. Her Crash was so goddamn sure of her loyalty. "Want me to ask her?"

Without really thinking about it, Harlow abandoned everything at the bar and went around it to cross the room. She could feel Parratt looking at her, Yarker too, and Hagan's anger was palpable, but she didn't take her attention away from the back of Ryske's head.

When Harlow reached him, she didn't speak, she just slid her hand onto his shoulder, giving him a silent signal that she was there with him. He didn't turn, and kept one arm around Ophelia, but with the other, he rested his hand over the back of hers on his shoulder.

The level of tension in the room rose. "You... witnessed this?" Yarker asked, leaving a space between his words as he frequently did, making it seem like everything surprised him.

"Harlow knows better," Hagan said, warning her with a glare. "Do not forget what I said."

Careful was the last thing she felt with Ryske's hand on hers. Hagan wanted her to be quiet, but it was beyond time for her to be open with Ryske.

"What? That you'd hurt him again if I didn't do as you said?" Harlow asked Hagan, which came with the bonus of explaining to Ryske why she was there. "I have done everything you asked. I am here because you demanded I join you."

Ryske understood what she was doing and ran with it. "Not her fault if it blows up in your face," he said.

Ophelia bounced to the edge of her seat and twisted around, tossing Ryske's arm away from her shoulders and pinning a glare on him. "Have you had sex with her? Have you?"

"I think it's been established that he sleeps with anything in a skirt," Hagan said.

Ignoring her brother, Ophelia kept her focus trained on Ryske. "Answer me, Ryske."

The fact that he said nothing was apparently all the answer Ophelia needed. She lunged forward and slapped him hard. Ryske absorbed the hit.

Ophelia got up, and ignoring everyone else in the room, she stormed to the door and slammed out of the room.

"I've achieved at least one of my goals," Hagan said.

Ryske exhaled at the inconvenience or Hagan's smugness, maybe both. "Separating me from Ophelia?" he asked, following his incredulity with a snicker. "Want to time how long it takes me to get both of them in bed together, doing things to each other and to me that you've only seen in the most depraved videos you drool over online?"

"Gentlemen," Yarker said, a sneer on his face. "We cannot allow our petty grievances to get in the way of the opportunity we have. Is sex going to be what prevents this from happening? Without each other, it's not possible. Jarvis, you know that we need Ryske. And, Ryske, you know that this chance has only been given to you because of your connections."

Harlow didn't know about the opportunity he'd been presented or what might prevent it. She didn't know what had brought these men together or if Ryske was there for genuine reasons or nefarious ones.

"I know I don't need to be stabbed," he said.

"Yes, that is worrying," Parratt said like he'd been pondering it since he last spoke. The expression he had turned on Hagan was curious too. "I think perhaps we should take this under advisement and meet again in a week."

This time when Parratt stood up, Yarker did too. "Yes," he said. "We'll be in touch."

Hagan stood up as the men began to move away from him. The woman from the bar scurried across to join them and the trio left the room together. Tense as the air had been before they left, it ratcheted up a thousand percent after everyone else was gone and Harlow was left alone with Hagan and Ryske.

Ryske took his time about getting to his feet. Unsure what move she should make, Harlow was still watching the door that had just closed and didn't think anything of him rising. Not until his shadow cast over her. He'd put himself in front of her, and was using his form to protect hers, just as he had done in the past.

The whole nature of the meeting and the aura in the room changed. The bullshit was gone. Ryske wasn't playing affable or even patient anymore. "You're not leaving with her," he growled, menace and daring reverberating through him.

Hagan laughed, but it wasn't in happiness. "I never intended to," he said, swaggering toward them. "She was a warning. I achieved what I wanted to."

"Yeah? You wanted Parratt and Yarker to question your sanity?"

"They can do that, I don't care. I know I have your vote no matter what."

Ryske didn't disguise his disgusted amusement. "What happened to make you think you have my loyalty?"

Hagan's arrogance repulsed her. "That woman, your woman, has been in my house for a week. Trapped. In need. And you didn't have a goddamn clue." Slipping something from his pocket, he tossed it onto the couch when he stood behind the furthest arm of it. "You come for me again and I won't release her next time. I can get to her. Both of you can deny it, but I know that means something. I've seen what you'll do for each other. To hurt you, all I have to do is hurt her."

"You motherfucker," Ryske spat and started toward Hagan.

Thinking quickly, Harlow grabbed for his wrist and pulled him back. Rushing around to get in front of him, she pressed her back into Ryske's torso. "No," she said. "That's what he wants. If you hurt him, he'll have his own evidence to present to Parratt and Yarker."

"Listen to your woman," Hagan said, starting for the door. "She's a smart one… way out of your league."

The smug smile and swagger that accompanied Hagan's words seared her, Harlow wasn't sure she'd ever felt such potent anger. "Go to hell, you bastard."

"I'll tell the men you say goodbye, shall I?" he asked.

"They will miss watching you shower and dress every day…"

Stunned, Harlow couldn't believe he'd been spying on her all this time. There was no need for anyone to watch her in the bathroom, she didn't have access to anything that could hurt anyone. He'd done it, or let his men do it, for the sheer hell of it, much like why he'd had Ryske stabbed.

"You fuck…" Ryske hissed, but she used all her strength to push against his body, holding him back.

Hagan laughed and departed, letting the door swing shut under its own weight.

The moment it was closed, Ryske grabbed her shoulders and spun her around to face him. "Crash," she murmured, grabbing for him.

"Did he hurt you?" he asked, checking her face, pushing her hair away to run his hands over her head and neck, then down her body.

There was something frantic about his touch, like he was just desperate to know she was in one piece.

"I'm okay," she said, trying to slip her hands onto his cheeks, but he took her wrists in turn to squeeze the length of her arms with his strong grip, still checking for injuries. "Oh, Ryske, I'm sorry. I'm so sorry, baby."

"No," he said, snatching her to him, holding her, squeezing her body tight. "I'm sorry. That fucker… He's right, we didn't even know—"

"Not that," she said, putting her hands to his chest to force some space between them.

"Whatever he did to you or had his men do, I—"

"I'm sorry, Crash," she said, trying to see through the tears that were blurring her eyes. "I'm so sorry for what I said, for how I made you feel. I… I don't feel that way. I know what kind of man you are. I know you wouldn't—"

"Shh," he said and flashed her a dazzling smile. Damn, he was good, he could switch it on, just like that. "It's forgotten. No idea what you're talking about." After a wink, his smile was gone. "Are you hurt?"

"We need to get out of here, Crash."

Nodding, he pushed her hair from her cheeks with both hands. "Okay, yes."

Ryske grabbed for her hand, probably to lead her out. Except Harlow didn't move with him when he tried to head for the door. In answer to his confusion, she scooped her free hand around the back of his neck, and pulled him down, seeking his kiss.

In the first moment of surprise, he was hesitant, making it obvious that he hadn't been expecting her to do something so intimate. Maybe it was the situation or the environment. She'd guess he was still in work mode, maybe in Ophelia mode, but that wasn't going to stop her from showing him how she felt or taking what she wanted.

What had happened this week had proved that anything, even the most unthinkable scenario, could happen at any moment. Harlow didn't want to be separated from him again and didn't want there to be question marks between them.

"That was nice," he said when she broke their kiss.

Nice. Hmm. Sounded like he meant it. But he was dubious, and she couldn't blame him given all the mixed signals she'd sent him. From the early days, she'd wanted him, physically reacted to him, but she'd pushed him away and made demands as soon as he tried to return the favor.

"I don't want any promises, Crash," she murmured, splaying her hand on his chest to nestle herself closer. "None except that you'll come home with me tonight."

"Hmm," he said and cleared his throat. "I guess whatever's in the water at Hagan's place works for me." Using his body to push her back, he peeked down his nose at her. "Are you drunk?" Grinning, she shook her head. "Well, baby, much as I'd love to take you up on that, I won't be going to your place tonight."

It hadn't even occurred to her that he might reject her. Yeah, maybe it had been arrogance, or naivety, but she'd really believed he wanted her and that he'd follow through.

"But I…"

"Come on," he said, taking her hand again to turn her around.

In a quick maneuver, he swiped something off the couch, presumably whatever Hagan had tossed there, and then led her out of the room. They didn't go back through the ballroom, they took a different route and ended up in a side alleyway where he presented a motorcycle.

Taking the helmet from the handlebar, he offered it to her. Harlow just blinked. "I… I can't go on that. I'm in a maxi dress."

Scanning her figure, he nodded. "I'm not sure what that is, but you look hot."

"Crash—"

"Lift it up," he said, tossing a leg over the bike. "Come on. It's just a quick trip."

Quicker than it would be in a nice, safe, comfortable car. Mumbling to herself about how crazy this was, Harlow pushed her hair back and pulled on the helmet. Ryske took off his jacket and swept it around her, helping her arms into the sleeves before gathering her skirt and helping her to bunch it up. Using him for balance, she climbed on, and squashed the skirt of her dress between them.

Wrapping her arms tight around him, she tried to see the positive that she was getting to hold Ryske again.

His changing his mind about being intimate with her could spell the end of their friendship. It couldn't last if she'd made the decision to go all in with him and all he wanted to do was fold and walk away.

Ryske got the bike going and she clung to him tighter as they whizzed through the streets. Hagan thought she was important, Ryske was putting up barriers, and Harlow was confused.

But she was safe and free, two things she wouldn't take for granted ever again.

TWENTY-THREE

FLOYD'S WAS THEIR destination.

Harlow wasn't surprised to find herself in the alley behind the bar after Ryske parked and helped her off the bike. He took her helmet from her hand and then laced their fingers together. She was still smoothing her hair when he led her around the side of the building, in the opposite direction to the one Noon had taken her. They went into a narrow alley that had a wall at the end. About halfway down, he stopped to unlock a side door and pushed her inside.

In a dark stairwell, her eyes needed a second to adjust to the lack of light before they noticed an internal door opposite them. As Harlow started toward it, Ryske took her waist and swung her left to face the stairs.

"Up," he said.

"Up?"

She hadn't expected the redirection but did as told and climbed the stairs. At the top was another door. Ryske came up behind her and leaned past her to open it. Harlow wasn't sure what she was expecting the upstairs of Floyd's to look like, so she just waited for it to be revealed.

Walking in to an open plan apartment, a very open plan, very large apartment, she discovered the crew's home.

There was a kitchen in the furthest left corner, that would be above the den she'd found Felipe in the last time she was here. A spiral staircase with a wrought iron banister led down from the far side of the kitchen. Doing her best to recall the downstairs layout, she guessed those stairs would lead to the curtain Ryske had appeared from in the den.

Next to the kitchen were the only walls in the place, other than those around the stairwell she and Ryske had just come from. They divided off what had to be two rooms because there were two doors.

She didn't dwell on what could be behind those doors after concluding they wouldn't be concealing bedrooms. Apparently, privacy was a myth to these men. Four double beds were on display in this space, two flanking either side of the stairwell she'd just emerged from. Around each bed were rails with curtains hanging on them, but all of the curtains were pulled back open.

Still taking in the details, she wanted to know where Ryske called home. In front of the kitchen, parallel to the substantial breakfast bar, was a long dining table where the crew must eat their meals. There were couches and arm chairs between that and the two beds to the left. To the other side, was a gym that contained a couple of machines, fully stocked weights racks and benches.

Yeah, this was a guys' pad.

"You live here?" she asked, though that was kind of obvious.

"We all do," he replied, pushing her deeper into the apartment. "Do you want something to drink?"

"No," she said, scrutinizing the place as he crossed it to go into the kitchen. "Shouldn't you tell someone you're back?"

"One of the guys will be around soon. They're always in and out."

No wonder it had been so easy for her to fall off their radar; they didn't worry much about each other's radars either.

"I should call work," she said and slipped her feet out of her shoes. Though the office would be closed, there were emergency numbers, and voicemail where she could leave a message. "Do you have a phone around here?"

Ryske was on the other side of the wide kitchen breakfast bar that separated the kitchen from the dining area. "He had you all week?"

She wasn't sure if he'd ignored her question because he didn't want to answer it or if he just hadn't heard her. Whatever the reason, she wasn't in the mood to argue.

"Yes," she said and pointed at the couch. "Can I sit down?"

As always, he was so laid back he was almost horizontal. "Do whatever the hell you want, Trink," he said, going to the sink to fill two glasses with water. "Let me check a few things out before you call anyone."

The sink was under the window in the counter that attached to the perpendicular breakfast bar. In the center of the kitchen was a small square island. Another long countertop ran along the opposite wall. At the end of that was the fridge, which stood flanking the opening to the kitchen across from the end of the breakfast bar.

Casting his jacket from her shoulders, Harlow sank onto the couch. "Why? What do you need to check out?"

Ryske came toward her. "If you've been missing all week and no one reported it, we have to figure out why."

He stopped in front of her to offer her a glass of water. "Gina wouldn't be in cahoots with…"

The words trailed off as her fingers touched the cool glass.

"What?"

Squinting, she tried to recall how things had played out. "I don't know, I… I went there on Monday because she told me to go. I thought it was a regular client meeting. But I… Hagan said he'd arranged with her for me to have the whole afternoon, which I thought was odd."

"It is," he said, sitting at her side after she took the glass from him. "He donates a bunch of money to different causes. Maybe your department is one of them."

"Maybe," she murmured, drifting on her ideas of the possibilities.

Just being free again was a relief. It had only been a

week, but already liberation felt like an adjustment. One thing had been so prominent in her thoughts during her captivity: Ryske. This was what she'd wanted… to be alone with Ryske again.

His attitude was almost professional, which couldn't be further from where her mind was in that minute. "Talk me through what happened," he said. "I'm gonna do whatever it takes to make this right."

"Talk…" she said and leaned forward to put her glass on the coffee table.

Twisting toward him, Harlow didn't say anything else. He'd told her once that conversation was a distraction. But she wasn't distracted anymore.

Loosening his tie, she tossed it aside, and began to unbutton his shirt. Harlow was not going to waste this chance.

"Baby, we don't—"

"I don't want to talk, Ryske," she said and pushed him against the back of the couch to climb onto his lap.

"Trink…"

Nuzzling his mouth, she took from him the kiss that she craved, and then demanded another. While their lips tasted and spoiled each other, she finished unbuttoning his shirt and pulled the tails from his pants so she could force the fabric from his shoulders.

"All I kept thinking about was that moment you walked away from me," she whispered. Exposing his torso, she dug her nails into his tats, shoulder and abs. "I don't want to play it safe anymore. Make me dangerous, Ryske."

Searching her gaze, he caught her hair with the back of his hand and wrist, sweeping it off his chest. "What did they do to you, Trink? Huh?"

With a shake of her head, she kissed him again. "I don't want to talk about that."

Arching her back meant breaking the kiss, but she had to straighten up to loosen the zipper beneath her arm.

"Baby, we don't—" He stopped talking when the click of zipper teeth opening crackled through the air. "Are you gonna take that off?" Slouching, he locked his fingers together behind his head. "I'll quit interrupting. Keep going."

Wearing a smile, she finished unzipping and gathered the dress up to take it off over her head. His eyes flared, fascinated by the sight of her figure. Even just in her underwear, Harlow didn't feel self-conscious, somehow he made her proud of her body.

Leaning forward, she tossed the dress over the back of the couch and tried to kiss him again. But he grabbed her waist and held her back, savoring the full view of her bared body. His grip tightened as his feral eyes traveled down and up, inspecting every inch of her.

"It's a damn shame you like it rough, baby. Your skin is like butter," he said, skimming a hand to the center of her torso and up to her cleavage.

Bowing forward, she rested her head against his. "It doesn't bruise easily," she whispered. "Take what you want, Crash. Take it from me."

A breath of silence passed. The thump of her heart shook within her chest. Invigorated and enthralled, she was consumed by a massive sense of exhilarating anticipation. This was going to happen. Harlow didn't have a damn clue what *this* was, but whatever it was... she was in it. Choosing to embrace a life that involved Ryske was going to be an adventure.

In a snap of movement, Ryske snatched her thighs and scooped her up to flip her onto her back on the couch without letting his body lose contact with hers. The press of him between her thighs made her groan as he slithered south, his lips tasting every new quivering corner they met.

"Promise me this minute, Crash," she sighed, arching her body into his mouth that was sampling her neck and descending to her upper chest. "Promise me the present."

Kissing the generous mounds of her breasts, he sent heat cascading through her. Harlow wanted this. She wanted more. Instinct made her knees bend. She pulled her legs high, sliding the soles of her feet around his hips. Tucking her toes into the waistband of his pants, she tried to push them down, but his belt frustrated her efforts.

"Mmm," he said in a show of approval. "You're flexible, baby."

Pilates was the reason for that. Explaining her workout routine was the last thing on her mind. "Take your pants off."

"Love a woman who knows what she wants."

His hand closed over her breast. Just the notion of his grip made her whimper for more. Harlow wanted his hands everywhere, wanted his forceful touch, wanted him to demand what he wanted from her.

That whimper just so happened to seep out of her in the same moment a rabble of voices rose from the direction of the kitchen.

The couch they were on was perpendicular to the dining table. Armchairs stood parallel to the dining table, and they would probably block the view of them from whoever was coming from the spiral stairs. But Harlow didn't care about being seen, she was too caught up in wriggling beneath Ryske and trying to squeeze her toes deeper under his belt to force his pants down his hips.

"Whoa, hey," one voice rose above the others. Maze. "Do you have a... does he have a... We have rules about women up here, asshole."

Ryske seemed to be tempering himself when he stopped kissing her. His eyes rose to the top of their sockets like he was counting to ten.

Harlow didn't want to let him go, and made that clear by resisting when he tried to pry her legs from around him. She whimpered and clenched. Strengthening his grip, Ryske pulled harder. But she didn't want to lose. This battle boosted her want. His strength, his power, it was what she wanted to feel.

Her mouth opened in a silent yowl of arousal that encouraged Ryske's intensity to keep fighting for control. Overpowering her, he won the battle and freed himself from the circle of her legs.

Laying an arm along the top of the couch, he held himself above her, taking a moment to admire and adore her laid out beneath him.

"Baby," she whispered, throwing a hand to his abdomen when he twisted around to look back at his colleagues.

Because they were in the kitchen and she was blocked by furniture, Harlow still hadn't seen them. But with Ryske caressing one of her legs, her thoughts stayed on the carnal.

"Kinda entertaining here, guys," Ryske said.

Harlow was impressed that he managed to sass. No, she was impressed that he'd managed to say anything at all. Her mind was too fuddled to think about forming sentences. Life got better when Ryske shifted onto his knees. Still twisted to look over his shoulder at his crew, he didn't notice her fingers moving towards his zipper.

"Uh, I don't fucking think so," Maze said. "Take her downstairs."

"Thought you were working tonight," Noon said.

The sound of someone socking someone else carried to her ears. "And if he's working her, you just screwed it up," Maze said.

"He wouldn't bring a woman he's working back here."

Seemed like maybe it was just Noon and Maze. Dover was probably still working downstairs. Didn't bother her, Harlow was happy loosening Ryske's pants.

"He knows better than to bring any woman back here," Maze said, without disguising the displeasure in his voice. "Least he should know better. Get her out of here, Ryske."

Rubbing her hand over the bulge she'd exposed, she bit her lip. "Can I take it out?" Harlow whispered, wondering how Ryske felt about public exposure. If he was successful in getting rid of the guys, she wanted to get right back to where they'd been heading. "I want to play, Crash."

She tried to slip her hand into his underwear. Ryske intercepted it to link their fingers together, doing the same with the other when she switched, giving him control of both her hands. Twisting and pulling did nothing but make her smile. Ryske was strong and he wasn't giving in.

"Guess, on the bright side, this means he's over Nightingale, right?" Noon said. "Isn't that what we've been telling him to do all week? Get over it or go get her."

"Do you think a random fuck is really the answer?" Maze asked. "What if that broad he's got on the couch is a crazy psycho? She's in our damn living room."

"Oh, she's crazy for sure," Ryske said.

Succeeding in wriggling a finger free of Ryske's control, the first thing Harlow did was respond to that gibe by poking her fingernail into one of the points on his abdominal tattoo.

"Then what's she doing in our living room?" Noon asked.

"Fucking our friend apparently," Maze said. "You didn't pay for it, did you? 'Cause, man, that's not the answer. It won't bring Nightingale back to you."

"Nightingale isn't as pure as you think," Ryske said, earning himself another prod.

Just that night, she'd been accused of being a hooker. And she had technically gone on a date with one man, and come home with his enemy. But that didn't make her impure… not exactly.

Having fun after a week of captivity felt overdue. The light, happy sensation couldn't last. Her attention snagged on the scar forming above Ryske's hip and her smile slipped.

That was where he'd been stabbed. His grip on her must have loosened because when she shook her hand, it was freed from his. Her fingertips grazed the scar as she thought about the night they'd met and how close she'd come to losing him.

"We need a report," Maze said. "Tell the girl to get lost. Dover's on his way up."

"She's not easy to get rid of," Ryske said.

He probably expected another fingernail stab, but she didn't want to hurt him. Adrift, reflecting on their past, she was only half listening anyway. Sex would be fantastic and it was what she wanted. But this was a chance at something else she'd wanted too. Answers were right there in that room. All she had to do was ask. Even if it took some cajoling, the worst they could do was say no. Harlow had to try.

Sitting up, she kissed Ryske's torso and gave him a push while untucking her leg from between him and the back of the couch. "We should tell them what happened," she murmured and stood up to stretch.

With her fingers interlinked, she straightened her arms and turned her palms toward the ceiling. "Hey, guys," she said, offering a finger wave when she released the tension of her body.

Noon and Maze were on the other side of the breakfast bar. Their expressions of impatience had given way to surprise.

Neither of the men spoke and she feared she'd somehow offended them. "What's wrong with them?" she asked Ryske while watching the two men in the kitchen.

"You're giving 'em a show, Trink," Ryske said, adjusting his slacks as he moved to sit on the edge of the couch. "You're almost naked, babe."

She hadn't been thinking about her apparel. But when she looked down at the pink plunge bra and thong she was wearing, she remembered the dress she'd tossed away. Blowing out disbelief, Harlow bent to retrieve Ryske's shirt from the floor.

Slipping her arms into the sleeves, she only did a couple of buttons up over her breasts. "They don't care about that," she said, climbing onto the couch, tucking her toes beneath Ryske's thigh and letting her bent knees rest across his lap.

Ryske slid an arm around her. "They're guys," he said, pushing her hair away from her shoulder to kiss the side of her neck. "They care."

"They must have seen a zillion women more naked than that," she said, tracing her index fingernail around his shoulder tattoo. "And I'm Nightingale. They don't think of me like… that."

Again, Ryske laughed. The men seemed amused too. Both were walking from the kitchen to the living room. "We debated putting a pillow on his face at Bale's, just to see which of us would be your second choice," Maze said, dropping into one of the armchairs that had its back to the dining table.

"So…" Noon said, waving a finger between them, and seating himself in the armchair next to Maze's. "Are you two like… a thing now?"

"Please," Maze said. "They've been a thing since the moment he crashed into her."

TWENTY-FOUR

HARLOW WAS SURE they were just teasing about the second choice thing, and she couldn't deny that there had been a spark between her and Ryske from the very beginning. Maze wasn't wrong about that. But what she and Ryske were was still ambiguous. They hadn't put language to it yet.

While she might have decided to drop the barriers she'd built between them, she hadn't really figured out what she wanted them to be, or what they could be.

"Fun as it would be to debate what Trink and I are," Ryske said, laying his hand on hers to flatten it on his chest, stalling her nails in their tracks. "We have bigger things to deal with."

"Like what?" Noon asked.

Maze sighed. "Guess tonight didn't go well. What's the report?"

Ryske shrugged. "Went exactly like we thought it would." He side-nodded toward her. "'Cept this one showed up. Ophelia played to having the competition around. And, Trink, man, she's a fucking natural in the field."

The pair in armchairs aimed their focus on her. "Why were you there?" Maze asked. "Work? Did you know Ryske would be there?"

"I knew he would be there," she said and licked her lips. "Well, I hoped he'd be there… It had been kind of implied to me that he would be." Harlow was aware that she wasn't making much sense. Telling them everything, and putting it in context, was more difficult than she'd realized it would be, which gave her more respect for why the crew weren't forthcoming with her. "Ryske wasn't why I was there… I… I didn't really have a choice."

"Hagan has been holding her since Monday," Ryske explained.

That surprised both Maze and Noon. Seeing their shock gave her confirmation that they hadn't known about her predicament. They'd been unaware; it wasn't that they just hadn't cared enough to do anything about it.

"What the fuck?" Maze said, shooting to his feet. "We've got to take that bastard down. That's two of ours he's come for!"

"Sounds like I'm missing one helluva party," Dover said.

Twisting to look over the back of the couch, Harlow saw him coming through the stairwell door she and Ryske had used. Crossing to them, he did a handshake thing with Ryske and then put a hand on the back of the couch to bow and kiss her cheek like he'd anticipated her presence.

"Hagan's been holding Nightingale," Noon said.

Dover paused on his way to the kitchen and turned to look at her for confirmation, so she nodded. "Did he hurt you?"

"Not physically," she said. "But the guy is an asshole."

"We could've told you that," Dover said and continued his walk into the kitchen where he opened the fridge.

"What are we going to do?" Maze asked.

"You're going to sit down," Dover said, closing the fridge to show he'd retrieved a beer. "And Nightingale is going to tell us exactly what happened."

Dover went to the dining table and sat in one of the chairs behind Noon and Maze. Her attention drifted to Ryske whose hand skimmed up her back and under her hair to give the back of her neck a squeeze.

"We're listening."

For some reason, she was nervous. Despite that, Harlow took a long, deep breath, and began telling her story, filling in as many details as she could about her week in Hagan's apartment. No one interrupted, they just listened, and for a time her words were the only sound in the air.

Ryske's hand had moved on her back once in a while, encouraging her on, reminding her that she wasn't alone. "Brash visited my room a few times. He liked to think he was taunting me and did get handsy," she said, stroking Ryske's chest when he tensed. "I don't think he really meant to do anything to me. I…" Her cheeks warmed at what she had to confess. To distract herself, she let her hand slip south on Ryske's torso to outline his ab tattoo with a fingernail. "I implied that I thought they were together."

"Who were together?" Maze asked.

"Brash and Hagan, I—"

The instant sound of masculine laughter cut her off. Ryske hooked an arm around her neck and pulled her forehead to his mouth.

"Bet he fucking loved that," Dover said.

Harlow shrugged. "I think getting close to me was Brash's way of trying to prove something. Like he thought I'd never question his sexuality again if he noticed my boobs enough."

"Sounds like he was trying too hard. I thought Animal was the one who took pleasure in pleasing Hagan," Ryske said. "Maybe I missed what the other goon felt."

"I was just teasing them," she said, patting Ryske.

Being this close to Ryske was enchanting. Having personal access to him was a gift and an honor. It was intimate to be this familiar with him and to be so accepted by his crew who seemed to view this situation as normal even though they'd never done it before. They'd hung out at her apartment plenty of times, but until that night, she'd never been in their home.

"You're good, Trink," Ryske said, kissing her head

again.

Something made her cup his jaw and turn to steal his mouth with her own. Maybe she just needed the comfort of his kiss, or maybe she wanted to remind him that he was allowed to do more than just kiss her hair. As proved by them writhing together on the couch earlier, he had access to more intimate parts of her.

Their eyes met after the kiss and without meaning to, she'd conveyed the latter message. His arm descended on her back until he was holding her hip and he pulled her closer, deeper onto his lap. Harlow moved her forehead to his, but he tipped his head back, rolling their mouths closer so they could kiss again.

"We figure out what changed there yet?" Dover asked.

Harlow was too interested in caressing Ryske and enjoying his kiss to worry about what Dover was saying. "Still refusing to come home with me?" she murmured, rubbing Ryske's chest. "Don't want it now I'm not putting up a fight?"

"Oh, I want it, baby," he said, his hand snaking under her shirt to cup her ass. "And I'm going to take it too."

That was poetry. A shiver joined her smile and she kissed him again, unable to restrain herself.

"She can't go home," Maze said.

That comment made her kiss slow.

"No," Dover said. "It's not safe."

"Not until we know why Hagan went after her."

Harlow broke the kiss and twisted to glare at the guys. "I can go home. I know why he came after me."

"Why?" all of them asked.

Touching her finger to the center of Ryske's chest, she made eye contact with each of the other men.

"Ryske?" Noon asked.

"Clyde," she said, curling her fingers until her fist was resting on Ryske's chest. "Hagan's man saw how this guy reacted to Clyde downstairs."

"And less then twenty-four hours later, he had you under lock and key," Dover said, thumping the side of his fist on the table. "Damnit."

"So that's why he was taunting me with you," Ryske said. "He wanted me to react."

She shrugged. "Guess he didn't bank on Ophelia distracting you."

Harlow hadn't asked about Anwen. She would. But she'd ask Ryske when they were alone, assuming that he'd give her a more honest answer without his crew scrutinizing him. Though, if she didn't feel she was getting the full truth, she would go to Dover or Maze. Noon would be a good source of information too, and he did tend to be more forthcoming. But he'd also be likely to tell Ryske she was prying.

"Distracting Ryske is Ophelia's favorite pastime," Maze muttered, but seemed to be contemplating something else.

All of the men were lost in their thoughts. Seeing them at work while not saying a word was odd. Each of them was making plans and trying to figure things out for themselves.

Turning her focus to Ryske, Harlow stroked his torso again and rested her face against his jaw. She hadn't told him about her conversation with Ophelia at the bar either, not just the Anwen bit, but the part where Ophelia had accused her of being in love with him. That same conversation had led Harlow to making some assumptions of her own about Ophelia's feelings.

It had been a long week and now that she was safe, exhaustion began to creep in. There were still so many unanswered questions, like what the million apiece was supposed to be for, and how Parratt and Yarker fitted into the equation.

"Are you going to call her?" Noon asked.

Ryske lost his hand in her hair, cupping the back of her skull. "Ophelia? Nah, not tonight. Tomorrow, maybe Monday."

"Always leave 'em wanting more," Noon said as though it was a line he and Ryske had used before, or maybe one Ryske had taught him.

That same sound of someone socking someone else made Harlow peek from the corner of her eye.

Noon was rubbing the back of his head, and Maze's hand was hovering just above it. "You think Ryske wants you saying shit like that in front of his girlfriend?"

"Is she his girlfriend?" Dover asked.

"What does that mean for the job?" Noon asked.

Three pairs of expectant eyes landed on her. Those were the ones she could see. At her side, she could feel expectation coming from Ryske too. These four men expected her to figure this out? Alone?

Harlow didn't know anything beyond her attraction and her feelings for the man at her side.

"I have no plans to steal Ryske away from you," she said, beginning to feel awkward enough about what they wanted from her that she pushed away from Ryske to climb onto her feet. "I'm going home… And I'm keeping your shirt." Going home in his shirt might seem to be an overstep, but she didn't want to put Hagan's dress back on. "Can someone loan me twenty bucks for a cab? I have literally nothing on me."

"Trinket," Ryske said, leaning forward to take her hand. She expected him to reassure her, to say something charming or soothing that would make her feel less self-conscious about their relationship or his friends' scrutiny of it. Instead, he used his matter of fact expression to shock her. "We're not gonna let you go home."

His thumb began to move on her knuckles, but she was too shocked by his words to let the caress settle her. Seeking the rest of the crew, she found the other three men were wearing the same resolute expressions.

"You… you're kidding, right?" Each shook their heads. Harlow snatched her hand away from Ryske to take a step back. "I came here because I trusted you… I told you what happened because I… I thought we were on the same side."

"We are," Ryske said.

Harlow shook her head. "You can't say that and then threaten to hold me prisoner."

"She can't go back to work either," Maze said. "Or contact anyone."

Ryske bent over to take his jacket from the floor, where it had fallen after she cast it off. He dipped his hand in his pocket to retrieve something that he then tossed to Maze.

"I'd guess he's planted something," Ryske said.

Maze turned the item over and over in his hands. Harlow gasped and pointed at him. "Oh my God, that's my phone! How did you—"

"Hagan left it on the couch," Ryske said. She recalled Hagan throwing something and leaving, then Ryske picking up that item as they'd departed. "We can't be sure it's secure, Maze will figure it out."

Her fists went to her hips. "Let me get this straight. You're keeping my phone and refusing to let me leave… that's exactly what Hagan did!"

Her outrage didn't affect any of the men's resolve. "Yeah, but you'll get sex here," Ryske said. "Incredible sex."

Her lips circled. She laughed and groaned at the same time. "Oh, ho, ho, I doubt that, buddy. I sure wouldn't hold my breath if I were you," she said, swatting his hand away when he tried to touch her thigh.

"Wow, it is like a real relationship," Noon said.

"He doesn't have to be the one who gives her sex, if it's only him she's pissed at," Maze said.

After winking at her, Maze's gaze moved to Ryske, who was probably glaring. Maze winked at him too and then laughed with Noon and Dover joining in a second later.

"Who should go first?" Dover asked.

"We could draw straws," Noon said.

"Rock, paper, scissors," Maze said.

The trio all shifted to bring their fists into a central position like they were really about to play. Ryske jumped in before they could. "Any of you even think about touching her, I'll castrate you then turn CI."

That was another laugh. Dover had said they'd been friends for a long time. Over the years, they'd got up to God only knew what. No doubt they had a lot of dirt on each other and the power to send the others to prison ten times over.

It might be a joke to them, but Harlow was less amused by their game given that they were threatening her.

"I don't know," she said, relaxing her hip and letting one hand fall to her side. Scanning the amused trio, she pretended to ponder her options. "I told Ryske I didn't want promises, which means, technically he can screw around as much as he likes… It can't be one rule for him and a different one for me. That means I'm still on the market, boys."

The three looked around at each other like they didn't quite know what to do. She was still pouting at them when Ryske snatched her wrist and yanked her down to his side.

Grabbing her chin, he pulled her face close to his. "I told you what I'd have done to that sap from your office if I'd been carrying a weapon," he growled.

Yes, Ryske said he'd have shot Clyde if he'd had a gun.

"So?" she said, trying to seem unimpressed though his tightening grip on her arm was making it difficult to concentrate. "You're not going to take down your own team."

His brows rose. "Test that theory," he hissed. "I won't let another man have you. Any man touches you, and I don't give a damn if he's on my crew or not, I'll slaughter him."

"You think I believe that?" she asked, tugging at his hand, trying to free her arm.

It was useless. He was too strong and damn, if she didn't find that hot. It was hard to hide her desire.

He leaned in closer, his teeth clenched. "Test me, Trinket."

But she wouldn't. Harlow wouldn't mess around with other members of his crew. That didn't mean it wasn't fun to play with him, fun to piss him off, and push his buttons.

Forcing his mouth over hers, he stifled her with his kiss. Though Harlow objected, she didn't really pull away. Eventually, he broke the kiss and dropped his hand, so she shoved away and leaped to her feet, wiping her mouth with the back of her hand.

Dover drew in a breath and blew it out. "And this is why we never had women on the team," he muttered.

"Until now," Maze said in the same tone.

Noon was the only one grinning. "This is gonna be fun!"

TWENTY-FIVE

RESIGNING HERSELF TO her fate, Harlow didn't argue when she was taken on a tour of the Floyd's apartment and discovered where the two doors led. One took her to what used to be the master suite. In its place was an extremely messy closet-office. Lined with dressers, rails of clothes and filing cabinets, there was a desk facing into the room under the window and on the opposite wall was a couch in front of the closets.

It didn't take a genius to figure out that it was the space where the crew dressed and where Dover did all of Floyd's paperwork.

The guys had a bed each in the main apartment space, hence the four double beds. Maze had asked her if she was tired, probably as a way to break the tension. Noon had started talking about the curtains that could be pulled around the beds, like this was some kind of hospital ward or something.

But she couldn't say she'd paid much attention. Harlow had explored the messy master, and then come out to storm through the second door into what turned out to be a huge bathroom. At least that room was clean…ish. There was a double vanity, large claw-footed tub, and a shower cubicle that contained only one shower head but was probably twice the size of a typical double-wide stall.

The pristine tile was beautiful and didn't match the state of the run down bar beneath the apartment, or the untidy living room it was attached to. Nothing was dirty, certainly not to the level of being noticeable, it just seemed disorganized. But, in that minute, she wasn't complaining.

The bathroom door didn't lock, it didn't even close properly. Harlow pushed it over as far as it would go and crossed to the vanity. Running her hands through her hair, she took a minute to look at her reflection and breathed out.

The makeup she'd put on earlier had faded. Her lips were still bright, but that was probably more about the kissing she'd done than the gloss she'd applied at Hagan's.

Bending over to splash water on her face, Harlow was pleased to be revitalized by the cool liquid. Nothing could wash away the melancholy of her life. This was it for her now. Harlow hadn't asked for any of this, but that didn't matter, she couldn't ignore it.

A sound made her peek over her shoulder. Ryske was coming in. He pushed the door into the frame, though it popped back out to hang open more than an inch. He didn't stop or go back to it, he came over, and sidled up behind her.

"Good?"

Harlow just rolled her eyes at his reflection and nodded at the toothbrushes. "Which is yours?"

Reaching over her, he plucked one from the cup behind the sink. She took it from him to begin brushing her teeth.

"You know why we're doing this," he said, sliding his hands onto her hips. Harlow pushed them away. "We want to protect you, Trink."

While she was brushing, she couldn't respond.

Finishing fast, Harlow had to bend over to spit and rinse out her mouth. His hands crept onto her hips again and he began to gather up the shirt that protected her body, so that when she stood up, her abdomen was exposed.

"Mm," he said, skimming one hand around to her bare stomach.

Massaging her there, he used the other hand to scoop

her hair away from her shoulder, giving him access to kiss and tease her neck.

Harlow tried to hold onto her anger, but her body was beginning to loosen. She had to grab control fast. Spinning to face him, she pressured his chest meaning to put space between them. Instead of taking the hint and backing off, Ryske got closer, coiling his arms around her to cup her ass and pull her to him.

"No," she said, pressing harder. "You can't do that. You can't come in here and kiss me like we're some established couple having a tiff. We are not an established couple; we're a very un-established couple."

But he didn't seem to hear her assertions. His eyes were heavy and his lips loose. "I could fuck you right here," he murmured, digging his fingers in deeper. "I want you so bad."

That was more expressive than the apathy she'd got from him on the couch. Except she couldn't let herself feel that expression; she had to use her senses and be strong about resisting his advances. If Harlow gave in, she'd never get her answers, or convey how unhappy she was with the restrictions he and his crew were putting on her.

"Tell me about Anwen."

Ryske's job involved him being able to absorb any development and go with it as though he'd expected it to happen.

This time. He failed.

Harlow wouldn't describe his expression as straight up shock. It was sort of a mixture of horror and outrage, while at the same time, subdued. Ryske knew he should be hiding his reaction; he just couldn't manage it.

He swallowed hard. Part of her did feel bad for cornering him like this. But the other part was determined to start making sense of this mess.

"Anwen is why he hates me," he mumbled.

"Explain it to me…" No response. "Crash?"

When he opened his mouth, no sound came out. His gaze flicked between her eyes and she recognized for the first time in her life what speechless looked like up close. Holding her silence, Harlow drew her lower lip into her mouth, hoping that he'd be honest with her, that he'd trust her.

"Fuck!" he exclaimed, making her jump. Shoving away, he marched the width of the room to stop by the bathtub. "That prick couldn't fucking resist."

Pacing the length of the bath, he ended up facing the wall in the space between the head of the tub and the shower stall. Placing both hands against the tile, he let his head droop between his straight arms.

Whoever this Anwen woman was, she meant something to him, or he felt something for her. There were so many possibilities, but one quickly came to the front of the pack.

"You love her," Harlow said, propping herself against the vanity.

"That what he told you?" he grumbled.

"Ophelia."

Another jab of shock. Spinning around, he locked his focus onto her. "Ophelia? How much time did you spend with her?"

"None," she said. "I met her for the first time tonight."

He took a step toward her. "What did she say?"

Harlow shook her head and a finger. "Oh, no, Crash, this is your turn. I'm asking the questions. Who was she?"

"Hagan's fiancé," he said and swallowed again.

This made him uncomfortable. Harlow couldn't say she was desperate to hear about Ryske being intimate with other women, but they needed this. To be together, they had to start getting past the raw attraction and focus on building trust.

Theirs would have to be deeper than most typical relationships because she'd have to hold onto her faith in them while watching him going out there to run cons. If Harlow couldn't believe that what he did for work meant nothing to him and that he'd always come home to her, this would never work.

"You slept with her." He nodded. "Why?"

"She was beautiful."

That honest, but basic answer, was a surprise. "That's it?" she asked. "It wasn't a job or a con, you just… had to have her?"

Concerned that it might have been stupid to embark on this conversation while they were in a fight about something else, Harlow hoped she hadn't made a mistake. Her being restricted from leaving Floyd's could cause a problem between them in itself without adding the tension of this on top.

Difficult as this might be for both of them, she'd put off getting answers too many times. Harlow had to listen to the uncomfortable truths. This was just the beginning; she doubted this was close to the last of the awkward revelations she'd have to hear. It would be good practice for her poker face.

"Hagan was running an auction," he said. "It was stupid. The money he raised was going to his newest property development, so it was going to him. It wasn't charity. The biggest donor was allowed to name the building that was in a prime position by the river next to the museum."

"When was this?"

"'Bout two years ago," he said, slipping his hands into his pockets. "We were tangled with these people and had donated a piece we needed to fence. It was a fake, but a good fake; gave us credibility in the crowd. Anyway…" Sucking in a long breath, he blew it out before continuing. "An associate of ours was interested in the sister lot and had a buyer on standby. The opportunity fell into our lap while we were in the middle of another job… it was a favor for a friend. We're not jewel thieves by nature. When we do get into that, we're more old-fashioned about it. You know, smash and grab… subtle, sophisticated smash and grab." He might have been making a joke but didn't crack a smile. "We had an investor at that event… a mark… Gil Parratt." The distorted-glass window by the shower was tall and skinny. It wasn't possible to see through it, but he looked that way anyway. "That was the night I met Anwen."

"Love at first sight?"

The first hint of a smile crept to his lips. Slow in its

ascent, it took its time to build, but by the time it was there, she couldn't doubt that the smile was one of nostalgia. "She glittered. It was impossible for men to take their eyes away from her. She was like… I don't know, it was like one of those Old Hollywood movies, you know? She sat there perched on the edge of her stool at the bar wearing this shiny dress, surrounded by guys who were clamoring for her attention."

"And you wanted to be the one who got it," she said, turning her back, but the broad mirror above the vanity made it impossible for her to get away from him. "I understand that competitiveness."

Her attention dropped to the sink. "Anwen pursued me," he said. Raising her head, Harlow landed her attention on his reflection that was a step closer than it had been before. "I saw her at the event, knew she was beautiful, but she wasn't part of the plan. I was there to network, keep my eye on the auction, leave with Parratt, charm him. I had to make myself seen at the after auction event, then get back to the auction hotel to do the switch of the sister piece for our buddy. Maze got me in, Noon got me out. Went like a dream."

"The switch?"

"The jewel our associate wanted, we had a fake for that too. It's always a good idea to leave the real deal on show for as long as possible. The event was over. Everyone had gone home. The piece would've been packed for shipping the next day. No one who does the packing is expecting a fake, probably wouldn't know the real deal if it bit them on the ass. So the piece is packed, goes on its way, and no one can prove when the switch was made."

She didn't want a lesson on how to commit theft. "And Anwen…"

"She was outside," he said. "Job was done. I got out. Noon was an alley over waiting. I was on my way out, my way home. I walked out of the hotel into the service alley on my way to meet Noon and ended up face to face with Anwen. She'd had some fight with Hagan and was pissed as all get out. She remembered me from the auction. I just wanted to get the hell out of there. Comforting angry women isn't my forte."

Already, Harlow could tell where this was going. "I

don't think there's anything that isn't your forte when it comes to women."

He didn't grace her comment with a reaction. "I had to get out of there, fast… so I did what I know."

"You slept with her."

Ryske raised his brows. "I fucked her," he said, adamant about the difference. "She wanted payback 'cause she thought Hagan was messing around on her. She said she was sick of his attitude. I don't know. I was only half listening, and had Noon yapping in my ear about what the hell was causing the delay. Maze was with him, tapped into security. They knew I was out of the building…"

"But you didn't make it to the getaway car."

"I made it," he said. "I was just delayed."

Because he was waylaid by Anwen… and having sex with her. The story was dubious. "That was her pursuit? She was crying in an alley, so you had sex with her? That's hardly a grand chase."

"No, that wasn't it. The pursuit came after," he said. "Far as I was concerned, that night was it. I didn't need to see her again. I'll be honest, I didn't even think about her again. In that alley, I thought on my feet, that's what I do."

"And if that involves sex, that's a bonus," she said, without meaning to sound so snide.

It wasn't fair to be sarcastic when he was being honest. Ryske had a past, and so did she. Neither of them were virgins. Harlow's contempt wasn't judgment, she was smart enough to recognize that her response was rooted in jealousy. Her life had never been one of abandon like that where she'd have sex in an alleyway just because the moment called for it.

Her life had been void of anything even close to adventure. Danger was a word used in books and movies. She'd never taken a risk in her life. Not a real one. Ryske and his crew were daring, living on the edge. In her studies, she'd read countless stories about people whose lives were cut short by prison or death because they chose that life.

But it was attractive, alluring, exciting, interesting, all of the things her life hadn't been.

The story wasn't finished, so he kept going. "I'd met

Ophelia before then. She didn't know me like she does now, but she'd been my in to the auction. She believed I was the quiet, rich entrepreneur I wanted her to believe I was."

"You seduced her first."

"No," he said, coming closer still, but staying out of reach, which she was grateful for. "We flirted. We've always flirted. But things get messy fast when you mix business and pleasure. I didn't need to screw anyone but the mark for that job… least not in the original plan. Ophelia was a business contact. To get close to Parratt, I needed a way into that circle. Ophelia was it. I gave her some advice to help her in her role with Hagan, one she doesn't have any more, but at the time, she was trying to make a name for herself in the company. I coached her, we flirted. Yeah, the relationship was fun, but that was it."

To him maybe, Ophelia had thought it was something more, or could've been something more. "How did Ophelia find out about you and Anwen?"

"They were best friends. Maze set up a digital answering service for us years ago. Means we can change the number any time and never have to answer calls. None of us carry phones. People want to talk to us, they leave messages, and we get back to them, ignore them, take action, whatever… Anwen got the number from Ophelia's phone, that call was a goddamn surprise, let me tell you… Anwen wanted a replay. At first, we ignored it. But Anwen called and called and called. Maze was about to change the number when Anwen left a message saying she was going to tell Hagan what had happened. She'd already told Ophelia. Shit was falling apart."

"So you had to see her again?"

He nodded. "To let her down gently, to tell her I didn't want trouble with Hagan, I didn't… Then I got there and…"

"You couldn't contain yourself."

He'd already said she was beautiful. It wouldn't have been easy to refuse the advances of any woman determined to have him. But if Anwen was as perfect as he'd implied, he wouldn't have put up much of a fight.

Harlow pictured him meeting Anwen in a hotel room

somewhere, walking in to find the beauty in some silky negligee, begging him to satisfy her. Ryske wasn't picky, as demonstrated by his early lust for her.

The only time Harlow had worn negligee she'd felt like an idiot. Rupert had bought some Victoria's Secret apparel and she'd tried it on. It looked fine, was softer than air. The trouble was, she didn't feel delicate and wasn't patient. Standing in front of Rupert while he "admired" her had just bored her.

"She threatened me," Ryske said, jarring Harlow out of her thoughts. "Said we had to keep going or she'd tell Hagan… I didn't want to be the guy who screwed other men's wives. We'd been working the con with Parratt since before the Hagan auction opportunity cropped up. Parratt was about to hand us more than half a million dollars. I couldn't risk that deal, we needed that money."

The reason he needed that money was interesting, but she could only pursue one line at a time. "So you… you and Anwen kept going? You had an affair with her."

"Yeah," he said. "For six months before he found out."

Stunned, her reaction was instant. "Six…" Spinning to face him, she expected some kind of contrition, but didn't find any. "How did he find out? Wasn't the point that he wasn't supposed to know?"

"The deal with Parratt was done by then. We had the money and I was out of their circle. Parratt never admitted we'd taken him for the half mill. Guess he was embarrassed. We strung him along for a while. Whenever I see him, I'm still convinced he thinks I'll come up with the goods."

"You told Hagan the truth?" she asked, wondering if the confession was his way of getting out of the affair.

Except, if they'd been sleeping together for six months, Ryske must have developed some kind of feelings for her.

"I didn't owe Hagan anything. That's always the way I feel if I'm in a married woman's bed, or an almost married woman's bed. I didn't make any pledge to their other half. But with women like that, women who would do that to their partner, I… there's always an element of…"

It was like he was searching for his meaning, but she got it. "Anger," she said. "Resentment. You can't understand why they would do that to someone they're supposed to love."

His head bobbed. Silence reigned for a few seconds. "Business, I understand, if everyone's on the same page. If it has a reason, a purpose, I get it. Sex is just sex; it can be just sex. But she was sleeping with me to hurt him, that's what it was about. Except… they would fight and he'd…"

Pushing the heels of her hands into the vanity, Harlow straightened. "Hit her? Did it get violent?"

"He'd have his men do it, Brash and Animal usually. Hagan doesn't like to get his hands dirty. So I understood her need to have control, to feel like she had some kind of control. When she was fucking me, she was trying to fuck out that hurt and her hatred for him, I get that."

"Why marry him?" she asked. "If she hated him so much, why was she still engaged to him?"

"Anwen came from nothing," he said. "Hagan has money. He was supporting her. Her parents were gone, she had no one. Her life was entwined with his, and if she even thought about leaving him… Let's just say, he's the kind of guy who holds a grudge. He'd never let her just walk away. He'd take it as a personal affront. She was stuck. She didn't have the power to get away from him. Even if she did, he had the power to pull her back every time."

"What happened when Hagan found out about you and Anwen?"

That answer was simple. Ryske looked her straight in the eye as he delivered it. "She killed herself."

TWENTY-SIX

THE END OF the story was so shocking and unexpected that her mouth fell open. After a stuttering moment of astonishment, Harlow pushed away from the vanity and went to him, wrapping her arms around his torso to hold him.

"I'm so sorry," she whispered. "Oh, Ryske, that's horrible. I'm so sorry… She committed suicide?"

He stroked a flat hand down her back over the length of her hair. "That's what Hagan will tell you."

Pushing away, she inspected his face. Did that mean… was he implying Hagan had hurt her… had Jarvis Hagan killed his own fiancée?

If Harlow needed any further proof that she was a terrible judge of character, she'd just got it. Harlow had deemed Hagan an asshole, but hadn't considered him dangerous. In one way, she was right, Ryske had said Hagan didn't do his own dirty work. But Hagan had the resources, and manpower, to end a person and he'd used them before, so he was definitely dangerous.

Ophelia had been right too. Such an experience would change a person.

Touching his face, Harlow wondered how Ryske had made it through such a difficult time. "If this was all two years ago, why are you still dealing with him?"

"After Anwen was gone, about eighteen months ago, we all went our separate ways. I thought that was it."

"Until?"

"Losing the half mill was embarrassing for Parratt, but he could afford to absorb the loss. Once he figured out the investment wasn't coming good, he'd said he wouldn't go to the cops on the proviso that when he needed something from me, I'd have to deliver. Helped that he couldn't prove anything illegal. He'd handed over the money and had no evidence I lied... But we let him say his piece, he wanted to save face after being taken for a ride. Sometimes pays when guys like him reach out."

Parratt had gotten him involved in this recent mess? Harlow wanted to know more. "Parratt reached out?"

"About six months after Anwen was gone, Parratt called in a favor and I had a chance to square things... I screwed that up..." She didn't understand how and he wasn't forthcoming. "The debt was still outstanding, but I didn't hear anything until a few months ago. Parratt left a message on the answering service. Maze has a program that checks the old numbers once in a while... He called in the chit."

Called in the chit, that had to be what the meeting tonight was about. Parratt was bringing Ryske into some deal. "Parratt called in a favor that's going to cost you a million dollars... where are you going to get a million dollars?"

One side of his mouth rose in a dashing smile that she recognized as the one he used on the con. "Cool mill is easy, babydoll."

Sometimes she lost herself in wondering how he could live such a capricious life. "How?"

Combing his fingers through her hair, he brushed it down the back of her shoulder. "We'll come up with it if we have to... might not be ours, but there will be numbers on the screen if there has to be."

Did that mean Maze would steal it or that he'd manufacture it? She didn't know, but it seemed the money wasn't the problem. "I don't understand. If this is about a deal with Parratt, what was the talk about Hagan competing and the gambling and—"

"Part of the reason Hagan wants in on the deal is because he's branching into less than... legitimate ventures. He bought a club. It's vital to this deal with Parratt, who needs... premises to make it work... That's what Hagan brings to the table. The premises.

"Don't think Hagan knew I was going to be involved until I showed up at one of their initial meetings. We hadn't seen each other since Anwen. I walked in there and I guess it all came back to him. We're a sort of consortium, you could say, everyone brings something to the table. Me, Hagan, Parratt, and Yarker... Ophelia was at that first meeting too."

"That's how you met with her again?"

He nodded. "She's responsible for Parratt getting me involved. She didn't say it, but I know her. Somewhere behind the scenes, I knew she was pulling some string somewhere... Like I said, she's not involved in Hagan's business anymore, not his legitimate business. This kinda shit gets her off."

Illegal shit, that's what he meant. Ophelia couldn't work with her brother in business, but she could in a crime syndicate.

"Parratt brought you in on this deal?" Harlow asked, wary of Parratt's motives. "Even though he knew what you did, that you conned him out of that investment money?"

"This new operation is a second chance to clean the slate. Couldn't say no to hearing them out... So we got together, me, Parratt, Yarker, and Hagan, who's been fuming about my involvement the whole time. This op is not small potatoes. Ponying up the money is a sign of our commitment." And Parratt would want a sign of that from Ryske in order to trust him. "Every man has his own responsibility in this op. Hagan provides the premises, but like you heard them say tonight, they need my... connections."

Speaking to Ryske was supposed to help her understand what was happening. There were serious layers to the operation and to the individual relationships.

Harlow understood that the Floyd's crew had scammed Parratt out of money. Ingratiating themselves with him had involved Ryske coaching Ophelia in business.

Ophelia had to believe there was some element of romance to their relationship as she'd taken him to her brother's auction.

Going to the auction had been twofold for them. They donated a fake item to give themselves credibility with Parratt, and stolen another item for an associate, whom she didn't know. While at the auction, Ryske had met Anwen. That had set in motion a series of events that she doubted he could've predicted. The affair, Anwen's suicide, Hagan's hatred.

If it wasn't for the debt he owed to Parratt, Ryske would probably have avoided Hagan forever. But Parratt needed Ryske's connections, and needed Hagan's premises, so the men were in business together. Given that Ryske had slept with Hagan's fiancée, it made sense that there was animosity. It even made sense that Ryske would dislike Hagan who had been violent with the woman he was supposed to love.

This wasn't over and she doubted that it would be any time soon.

With this new information, something else became clear. Ryske had sold her a bill of goods. This wasn't about any professional rivalry. The men were embroiled in the same operation, Parratt's operation, which she didn't yet understand. But it wasn't about Hagan's premises taking Floyd's business.

Figuring that out changed so much about her view of their previous conversations. "It was a lie… You, who always said you couldn't lie to me, lied to me… What you and the guys told me about Hagan trying to take Floyd's business, being in competition with you… it was a lie?"

He didn't admit it straight out, choosing instead to offer an explanation for what had happened the night they met. "I didn't want you involved in any of this, Trink… Parratt's operation, it's intriguing, and playing along will settle the score. We won't owe him anymore. Having Hagan involved makes it risky… Me and the guys knew Hagan was pissed about Anwen, and we have no friends in Parratt's operation, none except Ophelia who can turn on a dime. We had to figure out if this could be a trap… Playing at Hagan's place gave me a chance to see how far he'd go for payback.

Losing was a strategic move. Parratt knows I never lose…"

Frustration didn't begin to explain how she felt about how casual he was with his own safety. "You're impugning Hagan's credibility, that's what it was about? You got stabbed because you wanted to shame him?"

"I wasn't supposed to get stabbed. I didn't know he'd… that Anwen would make him…"

"You underestimated how much he hated you."

"I knew he was bitter at that first meeting… the night Parratt pitched the scheme to us. After Hagan saw me, it didn't even matter to him what the setup was, he wouldn't back down. As long as I was in, he was going to be in. Guess he sees this as his chance to get even with me…"

It was a hot mess and he was in deep. Harlow was tempted to ask Ryske to walk away from it all, but she doubted Hagan would give up even if he did. "You said Ophelia was your in at Hagan's club?"

"After the first consortium meeting was done, I was heading out. Ophelia intercepted me… we had a drink… reminisced."

"About Anwen?" While he raised a shoulder in a half shrug, she let her fingers caress his stubble. "Crash."

The whispered moniker was supposed to soothe him, but he moved out of her arms and turned away again. "Ophelia's relationship with Hagan was never the same after Anwen. She said she kept up appearances, but she has a lot of resentment toward him… That night, she asked me to ruin him, asked for my help."

And that's how Ophelia had become their inside man. Ophelia was feeding Ryske information about Hagan because she wanted to avenge her best friend.

After Parratt's failed investment, Ryske and Anwen's affair, and Ryske's sudden disappearance from their social scene, Ophelia must have figured out he wasn't what he'd originally presented himself to be. Or maybe Ryske had been honest with Anwen. Pillow talk could lead to all kinds of confessions. If the best friends had been close, Anwen might have revealed the truth to Ophelia.

Parratt knew it, and by association, Yarker and Hagan

did too. Of course, Hagan's beef was more personal than professional. In whatever way it had come out, all of the players knew Ryske wasn't any kind of benign, rich entrepreneur.

Imagining Ophelia's plea and how Ryske might have reacted to it, Harlow made an educated guess. "You said yes."

"She knows I have no love for the guy," he said, turning to face her again. "But I'm not interested in vendettas, that shit can ruin a guy."

So Ophelia hadn't recruited him to her cause, not all the way. "How did she take it when you told her that?"

"She wasn't happy, but said she wasn't going to give up trying to enlist me… Since then she's been a part of the meetings with her brother and the others. Somewhere along the way, she told Hagan we're sleeping together. Taunting him with me gives her some kind of satisfaction. He thinks we're dating, casual, fuck buddies, into each other, serious, I don't know. I let her run with it and don't correct his assumptions or contradict her in public."

Much like he didn't want others to do to him, made sense. Ryske followed the *'go with it'* attitude.

"Why lose? Why push him into hurting you?"

He inhaled. "Hagan's club, he calls it Windsor's… Anwen's last name was Windsor." Saying that seemed to give him reason to pause. Harlow didn't push and let Ryske decide when he was ready to continue. "Hagan started these poker nights, tournaments with unofficial stakes in the place he bought uptown."

"What does that mean?"

He licked his lips. "Anything can go on the table. If there's no money, favors can be traded, deals can be signed, businesses handed over, cars, homes, family, anything."

"Family?"

He laughed, probably at her shock. "Yeah. We're talking businessmen here, some have reputations for being good in specific areas. So a father may barter a son's services to negotiate a deal or to work with a competitor, that sort of thing. Basically, anything can be put on the table. As long as everyone else agrees, matches the bet or raises it, it is allowed."

"Anything," she muttered, wondering what would possess someone to take a risk on something they cared about.

"Sometimes it's just money, the nights usually start that way as a warm up. Later, the players want variety. These are men who like to keep things interesting and men with egos the size of the Pacific. Some go in with an agenda, others wait to strike vulnerabilities they find. When an opponent has a few drinks in them and the night grows stagnant, anyone can suggest or request anything… Sometimes they're taunted into it, other times, they really believe they're invincible, so they will put anything on the table."

"I would be terrified," she said.

Ryske shrugged, indicating he didn't think it was a big deal, or at least wasn't moved by it. "These men have this stuff to lose," he said. "They don't know fear like we do… or like I do. They don't know poverty and can afford to lose pretty much everything and still have the capital to start again. They go for the thrill, the excitement. They don't want a regular card game, there's no adrenaline in losing, even if it's millions. Put your daughter or your family's fifth generation corporation on the table? Those are real stakes."

"And you went to this Windsor's card game? What did you have to lose? How did you get in?"

"Ophelia," he said. "She likes to go and watch these guys bet the bank. Guess she has a bit of a sadistic streak. Nothing makes her happier than seeing a guy lose it all." He smiled. Though it was tighter than the smile he'd worn for Anwen, Harlow got the sense that he enjoyed Ophelia too. "I can identify with that."

"They let you bet money?"

He nodded. "I said I was there just to get a feel for it… if it's going to be a part of the consortium op, I need to know it'll hold up… Hagan didn't know I was there at first. I went in with Ophelia on my arm and sat at a table of strangers. 'Cause they thought I was a rookie, the players just assumed I wouldn't have the balls for it… I was up when Hagan discovered I was there… he doesn't usually play. That night. He did."

Despite him saying vendettas could ruin a man, Ryske

had got into a pissing contest, which had gotten him stabbed. "Because you were there. Hagan played because you were there."

"Probably."

Heading back to the vanity, she thought about the night and tried to put the pieces together. Ryske had gone to Windsor's with the intention of getting into Hagan's head.

Having Ophelia as his date, the sister of the club's owner, meant no one would question his presence. Ophelia probably fawned over him all night, irritating the bejeezus out of Hagan after he sat at the table. Everything had gone to plan. Though, it was still a crazy plan, given that it had gotten him stabbed.

"But you lost," she said, folding her arms when she turned to prop herself on the vanity again. "You said that was part of the plan. Why would you want to lose to—"

"Losing to Hagan is about pushing him to his limit. If he loses his shit, we know how reliable he is as a business partner. So far, he's not doing a great job of putting the past behind him."

"You want to discredit him in front of Parratt," she said and he swept a hand toward her like she was right. "But… doesn't losing to him make you look unreliable? If you can't come up with ten grand…"

"Not having ten grand in my back pocket is not the same thing as not having it," he said. "I could've put my hands on it. The idea was to be cocky, smug… glib, disrespectful…"

"You wanted to provoke him," she said. "And he took the bait."

"Always does."

Shaking her head, she felt almost maternal in reaching a conclusion. "You play, take your risks… It's all one big game," she said. "You didn't bank on getting a knife in your gut, did you?"

"I'd say that's what I get for sleeping with the man's fiancée," he said. "He has a lot of pent up anger toward me. We knew it. We just didn't know it was homicidal anger until that moment."

Provoking Hagan wasn't only about checking how

reliable he was as a business partner. Sure, Ryske wanted to put eyes on the club that was going to be part of this consortium op. But Harlow had a feeling Ryske had some pent up anger of his own too.

Whatever his feelings for Anwen, for months, he'd had to listen to tales of her suffering at the hands of Hagan's men, on her fiancé's orders. Then he'd have learned she had killed herself. That wasn't something anyone just got over. Maybe he hadn't admitted it to his crew, or even to himself, but she'd guess Ryske wanted to lash out and hurt Hagan for hurting someone he cared about.

He couldn't have been expecting a potential mortal injury though, that had to be why he'd gone on his own. Ryske was an imp, mischievous and often cocky. He'd have told the guys he was taking Ophelia out to Windsor's and probably expected to have a good time taunting Hagan rather than ending the night bleeding out.

"Hagan did that in front of people?"

"No," he said, scoffing out a laugh. "He didn't do it at all. He took me into another room with Brash and Animal. We got into it. I got to see first-hand what Anwen talked about. Hagan didn't throw any punches, he ordered Animal to do it. We were fighting when Brash came in under Animal's arm, that's when the knife went in… I didn't think it was a big deal, but I knew enough to get out of there."

Recalling what she'd learned in Bale's when Ryske was recuperating, pieces started to slide together. "You ran around all over the place before heading back to Floyd's."

"I was slowing down, getting dizzy. When my vision started to blur, that's when I knew something wasn't right."

"You're an idiot," she said, but didn't budge when he came up to her.

"Don't know about that," he said. "If I'd been with it, I'd have avoided running into the babe who walked in front of me. Usually I'm quite nimble."

Nimble or not, it would've taken some skill to avoid their collision, but she agreed that his physical state was what led to them making this connection. Whether he'd crashed into her or not, he'd have been able to recover and keep moving if he'd been at full strength. That stab wound brought them together.

He might be used to working by himself when he had to, but while Hagan was involved, Harlow didn't like the idea of Ryske not having backup.

"Someone should be with you when you're out there," she said.

"That an offer?"

An offer to be in the field with him? If he needed someone to watch his back, she would do it if no one else was available. Except Harlow wasn't a master criminal or secret ninja, so she didn't know how much help she'd be.

Whatever the future brought, she wanted a better look at the past to satisfy her curiosity. For weeks, she'd helped to care for his wound, and looking after him wasn't a habit easily broken.

"Can I look at it?" she asked. "Your scar?"

With a single nod, he inched back to let her crouch in front of him. Peeling back his pants, she revealed the injury that had brought them together. It had healed and was looking clean. She was pleased that Bale was so good at what he did because although there would always be a scar, there were no signs that it would cause Ryske long-term problems.

"Oh, shit, I should've known." Peeking around Ryske's leg, Harlow saw Maze in the bathroom doorway with Noon at his side. "Can you blow him in the closet? The rest of us need to use this room too."

They had been occupying the bathroom for a while, but they were talking, not… the other thing.

Ryske took her hand to help her up to her feet. "She can blow me any place she likes, any time she likes," he said.

Harlow slipped her hand out of Ryske's. "She's not blowing you anywhere any time," she said, and eyed each man again. "Are you ready to let me go home yet?"

All of them shook their heads.

"We're not that bad to live with," Noon said.

"Four guys? Four slobs? No, I'm sure it will be wonderful," she said, fastening another button on her shirt.

"You ready for bed?" Noon asked. "I can show you

the setup. Dover and Ryske are in opposite corners, Maze and me sleep on either side of the stairwell."

"Why are you telling her that?" Maze asked, crossing to the toilet that was in the corner beside the window. "So she can pick which of us she wants to bunk in with? You taking bets?"

"You'd all lose," she said, twisting to prop her hip on the vanity when it became clear Maze was going to pee whether the room was full of people or not.

In an apartment with three other guys and a bathroom door that didn't close, she guessed they lost their modesty quickly. This crew had grown up together since they were kids. It was no surprise they acted as brothers would.

"We would?" Ryske asked. "You're not sleeping downstairs."

"Don't trust me not to sneak out?" she asked, arching a brow.

"That and the bar is still open," he said. "You're not going downstairs to the den dressed like that. Guys from the bar wander in there all the time."

She cast a quick glance at herself in the mirror then blinked innocence at him. "I can take the shirt off if it pleases the crowd."

"Hilarious," he said, grabbing the back of her neck to push her toward the door.

Noon got out of the way in a hurry. Ryske angled her right and guided her across the apartment to the bed in the furthest corner. Thrusting her forward, he gave her no choice but to fall onto the bed. Although the shirt flew up to reveal her ass, she was quick to pull it down and flipped over to sit in the middle of the mattress.

"What the hell are you—"

"This is your bed," Ryske said and opened his arms. "Harlow Sweeting, meet the place you're going to sleep for the rest of your life."

"The rest of my life?" she asked, pushing her hair up off her face. "Do you think that it will take that long to get Hagan off my tail?"

Ryske didn't answer, just raised both brows and

turned his back on her. Dover wasn't in the room anymore, she guessed he'd gone back down to the bar. Maze and Noon were still in the bathroom. The door was open, as apparently it always was, but she and Ryske were alone.

Going to the kitchen, Ryske retrieved a fresh glass of water. After he brought it back to put it on the nightstand, he took off his pants and tossed them to the chair at the end of the bed.

"Move over."

"You are not getting in this bed," she said, pulling down the covers to tuck herself beneath them. "The jailor does not get to have sex with his prisoner."

"Oh, yes, he does," he said, sitting on the edge of the bed. "Perks of the job."

He reached for her, but she slapped his hand away. "Couch," she said, pointing past him.

Opening his mouth in a display of surprise, he blinked. "Are you for real? A half hour ago, you were all over me."

"A half hour ago I wasn't your captive," she said. "This is your job. You want to protect me? Great. But I'm not happy, Crash, and unhappy Harlow isn't horny."

A snort of a laugh came from the other side of the room. Maze was emerging from the bathroom. When he caught them glaring, he held up both hands. "Hey, I'm saying nothing... other than you sound like my parents."

Ryske sneered. "You're funny, funny guy. Let me work, we're getting busy over here."

Intrigued, Harlow wanted to ask more about Maze's parents. But when Ryske turned back to her, she cleared her curiosity and returned to frowning. "I'm serious, Ryske. You're not sleeping here. I gave up my bed to you for a week, now it's time to return the favor. I'll stay, I'm not going to make a big deal of it, but I am not happy with the way you guys handled this... Besides, it's not like we can have sex when we're sharing a room with three other guys."

Undeterred, Ryske startled her by leaning in until his mouth was within an inch of hers. "You'll get used to it, Trink. Because soon we're gonna be having a lot of it, right here," he said, bouncing his fist on the bed. "You're gonna love it and they're gonna hear every whimper."

Squashing his mouth to hers, he stole a kiss. Harlow shoved him away hard, but he just smirked and winked before leaving the bed and pulling the curtain across the end to block out the living room and kitchen. She could still see the bed next to hers and the back of the apartment. This was as close to privacy as they'd get.

Harlow had been ready to give herself to Ryske, but wasn't sure she'd be able to do it with an audience.

Maze had said women weren't allowed in the apartment, which made sense given it was so open plan. If any of the guys on the Floyd's crew wanted to entertain a girlfriend, it would be less complicated for them to go to wherever the woman lived. The rule would also reduce the chances of a female getting in their business and making it difficult for the crew to move around and talk like they had to when they were in the midst of a job.

Allowing Harlow to be present implied she was different.

Women weren't allowed there, but she was there. Not only was she there, but they were telling her she wasn't allowed to leave.

Any paperwork lying around, she'd be able to read. Conversations about a job? She'd be there to overhear them. Either these men trusted her immensely, or there was something else going on that she didn't see.

TWENTY-SEVEN

HARLOW WOKE UP relaxed and happier than she had for days.

But the noises she registered before opening her eyes took care of that ease fast. A TV was on. There was a sound like someone was humming or singing under their breath. She could hear water too. But it was the reverberation of coffee beans grinding that made her sit up.

Climbing out of bed, there was no point in being self-conscious about only wearing her panties and Ryske's shirt. She couldn't change; she had nothing else to wear.

Running her fingers through her wild hair that liked to do its own thing in the mornings, Harlow stretched. No doubt her cheeks were flushed and her eyes heavy, but the draw of coffee was too powerful to ignore.

Creeping around the curtain, she noticed the bathroom door was open. In the living room, the wall-mounted TV was on, but there was no one watching it. Dover and Noon were in the kitchen. The former seemed to be in charge of coffee as he was standing by the machine that was on the counter by the fridge, while the latter was at the island spreading something on toast.

"Morning," Dover said when she tiptoed up at his

side to peek at the coffee.

Harlow was so focused on the java that she almost missed him dipping to kiss her cheek. "Is it ready?"

"Couple more minutes," he said, showing his amusement with a half-smile. "Nightingale's a caffeine addict."

"Oh, you have no idea," she said and bent over, propping her elbows on the counter to watch the coffee drip through without even caring her panties were probably on show.

"Ryske is in the shower," Noon offered. Harlow just huffed and kept watching the coffee. "Maze is at work."

"Work?" she asked and straightened up to look at them. "Where does he work?"

Dover put an arm around her shoulders, so she slid hers around his waist. It was nice to have a broad, solid man to lean on before breakfast. "He does freelance tech support."

Rolling her eyes, she yawned. "How come when you guys tell me things, I always get the feeling you're not really saying what you're saying?"

"Because you're a smart girl, Nightingale," Dover said and bowed to kiss the top of her head.

She flashed him a smile. "You smell good in the morning."

Narrowing an eye on her, he feigned suspicion. "Hitting on me, babe?"

"Maybe after coffee," she said and pushed away to stretch again. "I'm going to wash my face. Call me when the coffee's ready."

Heading out of the kitchen, she swung a left and went into the bathroom. Even though the shower was on and occupied, the door didn't even pretend to be closed. The room was filled with steam. She'd guess Maze had been in too; Dover had sure smelled clean. This building had to have a great water tank to accommodate all the bodies that had to shower each day.

The mirror was fogged, but she leaned over the sink and used the arm of her shirt to wipe the mist away. Staying close, she checked her skin and picked out Ryske's toothbrush to brush her teeth again. She had just finished and bowed to splash water on her face when she heard the whistle.

Peeking over her shoulder, she spotted Ryske in the shower. He'd swiped away some of the mist from the glass, and was looking out at her. "Morning, beautiful."

"Good morning," she said, turning to the mirror again, tucking her hair behind both ears. "I came to get washed."

"Easiest to do that in here. I have water… and soap… and hands ready to lather you up…"

The man never missed an opportunity to make a move. "I'll lather myself when you're done."

"Doubling up saves water," he said. "You'll get the full package with me."

Harlow ignored him until the window he'd cleared of fog began to mist again. Guessing he'd gone back to his shower, she went for a quick pee and washed her hands.

In the shower, Ryske was muttering the words of a song she couldn't figure out. She'd never have pegged him as the type to sing in the shower. She couldn't remember him doing it at her place. Maybe this was a one off. Being trapped at Floyd's would give her the chance to find out personal, maybe intimate things about Ryske, and the rest of his crew.

Whatever was going on between them, they just couldn't seem to stop growing closer. Fate, or whatever higher power was screwing with them, seemed determined to keep Harlow in Ryske's path. The man had his own gravitational field and she was caught in it.

Not that Ryske was averse to having her around. If she hadn't put the brakes on the previous night, he'd have joined her in bed. The man was brazen, happy to take liberties with women, to make his interest known. There was no shame in him.

Wondering how often others matched his confidence or gave him a taste of his own medicine, Harlow thought it was time someone put him on the spot in return. Leaving the sink, she felt herself drawn closer to the oblivious man in the shower.

Hoping to take him by surprise, she turned on her

discerning eye, and slid back the shower door. Ryske whipped around fast, but he wasn't shocked to see her. A half-smile formed in time with the glow of a satisfied feral light in his gaze.

Lunging forward, he grabbed her wrist and yanked her into the water.

"Crash!" she shrieked.

Water cascaded through her hair and into her mouth, silencing her.

His fingers were already working on the buttons of her shirt while she sputtered the water from her lungs. "Oh, what a shame," he said without an ounce of sincerity. "Your shirt is wet, Trink. Let me help you with that."

He peeled it from her shoulders and lobbed the sopping lump of fabric into the far corner. She'd taken off her bra in bed last night, and he didn't waste any time cupping her breasts or bowing to kiss them.

"No," she said when he hooked his thumbs into her panties and bent to draw them down her legs. Though she'd objected, she held his shoulders for balance as he guided her feet out of them. "I don't like shower sex."

Throwing the panties up over the top of the shower stall, they landed somewhere in the bathroom far out of her reach.

"You haven't done it with the right guy," he said, taking her hips to back her up against the wall.

Ryske tried to find her mouth, but she tilted her head out of the way, so he settled for her neck instead. "I'm not doing it with you either. Showers are for washing, not for sex."

"I said I'd take care of that for you too," he said, grabbing a bottle of his shower gel to lather the soap between his hands, which he proceeded to run over her body.

"Ryske," she said, trying to sound unimpressed.

The amount of time he spent on her breasts and ass made her want to laugh. He was like a kid getting his first chance to play with the toy that had been wrapped under the tree and out of his reach for a month.

"Want to wash your hair too?"

As if to distract her, he thrust a bottle of shampoo

into her hands. It wasn't her usual brand; it wasn't a brand she recognized at all. Harlow was still reading the label when she noticed Ryske pouring more soap into his hands.

"Ryske," she said again because her body was more than clean.

Ryske didn't heed her tone, he just leaned in to kiss her and went on soaping her body. The length of his intimidating erection hung between them. Her gaze snagged on it when he returned to watching his hands run across her body. Harlow swallowed away her trepidation. If he tried to come anywhere near her with that in here, there would definitely be an accident.

Deciding to distract herself with the shampoo and to let him keep soaping her as it kept his hands busy, Harlow washed her hair and let the suds wash away. It only took a few minutes and she thought when the soapy foam was gone, they'd both be finished.

Ryske had other ideas and pinned her to the wall instead. "Now, let me show you how a real man does it," he mumbled in her ear and scooped her sopping hair out of the way to close his mouth around the curve of her neck where it met her shoulder.

Opening her hands on the wall that was holding her up, she didn't want to encourage him. "Shower sex is dangerous. With your luck, if you try it, you'll fall and crack your skull."

"Not this hard head, baby," he said, his hand snaked down from her breast to cup her between her thighs.

Sliding a finger through her folds, he circled her opening then curled his digit to begin stroking her clit. "I said no," she whispered.

Her head fell back against the tiled wall and her eyes closed. She said the words, but there was no conviction in them.

"I heard you, Trink," he murmured and kissed her jaw. "God, you tease me."

Rolling her head on the wall in a lazy shake, her resolve weakened. "No."

"No?" he said and trailed his lips down to her neck.

"To me… or the tease?"

Harlow couldn't think straight. Being so close to him felt so good. Being touched by him… "No," she said again and his finger slid into her. A long breath of euphoria slipped from her lips. "Oh, damn you, Crash."

"Feel good?"

Harlow could hardly manage to listen, but she forced herself to respond. "Mm."

"I promised to make you feel good, didn't I, baby?"

His lips touched hers, just for a second, while his hand still managed to work her clit and finger fuck her at the same time. "I'm mad at you. I said no sex."

"This isn't full sex."

The smile in his voice betrayed how she amused him, but she couldn't open her eyes to see it. Semantics gave her an out. "Your hand can have sex with me," she said, moaning and moving with his touch. "Oh, fuck, you're good at that."

"My mouth's good at it too," he said. "My tongue will feel better down there."

As if to convince her, he kissed her again, this time slipping his tongue between her lips, giving her a sample of the delights her pussy could look forward to if she let him loose. His hand didn't miss a beat and she was right on the edge of orgasm, so close that she was beginning to lose the ability to refuse him anything.

"You both in there?"

The third voice shattered her haze and made Harlow gasp and shove at Ryske's chest, separating them.

For a few seconds, she couldn't remember what had been happening. With wide eyes she blinked left and right trying to convince herself that she hadn't actually just been caught in flagrante delicto.

"Noon, fuck off," Ryske said, sliding a hand up the wall and leaning in again, pressing her to the tile.

Harlow shook her head and pushed at him. Losing herself to him hadn't been her intention when she'd slid open the stall. His friend had done her a favor by bringing her back to her senses.

It sounded like Noon was peeing. "One bathroom,

man," he said.

These men didn't seem to have any boundaries. But she couldn't judge them given where she was and what she'd been about to do. Resting her forehead on the heel of her hand, she couldn't believe common sense had abandoned her.

"One girl, and she's mine," Ryske responded to the man beyond their glass walls.

Noon laughed. "Don't see anyone fighting you for her," he said and flushed.

"Won't keep her long if you bastards force me to neglect her needs."

Harlow nudged him away when he tried to reach for her again. "I'll take care of my own needs."

Ryske groaned. "Oh, I'd love to see that, Trinket. Promise me a front row seat?"

She just scowled at him, but he grinned.

Noon interrupted again. "Dover said to tell you the coffee's ready, Nightingale."

She took a step backward toward the open shower door. "Baby, come on," Ryske said, snagging her wrist.

Harlow shook her head. "I can't," she whispered, begging him to let her go.

Sealing his lips to take a deep breath through his nose, he reached back over his shoulder to slide his towel off the top of the screen behind him. Handing it over to her, he was careful not to get it wet in the spray.

"You'll enjoy it with me, Trink," he said and winked while she wrapped herself in the towel. "Soon."

There were no rules in this abode. The unrestricted movement and open living shocked her less than her own fickleness with Ryske. It was a bad idea. A good idea. She said stop then encouraged him. Ryske wanted her and she was attracted to him. What were they doing? Where was this going?

Harlow didn't believe in giving a man mixed signals. She liked to be open and honest and believed in communication. But Ryske was... she didn't know what the hell she was doing with him.

She was tucking the corner of the towel between her

breasts when she left the stall. Noon was brushing his teeth and bobbed his brows at her as she crossed to the door. Harlow offered him a tight smile and kept on walking.

TWENTY-EIGHT

DOVER WAS STILL in the kitchen when Harlow got there. The first thing she saw when she rounded the fridge was him holding up a steaming mug of black coffee. She might have kissed him if his expression hadn't morphed to confusion.

"Take a shower?"

"Something like that," she said and accepted the coffee. Dover sat at the breakfast bar and pressed some buttons on a tablet laid there to open a news app. "I should call work."

"Maze is going to check that out. He's been in their system. You've been marked as being on personal leave this week."

Whatever this week had been, it wasn't personal leave, and she hadn't requested it. Trying to figure out why her boss would put something like that on an official record when it wasn't true, Harlow kept drinking her coffee.

Noon appeared around the corner from the bathroom. "When you're dressed, I'll take you over to your place to pick up your stuff," he said.

She hadn't expected to get a chance to go to her apartment, and looked at Dover, expecting him to object. It took Dover a second to register the silence. He raised his eyes from his app to see her waiting for his reaction.

"The rule is you're not allowed to go anywhere without one of us," Dover said and must have seen her surprise deepen. "You didn't like the idea of being stuck in here twenty-four seven… don't think I would either."

Rushing around the breakfast bar, she hugged Dover as tight as she could without putting down her coffee. She'd still rather have her independence and would fight for it any chance she got. But being protected by Ryske's crew was nothing like being locked up by Hagan.

"You watch those wandering hands of his, Trink."

Ryske's voice made her straighten from the hug, but it was Noon's groan that made her turn around. "Do you gotta wave that thing around?"

In his full naked glory, Ryske went to the coffee machine, but found the pot almost empty, so he came over to take her cup. Dover didn't seem to notice, or at least he didn't care about, Ryske's nudity.

"You've got to be used to seeing it by now," Dover muttered, going back to reading a story on his app. "Nightingale, you'll find out there's not a lot of boundaries around here."

Apparently not. "I haven't found one yet," she said.

"There is one," Ryske said, drinking from her mug. "An important one."

"One?" she asked, taking the mug when he gave it back to her. "Where?"

Using his body to push her against the curved edge of the breakfast bar, he slipped a hand between the flaps of her towel. "A threshold not to be crossed… Right here."

His fingertips just touched her pussy. Smacking both her hands to his chest, she shoved him back. "Whoa," she said.

"A boundary for them, not a boundary for me," he said, trying to reach for her, but she slapped his hand away.

"I'm going to get changed," Harlow said, pinning a glare on him.

Ever confident, Ryske grinned at her.

Everything he did seemed designed to seduce or tease

her. He might have touched her in intimate places, but that didn't mean she wanted him to pick up where he left off with his friends watching.

Leaving the kitchen, she took her coffee into the room deemed the closet. It was a huge space, at least seventeen feet by twelve. Although it had once been intended as a bedroom, it wasn't one anymore. There were racks of clothes and drawers, with overflowing hampers and a scattering of cufflinks and watches by the only mirror in the place.

It was a messy room, even the area rug was crooked. The filing cabinets were closed, but there were files piled on top and a mess of paperwork on the desk, which seemed to also be hiding a computer and printer. The couch in front of the closets faced into the room; it had a scattering of clothes on it too. These men weren't poster boys for cleaning up after themselves.

The only way Harlow would have any chance of finding something clean to wear was to go searching through the drawers. Usually, she'd find such an invasion of someone else's privacy distasteful. But when it was that or go outside in a towel, she'd pick the former every time.

Of the half a dozen dressers in the room, none of them matched. They did have one thing in common, they all looked kind of beat up. All were chest height or there about and broad enough to contain a wide selection of apparel.

Putting her coffee on top of one of the dressers, she began to peek in drawers. Leaving the underwear alone, she didn't think there was any need for her to put on boxer-briefs, which seemed to be the choice of each man.

Shoes would be a problem. She'd have to wear her heels from last night.

"Your dress is right here."

Turning away from the drawer she was exploring, Harlow discovered Ryske by the door, still naked, but holding up her dress.

"I don't want to see that thing ever again," she said, thinking she should've retrieved her bra from next to Ryske's bed.

Heading for the door to do just that, she expected him to step aside, but he didn't, which forced her to stop and meet his eye. "What I told you last night… Anwen and I, it was… complicated." Raising his curled fingers to her jaw, he traced them across her skin, but she tilted her head away from his caress. "That doesn't change this."

"Doesn't it?" she asked, taking his wrist to guide his hand away from her face. "You were honest with me, but… there's something I didn't tell you."

Though his expression became more serious, he didn't back off. "Nothing you could say would change how I feel about you, Trink."

She believed him. Even knowing that he lied for a living, she didn't believe he was insincere about his attraction to her. "This isn't about our feelings… about us… it's…"

His frown deepened and he shook his head once. "I don't…"

"Ophelia," she said. "She's in love with you."

The tension left him at the same time as the concern seeped away; he cupped her head, her ear in the crook between his thumb and forefinger. "She's not your competition, Trink. That slap, it was part of the con. She wants her brother to think we're together, she had to act jealous. I want to rile her brother, to provoke a reaction… I want him on a hair trigger with me, that's why—"

"She loves you, Ryske," she said. "I'm not telling you to act on it, but it does change things."

Ryske was still shaking his head. "Baby, we've never been together."

The warning wasn't rooted in jealousy. He didn't see the trouble that could lie ahead. "You need her on your side. A scorned woman can be a dangerous thing."

"What are you saying?"

Stepping in close, she tilted her head back to murmur, "Watch your ass, Crash. I'm saying you have to watch your ass."

On a slow blink, the corner of his mouth rose. "Always do, Trinket."

Dipping down, he covered her mouth with his.

Harlow closed her eyes and let herself enjoy the feel of him. His kiss was powerful in its delicacy. There was no denying that he was practiced, and not just in kissing. Ryske knew what women wanted, how to make them feel like they were the most valued thing on the planet, and she was not immune.

In that moment, basking in his kiss, Harlow felt like the only female who existed. He didn't push, didn't force himself harder against her. Cupping her head, he held her with a gentle insistence, tipping her head to the side to consume more of her with his tender mouth.

Their kisses were usually urgent or anger fueled. This wasn't like that. It was soft, slow, full of need and yet filled with wonder. She didn't feel him untucking her towel or hear it falling to the floor. The first Harlow was aware of her nudity was the sensation of his hand skimming up her bare waist. Cradling her breast, he brushed his thumb over the apex, tormenting her nipple to a peak while his mouth kept softening her resolve.

"I'd wait an eternity to be inside you," he murmured, tilting her head the other way to kiss her from a new angle. "Just tell me I'll have you."

His body didn't seem to agree with the idea of waiting; she'd felt the welcome intrusion of his dick against her since they'd started kissing. There was no time for her to respond or tease. He clamped one strong arm around her waist, pinning her body to his to pick her up off her feet. Without raising her higher to wrap her legs around him, he locked their gazes and began to walk across the room.

When her spine met one of the dressers, he put her back on her feet. "Crash—"

He cut her off with a kiss and winked on his way down to his knees. She stayed still and mute until he picked up her ankle and directed it around to his back, hooking her knee over his shoulder. His lips kissed each angle of her groin before his tongue slid between her folds, searching for her clit.

When he found it a moment later, she gasped. Her head fell back and she whimpered at the sensation of his mouth licking and sucking on her. His focus started on her clit, tantalizing the flesh until it tingled and sparked with the need for release.

Using one arm to steady herself on the dresser, the other fell into his damp hair, scrunching and kneading as he increased her pleasure. His mouth slid lower, and he slipped his tongue into her. Circling and delving deeper, he fucked her with his mouth.

Harlow didn't want casual. But for all she knew, that's what this was for him. He'd told her himself that when he wanted to comfort Anwen, he'd had sex with her because it was what he knew how to do.

In her opinion, he didn't give himself enough credit. What he made her feel was more than sex, and more than casual. But maybe this was what Anwen had felt with him too. Maybe he made every woman feel this way.

Harlow had told him no promises, so it wasn't like she could push for more. Ryske had been clear that he had no more than pleasure to give her.

Even as her teeth dug deep into her lip and she tried her hardest to hold onto the scream that wanted to leave her lungs, Harlow dedicated herself to him. It was insane to feel such an intense draw to a man. But she couldn't deny feeling it.

Ryske had told her he couldn't make her a promise he might break. He might be a criminal, but he had his own moral code, and doing that with her went against it. With her. He'd said that breaking promises to *her* would bother him.

Maybe it was a con and he told every woman they were different. So many maybes. Harlow wanted to believe he'd meant what he said when he told her he couldn't feed her lines.

Reasoning and rational fled her mind when Ryske returned his effort to her clit. He sucked harder this time and flicked his tongue over her with finessed speed, giving all his focus and force to that tiny corner of her being.

Everything else vanished. There was no stress. No family pressure. No career worries. No college assignments. No Hagan. No Ophelia. No Anwen.

Just this man and her.

Yelping, she tightened her hold on his hair when

orgasm slammed into her. Restraint was lost and her mouth opened in the cry of climax. It hadn't taken long, but he'd warmed her up in the shower and he didn't seem to be the type to leave anything undone.

Heat inside her head made her thoughts blur and she felt groggy, like she'd just woken from a deep sleep.

Ryske rose in front of her and brushed her hair away from her face. "I could've done that in the shower," he murmured. "That wouldn't have been so bad, would it?"

Crooking her arms between them, she nestled against him when he wrapped both arms around her. "I wish you had a bedroom."

"We're alone right here," he said.

Smiling, he started to descend for a kiss. As if on cue, the door opened, making her gasp. Only Ryske's body concealed hers from the view of whoever was in the doorway. He turned his scowl on, twisting to land it on whoever had interrupted them.

"We've got to get going," Noon said. "I have that other thing to do later."

Ryske nodded once and the door closed, so she guessed that Noon was gone. "It's amazing none of you can keep a girl when this is what she has to put up with."

"None of us ever brought a girl here," he said and kissed her forehead. "I'll talk to him."

Leaving her by the dresser, he went to another and pulled out his clothes to begin dressing.

Harlow stayed there, folding her hands against the wood at her back. "None of you?"

He glanced at her. "None—yeah, well, not since we were kids and Floyd was around. We were dumb teenagers back then, desperate to cop a feel."

Her lips curled until a laugh slipped out. "And that's different than now… how?" He tossed a wink her way. "Guess I should say I'm privileged."

Grabbing a shirt from a rack close to him, he pulled a pair of sweats from another drawer and tossed both to her. "Didn't have much choice with you."

She began to put on the apparel he'd thrown her way

while he finished dressing. "Wow, you know how to make a woman feel special."

"Think I just did," he said. Straightening after he finished pulling on his socks, he wiped the corner of his mouth like he'd just finished a meal. "You taste good, Trink."

"Yeah, well, don't get used to it," she said, crouching to fold up the sweats. She was going to look ridiculous, but at least she only had to get from here to Noon's car and then into her apartment. "How long do you think I'll be here?"

Ryske ignored that last question and addressed the first thing she'd said. "You don't like oral?"

Eyeing the desk, she crossed the room and pushed aside some papers to look for a rubber band. She didn't like tying her hair up with them, but it would be better than leaving it loose in the wind.

Harlow sat in the desk chair to finger-comb her hair before scooping it up into a loose messy chignon. "I think as long as all this is going on, we have other things to focus on, don't you?"

Coming around to prop himself against the front of the desk, he folded his arms. "This is life, baby," he said, bending over to kiss her. "If we wait until there's none of *this* going on, we'll never get it on."

She wrinkled her nose and tipped her head back to tease him. "Really bothers you that we haven't had sex, doesn't it?"

"Shh," he said in a mock panic. "Don't say that around here, someone might hear you."

"Wouldn't want to dent that reputation of yours."

Bowing again, he tried to kiss her, but she leaned away. "We could take care of the oversight right now."

Struggling to hold onto her laugh, Harlow was about to let him kiss her when the door opened again.

Ryske groaned. "Right! Fuck, Noon! We get it, you want to leave!" he called and glared back at his friend. "Remind me never to miss an opportunity to cock-block you."

The poor guy was standing there stunned by his friend's outburst.

Ryske took her hand and slid his other arm around her. "You're coming?" she asked when he pulled her to her feet and began to guide her to the door.

"Not as long as Noon's got the chance to keep my dick out of your pussy," Ryske grumbled, tossing another scowl at his friend as he guided her out of the room. "Prick."

She knew he didn't mean it, and Noon didn't really mean to interrupt them. Everyone was in close quarters, and she was sure they'd get used to living together. After all, it was only temporary.

Once Hagan was dealt with and they'd figured out how to free her from his scope, Harlow would be able to go back to her life and Ryske's crew could do the same.

TWENTY-NINE

IT FELT LIKE an age since she'd seen her apartment. Harlow hadn't lived there for long, so it wasn't like she had a deep emotional attachment to the place. Still, it was nice to see that everything was where she'd left it.

Wasting no time, Harlow got a suitcase and a sports bag out of the closet and began to pack her clothes. Ryske had made himself at home, leaping onto her bed to stretch his legs out while he leafed through the textbook she'd left on the nightstand.

Noon loitered in the bedroom archway. "When was the last time you saw Rupert?"

Harlow opened out her suitcase on the bed next to the sports bag, letting the lid fall onto Ryske's legs. "Uh… a few weeks ago."

"But he works here in the city, right? Where does he live?"

Taking some things out of the nightstand, she put them in the sports bag. "He works at Sweeting Securities," she said, retrieving shoes from the closet. "So, yes, he works in the city… with my father. But he lives near my parents in the suburbs."

"That's got to be a helluva commute."

"Only an hour or so either way," she said, tossing Hagan's shoes into the corner and shirking her sweatpants. Grabbing a skirt from a drawer, she wriggled into it under her shirt. After putting on her own shoes, she went to the dresser to collect more of her things. "How long am I going to be staying at Floyd's? I never got an answer before."

Ryske turned the page of the book and tucked his hand behind his head again. "Bring everything silky or lacy you've got."

"I don't wear lace," she said and went into the closet.

"You should wear lace," Ryske called after her. "Want to stop at Victoria's Secret on the way home?"

Popping her head out of the closet, she pinned a glare on him, wondering if it would be wrong to swear at him for something her former fiancé had done to piss her off. "I dumped the last man who bought me lingerie."

As he arched a questioning brow, his chin rose. But Harlow didn't respond to his silent query because Noon spoke again. "You lived with him, didn't you? You were going to marry him, you must have lived together."

With her stare locked on Ryske, it took Harlow a minute to catch on to what Noon was talking about. Shaking her head to force her gaze away from the man strewn on her bed, Harlow refocused. Ryske went back to his reading.

"Rupert?" she asked. "Yes, we lived together for about a year. We moved in together after he proposed."

"Why are we talking about her jackass of an ex? The guy's a fucktard who cheated on her. He's a waste of air." Ryske peeked at her over the top of the textbook. "He did cheat on you, right?"

Wrinkling her nose, she shook her head, which made interest deepen his expression. "No, he did not cheat on me," she asserted. "Geez, Ryske, what a thing to say to a woman you were intimate with this morning. Was it that bad?"

Slapping the textbook shut, he sat upright. "No, baby. Shit, I'll eat you right here. Right in front of Noon, if that's what you want."

Leaning over the top of her bags, she took the textbook from him and put it inside. "I don't want you to eat me at all and I definitely don't want your friend to watch."

Settling back against the pillows, Ryske made himself comfortable again. "He's less my friend now than he was before he started interrupting us every time you're naked. But you better get used to him watching, his bed is right next to ours."

"Reminding me of that only makes it less likely you'll ever be allowed into that bed with me. I'm not sharing with you if you won't promise to keep your hands to yourself."

"You said no promises," he said, so cocky and proud of himself.

Harlow had said that. To her, it was less about promises and more about decency. "It would be the gentlemanly thing to do."

His mouth opened wide. "Oh! Okay, yeah, I see what happened. You forgot you got with a criminal." He smiled. "There's not much that will stop me from getting what I want. The law won't do it. Your lame objections sure won't and if you're relying on me being a gentleman…" Sneering, he shook his head. "You've gotta find yourself another guy, baby, 'cause playing dirty is what I do."

"You're saying if I'm in your bed, I have to let you into my panties?"

He laughed. "Baby, I'm saying if you're in my bed, you won't be wearing panties. Panties are banned on women as beautiful as you."

"Given the lack of rules in your place, I can't even keep a straight face while trying to buy that BS you're selling. And I wore panties in your bed last night."

"That's gonna be the exception."

"Whose choice was it not to live in the city?" Noon asked.

Tearing her attention from Ryske again, Harlow tried to work out what the hell Noon was talking about. "I don't know what—"

"Rupert," Noon said. "You must have talked about it."

Closing her eyes for a second, Harlow was trying to follow this conversation, the one with Ryske, and pack her things all at the same time. "He wanted to stay in suburbia, near my parents, and my job was there."

"Again with the ex," Ryske said. "If you've got a hard on for the guy, ask him out, Noon. What the fuck? Why are you talking about him so much?"

Noon lounged against the frame of the archway. "Just thinking, it might make sense for Nightingale to crash with him instead of us. She dumped him, and she's hot, so he must still be into her. He'd take care of her."

Sitting up again, Ryske locked his straight arms behind him to support his weight. "You want my girl to go and sleep with the ex who wants to fuck her? Why the hell would I let that happen?"

That wasn't the first time he'd referred to her as his girl. The glow of that flattery was somewhat reduced by his use of the word "let." Harlow didn't want the man she ended up with to think she needed his permission for anything. Ryske might not be her white picket fence guy, as he'd admitted himself, but he was her right now guy.

Playing with him was a good way to make her point. "Rupert never did get his goodbye lay," she said. Contemplating it, she reached over to close the flap of her suitcase. "Might be nostalgic and romantic to do it in our bed again."

Inhaling a deep breath, Ryske slid onto his back and linked his hands behind his head.

"You're cool with that, Ryske?" Noon asked, dubious like he didn't quite believe it. "Seems like you're cool with it."

Ryske's eyes shut. "I'm picturing what it will be like to decapitate a guy while his hands are on my girl."

"I know you're not talking about me because I don't belong to anyone," Harlow said, backing toward the closet.

"And I know you're not going anywhere near your ex," Ryske said, tipping his head to glare at Noon. "You're an asshole for suggesting it."

"We're not in the protection business," Noon said. "I'm thinking about what's best for Nightingale. We can take care of ourselves and each other, but—"

Ryske straightened to lift his arm, presenting the line

of stars on the back of his right forearm. "What's that?" he said. "Highs and lows until we're dirt in the ground." Noon seemed nervous when he glanced at her. "That's right. You fucking watch who you're casting out—"

"No, man, I wasn't—"

"I'll let you men duke it out," Harlow said to the quarreling pair.

Heading into her closet, Harlow took her time about selecting clothes and things she'd need for a stay at Floyd's. Whether it was a few days or a few weeks, Harlow wanted to be prepared for whatever might crop up and would always rather bring too much than too little. Anything she took to Floyd's, she'd be able to bring back when this was over.

Retrieving things from her closet, she put them in the suitcase and then went into the bathroom to pack up what she needed from there. Checking through what she'd stowed in her luggage to ensure that she had everything, Harlow didn't pay much attention to Ryske and Noon's conversation, which had moved onto something else.

She changed her top and left Ryske's clothes in her closet. The possibility that his possessions might find a home among hers was appealing. It was sentimental, but she would get away with it. He was a guy, he wouldn't notice a missing shirt or pair of sweatpants.

Both men were seated on the bed now, Ryske against the headboard and Noon at the end with his feet still on the floor. Neither looked her way when she passed by to go into the living room to gather her college things together.

Her books would give her something to do during her indefinite time at Floyd's. No reason she couldn't keep studying there. Some of her assignments were almost overdue, she'd have to buckle down.

In the living room, sorting through papers, Harlow was interrupted by a knock on the front door. Unsure who it could be given that no one would know she was home, Harlow looked up from the desk, glanced back toward the bedroom, and then cursed herself for being dubious. It was a knock on her own door, why should she be suspicious of that?

The peephole helped her out, Harlow checked it to

see who was on her threshold. Though, she couldn't have been more surprised to identify who it was.

Opening the door, she didn't have time to speak before he came barreling inside. "Harlow!" he exclaimed, storming through the kitchen to stop in the middle of the living room. "Where the hell have you been?"

"Please, come in, why don't you, Clyde?" she said, swinging the door into its frame as she turned to face him. "What are you doing here?"

"I've been coming every day! I don't know what happened. Does this have something to do with what happened in Floyd's? I was mad. I was. I don't deny it. I planned to avoid you. But… I heard you were in the office on Monday and then, you disappeared. What happened?"

"What did you hear?"

"Gina just…"

Ryske and Noon came sauntering out of her bedroom. She didn't know if they meant to look as menacing as they did, but they didn't make a welcoming picture. At least they wouldn't for the nervous Clyde who stumbled and had to grab for the back of the couch to stop himself from falling on his ass.

"Look, Noon, prey," Ryske said.

Clyde pulled himself closer to the couch.

Noon laughed. "Just in time for lunch."

"Stop it," she said. "Both of you. Clyde don't—"

"You have two… two men in your bedroom?" Clyde asked.

Well if that didn't just offend the shit right out of her. Opening her mouth, Harlow wrinkled her nose a little, but Ryske just laughed. "Yep, she's a dirty, dirty girl, with a voracious appetite. Sometimes I have to pimp her out 'cause I can't keep up. I'm always there to watch… make sure she doesn't get too excited and damage the johns."

"Are you kidding me?" she demanded. "Don't say things like that! He's my colleague, he might believe you!"

"Trinket, if you think you're ever going back to that office, you haven't been paying attention."

He could deliver shocking news in a matter of fact

way. Maybe instead of spending so much time making out, they should've spent a little more time talking. There had been time this morning that she could have asked why they weren't letting her go back to the office or what Dover had meant about Maze checking out her work.

Never had Harlow assumed going back to work would be off the agenda forever. In his defense, Ryske wasn't telling her she couldn't go back to work, just that she couldn't go back to *that* workplace. At least, that better be what he was saying. If Ryske was implying that she should stay home while he took care of her, she'd dump him faster than she dumped Rupert.

"What is going on?" Clyde asked.

"None of your business, Flaxman," Ryske said.

So Clyde was his first name and somehow Ryske had known that about her colleague before she did. Asking his name had been on her agenda, she just hadn't got around to it.

In that minute, something else occurred to her and she paused to squint at the guy who'd been eating her out that morning. Harlow had no idea what his full name was. He'd told her Ryske was his name, but his first or last? And what was his other name?

Another knock at the door made her reverse. This one was melodic and familiar. It sounded like the knock Dover had used to request entry to Bale's on the night she'd met the crew.

Guessing the new guest was a friend, she didn't bother to check the peephole. Declaring his identity through the knock helped her out, no way did she want to take her frown off the man who was growling at Clyde.

Opening the front door without turning around, she figured even if she was wrong about the intentions of whoever was on the other side, Ryske and Noon could probably handle the visitor if the need arose. And Clyde was always around to call the cops if things got desperate.

Turned out, she didn't have to be concerned. Maze was the guest who walked around her, pausing to kiss the top of her head.

"Hey, look at that, Trink," Ryske said. "Your next appointment is here. It's a grand for the hour. No extras. Extras cost more."

Maze was probably confused, but Harlow smiled. "Wow, I'm expensive."

"Just like you always told me," Ryske said and winked.

Staying with her at the door, Maze slid an arm around her shoulders, giving her some of his weight. His burden was reassuring, and made her feel secure, even if he was crushing her a little. Harlow didn't know why he was there or what had happened at his work to bring him home early. Though, like she'd said to Dover, she doubted what Maze classed as a job was anything close to a regular nine to five. The word "freelance" had given it away for her.

"Should we take this asshole with us?" Noon asked.

She thought for a second they were talking about Maze, but Noon was actually pointing at Clyde. "Take him where?"

"Yeah, take me where," Clyde said, his pallor noticeably paling.

"Away from my girl," Ryske said. "You don't get any cookies."

Her man was so random. Wait, no, she had to remind herself she wasn't pleased with him treating her friend this way. There was no thinking of him as 'her man' while he was being an unreasonable asshole.

Harlow didn't need to be saved from Clyde, especially not before he'd filled her in. "He hasn't told us what Gina said yet," she said.

Everyone paused to look at Clyde. "I... I..."

"You, you, yeah," Ryske said. "Speak."

When he took a step toward Clyde, her friend gasped.

"Crash, would you stop making him nervous," she said, pushing away from Maze to go over and stand in front of Ryske, as a shield for the colleague she faced. "He won't hurt you, Clyde."

Ryske took her shoulders and pulled her back a step. "Long as he's not within ten feet of you, I won't."

Harlow chose to ignore him. "What did Gina tell you about where I was?"

"Just that you were taking some personal time," Clyde said. "The office was whispering about your absence. You haven't been with us long. There was that Felipe thing and then you disappeared."

"But we found him," she said. "Did they think I had been suspended for something?"

"I think they thought you couldn't cut it."

THIRTY

IN DISBELIEF, Harlow sagged against Ryske who was still holding her shoulders. Although she might be new to that specific department, she had worked social work for years. Runaways were common, bereavement happened all the time. Harlow was no rookie and had supported kids and parents through all kinds of fraught and tragic circumstances.

The man at her back squeezed her shoulders, maybe sensing how Clyde's statement hurt her. "Shows no one in that department has a fucking clue who you are, Trink," Ryske said, pulling her back to kiss her head. "My girl's a fucking rock in any situation, Sap."

Even the most dire of situations as Ryske knew firsthand. Much as she appreciated his support, Ryske was biased, she had saved his life.

"I didn't think you'd folded," Clyde said, quick to assert his faith in her.

To further prove it, he reached for her, probably to offer some kind of physical comfort too. Just attempting it was enough to make Ryske pull her back against his chest. Being possessive was just ridiculous. Clyde was nowhere near touching her, but apparently he was too near for Ryske's liking.

"You know, Crash," she said over her shoulder, sharing her observation. "Your boys kiss me and touch me all the time. I've never seen you even blink about that."

"My boys wouldn't compromise you," Ryske said with a growl of impatient irritation. "That fucker would."

She rolled her eyes and mouthed an apology to Clyde who smiled in response. "I was naked when Noon walked in on us this morning."

"He's already erased whatever he saw from his memory," Ryske said, making her laugh even though he wasn't joking.

In the field of her peripheral vision, Noon passed on his journey to Maze and saluted in agreement. The pair did their familiar huddle thing, exchanging murmurs, blocking out the rest of them.

"You have some warped rules, baby," she said, taking Ryske's hand from her shoulder to pull it around her collarbone so she could dip to kiss his forearm.

"You really are with him?" Clyde asked, his eyes narrowed like he couldn't quite believe it.

"You got a problem with that, Sap?" Ryske snarled.

Harlow dug her nails into his wrist to quiet him. "I don't know what I am with Ryske," she said to Clyde. "But I do know it wouldn't be smart to cross him."

The second part didn't register to Ryske because he was stuck on the first. "You don't know what you are with me," he said with a tone of incredulity.

Maze raised his forearm to tap an imaginary watch. "We've got a reservation, Night. Gotta hustle."

No one had clued Harlow in on the plan. If she'd guessed on it, she'd have said Floyd's was her next destination. A date with Maze wouldn't have crossed her mind. "We… we have a reservation?"

"Yeah, Maze is going to take you for food," Ryske said, guiding her around to face him while Maze and Noon headed into her bedroom.

"Noon and me got a place to be," Ryske said. "Stick with Maze, he'll bring you home after." Searching him, she got a flashback of the night he'd left her here alone. "I'll see you later."

It was like he could read her mind. Those last four words were deliberate. They weren't a casual "see you later" they were giving her the message, *I can hear what you're thinking and I'm thinking it too.*

"Why is now different?" she asked, fingering the hem of his tee-shirt.

"Because of this," he said and bowed to kiss her.

Harlow let her head fall back to better experience the texture of his mouth and the insistence of his tongue.

His kiss was so good it kicked her off-balance. "Oh, Crash," she whispered, her eyes still closed, her mind swimming.

"I'll stay if you want me to," he murmured on her mouth, tucking her hair behind her ear. "You have the one thing it takes to stop me walking out that door."

Her lips curled up. "I thought it wasn't safe here."

"I'd take the risk for that."

Laughing, she slid her arms up around him and pulled him down for another kiss. There had been a time when she'd told him to keep his lips away from her, that they would never be together. It was a vague, distant memory and one that she didn't like to dwell on.

Harlow had been falling for this guy since the moment he'd fallen on her. Fighting it would've been smart, distancing herself would've been safer. Except, she'd been ensnared by the allure of him, and probably wouldn't have been able to free herself from his web if she'd wanted to.

Mumbling his approval, Ryske wrapped both arms around her torso and raised her off her feet, kissing her. One of his arms kept its grip but angled so he could cup her ass, squeezing her hard and letting her feel just how happy he was to be kissing her.

"No time for that," Noon said from beside them.

Breaking the kiss, both she and Ryske turned to him. "You seriously want me to kick your ass today, don't you?" Ryske said to his friend.

Noon just smirked, making her wonder if his interruptions weren't some kind of prank arranged by his supposedly supportive crew.

"You've got your own appointment to keep," Maze said.

Ryske lowered her onto her feet, but kept one arm tight around her while he raised the other to check his watch. The timepiece was above the double-wrapped leather band on his wrist. Touching the edge of the engraved metal that circled one strand of the wristband, Harlow thought about the night Bale had read its words to her.

"Carpe noctem," she whispered, just loud enough for him to hear.

His focus lowered to her. "We sure will, Trinket… We are gonna own the world."

There was so much meaning and innuendo behind his tone that it became profound. She might have said something in response, but when her attention ascended, she noticed Maze and Noon were nearby with her luggage.

Harlow had been told to hustle. Instead, she'd stood basking in the man holding her. Time to get with it. "Oh," she said. Pushing away from Ryske, she hurried to the desk to scoop up her books. "I need these too."

Maze put her suitcase down. She crouched to open it up and put her books inside, using Maze's legs as a stand for the back of the case. "She just kneels in front of any guy, doesn't she?" he asked.

"I'm gonna start a list," Ryske said. Harlow glanced over his shoulder to see him run a ragged hand through his hair. "I shouldn't let you punks get in my head."

"Yeah, you should really know better than that," Maze said, leaning over to sock his buddy's shoulder. After enjoying the frazzled Ryske for another few seconds, Maze's focus dropped to her. "You done yet, Princess?"

"Where are we going to eat?" she asked, zipping up her case.

"Sushi," Maze said.

The answer made her grin up at him.

"Yeah, he's the only one of us who'll eat that posh shit," Noon said. "You want cheap Chinese or greasy burgers, call me."

"I could take you to lunch, Harlow," Clyde said, drawing everyone's attention. "We could catch up with—"

"Ha, Flaxman's funny, who knew," Ryske said on a fake laugh, which his crew joined. Three seconds later, the sound died, giving way to an abrupt cold silence and a trio of glares. "Think about trying to get her alone and she won't be the only one missing from your department."

Surging to her feet, Harlow smacked his chest. "What did I tell you about scaring him?"

In response to her scolding, Ryske's hand shot up to her throat, squeezing her tight. "I don't have time to play this game with you now," he growled. "But I'm thinking you might want to be punished later."

Maze picked up the case and Noon handed him the sports bag too. Harlow didn't see it, her eyes were trained to Ryske's, but she heard the movement.

"Time to go, Flaxman," Noon said.

"Wait, you can't just leave her there with him like that," Clyde said.

She'd guess they were going toward the door because the sound seemed to be receding. "He can handle her," Noon said. "She always leaves him in one piece and a few bruises never hurt any guy."

That suggested she was going to be the aggressor putting Ryske in his place. Though, that might make sense because technically Harlow had hit Ryske first. But if anything was going to end up bruised, it was going to be her throat in the force of that grip.

She relished every second.

Damnit, her man knew what his forceful actions did to her hormones. It was intoxicating to be held under his strength, overpowered, yet still in complete control. Control. Even with his superior ability, Harlow was confident in her influence over him.

The front door closed. The room fell into silence. The air crackled with a desire thicker and more potent than the need they hadn't sated.

Ryske looked angry, but he wasn't. He was turning her on and he knew it. Harlow couldn't deny it, she was weak in the face of his strength, but only because it proved to her what this man was capable of. Her capability was in holding sway over him. She had her own power because he gave it to her.

Without so much as blinking, she angled her body closer, reaching for him. Unbuckling his belt, she did her best not to smile when she read his subtle flicker of surprise.

Ryske did a good job of not reacting when she opened his jeans and slid her hand inside to rub the reaction that had persisted since he'd been kissing her. The change in his breathing betrayed that her actions were having an effect. His lips got narrower. He pressed them tighter together as she curled the fingers of her free hand around his strong wrist.

Guiding his curved hand away from her throat, Harlow didn't want it to leave her body, she just wanted to reposition it. Ryske didn't argue when she directed it around to the crown of her head.

Rising to her tiptoes, he lowered his chin to accept her kiss. "Tighter," she whispered when his mouth was a few millimeters from hers.

Tensing his fingers in her hair, they tangled in her locks, tugging on the strands, sending a sting through her scalp that made her hiss in satisfaction. His nostrils flared a little when he smiled, showing her that he was enjoying this as much as her.

Harlow winked at him and unlocked her knees, sinking down in front of him to breathe his dick into her mouth. Ryske hissed, a loud, almost pained noise, but she took it as a positive sign because his fingers clamped even tighter in her hair.

Her experience giving head was limited to a small number of men. Ryske was larger than Rupert, who'd been the only man she'd pleasured with her mouth for a long time. Harlow's drive to please the man in her mouth now made her work harder.

Until Ryske, giving head had never given her pleasure. Something about this was arousing her though. Maybe it was the sensation of his fingers matting her hair or him hitting the back of her throat every time she sucked him into her. Harlow felt powerful and strong and alive, more than she remembered feeling before.

Ryske took risks, he was a danger to society and, in a lot of ways, to himself, because of the risks he took. But he was no danger to her.

Pulling his jeans further down, she kissed his thighs, up to his scar that she brushed her lips across, making quick eye contact with him before descending to his groin. Kissing him there, she kissed his shaft, licked him, and sucked him once, working him with her hands while she gave his balls a little love.

There was no way for her to know how many other women had done this for him. Dozens, maybe, hundreds, perhaps more. Ryske probably couldn't even tell her the number. But there, with him in that second, she knew he belonged to her.

They couldn't make promises or define what this was, but in these times they were together, alone together, there was nothing more powerful than their connection.

He swore and began to take more control of her advance and withdraw. His other hand joined the first and he pushed forward, coming hard against the back of her tongue with a hiss that made her hold her breath.

Swallowing until his seed was all gone, Harlow took her time about letting him leave her mouth. She didn't move away, just rested her head on his thigh.

"We should say goodbye like that every time," Ryske said. His breathing was still shaky, but she could hear that he was smiling, which made her smile too. "You're incredible, Trinket."

The front door opened. "What the hell is—oh, fuck!"

Noon's exclamation made her smile grow.

"You've got to be shitting me," Ryske snapped.

"Least you got to finish," she said, taking his hand so he could help her to her feet.

"You guys have a lot of sex," Noon said.

That was ironic given that they hadn't done anything but oral. She and Ryske shared a private smile as she moved in close to tuck him away and fasten his jeans again.

"You got a problem with that?" Ryske asked Noon, stroking a hand down the side of her face.

"No, I'm saying, you act like I'm doing this shit on purpose. But, the truth is, if you guys are alone, you're gonna be doing… something. So it's hard to avoid."

And Noon was the one usually sent to deliver messages. If anyone was going to be interrupting, it was going to be him.

"It's okay, honey," she said, turning her back on Ryske to address Noon. "We were just saying goodbye."

"Wish someone would say goodbye to me like that," Noon muttered.

She felt a little bad for him, but doubted any of the crew had to worry about a lack of female companionship. Each of them was hot and dangerous in their own way. Though, while this mess with Hagan was going on, they probably didn't have a lot of time to socialize. If they weren't allowed women upstairs in Floyd's, they'd have to go back to the woman's home and that meant separating from the group, from the pack, something else that wasn't smart.

"I'll call someone to say goodbye to you tonight, how's that?" Ryske asked, bowing to kiss her shoulder before taking her hand to lead her toward the door.

Ryske had been the one to unlock her apartment and still had her key. Something Harlow only remembered when he took it out of his pocket.

"Cindy?" Noon asked, opening the front door.

"Cindy's in Sydney," Ryske said.

"Whitney?"

"Married," Ryske said, holding the door open for her. Harlow stepped into the hallway and Ryske closed the door to lock it up. "So that's a maybe… I'll call her." He tucked the key into his pocket and put an arm around her. The three of them started for the stairway. "You know who is in town?"

"Who?" Noon asked.

"Svetlana," Ryske said.

Noon paused at the top of the stairs. Harlow read Ryske's smirk. He kept it trained on the stairs, pretending not to notice his friend's reaction, though she didn't doubt that he had.

They descended and were all the way down the first flight before Noon came thundering after them. "Is—"

"Lyudmila with her? Yes, she is," Ryske said.

"How the hell do you know that?" Noon asked. "Why haven't they been over to party?"

"She called me last week, that's how I know," Ryske said, opening the alleyway door for her. Maze was out there alone, sitting shotgun in the car with his window rolled down and his elbow on the sill. "And I told them not to come over."

"What?" Noon said with such horror Maze looked up.

"What's going on?" Maze asked.

Noon went around to get in the driver's seat while Ryske tucked her into the back of the car. Noon started driving, but threw his passenger a look of shock. "Ryske told the twins not to come party."

"I know, he told me," Maze said, less horrified than Noon.

Ryske was laughing when he pulled her close to tuck her under his arm. "I'll call and find out where they're staying. You can go hang with them, have them both to yourself."

"Won't Zance..."

"What?" Ryske asked. "Not like they were exclusive."

"No, 'cause she was fucking you every chance she got," Maze said.

"We've shared women before," Ryske said. "Never bothered him. Never bothered me."

"I don't think there's a damn woman on the planet you haven't shared with one guy or another," Maze said and there was a moment of silence. "You never did the threesome thing... did you?"

"Svet and Zance? No," Ryske said. "Svet and Lyud..."

He didn't finish the sentence, but he didn't have to. Having a threesome was something she'd expect from him, but finding out he'd had one with sisters was both horrifying and impressive in about equal measure.

"Their numbers are in the lockbox in the desk," Maze

said. "The key's hanging on the back of the closet door, it's not like he makes a secret of it. You can raid Ryske's catalog any time. There are thousands of women in there. Just drop his name, they'll come a'runnin'."

"They're more likely to show if he calls," Noon grumbled.

"I'm not a pimp," Ryske said in a kind of sing-song voice though there was humor in his tone. "You want it, you work for it. The rest of us have to."

Noon snorted and even Maze laughed. "You've never had to work for sex in your life."

It was a good thing that the guys were in the front, because Harlow's lips began to rise. Ryske tightened his hold on her and buried his mouth in her hair. "Not a word, Trink."

Still smiling, she dug her nails into him in a kind of teasing response.

"Bet Dover doesn't know the twins are in town," Noon muttered, checking a junction before pulling out. "We always make a mint when we have the girls in on a Friday."

Friday was the main event in Floyd's, the night they made the most amount of money in their basement casino. Harlow had thought it was just gambling that went on down there. Though, she hadn't been down to check the place out and hadn't thought to ask too many questions.

"They're dancers?" she asked, tipping her head back.

Ryske kissed her forehead and kept his eyes ahead. "Hookers, baby."

They had hookers in Floyd's? She'd had no idea. "So you *are* a pimp?"

Maze made a sound of amusement, and Ryske pulled her closer, nuzzling her hair. "Svet is a madam, Lyud backs her up… Whatever they make is theirs. We just give them a place to operate."

"A safe place to operate," Maze said and twisted to look at them. "How did we get to talking about the twins anyway?"

"Noon is lonely," Ryske said, tilting his head toward the driver.

Maze gave Ryske a look she couldn't interpret, but

she felt the man holding her nod.

Turning back to the front, Maze slouched in his seat. "You like sushi, Nightingale?"

"Uh, yeah, I do."

And just like that the conversation moved on. Harlow still had questions, but when did she not? These men had complicated lives and histories more intricate than she'd be able to follow. She'd been naïve not to consider her life simple, as it had been before anyway.

Growing up in a semi-affluent family, she'd had an excellent education, always been safe, and for the most part, she'd been happy, even if she'd never quite fitted in.

College and Rupert were just extensions of that typical existence. She had lived a simple life and even in spite of her work, she'd never fully understood what doing anything to survive really meant, not until she met Ryske and his crew.

Twisting around, she angled until she could look up at Ryske who was saying something to Maze about Dover's issue with a liquor supplier and how they might have to pay the guy a visit later.

Ryske would do anything to survive. Noon and Dover were the same. Maze was more of an enigma. Having lunch with him would give her a chance to learn more about the man she hadn't spent much alone time with.

Pushing up, she cut Ryske off in the middle of the sentence by kissing him. At first, he was too stunned to respond, but it didn't take him long to catch up. He smoothed a hand over her cheek, and when he lost his hand in her hair, she leaned back.

The question of why was in his eyes, but she didn't answer it, she just turned again and rested her head against him, closing her eyes. They'd probably get to the restaurant in a couple of minutes and Maze would keep her occupied while Ryske went to whatever appointment he had to keep with Noon.

Harlow didn't know where the pair were going. Wherever it was, they'd keep each other safe. Unless she became more embedded in the group that was probably all she could ever hope to understand.

THIRTY-ONE

LUNCH WITH MAZE had been enlightening.

Turned out, when he was eleven, Maze had been adopted by an affluent couple who lived on a vast estate not a million miles from Harlow's modest middle-class family home. The Rowes were members of the same country club as her parents. Harlow had never met either of them, but that was no surprise, the country club wasn't exactly her favorite scene.

In his early years, Maze had bounced around a bunch of foster homes in the Floyd's neighborhood and didn't take the best attitude to his new home with him. In fact, from the sounds of things, he'd carried a massive chip on his shoulder.

Eleven was a late age for adoption. Usually people, especially those with means, would choose a baby over an almost teen. Maze had been lucky, though he hadn't seen it that way when being ripped from his neighborhood and everyone he cared about.

His perspective on life was unique. He had experience from both sides having spent the first part of his childhood around abject poverty, and his teen years receiving the benefit of the best things life could offer… when he wasn't busy shunning the luxury available to him.

His adoptive father was less involved in his

upbringing than his mother, Amelie, who doted on him. In some of the stories Maze told, it sounded almost like his mother treated him as a pet rather than a child. His father certainly did because although Maze was given a good, private education, he wasn't offered a position in his father's successful company. Though through the course of the story, Maze made it clear that he hadn't wanted one anyway.

Maze said he had tried to fit in, which was why he'd agreed to the adoption. The dream for any good-for-nothing orphan kid was to be submerged in lavishness and indulged in every way. But he'd never settled. A rift had grown in the family when he'd bonded more with the household staff than the elite socialites his parents wanted him to associate with.

Parents and child argued, deepening the rift, which hadn't been helped when Maze began inviting his old street friends back to the mansion to play on the estate and with the vast array of tech he'd been spoiled with.

Floyd had taken him in during his pre-teen foster years. Maze's residence at the bar was unofficial, but it was his home of choice. Almost as soon as he was placed with a new foster family, Maze would run away back to Floyd's. The placement family wouldn't put up a fight as they'd inevitably care more about the stipend than him. Harlow liked to think that such a thing wasn't as widespread these days, but it wasn't the first time she'd heard the tale, not by a long shot.

The trend continued after the adoption. Whenever Maze ran away from his adoptive family, the Rowes, he'd go back to Floyd's. Dover's father had been a steadying influence for him, and other strays as well.

Maze talked about Ryske too. Noon had told him that Ryske was open with her, and that seemed to open the doors for all of them to be honest about their joint pasts.

He talked about how Floyd's had been the regular haunt of Ryske's father. Floyd would take pity on the young Ryske when his father drank himself into a stupor, letting him hang out and often sleep in the den overnight. Floyd made a conscious choice to serve Ryske's father even when the man was blitzed. That way he could know Ryske was safe. The alternative would be to boot Ryske's dad out and leave the kid at the mercy of his father's violence.

If the boys hadn't met at the bar, they'd have met at the school where they'd also crossed paths when they bothered to show up for lessons. Though Maze had been moved from one school to another and back so many times that he lost count. Floyd's, and his friendships with Dover and Ryske, were the only constants he had known.

Understanding more about how the crew were connected to each other helped her to see why they were so loyal and how that loyalty would never be broken. They cared a lot for each other and she cared a lot for them.

Cared, yes. But, boy, was she bored.

After lunch, Maze had dropped her off with Dover at Floyd's and gone to do whatever he did. So Harlow had spent the rest of the day alone in the apartment catching up with her college work.

While it was nice to lose herself to the concentration required for college, she couldn't maintain it after night fell and sound rose from the bar below.

Taking a long shower and blow-drying her hair, she took her time about putting on makeup and one of her favorite dresses. Getting herself ready killed some time that apparently she had a lot of.

No one had come to check on her, and she couldn't stay upstairs forever. Harlow was getting bored and wanted to be useful, or at least part of the fun. So donning some shoes, she went on the hunt, creeping down the spiral stairs.

The first person she found was Felipe. In the den, sitting in the middle of the couch, stuffing his face with potato chips, he was watching something on the TV with the volume up high.

"Miss Sweeting," he exclaimed, crumbs of the chips spouting from his mouth.

"Hello, Felipe. Are you okay?"

Going over to sit next to him, she propped herself on the edge of the couch and ran a hand over his hair. He didn't recoil, even though he probably thought she was weird for stroking him. Smiling at her, he closed up the chips and wiped crumbs from his hands onto his jeans.

Something compelled him to explain his presence. "My mom's at work 'til midnight. I've been working today. Mr. Dover lets me watch TV in here after 'cause ours is out. Do you need something?"

"No, honey," she said. "Are you going to be here tomorrow?" He nodded. "I've got something I want you to help me with. Will you do that?"

He nodded again. "Do you live here now? You're in love with Mr. Ryske, aren't you?"

Moistening her lips, she didn't expect that restraining her smile was going to be so difficult. "Mr. Ryske is very special to me," she said. "And I'll be staying for a while. So if you need anything, you can talk to me, okay?"

"Yes, Miss Sweeting."

"Good boy," she said, patting his hand.

As his social worker, she wasn't supposed to touch so much. But she wasn't sure she was his social worker anymore. She wasn't sure she was anyone's.

Leaving him to enjoy his movie on the TV, Harlow got up to head into the bar. The moment she left the den, the noise of Floyd's hit her. Passing the restrooms, she decided to go to the left and hop up behind the bar as opposed to going around the front of it.

The place was busy, but it was dark, so she couldn't pick out who anyone was. Music played on the jukebox and the usual smell of beer and sweat permeated. It wasn't exactly a pleasant smell, but there was comfort in it now that it had become so familiar to her.

Rounding the corner of the L-shaped bar, she found Dover talking to a bunch of guys crowded on the customer side of the bar. The drinkers noticed her before Dover did. His hands were propped on the bar, far apart, supporting his weight. Ducking under Dover's arm, she wrapped both arms around his torso, taking him by surprise.

"Oh, who's the hottie?" one of the patrons asked.

"I want a go after you're done," the second said.

"Sorry, guys, this one's not mine to give," Dover said, resting an arm around her. "You've got to talk to Ryske if you want to take a run at her. Without his say so, you'll get your ass handed to you if you think about feeding this girl a line."

This was a different world. She'd known that. But hadn't known that a guy could hit on an involved woman as long as he got the approval of the man she was involved with… or maybe they were just playing, she wasn't really sure.

The trio on the other side of the bar were still eyeing her. Even though they were bulky and covered in tattoos, she didn't feel intimidated. Floyd's was one of the first places she'd been warned about when taking up her work in this neighborhood; she used to adjust her route to avoid it. Now, Harlow was sleeping there and considered the place a sanctuary and a comfort.

"He's always the guy, isn't he," the third patron said.

"Always is," Dover said and pointed at each of the guys. "These guys here work certain nights for us, we call 'em Tom, Dick, and Larry… Guys, this is Nightingale."

Certain nights, she took that to mean on nights they were busiest, like Fridays.

"Charmed," the one on the end, Tom, said, making the other two laugh.

"Don't fall for it," Dick said, giving Tom a shove. "He's as rough as they come."

"Hey, she likes Ryske," Larry said. "I say that's got to mean she likes it rough."

The guys jeered, making comments on Ryske's long list of exes and how he'd been with women who seemed to like all sorts.

Dover turned toward her, bringing her into a mini-huddle. "You need something, Nightingale?" he asked. "Problem upstairs?"

"No," she said. "Can I borrow Felipe tomorrow? We're going to organize your paperwork."

He circled his arms around her, letting them hang loose behind her as his fingers linked. "The kid's not allowed upstairs."

"We'll do it in the den," she said and widened her smile to a pout. "If that's okay with you."

"That pouty thing might work with Ryske, but I know it's not going anywhere for me," he said and she raised her shoulders in a shrug, making him smile. "But I guess… it is pretty to look at. You can have the kid."

"Thank you."

Tucking her hair behind her ear, his touch was like that of a big brother. "That it? You should go back upstairs. Ryske and Maze are still out. Noon will be back in a while."

Doing whatever it was they did when they were out at night, as they frequently were. "I want to help," she said, inspecting the bottles behind the bar. "Let me work."

His brows almost shot off the top of his head. "What the… You want to work the bar?"

Grinning, she nodded. "Or I can serve."

"Floyd's has never had table service," he said. "And I'm here on my own tonight. You think I want to take the risk of you out there where hands can wander?"

Big brotherly and protective. That may have had something to do with his friend's reaction last time a man outside the crew had touched her.

"Hands don't worry me," she said. "If I get in trouble, I'll go upstairs."

"You'll cause a riot."

Clyde wouldn't be showing up again. There would be no need for anyone else to be near enough to cause a problem for Ryske. "I promise not to flirt," she said, biting her lip, wishing he'd agree. Though it looked like he might be coming around, he wasn't there yet. "I can pour drinks back here if you want…" Letting go of him, she ran a finger along a bunch of bottles. "I've never worked bar. You can teach me."

Obviously that idea was more attractive to her than it was to him. "Table service sounds great," he said, taking her waist to pull her away from the bottles. "Go find yourself something to write on in the store room, and get out there."

Excitement made Harlow squeal. Bouncing up, she grabbed his neck so she could pull him down to kiss him. Giving her something to do might not seem like a big deal to him, but she'd always rather be busy than twiddling her thumbs.

Working bar in this kind of place hadn't even been on her radar before meeting Ryske. If she succeeded, and did it well, it could bring her a step closer to being accepted in this world. To have any kind of future, or relationship, with Ryske, she'd have to become a familiar face around Floyd's. The last thing she wanted was to be the oddity in the corner who no one understood.

Harlow didn't see herself as superior; her family's money was insignificant as far as she was concerned. If Maze, whose family were worth a vast amount more than hers, could be accepted around here, there was hope for her. Connecting with people meant something to her and Ryske was giving her the chance to connect with people in his world by opening the door for her.

Their relationship hadn't been defined and probably never would be. Ryske couldn't promise himself to her, but she could promise herself to him. Being welcome in his world meant more to her than he could ever know. Working for Dover was just the first step.

***

DOVER HADN'T BEEN wrong about the customers wandering hands, but Harlow had done her best to control, and avoid, them. Anytime anyone thought about doing more than putting a hand on her waist… or her thigh… or her ass, she'd hear someone say something about her seeing Ryske and the hand would disappear. Didn't take her long to pick up on the trend. Talking about Ryske whenever anyone was getting too close got her away from any close calls.

The bell to signal last call had rung a few minutes ago and although some patrons were still finishing drinks, most were beginning to leave. Harlow gathered up a bunch of dirty glasses and bottles to take them back over to the bar.

Moving around a crowd that were heading toward the door, she saw Ryske and Maze on this side of the bar, leaning over to huddle with Dover who was on the other side. Noon had come back a while ago and taken Felipe back to his mom's.

She pushed the bottles and glasses onto the bar and crept over to smack Ryske's ass, taking him by surprise.

Grinning, she laughed when he scooped an arm around her waist to haul her against his side.

"Can't keep your hands off the goods. Can you, babydoll?" he said, sweeping her hair away from her face. "What are you doing down here?"

"I'm your friendly neighborhood server," she said, stroking his face. "Can I have a kiss? Do we have a mark in the room?"

"Only mark on my agenda tonight is you," he said and bowed to kiss her.

Curling her fingers into the edges of his jacket, she pressured him down, holding onto the kiss even when he tried to pull away. Slipping a hand to the back of his neck, she held him close, delving her tongue deeper into his mouth.

Her intention had been to show the room that the rumors were true, that she was with Ryske. But she lost sight of that aim when he took her into his arms and reminded her of who she was dealing with by tightening his hold and pinning her to the bar.

In a desperate attempt to hold onto her sanity, Harlow pushed away with both hands and slid out from in front of him. Ryske didn't let her go far. His arm snaked around her to pick her up and seat her on a stool.

Keeping his arm around her, he propped his hip on the seat between her thighs. "You want to explain to me why my girl is working your bar?" Ryske asked Dover.

"She asked."

"He's right," Harlow said, sliding a hand under Ryske's jacket to hold herself against him. "I did ask and I've had fun."

"So much fun that you needed me to put my mark on you the minute I got here," he said and exhaled. "I'm taking you upstairs and we're not coming down for the rest of the night."

The night was basically over anyway. Once Dover was done with clean up, everyone would be coming upstairs to chill or sleep. So Harlow let Ryske take control.

THIRTY-TWO

DOVER HANDED RYSKE a bottle of wine over the bar and Ryske made short work of taking Harlow upstairs to pour her a generous glass.

Propping herself on a stool at the breakfast bar, she drank her wine and watched Ryske open a bottle of beer for himself. "Did you have a productive day?"

"Look, Trink," he said, coming over to sit facing her on another stool. "I appreciate you chipping in. But it's probably not safe for you to be working downstairs."

Protection could only go so far. They couldn't wrap her in cotton wool. Harlow still wanted to live and Floyd's was safe for her, of that she was certain.

"I had fun," she said, guessing that Ryske had avoided her question because he didn't want to tell her what he'd been doing that day. The change of subject was an obvious deflection. "And no one hurt me. If anyone thought about hitting on me, I told them I was involved with someone."

Though she'd stopped short of putting any kind of label on it and avoided terms like "boyfriend" or "partner" like the plague.

He smirked. "That wouldn't stop any of the assholes who come in here."

Smiling in a semi-pout, she was happy to contradict him. "It did when someone mentioned your name."

On a shrug, he conceded a fraction of ground. "Yeah, I guess that would work," he mumbled and slurped from his bottle. "But, Trink, seriously, it's not the ones who ask that worry me."

With Dover always within earshot, she couldn't imagine what Ryske was concerned about. It was nice that he cared enough to be concerned, but if she'd ever felt unsafe or in danger, Dover was right there.

"I'm not worried," she said, sliding a hand onto his thigh. "Will you tell me about your day?"

"Nothing to tell," he said, keeping a hand curved around his beer bottle after propping it on the breakfast bar. "Noon and I took care of some business, got some food, split. Maze and me met up, we took care of some other business."

That wasn't informative. Being vague was Ryske's specialty. Harlow was learning that it paid better not to let him get away with it. "What kind of business?" she asked, and remembered something else she wanted to bring up. "Oh, don't forget you have to talk to Ophelia tomorrow, make sure she's not upset."

"I was with her tonight. We're good. We made up."

Ryske had been with Ophelia. Did that mean they'd been alone? And what did he mean by "made up"? It sent a chill down Harlow's spine to think about what Ryske might have done with Ophelia Hagan to keep her on side and reassure her about his relationship with the "hooker" her brother had brought to the hotel meeting.

Watching Ryske take another drink of beer, Harlow wondered if she was being paranoid about his lack of eye contact. "Did you talk to her about me?"

"Little bit," he said, putting his bottle down again. "Babe…" His jaw went one way and his eyes the other. "Why don't you ask me what you want to know? You want to know if I fucked her."

He stated it without understanding that couldn't be further away from what she wanted. "No, actually," she said, leaping off her stool and walking toward the living room. "The last thing I want to hear about is you sleeping with other women. Did it cross my mind that maybe you had sex with her? Yes. Do I want you to confirm or deny it? No, definitely not."

Harlow didn't know what would be worse to hear, his honesty that he had or the potential dishonesty that he hadn't. What if she didn't believe him? Even if he hadn't and told her that the meeting was platonic, there was always a chance that he wouldn't sell it or she wouldn't let herself believe it. The lie might be worse than the sex.

"So what do you want?"

Stopping in front of the couch, Harlow spun around with her arms open to find him sans beer standing at the head of the dining table. "I don't know, Ryske. Maybe I just don't like the idea of you talking to other women about me. Or maybe it's frustrating that Ophelia knows more about what we are than I do."

"What the fuck does that mean?" he asked, leaping a step in her direction. "And, while we're at it, what the fuck was that 'I don't know what I am with him' today with Flaxman? What is that? Keeping your options open or do you just enjoy seeing me beat on guys for you?"

The idea she'd encourage Ryske to hurt Clyde was laughable, but cracking a smile was beyond her capability when she was this agitated. "I don't need you to beat on anyone for me," she asserted. "But every time, round and round in my head, it hits me. I have no idea what this is."

"What do you want it to be?"

Her arms ascended again, then flopped to her sides. "I don't even know the answer to that. I know I'm attracted to you. I know I care about you, but… I know you'll never be able to be faithful to me. I know you'll never want to marry me or live with me, so… what can it be?"

Coming toward her, he seemed softer when he picked up her hand. "Special," he said. "It can be special. It *is* special." Scooping a hand around her jaw, he tracked the pad of his thumb back and forth on her cheekbone. "You're special to me, Trinket. More special than I think any other woman has ever been in my life."

Covering his hand with hers, she tried to pull it down. The delicacy of his touch was making her forget how important definitions were. "How can you say that? I'm no different."

"You are different," he said, edging closer. "Since you've been in my life, I haven't thought about another woman. Sex was never that important to me. I didn't seek it out, I just took it if it was around. You've changed that. You're smart and sexy. You have morals that make me consider consequences… one consequence anyway… If I touch another woman, you'll look at me differently. It'll hurt you… I don't want to hurt you, Trink."

Warmth crept into her eyes, which was why she kept her focus pinned on his chest. "But everything else I said was true, wasn't it?" she asked. "We can't define this. We can't have a relationship."

"Not a traditional one."

Swallowing hard, she made herself look at him. That might be an explanation he could live with, Harlow needed more. "We can be together, without being together."

"I can promise you—"

"Don't," she said, touching his lips. "I don't want to be someone who forces you to do anything against your will."

Taking her hand from his mouth, he flattened it on his chest over his heart. "This will never belong to anyone else. I will do everything in my power to protect you. Whatever it takes, whatever I have to sacrifice, I will make sure that you are shielded from anything that could hurt you."

"That's why I'm here," she said on a sigh, resigned to this being the way it was. "I'm here because you guys want to protect me from Hagan, not because I'm special to you… But Hagan released me, he didn't put up a fight. Did it ever occur to you that maybe he wants you to be preoccupied with me?"

Ryske was one step ahead. "Yes," he said. "That's why I spent the evening distracting Ophelia so Maze could trawl Hagan's systems. Not only do we know where he's getting his million from, but he may have contributed to ours too."

Though he looked proud of himself, fear made her

steal her hand back. "Is that smart? You already owe him ten grand. If he finds out—"

"He won't find out and I won't tell Maze you just insulted him. He knows how to cover his tracks."

"I'm worried about you, Ryske. I'm worried about all of you. This is dangerous. I shouldn't have to remind you of that."

"This is what we do," he said, bending his arm to show her the four stars on the back of his forearm, he ran a fingertip down the middle of the row. "Highs and lows until we're dirt in the ground."

"I don't know what they are."

"One for each of the guys," he said, touching each of the stars. "I want you to stick around, Trink. I want to add another to the line."

His finger stopped on the blank space on the back of his wrist. For her, did he mean another star to represent her? "You want me to… I can't be on your crew."

"It's dangerous, like you said, but we'll keep you safe, baby. You won't ever be asked to do anything that could hurt you. I… I've woken up without knowing where you are, thinking of you, wondering what you're doing. I don't want to wonder. I want to roll over and see you're right there beside me."

Every morning? That would mean living together. Harlow didn't know whether to be scared or flattered. All she knew about crime had come from books… and her experience since being with Ryske.

"I don't know what to say."

"Think about it," he said as noise from the stairway indicated they were about to have company. "I know what I'm asking you. I know it's a big decision."

The rabble got to the top of the stairs. "Hey! We're gonna get drunk!" Noon called out. "Who's in?"

Her alone with four men, who were drinking, and not known for their integrity. Harlow smiled and swept Ryske aside while raising her arm. "I'm in."

***

"YOU JUST WALKED out?" Noon asked.

Seated in the middle of the couch, Harlow had Noon at one side and Maze at the other. Ryske and Dover were in armchairs that stood in front of the dining table, facing toward the end of Ryske's bed on the other side of the room.

"Yes," she said and shrugged, dipping her fingertip in her wine.

"And he told you to keep that?" Noon asked, looking at the diamond engagement ring Dover was inspecting. "What do you think it's worth?"

Harlow opened her mouth to answer, though all she'd been going to say was that she didn't know. Her voice never made it out of her throat, Dover's was the one to fill the air. "Platinum setting, cushion cut, very good cut, clarity's not perfect, but color's definitely in the colorless range, and it's around five carats... upwards of seventy, eighty grand."

Maze whistled. "Nice. It would be a four month op to swipe something like that," he said.

"Keep it," she said, leaning forward to pick up the wine bottle only to find it was empty.

"Keep it?" Noon asked, incredulous and excited in equal measure. "For real?"

"What am I going to do with it?" she asked. "Rupert didn't want it back. I can't wear it. It's just a reminder every time I open my jewelry box."

"A reminder of what?" Maze asked.

After emptying her glass into her throat, she put it on the coffee table. "Of lessons learned."

Sounded profound when in truth it was just reality. Being with Rupert hadn't been horrible, but it was an education that she didn't plan on forgetting.

"You miss him?" Dover asked.

Sitting back, she tucked her feet up on the edge of the couch. "Sometimes," she said. "We were together for six years... he knew me better than anyone else ever has."

"Not well enough to know you weren't interested in being a fifties wife," Maze said.

She shrugged. "You said your parents wanted the

same kind of life for you. I guess it's not that unusual of an aspiration. It just wasn't mine."

"If he won't keep it, I will," Noon said, lunging over her to snag the ring from Dover.

His exuberance made her laugh. She was still laughing at him when Dover put an arm around her shoulders to pull her against his chest. "What is your aspiration, Nightingale?"

The effects of the wine were making her sleepy. Happy to rest against his solid form, she arched her back and yawned. "To be wild, and crazy, and irresponsible. I want to drink, and party, and have sex in insane places." She was already grinning, but it was when the other three turned to look at Ryske that she laughed. "I wasn't propositioning him."

"Don't think you have to," Maze muttered. "I think he'd do you anywhere."

"Anywhere Noon could walk in and catch them at it," Dover said. "I'm sure they set it up that way just to remind him he ain't getting any."

"Don't see them lining up for you," Noon said, lunging over her to try smacking Dover who just laughed harder and used her as a shield.

"I forget, Ryske," Dover said. "What did the twins say when you told them Noon needed company?"

Standing up, Ryske smirked. "Poor kid's taken enough of a beating for one day and his night isn't about to get any better."

Coming over to stand in front of her, Ryske bent to take her hands and pulled her onto her feet. "It isn't?" she asked, letting him push her along, their joined hands on her hips. "Why not?"

Drawing her back, he whispered above her ear. "Because he's going to have to listen to you screaming for me all night."

"We're not having sex," she said.

Ryske pushed her to the side of their bed, blocking her in while he reached over to draw the curtain at the foot of the bed closed. The guys whooped and catcalled. There was a second curtain between the two nightstands that separated Ryske's bed from Noon's. He guided that down to meet the straight one at the bottom, concealing them from the view of the others.

The wine had loosened her up. When Ryske started to undress her, she admitted to herself that she kind of liked it. "We're gonna start fulfilling your aspirations right here."

"Strange places doesn't mean in front of an audience," she said, deciding to work on removing his clothes, since he was taking care of hers. "We can make out."

"Good," he said, snatching her hips to thrust her backwards onto the bed. "That's the only in I need."

Disoriented, Harlow was still getting used to being naked when he finished stripping and climbed on top of her, kissing his way from her knee to her cleavage. "I don't know how much time you spent with girls in high school," she said, running her hands through his hair while he feasted on her breasts. "But this goes way beyond making out."

Lifting his head, his feral eyes were unapologetic. "You didn't restrict which part of your body I could make out with.

Rising up, he grabbed her knees to pull them apart and dipped down to kiss the most intimate corner of her body. "Oh, boy," she sighed and grabbed a pillow to squash it into her face in hopes it would block the sounds of ecstasy seeping from her lips.

Ryske wasn't subtle; he took liberties wherever he could. Harlow would just have to get used to the fact that being with a criminal meant rules were always going to be optional not mandatory.

THIRTY-THREE

FOR ALMOST A week, they settled into a routine that involved her naked in bed with Ryske every night, and her laughing at him for trying every way he knew how to get inside her, literally. His patience was stretched so thin that he seemed to be in a perpetual bad mood with her.

Harlow hadn't let them go further than oral. Each morning, he got his in the shower. The closest thing they got to privacy was behind those steamy glass walls. It was amazing how quickly she'd become accustomed to their living arrangements and how the men just walked into the bathroom whenever they felt like it, whether she or Ryske were in the midst of orgasm or not.

Bedtime was harder. In the intimacy of the small hours, she didn't talk to Ryske about what he'd said. Because she was aware of the other men sleeping in the room, it wasn't easy to relax and be with him the way a girlfriend might be in bed with her man. Not because she didn't trust the other men, she did, but she didn't want Ryske's friends to hear her questioning him or them whispering sweet nothings.

Spending time with Felipe was a lot of fun. During the day, she worked with the youngster to organize the Floyd's paperwork or did her college assignments. The guys loved to stop and offer the wisdom of their experience if they passed by when her books were open. Essays on motivation, logistics, and after-effects were certainly easier with subjects around who were eager to provide case studies.

At night, Ryske went out with one or more of the guys, while she served in Floyd's where she was beginning to make friends with the regulars and Dover's other employees.

On Friday night, seated on the closet couch, Harlow was buckling her shoe around her ankle when the closet door opened. Ryske came in naked, with a towel slung around the back of his neck rather than around his hips, where any other normal guy would wear it.

"I thought you were gone," she said, sitting up straight.

"I was, I came back," he said, dropping the towel and retrieving a pair of jeans from a drawer.

Smiling at his lack of underwear, she leaned back on the couch. "I don't need you to make my job any easier," she said, nodding at his groin when he turned toward her pulling on the jeans. "You're going smokeless."

"Hoping to get laid," he said, buttoning his fly.

That explanation changed her mood. Hiding how uncomfortable it made her to think of him on a job that involved getting intimate with another woman wasn't easy. Fearing he might be able to read her, she thought it best to change the subject.

Pouncing to her feet, Harlow smoothed her skirt and pasted on a grin. "How do I look? Like a pro?"

He finished buttoning and folded his arms across his chest, taking his time about checking her out. "Nothing like a pro, baby..." That answer disappointed her. Her smile dropped, making his rise. "You're too classy for that shit, Trink."

Breathing out, she relaxed. "Good save," she said and sidestepped toward the door. "Have a good night."

"Hey," he said, darting across the room to get in front of her, blocking her exit. "You don't have to work tonight."

"You tell me that every night."

Harlow tried to get around him, but he got in her way

again. "No, I mean, I've got us a room."

Confused, she had no idea what he was trying to say. "A room? Where? For what?"

Coiling his arms around her, he pulled her body against his. The way he bent his knees to get closer to her level was familiar to her now. This was a prelude to a kiss, which was his prologue to seduction… or attempted seduction.

"I'm gonna buy you dinner," he murmured, the deep tone vibrating from him through to her bones. "Load you up with a few drinks, loosen you up and then…"

Leaning in, he pressed his mouth to hers.

Suspicion kept her from accepting his kiss for what it was. Pushing him back, she squinted to examine him, trying to figure out what this was about. These were work hours, they didn't get intimate during work hours.

"What's going on, Ryske? You always have business at night, why is tonight any…" Figuring it out, her eyes ascended as her head began to nod. "It's Friday."

"Yeah, baby—"

"You want me out while the basement is open," she said, giving him a shove to free herself from his embrace. "What is it about that place? All week you've been keeping me out of there. What is it you don't want me to see?"

"It's not that we don't want you to see it," he said.

"You don't trust me?"

That statement almost seemed to offend him and he jumped onto the defensive. "It's called plausible deniability, Trink. Me and the guys might end up in front of a judge one day for what we do down there. We've made our peace with it. All of us. We've made that choice. But you? No, I won't have it. You will never do time behind bars for this crew. Not as long as I have any say in it."

Folding her arms, she glared. "So all that stuff you said last weekend about me being part of the team." Tapping her wrist, she indicated an invisible star. "That was bullshit? Your attempt to speed up your journey into my panties."

"No," he said. "I don't need tricks. If I'd wanted in that bad, I'd have forced myself on you." Seizing her wrist, he yanked her to him. "Do you think the guys would've stopped me?"

Tugging her wrist out of his grip, her anger made her back away. Rape wasn't in Ryske's repertoire and the guys would've stopped him if he had considered taking things too far with her. His crew knew as well as she did that Ryske was incapable of violating her. He knew how to go to the edge, but never went too far. His instinct was attuned to hers.

This was his attempt to arouse her with his domination, which would usually work. Harlow had to see past their desire. One of them had to keep them on track. "No, that won't work this time, Crash. Yes, I get turned on when you're forceful, but I can't do this anymore. I can't do this halfway thing. You have to tell me, all or nothing? I can't just go with it anymore."

"You're the one who hasn't answered me," he argued. "I told you what I wanted, you didn't answer me, and then spent the night talking about your ex. You want to be with me? You've gotta prove it."

Shocked by his vehemence, she was close to speechless. "P… prove it?"

His scowl was fierce. "Yeah, you're Miss Goody Two Shoes, right? Miss Books and College Assignments can't be with a guy like me. You've picked your path. You have a future ahead of you; a good one. I said you were excited by the thrill of me, but you're terrified of it too and you know what, Trink? You should be!"

His anger was enveloped in disappointment too. Hearing the truth coming from his mouth, she realized he was telling her what she hadn't wanted to admit to herself. All this time, Ryske had been playing with her.

Her dejection wasn't a simple thing to overcome, but Harlow did her best to stand tall even in the face of it. "You don't know what you're talking about."

"Don't I, baby?" he asked. "Why haven't we gone all the way, huh?"

"We share a room with the guys."

He spat out his disbelief like it was disgust. "They think we started screwing when I was holed up at Bale's. If you wanted it, you'd have let me take it. We've had plenty of chances. We could've slept in here or down in the den. But you don't want it. I know I turn you on, that's fucking obvious every minute. But your feelings for me fucking terrify you."

Throwing that in her face was some bullshit that she wouldn't let him get away with. "Oh, yeah, and what's your excuse? You're so sure you could've had me, why haven't you? And don't give me some bullshit about respect or consent. You pride yourself on being an arrogant asshole, and taking sex any time it's on offer. Why haven't you taken it from me?"

Arguing wasn't a new phenomenon for them. But it only seemed to get to this fierce panting stage when they were talking about them. It was the hardest thing for them to talk about, the most difficult thing to face.

"Are you offering it?" he snapped.

Opening her arms, Harlow said nothing, daring him to come and take it. For half a beat, it looked like he was going to move, but his tension vanished when he deflated.

"I knew it," she said, accepting that he wasn't going to follow through. "I was a distraction. You wanted to know if you could make the naïve goody two shoes fall for you. This was all just an exercise, a way to hone your skills. Well done. I fell for it, Grifter."

Going for the exit, Harlow was ready to get the hell out of this place and away from this man.

"Where are you going?" he asked.

Passing him without a second glance, she opened the door. "The best thing about this conversation? I now know that I don't owe you a goddamn thing. I don't have to tell you a damn thing either."

Leaving the closet, she held her resolve as she crossed the apartment and went into the stairwell. Harlow wasn't going to take the risk of going out through the bar where she could more easily be stopped.

The stairwell wasn't used by customers during the week, so she didn't really think about the people who may be coming in the side entrance to head for the basement. They became a frustrating obstacle in her way. Ignoring the odd looks customers cast her way, she pushed through the people who were trying to get in.

All she wanted was to be out of there. As far from Floyd's as she could get. Hurrying down the alley, she could only leave by the rear parking area, which had more than a dozen vehicles in it that night. Usually empty but for the crew's vehicles, the increase of occupied spaces was further evidence that tonight was different.

But that wasn't her business, and she wasn't going to dwell on it. Her goal was to get the hell out of there. Hagan hadn't come for her since letting her leave the hotel with Ryske. She'd seen no evidence that she was in danger anymore.

Maneuvering around a couple of vehicles, Harlow thought she was home free with a clear shot out.

A car door opened and Maze stepped out into her path. "Nightingale, what's—"

"Get out of my way, Maze."

"No," he said, grabbing her wrist when she tried to march on past him. "I'm eyes out here, but Noon's inside. If there's somewhere you need to be—"

"Yes, there is somewhere I need to go."

Taking her shoulders, there was real concern on his face when he asked. "Where?"

"Away from here," she said, throwing his hands from her body. "You were right, okay? You were all right. I'm not cut out for this. The dumb, naïve little middle-class princess is going to run on home, back to the life she was supposed to live. I'll go back to the ex, get knocked up, and live miserably ever after, just like you all want."

Spinning around, she stormed away, skirting a couple more cars to get away from Maze to head for the opposite street. She didn't even get to the corner before Maze caught up at her side.

"If you want to dump Ryske and turn your back on your crew, that's just fine. But I'll lock you up in the basement myself before I'll let you go back to the prick who couldn't keep you happy."

"Least I could keep that prick happy," she said without missing a step. "Maybe he's the only man I'll ever understand."

Maze matched her speed with little effort. "I know Ryske can spin a lot of plates, but with you he's… well, he's about as straightforward as I've ever seen him. I don't know what happened between you two, but me and the guys, we keep saying he's an open book with you. He's never had his poker face fail him so much. He just can't keep his cards hidden."

She didn't know what any of that meant and wasn't interested in figuring it out. On her trek down the next block, she tried to gather some enthusiasm about the idea of going back to the life she'd left. Her parents had told her that she wouldn't make it in the city. Moving home would prove their point.

Maze was still there beside her, keeping pace, frustrating her. "Are you going to follow me all the way home?"

"If I have to," he said. "You know the rules, you're not supposed to go anywhere without one of us."

"Then prepare to meet my parents and my boyfriend."

Rupert wasn't exactly her boyfriend yet. If she went back to him and told him she'd be everything he wanted her to be, he wouldn't reject her. Not like Ryske had.

"I've met your boyfriend." Maze was talking about Ryske, not Rupert. "I've known him longer than you have and he's not the type to give up easy… He says stupid stuff all the time. You *know* that, he says stupid stuff to you. I've never seen you react like this. Usually, you know exactly how to play him at his own game."

Snorting out a semi-laugh, she couldn't rid herself of her rage. "Oh, I did. I played him right back and found out the truth."

"What truth?" he asked. When she didn't answer, he took her arm to pull her to a halt. "Damn it, Nightingale. What did he say?"

"This has been a game, all along. I've been a distraction, a way to hone his skills."

Shocked, his fingers drifted away from her arm. In his moment of reflection, Harlow got the chance to absorb where they were. This was the spot where it had started. They were standing at the end of the alley where Ryske had first crashed into her.

Maze's shock wasn't rooted in the same place as hers. "He loves you," he said, while she was still off balance trying not to think too hard about the night she met Ryske. "That's why he's acting like a jerk. Ryske has never been in love, always said he was impervious, which was how he could seduce any woman and never get attached. But in you, he found something pure. Not innocent, no, you're anything but that." He touched her cheek. "You have fire and grit, two things that he admires. You've never been afraid of anything and he's drawn to that fearless quality. You didn't look down your nose at us or where we live. You've accepted everything about our lives, about his life. He loves you."

She edged away from his caress. "No, he doesn't. We might all live together, but you guys don't know the truth of our relationship, of what we are."

"I don't doubt that. No one outside a relationship knows the full truth of what's going on in it."

"You might think he loves me; the guys might think it too. It's not the truth." Conceding a sigh, she tried to calm down. None of this was Maze's fault. "Maybe it wasn't all a game. But there's one truth that none of us can deny. There's no future for us. For Ryske and I. All there can ever be is sex. As long as he does what he does, that's all he can offer me. And before you freak out, I wouldn't ask him to give up the con. He loves what he does. But there's no space in his life for me."

Maze took one step back. A solemn air descended around him. "You're right."

She nodded once, letting the sadness of that truth weigh her down. "I know I am. I don't fit in his world and I won't ask his world to fit around me."

"You have to get out," Maze said, like he was putting pieces together. "You have to be free to move on with your life without him pulling you back."

"I didn't say—"

"Come on," he said, putting an arm around her to

guide her in the direction of Floyd's again.

"Where are we going?"

"We're going to make sure you're safe," he said. "We can't split our resources. You'll have to stay at Floyd's until this is over—"

"Maze," she said, shrugging his arm away. "I can't. I'm done making a fool of myself with him."

"You won't," he said, holding up both hands to soothe her. "This will only be for another day or two. Ryske will make it clear to Hagan at the meet tomorrow that you're a non-factor."

That didn't do much for her ego. Harlow folded her arms. "How will he do that?"

For just a second, he was at a loss. "I don't know," he said and hazarded a possibility. "He'll propose to Ophelia or something. Yeah. That will work. She'll play along and it will get us a step closer to our goal, Ophelia too."

The way to save herself was to let the man who'd entranced her betroth himself to another woman? The situation just kept getting more complicated. Harlow didn't know how they all kept up with the twists and turns of the job.

Maze put his arm around her to start them walking again.

This time, she didn't resist. Making the crew's life more difficult wasn't going to help anyone. "I won't sleep with him again."

"You won't have to," he said. "If he won't give up his bed to you, you can have mine."

Harlow didn't want to go back to Floyd's, but returning to her parents wasn't an attractive prospect either. In a way, it was impressive just how big a mess she could make of her life in such a short time. Harlow might not be a pro in Ryske's eyes, but she was in hers. Except, being a professional screw up was nothing to be proud of.

THIRTY-FOUR

RYSKE HADN'T EVEN been there when they got back to Floyd's. Maze had walked Harlow back upstairs to the apartment, made her promise not to leave again, and then he'd gone back to work.

Her tantrum might have seemed juvenile, but she had fully intended to walk away for good. Their lives would be a lot easier if they didn't have her to worry about. Distracting Maze from his job was unfair too. Chaos seemed to be encroaching on Harlow from all sides. Everything was telling her she wasn't cut out for life with Ryske.

His crew needed to maintain a level head. They had to put their own feelings aside when there was an event or a job because they relied on each other. Even when they were mad, they'd still give their lives for each other. Keeping her feelings in check around Ryske wasn't her specialty.

Making a decision to stay out of the way, Harlow slept on the closet couch and no one disturbed her. Even in the morning, none of the guys came into the closet, not that she was aware of. Either they'd snuck in to dress before she was awake or they had grabbed whatever was in the downstairs laundry.

Proving that they were ready to be rid of her, no one

was in the apartment when she crept out of the closet in the morning. There had obviously been an agreement that they give her a wide berth until they could get rid of her.

Harlow didn't see anyone at all until the Saturday night. Studying at the cleared desk in the closet, she was keeping a low profile.

But this was a public space and she couldn't expect to be alone forever, as proved when Ryske came in wearing a towel, much as he had the previous night. His modesty hadn't increased just because they were at odds.

Making eye contact, they paused. "I'll give you your privacy," she said, closing her book and tucking it under her arm as she stood up.

Ryske walked in the direction of the dressers. She headed for the door.

"Maze is wrong," he said, just before she got to the exit.

The statement made her face him. He had his back to her and was taking underwear from the drawer that he proceeded to pull on.

"Wrong about what?"

"About where you should be," he said, going to a rail in the corner to begin donning a suit. "Your ex didn't make you happy, but he didn't make you unsafe. One's more important than the other."

"You think I should go back to Rupert," she stated, folding her arms around her textbook.

Putting on his pants, he didn't fasten them, and took a shirt from a hanger. Threading one arm into a sleeve and then the other, she was disappointed in herself for noticing that he was covering up the impressive body he'd once let her play with.

"You dumped him, not the other way around," Ryske said. "You were together for years and have been broken up for months. But he's not hooking up with anyone else... Noon was right, he's hung up on you. Your ex will take you back."

Hugging the book tighter to her chest, she tilted her head. "And that's what you want because that's what will get me off your plate."

"That's not what I said. With you, I say what I mean. He'll keep you safe. You'll be content."

"But not happy," she said, watching him continue to dress. "And what about you? What will you do?"

"Go with it," he said, seeking cufflinks. "It's what us on this side of town do."

"Go with it."

He nodded. "Yep."

This seemed like just another day at the office. Ryske was so unfazed that if it wasn't so heart wrenching, she might appreciate the insight into his inner self. All of this was happening, but he took it in his stride. Reading a situation, adjusting, and making a strategy. Planning her future was a single step in a mission that he'd probably never think about again after she was gone.

Even knowing that this was when she was supposed to turn and walk away, Harlow was too intrigued to just let it go.

Instead of departing, she took a step toward him. "Did you ever feel anything for me? Anything at all?"

"Trink, I care about you, but—"

"No," she said, tossing the book onto the couch. "Don't use that patronizing appeasement voice with me. Don't switch it on and think you can soothe me. Just look me in the eye and tell me the goddamn truth. Did you ever feel anything for me?"

The situation made her angry and that pounding emotion was made worse when something like pain appeared in his gaze. "Baby, I have nothing to offer you."

That stark truth took her anger. "I didn't want anything," she said, touched by his sincerity. "Nothing but you."

Clenching his teeth, he garnered some anger of his own. "I won't do it to you. I won't drag you down to my level. You don't belong with the scum in the gutter. You should be soaring with the birds, Nightingale."

But she couldn't claim to be Nightingale, not if she was being cast out of the crew. Reality caught up with her.

Maze's suggestion was no longer a distant prospect, it was coming to pass. The suit, the cufflinks, Ryske was going out, somewhere nice… he was making an effort with the goal of keeping her safe.

"You're going to do it, aren't you?" she said, suddenly cold. "You're going to propose to her."

As was his way with awkward questions, he avoided giving her a direct answer. "I'm going to make Hagan see that you are inconsequential. You won't be in danger after tonight."

Narrowing what was left of the physical space between them to rest her hand on his chest, she made eye contact. "And am I?" she asked. "Inconsequential?"

Laying his hand over hers as he had once before, he pressed her palm into him. "That will never belong to anyone else."

Even in spite of their argument the previous night, she wanted to believe him. "Crash—"

"We're through, Harlow," he said, losing his patience. "You're going back to your safe, mundane existence in the suburbs. You will never be hurt by my world again."

Hitching her chin up, she slid her hand out from under his. "And if I say I won't go?"

"Why wouldn't you go?" he asked, taking a jacket and tie from the rack. "The city ate you up and spat you out. You weren't built for the wrong site of the tracks, babydoll." He winked and flashed her his dashing, professional smile. "Time to tuck that tail and go home. There's nothing left for you here."

Pushing her buttons was so easy for him. Maybe he didn't realize that provoking her only fired her determination. The trouble was… he was right. Everything he'd said was true.

Ryske went past her to head out of the closet and off to his meeting with Hagan. All she could do was stumble backwards until the couch caught her.

Harlow was going home. The adventure was over.

THIRTY-FIVE

AN HOUR OR SO after Ryske had left, Harlow heard Felipe shouting up the spiral stairs. The youngster called her name, so she quickly finished applying her lip gloss and tossed the tube aside before heading toward his voice.

Telling herself to be confident and optimistic, she ran down the stairs, brushing a hand across Felipe's cheek as she passed him to float across the den.

"Someone's here for you," Felipe said.

Harlow hadn't so much as paused and twirled to face him as she opened the den door. "I know, honey."

"Dover doesn't look happy."

Peeking around the den door, her grin grew cheerier. "Do I look like I give a crap?"

If she was stuck in Floyd's until Ryske finished weaving his magic, then her only option was to see her friends there. Dover didn't have to like the people she socialized with, but he did have to bite his tongue, just like he had when Hagan sent his men in to spy.

Harlow flounced into the bar. She wasn't working tonight; no point when she was going to be kicked out as soon as the crew could get away with ousting her. All that was left was for her to say goodbye to the friends she had made in the city. In honor of her forced farewell, she'd snagged her clean cellphone from the closet desk and made plans. No one had told her that she couldn't invite people to drink with her.

Rounding the bar on the patrons' side, Harlow wasn't surprised to find that Clyde was nervous. Seated on the stool he'd occupied the last time he was there, he was looking left and right, vigilant, probably because he'd been caught so unawares the last time.

Reaching her friend, she put a hand on Clyde's shoulder to lean in and kiss his cheek. "He's not here," she said.

Clyde blinked, probably surprised by her familiarity, but he didn't say anything. Harlow leaned over the bar to wave at Dover's bartender, Lowan, and ordered them some drinks.

"He… he's not here?" Clyde asked. She shook her head, seating herself on the stool next to his. "Why did you call me?"

The only reason she'd been able to call Clyde was because Ryske had revealed his last name, which let her look him up.

"I'm heading out of town tomorrow," she said. "I emailed my notice to Gina."

Harlow hadn't been in the office for weeks, so she doubted her resignation was any surprise to her former boss.

It was more of a shock to Clyde. "You… why?"

Lowan brought over their drinks and didn't even try to ask for payment. Grabbing the glass, Harlow began to gulp down the alcohol. Having already destroyed half a bottle of wine upstairs, her reserve was long gone.

"That's part of the reason I called you," she said, touching her moist lip. "A friend of mine found out Gina has done quite a few favors for a specific guy who gives a lot of money to the department… the favors aren't always in our clients' interest… or in the employees' interest. I wanted to tell you to watch your back."

Dover's voice came from behind her. "Can I talk to you?"

Framing his words as a question seemed ridiculous given that at the same time he said them, he grabbed her elbow and hauled her off her stool. Harlow barely had time to put down her glass before she was being dragged away from Clyde.

About ten feet from the bar, Dover stopped and whirled her around to face him.

"Is there a problem?" she asked, picking lint from Dover's sleeve.

"Are you nuts?" he hissed. "What's this asshole doing here? Ryske is going to—"

"Do nothing," she said. "Because by the time he's back Clyde will be gone. Besides, he and I talked and agreed we're through, so it's all good."

She patted his chest and tried to go back to Clyde, but Dover caught her arm to pull her back again. "You're through?"

Smiling, she nodded. The last thing she needed to do was show the melancholy that was tearing her apart. Instead, Harlow chose to stick with blind optimism. "After tonight you'll be free of me forever. I'm going back home. I wanted to say goodbye to the closest thing I had to a friend in the city. I don't think that's wrong. I want to say goodbye to Bale too… maybe I'll write him a letter."

Dover seemed stunned for a moment, but pulled himself together. "Well, you're, uh… you're in luck. He got back into town last night. He's coming over later."

"Excellent," she said, patting him again. "Perfect."

Inviting Clyde for a drink wasn't meant to lead to a night of partying. Saying goodbye, and delivering the warning about Gina, were her motivations. This wasn't game playing. After going back to her parents' home the following day, she'd never have any reason to see Clyde again.

She'd never see any of them again.

Dover didn't stop her again. Harlow went back to the bar and got another drink for herself and for Clyde. Her ex-colleague needed the courage even in spite of her constant reassurance that Ryske wasn't around and wouldn't be bursting in to beat him up. After maybe the twentieth time of reiterating that she and Ryske were no longer an item, Clyde began to relax, and they finally had a chance to talk.

She didn't even notice the hours passing and lost track of how many glasses of wine she'd had. With nothing but the prospect of tension and grief ahead of her, the escape into this temporary fun was welcome.

Harlow's night got better when someone touched her waist. Turning to see who was there, she found herself in the half-embrace of a familiar man.

"Bale!" she exclaimed putting down her glass to leap into his arms. "Oh, I missed you! Where have you been, Doctor Urban?"

"It's a long story," he said, keeping an arm around her. "Who's your friend?"

"An ex-colleague," she said, picking up her wine again. "I quit my job."

With his fingertips, he gathered her hair from her temple to tuck it behind her ear. "I know, I've been talking to Dover... do I need to order a psych exam? I thought you loved your job."

"I did, until I realized it was a crock of shit." Tipping her head back, Harlow finished her wine and pushed the glass over the bar. "Nobody's who they say they are. Have you noticed that? How people are just bone-deep liars? Men and women alike. Everyone's out for themselves... Men are real bastards... Fucking bastards."

"Okay, I think that's enough liquor for you, lady," Bale said, shaking his head at Lowan.

She pouted at him. "You are a party pooper. I was so desperate to see you before I left... now I think you should go back to your conversation with Dover."

"I think you should tell me what Ryske did to upset you," Bale said.

Tutting, and sagging to the side, she noticed how Clyde paled at the mention of the person she'd worked hard to expel from their discussions. "Why is everything about that bastard? Can't I just be drunk because I'm drunk and not because he stole my heart and stomped all over it?" Smacking a hand on the bar, she twisted out of Bale's arms in her attempt to seek out the bartender. "I need more alcohol, Lowan!"

"No, you don't," Bale said.

The bartender, Lowan, was standing at the curve of the bar doing his best not to look in her direction, which was an obvious ploy because she was being loud enough that everyone else was looking at her.

"What am I doing?" she said, realizing her error. "I don't need your permission. I don't need anyone's damn permission! I know where the alcohol is. What is Dover going to do if I help myself? Call the cops?" Spitting out a laugh, she slunk out from between Bale and the bar. Taking a moment to wobble on her shaky legs, Harlow slapped at both Clyde and Bale as they tried to steady her. "I don't need help. Leave me. Leave me!"

After they let her go, she immediately lost her balance and stumbled to the side. She might have hit the floor if someone else hadn't caught her.

When she blinked up at the face belonging to the arms around her that had prevented her fall, Harlow went from grateful to resentful in a heartbeat. "Oh look," she sneered. "It's the man who gets the trophy for it."

"It?" Ryske asked.

"Leaving me," she said and shoved at him to get out of his arms. "I don't need your damn help either."

Holding onto Bale for balance, she dipped down to pull off one heel and then the other. Her legs might be shaky, but steadying herself would be easier without the shoes.

"She's drunk," Ryske muttered, making eye contact with the doctor behind her.

She raised a spike heel to wave it in his face. "Don't do that. Don't talk about me as though I'm not here. In twenty-four hours you'll have your wish and I'll be gone forever, then all of you can erase me from your memories..."

Bale's hand closed over the back of hers to remove the shoe from her grip. "You're going to take his eye out with that thing."

"He doesn't need his eyes," she grumbled. "Long as his dick works, he'll be just fine." Bale took both shoes from her, but she didn't care, Harlow was too busy glaring at Ryske who she hadn't expected to see so soon. Not given what he was supposed to be doing. Raising both arms, she pasted on a wide smile. "And congratulations are in order, everyone! One of our very own has chosen to sacrifice his freedom for love! Yes, he's engaged!" Those in the vicinity clapped or jeered, and she slapped Ryske's arm. "I can't ask to look at the ring. I don't know what you're supposed to say to a newly engaged man, so congratulations will have to do."

"Trink—"

"Don't Trink me," she hissed without caring that his anger seemed to be as potent as hers.

Sweeping Ryske aside, she muttered to herself about how out of line he was on her walk along the length of the bar and around to behind it. Lowan didn't even get in her way when she went past him. God help the Aussie if he had.

It didn't take her long to retrieve the wine from the fridge.

Still muttering to herself, Harlow knew she was drunk, and knew she was making a scene. But, fuck it, this was her last night in these people's lives. They were casting her out. She was being ousted. She wasn't good enough for them.

Twisting the corkscrew into the top of the bottle, Harlow didn't recall being aware of anything beyond her own thoughts. Bale might have been telling her not to drink more. Clyde might have been agreeing that it wasn't a good idea.

Only one thing stood out clear as crystal. In the time it took her glance to ascend past the duo, everything seemed to slow down.

Maybe she'd heard his name being called. Harlow couldn't remember that either. All she remembered was raising her chin, seeking something out. Whatever had drawn her attention got Ryske's too; he turned toward the door at the same time she did.

Everything happened in slow motion, yet it happened so fast. Harlow had just registered that the man standing inside the Floyd's entrance was Alleyman when a flash of light blinded her. It was just a second in time, and she didn't hear a bang, at least she didn't remember one.

She didn't remember hearing anything. Everything went silent until her ears began to ring. Activity exploded in every direction. People leaped from their seats, scrambling around falling furniture and probably screaming too, but she heard nothing.

Alleyman fled. She barely noticed his departure in her peripheral vision as her gaze swung back around to Ryske.

Did she know?

Harlow couldn't hold onto a thought. Nothing seemed significant. Not the pounding of her heart. Not the sickness in her belly or the adrenaline that diluted the alcohol in her bloodstream.

Nothing until the second her eyes met his.

Ryske was there where he had been, six feet from the bar. Completely still though chaos besieged him. Piling toward the door, everyone wanted to get out of there. They wanted to get away from what had happened. Was it danger? Were they afraid?

She hadn't figured out what had happened, where the flash had come from, or why Alleyman had even appeared... or maybe she just hadn't acknowledged the truth to herself.

At first, Ryske seemed calm. Dumb confusion swept over him and she felt it too. Something had scared all these people, but all she'd seen was a small burst of light, a brief spark of...

Ryske's hand rose. She hadn't taken her eyes from his, but she was somehow aware of the movement. Numb, nothing made sense and she identified with his confusion. This was bizarre. Something was happening that she didn't understand.

Ryske's eyes dropped from hers to focus on his fingertips. Following his gaze, she saw what he did in the same moment he saw it.

His fingers were red... why were they...

It wasn't just his fingers. There was a stain on his shirt... on his chest...

Undiluted terror struck her with the force of a big rig.

The world was still on mute, but Harlow opened her mouth in a scream that didn't seem to make it out of her lungs or at least it didn't make it to her ears. Whether the sound came out or not, Bale and Clyde turned away from the bar just as Ryske began to descend.

THIRTY-SIX

ABANDONING THE WINE, Harlow sprinted around the bar, throwing aside anyone or anything that got in her way.

It wasn't until she collapsed onto her knees at Ryske's side that she started to hear again. Grabbing up his hand and clutching it to her chest, she fixated on his eyes, ignoring how Bale ripped open Ryske's shirt and Clyde on the phone to 9-1-1.

Although his lips were moving, she didn't even attempt to decipher Ryske's specific words. Without hearing them, she knew he'd be trying to give instructions not to call 9-1-1, just like he had on the night they'd met. But if 9-1-1 was going to save his life, she wasn't going to express his wishes for him.

Stroking his hair from his face, she bowed to kiss him. "You're going to be okay, Crash," she said, taking his hand to her mouth. "You're going to be okay, baby."

Ryske was clinging to her so tight. His mouth opened again, but not to talk. The distress in his gaze was matched by the panic of his grip. He was wheezing, failing to get a breath. Trying to inhale and wincing, he tried again, but got nothing.

"He can't breathe," she said, searching Ryske's gaze. "He can't breathe! Bale!"

"His lung's collapsed," Bale said.

All of a sudden, a med bag was dropped at the doctor's side and he got to work. Someone gripped her shoulders and hunkered down at her side. She guessed it was one of the guys, but she wouldn't take her eyes from Ryske's.

Blood stained the corner of his mouth. "You always have to be the center of attention, don't you?" she said, her vision blurring. "If you wanted me to stop being mad at you, flowers would've worked."

Pain welled in her chest. Blood soaked his torso, she tried not to look at it, not to see it, but the stain was growing every second. It colored his lips too. With a quick brush of her hand, she swiped it away when it trickled from his mouth.

"You're gonna be okay, man," Dover said behind her.

Harlow could hear sirens, and wished they'd hurry up and get louder. Clutching his hand to her mouth, she kept kissing him, praying that Bale being present gave them a fighting chance. But Ryske was losing color.

"Crash," she whispered, moving his hand to curl his fingers around her throat. For the first time, he didn't take over, didn't grip her. "Tighter... Please, baby... Tighter."

Tears dripped from her face onto his arm. The agony of fear ate her up. His weak fingers tensed for half a second. But when they almost immediately loosened, she yelped.

Sinking lower until her face was on his shoulder, Harlow guided his hand around to the back of her head to try twining his fingers into her locks. All she wanted was the illusion that everything was okay. If she could just get a response, some acknowledgement that he was still with her, she had hope.

"Tighter, Crash," she cried. "Please!"

Nothing happened.

Filled with vehemence, and perhaps naïve determination, she sat up again, holding his hand in her cleavage. "You are going to make it! I am not going to let you do this to me, you bastard!"

"Harlow," she heard Dover say her name just a second before Bale called out.

The EMTs were here.

The Floyd's patrons were gone, yet someone tried to pull her away while Bale barked orders at the paramedics.

"No," she screamed. "No!"

Tears made it impossible for her to decipher details. The pressure in her chest was restricting her breathing. Everything was frantic. She was losing her grip.

The only thing she needed. The thing that made sense to her. Was Ryske. Her Crash. No one was going to take her away from him. No one. They got him onto a gurney and then he was being wheeled out.

Hope. The professionals had him. They'd fix him. Make him better.

Harlow tried to follow, but she was tugged back.

"No, Nightingale, you can't!" Noon called.

She hadn't even known he was present, but when she whipped around, there he was with Dover at his side.

Yanking her arm away from Dover's grip, she started to walk backwards. "No one will take me from him."

"The cops will—"

"Fuck the cops," she said and thrust an arm toward the door. "That's my man out there!"

The pleading determination in her voice must have been enough to convince them of her certainty because neither pursued her when she turned to dash out to the street.

Bale was inside the back of the ambulance, about to close the doors, when he saw her.

"Please," she mouthed and he didn't make her say anything else.

Stepping aside, the doc helped her to climb in beside him. Moving up the side of the gurney, she sat on the bench by Ryske's head, doing her best to stay out of the way.

Picking up Ryske's hand again, Harlow kissed his knuckles and smiled at him. "You didn't think it would be that easy to get rid of me," she said, doing her best to focus on him and ignore the blood that seemed so much starker in this florescent environment.

His other hand moved. Though his eyes were barely more than slits, Ryske was with it enough to pull the mask down from his nose and mouth to talk. "The cops," he mumbled.

"Oh, shut up," she said, putting the mask back on him. "You think I give a damn about them? I'll tell them I did this myself and after ten minutes alone with you they'll understand exactly why."

"Hospital's three minutes out," Bale said. "We're doing good."

That was the first piece of positive news and although she wouldn't breathe out a sigh of relief just yet, Harlow did feel her smile becoming more genuine. Dipping down, she kissed Ryske's forehead and cheek.

He moved their joined hands onto his chest, pushing it toward his tattoo. Harlow knew what he was asking for. Like it was a comfort he needed, she started to draw around the edges of his shoulder tattoo with her fingernails.

In spite of the angle being a little awkward, she tossed her hair out the way and laid her head down by his, not giving him any of her weight, but fostering their intimacy, getting close enough to let him feel this was normal.

They'd done it so many times. Almost every night this week. Lying together in his bed, saying nothing, just appreciating each other while she drew her nails around his tattoos in a silent display of affection.

His other hand moved again and she felt the elastic strap of the oxygen mask catch in her hair. "Stop moving, Ryske," Bale said. "There's no exit wound, and you're still bleeding." Ignoring the doctor, Ryske seemed determined to lift the mask. "Don't pretend your ears aren't working, 'cause I know they are, I'm the doctor."

Bale was distracted by something on a machine that she couldn't see. But Harlow did note the look of concern that crossed his face just a moment before the EMT shifted.

"I love you."

The croaked words were so faint that she almost missed them. At first, Harlow was too busy frowning at Bale's worried expression to realize who had spoken or what had been said.

Once the words filtered through, she sat up just enough to twist and meet Ryske's eyes. "Me?" she whispered.

"You... you love me?"

Though it was a weak attempt, Ryske tried to smile. It seemed that he was struggling for breath again. Worry began to thump around her heart. Harlow wanted to do something, to take his pain away, to make him better. But she was at a loss.

Despite the pain in his eyes, he winked at her slowly. "I love you, Trinket... and I... I'm sorry."

His face loosened and his eyes slid shut. She couldn't... couldn't...

Something began to beep, then there was a second beep in a different pitch. Manic in conveying the panic, the frantic noise was terrifying in its urgency.

"He's in arrest," someone declared and she was shoved aside.

Bale and the EMT were working, doing CPR, calling out to each other, busy and efficient in their practice. Harlow couldn't think. She was numb, stunned, dazed, shaking, helpless.

"We're losing him!"

A long, constant drone took dominance of the air. Certain in its finality... That sound, Ryske was... flat line.

Squashed in the corner, she didn't have a lot of space. There was just enough for her to drop her forehead onto Ryske's, to cradle his head, to cling to him like she could offer the life that was being stolen from him.

"No," she wept without caring about her tears or her running nose. "Don't... Please don't leave me, Crash. I'm sorry... I'm sorry! Don't leave me..."

The ambulance came to a lurching halt and the doors flew open. Ryske was taken from her in a flurry of activity. Harlow was quick to hurry out too, chasing after him as half a dozen people rushed in to begin working on him.

Someone caught her arm, yanking her to a halt. Fixated on his gurney disappearing down a corridor, all she could do was watch as her Crash vanished from her sight into a room.

"Ma'am," someone said. "Ma'am... are you family?"

Tearing her attention away from the nothingness left

in the corridor, Harlow found herself blinking at a sympathetic, but stern, nurse.

"Ma'am, are you family?"

Harlow didn't know how to respond. Was she family? She didn't know. She didn't know which way was up right now. Didn't know her own name. "I… I can't breathe," she gasped.

"Ma'am, are you okay?"

Her nose was burning, her eyes blurred. She couldn't think, couldn't function. Working hard to draw in a breath, she let out all of her pain and anguish in a scream so loud it silenced the bustling ER.

Panting, Harlow recognized the sensation of a panic attack, but she couldn't stop it, couldn't keep the deluge of truth from sapping her sanity.

"I… I can't lose him," she said, grabbing for the nurse. Her head was beginning to spin. Air wouldn't fill her lungs. Breathing was beyond her ability. "I… I can't. He's my everything… Everything and I… I didn't tell him…"

Yelping, the ache of her fear clenched her heart. Weakness began to ascend through her.

"We need a doctor here," the nurse said over her shoulder.

Harlow's knees buckled. "No." A strong masculine voice came from her side. Before she could collapse, she was swept off her feet. "She's gonna be just fine."

Harlow didn't even know who'd picked her up, she cried and clung to whoever he was. It didn't matter if he was friend or foe. If she lost Ryske, there wouldn't be any point to her living anymore.

Taken outside into the night air, she was carried out of the ambulance bay and bundled into a car.

"How is she?"

Rolling her head on the shoulder of the person still holding her, she looked up to find herself in Maze's arms.

Tucking her hair behind her ear, he peered into her. "He's going to be fine," Maze said. "You need to keep it together."

"He died," she whispered.

Maze's smile vanished. "He…what?"

"In the ambulance… he died."

Sitting there, wherever they were, in the car with Maze, Dover, and Noon, she cried and panicked, and begged to be let go. But they wouldn't relent and kept her trapped in the vehicle. Persuading her that staying together was what Ryske would want, the crew calmed her and encouraged her to stay put.

No one said much else in the long, tense wait.

Time didn't bring back feeling and it did nothing for her hope. One minute Harlow would convince herself it was a good thing that Bale was taking his time, that at least there was something for him to work on. The next she'd think the doctor was just too afraid to come and tell them that Ryske was gone for good.

She'd been staring at the back of the seat in front of her for God knew how long. It felt like days. None of them had moved or said anything for quite a while.

Suddenly, Noon sat straighter. "Bale."

Shifting at the same time, they all adjusted to look out the windshield. That was the first time she really registered that they were tucked in the shadow, parked in an alley on the opposite side of the street from the ambulance bay.

Bale was striding up the ambulance bay and seemed to know where to find them. He crossed the street to head in their direction.

Dover got out of the front passenger seat first, going to intercept the doctor. Noon twisted to make eye contact with Maze.

Harlow tried to get out, but Maze grabbed onto her. "No," he said. "Let Dover talk to him."

Looking out the window, she watched Dover meet Bale. The men stood face to face, talking near the mouth of the alley. The waiting drove her crazy. What could be taking so long? She couldn't see a damn inch of either of their faces. Dover had his back to them, blocking everything out.

"No," she said, shoving away from Maze to clamber over the backseat. "I have to know."

Neither of them could get to her fast enough to stop

her from getting out. As soon as her bare feet hit asphalt, Harlow hurried toward the duo at the alley entrance.

"Where is he, Bale? I need to see him," she said before she got there.

Her voice made Dover turn. The ashen look on the bartender's face wiped the smile from her face. Searching him for any hope, she came up short. Turning to the doctor, desperate to find some in him, she wasn't satisfied.

Bale had probably delivered bad news to dozens of families, maybe hundreds. But she didn't think he'd have tears in his eyes every time he did it.

Fearing that his sorrow could only mean one thing, her heart shattered. "No," she whispered, her lips cracking. "No... No, I don't believe it."

Walking past both men, she picked up her pace until after a few steps, she was running. The car horns that blared when she burst out across the street at a flat run meant nothing to her.

She couldn't accept it. Wouldn't accept it. Not without seeing it with her own eyes.

"Harlow!" Bale called from somewhere behind her.

Focused on her goal, she didn't slow. Running to the end of the ambulance bay, she rushed into the emergency room and headed in the direction she'd seen Ryske go. Most people got out of her way, and she dodged those who didn't.

It wasn't until she got to the double doors of the trauma room that she stopped. Registering the details of what was encapsulated before her, Harlow's whole world crashed.

The machines were off. Blood and a mess of medical paraphernalia was scattered and smudged across the floor.

There, in the middle of it all, was Ryske.

Crash.

Pale. His eyes were closed. His body still. The sheet was pulled up to his throat. She couldn't see much else, but there was no doubting it was him.

"Ma'am—"

"Leave her," Bale said, and came up to her side. "Harlow..."

"He can't be gone," she whispered, touching the

glass. "I didn't get to tell him."

"Harlow, you can see him if you want, but you should let me clean up in there first…"

"No," she said, shoving through the doors to stride inside.

Bale caught the door to follow her, but he didn't have to worry about pulling her back. Harlow stopped midway to the bed. There he was, her formidable Ryske… how could he be gone… how could the world still be turning when he was no longer breathing?

"The cops will be here in a minute," Bale said, standing at her shoulder. "He wouldn't want you facing them. I'll tell them it was a drive by. He was caught in the crossfire. I was a passerby… Can you say the same thing? After the way you reacted in the ambulance and here…"

The guys would stay if she did. That would lead to their house coming down on their heads. Harlow might get a slap on the wrist, but she hadn't engaged in anything illegal or immoral, other than her initial failure to call 9-1-1.

Ryske's crew couldn't say the same thing. They'd have to answer questions about who shot Ryske and why he was targeted. Bale would probably end up having to explain why he'd been practicing medicine in his bedroom.

Harlow didn't want that, Ryske wouldn't either.

But walking away from the man laid out before her felt wrong. "I can't just… I can't just leave him."

"I'll take care of him," he said. "But you have to say goodbye… You have to do it fast."

The point of her evening had been to bid farewell to those she'd met in the city. No one was supposed to die. Ryske wasn't even on the list of people she'd planned to say goodbye to. She'd been angry with him. So angry. Now it all seemed so pointless. They'd wasted so much time.

Curling her lips into her mouth, she took a step forward and another until she was within touching distance. Extending a finger, she grazed her nail on the sheet over where his shoulder tattoo would be.

"Harlow, there's no time to—"

"Take advantage," she whispered, letting her hand

rise to Ryske's hair. "He'd be disappointed."

"Yeah, he would," Bale said. "He'd be more pissed if you let the cops get hold of you."

"Guess you were right, Crash," she murmured. "There is nothing left for me here."

Bowing over him, she grazed her lips on his. Before she could succumb to her urge to throw herself on top of him and wail, Bale took her shoulders and eased her away. Pulling her backwards across the room, he drew her out of the swing doors.

Resisting as the door swung closed again, Harlow didn't want to take her eyes away from the man who'd come to mean so much to her. "I don't think I can leave him."

Something touched her hand, making her look down. Bale was slipping something into her fingers. It was the braided leather band Ryske always wore around his wrist.

"It was all he had on him," Bale said, stroking her hair. A tear fell onto her hand by the engraved metal cylinder. "You're not leaving him. You're going to take him with you." Tipping her chin up, she wasn't sure if the doctor's eyes were still wet or not because her own tears were blurring her vision so much. "Everywhere you go, he'll be in your heart."

Shaking her head, she looked down at the bracelet in her hand. "I don't know… I don't know how…" Clutching it tight, she was surprised to feel ridges on the underside. Opening her hand again, she turned the cylinder to see there was another engraving on the other side. "Felix culpa."

Bale put an arm around her. "It means fortunate fall." Breathing out, a faint smile moved her lips. "He got it added… after you…"

Surprise made her look up quickly and he smiled.

Harlow had said some horrific things to Ryske. They'd been at loggerheads. She'd been about to leave and believed that he wanted her out of his life. All the while he'd harbored feelings for her and she hadn't let herself trust them. They'd missed out on everything; lost the only chance they'd had to be together.

Licking her lips, she couldn't imagine how she'd go on. "What do I do now?"

"The only thing he ever wanted was for you to be safe. Be safe, Harlow Sweeting, and his sacrifice won't have been for nothing."

Letting Bale lead her away from the trauma room doors, Harlow concentrated on looping the bracelet around her wrist. Once it was on, she held it against her chest. Ryske wouldn't want her to cry, he wouldn't want her to be hurt, but she'd disappoint him on both fronts.

Her hero's life was over, and hers was changed forever. But he'd given her a gift and shown her what real love was. Harlow wouldn't forget that and wouldn't disappoint his memory.

Ryske had been hers and a part of her would always be his. No one and nothing could take that away, not even death.

TO BE CONTINUED...

Thank you for reading this tale!
If you can, please take the time to review.

~

Ask your local library for more Scarlett Finn novels!

~

For all things Scarlett Finn
check out:

www.scarlettfinn.com

BOOK TWO

GO IT ALONE
SCARLETT FINN

OUT NOW!